The

# CURSE of the MEKORI

# The CURSE of the MEKORI

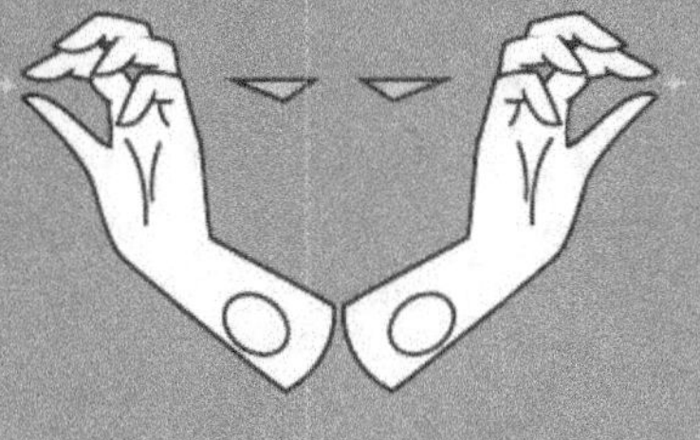

## BROOKE CLONTS

SECOND STAR PRESS

Second Star Press, LLC
support@secondstar.press
www.secondstar.press

Edited by Kelley Riegert, Fiona McLaren, and Kim Autrey
Proofreading by EditElle - Writing & Editing Services
Front cover design by Ben Dougal
Interior design by Francine Platt, Eden Graphics, Inc.




Ebook ISBN 9798985171945
Paperback ISBN 9798985171969

Hardback ISBN 9798985171952
Audiobook ISBN 9798985171976
Library of Congress Control Number: 2022921518

Manufactured in the United States of America

First Edition January 2023

To my sisters.

Because they keep me semi-normal.

## AUTHOR'S NOTE:

DEAR READER, this story brings in the history of the Gunpowder Plot and the Pendle Witch Trials. I encourage you to do your own research to discover what's historically accurate, and what I have twisted for the purpose of this story.

Please note: This story contains graphic violence, homicide, and instances of accidental self-harm. Please only read if you are safe to do so.

# PROLOGUE

✦ ❖ ✦

*Lancaster, England—Year 1613*

THE CANDLE BURNS LOW. A drop of hot wax slides down its side as Thomas Potts squints to read an account of court proceedings by the waning light.

*It's too late.*

He exhales and drops the document.

Opened bottles of dried ink sit in neglected corners of the mahogany bureau in his private office. Beneath his feet, a thick, patterned rug stretches across the wooden floorboards and forms haunting shapes, like outstretched hands to claim him in his misery.

Altham awaits the final draft, which means Potts can't postpone this day any longer.

Potts looks up and stares into nothingness as the candle's flame flickers. Shadow faces leer at him on the walls. If he looks too closely, they might resemble the innocents he helped accuse only one year ago, so he doesn't look.

Pages of words are strewn before him. Many of them bear scratches over the letters and blots of ink from when Potts ruined them in a weak moment, though he could not erase them.

He finishes reviewing the last page of his record and pushes it away. The records call his employer a hero for initiating the witch trials, though the actual witches escaped. An innocent testified against herself for practicing witchcraft and was hung, which horrified Potts so much he couldn't sleep for years. To this day, he has no idea why she chose to do such a thing. The witch tree pendant, once known as the last protection against the queen witch, has vanished, perhaps forever.

The manuscript pretends victory and mentions none of this. Every page is a lie…and he wrote it.

*I'm a victim, too.*

A chill creeps through his shaking fingers, and he closes the leather-bound book with a snap.

Finished. Done. He can alter nothing.

The door creaks open behind him, and the light of another candle brightens the room.

His son, William, hovers in the doorway, knobby kneed with wide, nervous eyes. "What do you think, sir?"

As much as Potts tries to hide his unease, William must sense it.

"It has been truly reported," Potts says. "It is fit and worthy to be published." He turns to extinguish the candle's flame before the shadows recognize the deceit in his words. As he ushers his young son into the hall, he leaves the room behind, purged by darkness.

"So, it is true? There are witches in our midst?"

"No longer, my lad." Another lie. "No longer."

# CHAPTER ONE

*October 13, 2016*

W ATER POURS IN SHEETS from the rain outside, the heat from the flower shop vents leaving ghosts on the windows. An assortment of fresh plants lines the shop, some in pots and others in cut and primed bouquets. The worn counter by the cash register gleams from my recent attack with Windex. No speck of dust survives my shifts.

My reputation at the store says I can make anything grow, but today, the lilies wilt in my hands even as I add fertilizer to the water. Customers walk around me, but I check my phone rather than look at them.

> I get off work at 9 p.m. Want to come over tonight? Sadie wants to see you.

It's the last message I sent Teddy, my boyfriend, but he hasn't responded. In fact, we rarely talk anymore, not like we used to.

I wait for the three dots that say he's texting me, but they don't come.

"Beautiful necklace."

I look up.

An elderly woman with silver hair and a thin nose gives me an apologetic smile. "Sorry, I didn't mean to disturb you, but it's a pretty tree. Does it mean something?"

"I'm not sure," I say. Putting on a smile, I tuck my phone into my pocket and drop the pendant I was fiddling with, the tree pendant necklace I've had since before I can remember. Someone found me wandering the streets of London when I was three years old, wearing this same necklace. The cool metal pokes my collarbone. "Can I help you?"

"I'm trying to find flowers for my granddaughter's dance recital tomorrow morning. Do you mind," she squints at my name tag, "Bryanna?"

I'm loath to leave my phone, but I can't refuse a request for help.

"I'd be happy to." I lead her toward a bouquet of carnations, popular for such occasions. "Is this what you're looking for?"

"No, I prefer roses. My granddaughter loves them."

Me, too. They have a dark fantasy vibe that rings of mist-riddled castles and ruby lips. I'd take them all home if I could.

"Can I show you some of my favorites?" I indicate a few bouquets I made yesterday that incorporate roses with a few unique flowers. "Do you know her favorite color?"

"Purple," the woman says. The wrinkles on her forehead soften as she smiles. "She likes purple and green."

I sneak a peek at my phone, but the screen remains black, rather than lighting up the way it would with a new notification.

"I know just what to get her," I say, fighting to keep my disappointment out of my voice.

I show her several bouquets, and she takes her time choosing one with hydrangeas. I take the bouquet to the back and peek at my phone again before adding more pieces of purples and greens to the flowers. As I cut the stems, I tie a lavender bow around them, and the older woman watches with a smile.

I'm glad she hasn't noticed how distracted I am.

Moving to finish her purchase, I hesitate. I want to apologize to this woman for my behavior and contribute to this little girl's special day. "They're on me," I say as I pass the bouquet to her.

The elderly woman's brow creases. "Are you sure?"

"Tell your granddaughter congratulations on her recital. Tell her a fellow dance enthusiast is cheering her from afar."

The corners of the older woman's eyes turn up. "Thank you. I see now why this place is more crowded when you're here."

After working here for two years, I'm glad to have such a reputation.

I smile at the compliment, but as soon as the older woman walks out the door, I can't help but glare at my stupid, motionless cell phone. Its cold, reflective surface could light up with a notification at any moment, and everything inside me wants it to.

I'm not giving the store the attention I usually do, but I can't put the phone down either.

Rather than look at empty messages, I open my email with restive fingers.

Every year before my birthday, I draft an email to a man my mom refers to as Professor Reeve. I don't need his help, but I want to know him, and I want him to know me. According to my mom, he found me as a toddler and, rather than contact social services, he located the best adoptive parents himself. My mom loves him so much for this that she named me after him, or at least based my name off his. While his first name is Bryan, mine is the more feminine "Bryanna."

*Professor Bryan Reeve.*

I've always itched to talk to the professor. Not only is Professor Reeve one of the most prestigious professors at a top English boarding school, but he's also a renowned lawyer. It's too coincidental that one of the best lawyers in England "found me" and handled my adoption case. And why choose an American family over a British one? My gut says there's more to the story.

My finger hovers over the send button, and my lip twinges as I bite down on the soft skin. I turned sixteen a few weeks ago, but it doesn't matter because I never sent the email.

While the professor connects with my adoptive parents every few years, he never speaks to me.

*Doesn't he want to get to know me?* The same question I've always asked myself bounces around my skull.

I want a relationship with him, and his indifference bothers me.

In my drafted emails, I don't ask questions. I don't ask for a response. I just list all the things I've done this year—minus my grades—so if he doesn't respond, at least the expectation isn't there. But I can never get myself to send the email and end up binging donuts instead.

The professor would want me to have good grades—he's a professor, after all—but I don't. My math teacher, Mrs. Allred, threatens me with failing grades on the daily.

Still looking at my phone, I reach for a vase of flowers to refill the water, but my fingers fumble with the handle and knock it over, pouring dirty water onto the tile floor.

*Curse it.*

My threadbare nerves rattle as I rush to the back room, grab a rag, and force a smile as I hurry past customers to the slip hazard.

I wipe the spill up and turn to the windows with my handy Windex to spray the ghosts, but the haze is mostly outside the glass, out of reach. Light from lampposts reflect off dark puddles outside.

At least I'm dry.

I set my phone on the counter as a car turns off the road, its headlights blinding me from the parking lot as it stops.

The door chimes, and Sadie, my older sister, sidles in, her dark hair recently bleached blonde. She wears leather boots, layers of sweaters, and soft pink lipstick—stylish to a fault and still my favorite person in the world.

She left for college a few months ago, and I don't see her often these days, but she drove a few hours to see me, and I'm sure she expected me home. She also expected Teddy to come to dinner earlier and to go with us to a movie. Neither of which happened.

She frowns from across the counter. "You didn't ask for today off?"

I give her a hug and hold on to her for a moment too long. "It's good to see you, too."

She pushes me away, her hands on my shoulders. "You didn't ask for today off?" she repeats. "Ben and I waited for you."

I shrug and avoid her eyes. "I'm sorry, I forgot."

Except I didn't, not for a moment.

"You didn't invite Teddy?" She surveys me with a knowing expression when I don't respond. "He ghosted you again, didn't he?"

I don't like to think of it that way, but I shrug again.

Sadie leans against the counter. "What a tool."

As her words sink in, I look away.

He's probably with his friends. Maybe he forgot, but the awful feeling in the pit of my stomach warns of something more. This isn't the first time he ignored my messages.

I remember the moment, two years ago, when he called me from his friend's phone to ask me out. I didn't think he knew my name. My whole body warmed with excitement, and I stuttered several times before I said "yes." He was cute and a member of the basketball team. The day we started dating, I suddenly had a swarm of new friends and party invites.

We've dated for two years, and he's become a comfortable sort of "cool" stamp. High school is easier with him at my side.

When I look up, Sadie picks my phone up from the counter and plays with it. She laughs. As she turns her back on me, my anxiety leaps into my throat. I shouldn't have given her the passcode to unlock my phone.

I attempt to reach around her and snatch my phone away, but she bounces out of reach. "Don't you dare call him!" I force the panic out of my voice. "I'll take care of it."

She laughs. "I'm not so sure. I'm not calling or texting him, don't worry. He's not worth my time. I'm just looking at this intriguing email you have. Why haven't you sent it?"

My breath catches as a horrible feeling expands inside me. I never exited the email I drafted to the professor. "You better not have—"

"I sent it." She turns and hands me my phone with a smile. "I made a few modifications before I did, though. I hope you're inter-ested in that school he teaches at because I asked if he's looking for new students. I hear they have a botanical garden. You'd probably love it." She winks.

She's lying. No way would she send such a message. And no way would a prestigious English boarding school accept an American high school student with average grades. I check my sent messages, and any hope I had drops to my toes. She isn't lying. She really did send it.

"Sadie, what were you thinking?" I demand, clutching my phone tight in my fist. "How could you? He hasn't spoken to me once, not ever. And you sent him this?"

She edited the email and basically made it a plea to get into the professor's school. "I'd really, really love a new experience like Lon-don, and I'd be the best student, I promise," I read aloud. "Seriously, Sadie? Seriously?" My voice rises as I talk, and Sadie's smile vanishes as fast as a drop of water in the desert sand. "Now he'll never want to talk to me."

My eyes burn, and I'm in danger of becoming a human fountain. This is humiliating.

Customers in the store turn with wide eyes, but I'm too upset to bother with them.

"I'm sorry, Bree." Sadie bites her lip. "I didn't realize this was such a big deal to you. I'll tell Ben to reschedule. Maybe he can set you up with someone…" she blanches, as if realizing now isn't the time for that, and scurries to the door. "Never mind. I'll catch you at home." Pausing in the doorway, she says, "I really am sorry. I just hope you know you deserve better." Then she closes the door behind her.

As soon as Sadie leaves, I pace around the shop, hovering over customers until they rush their purchases and go. I'm done here; I want to go home. My phone laughs at me from the counter as I draft a follow-up email in my head. I'll explain everything and apologize, but as soon as I abandon my closing duties to type the message out,

I can't bring myself to send another email for fear of making things worse.

I drive home after my shift ends and can't turn off the thoughts cycling in my head. What if Professor Reeve actually responds? I'm not sure I want him to, but if he doesn't, I'll be more than disappointed.

*I'd be the best student, I promise…I sound like a suck-up.*

Lying in bed, my mind won't shut off.

Sadie would say I'm obsessing.

I don't care. I'm mad at her, anyway.

I finally fall asleep and wake to the ping of a new notification.

# CHAPTER TWO

MY NOTIFICATIONS alert me of a new email. I don't wait to open it, though I dread its contents. After years of wishing for some form of contact, I can't allow one more second to pass without unveiling some piece of the professor's character.

From: Chelsea Craig
To: Bryanna DeLacey
Subject: RE: It's Me...

Bryanna, this is Headmistress Craig, Professor Reeve's boss. Professor Reeve is currently out of town, and his assistant forwarded your message to me. I've heard all about you, and I'm so excited that you want to meet Bryan and join us at our school! We have a new programme that opened up, and I think Bryan or I just might be able to pull some strings and get you in. If you don't mind, I'll contact your parents for arrangements. I believe Bryan's assistant has your mum's number listed in his close contacts.

Cheers!

Chelsea Craig
Headmistress, Administration
Burnley Boarding School, UK

I stare at the signature at the bottom, my limbs heavy and drooping, as if I might collapse into the letters on my screen. Professor Reeve wasn't the one to respond to my email, which may mean he never saw it. While I'm glad he didn't see Sadie's version of my message, it means the mystery surrounding him maintains a strong footing. It's also odd that Chelsea Craig responded so quickly when Reeve never reached out himself. Perhaps she doesn't know Reeve keeps his distance.

On top of that, Chelsea Craig's belief that I might get in is laughable, though, despite myself, a glimmer of hope bubbles up, alongside a bit of apprehension.

*What if?*

What if I went to school in England? What if I had the opportunity to research my heritage? That would require me actually going to England, which is unthinkable when I'm comfortable where I am. Of course, I can't go.

I can't think about this any longer.

Exiting the email, I stomp up the stairs to the breakfast table and show my father, who reads what Sadie wrote with a solemn face.

"Sadie sent this?" he asks. Wrinkles line his forehead, and a tangled beard the color of freshly churned dirt nearly touches his collarbone.

"Yes."

His shocked expression validates my anger and makes me want to cry all over again, except I don't.

"We'll talk about this after you get home from school," he says.

I hold him by his promise. After a day spent looking for Teddy and not finding him anywhere, I return home even more frustrated, and with the full expectation of having that email addressed.

My family gathers for dinner around the log table my father made, its surface rough and pockmarked, just as the last few days of my life have been. I stare at the email rather than look at Sadie, even as the steam billowing from my bowl of soup ebbs to nothing. Rather than eat, I try to control the heat rising in my blood.

"What's wrong with you?" My brother, Henry, pokes my arm, but I ignore him.

My older brother, Xander, sits on the other side of Henry and watches me with more interest than I like. He goes to the same college Sadie does and returned with her for a short visit.

I still can't believe Sadie sent that email.

Henry prods harder. "Spacing out again?"

"Stop touching me." I shove him off.

"Leave your sister alone," Mom says in the breezy voice she uses when she's said the same words a thousand times before.

Mom and Dad eat slowly, raising their spoons to their lips and blowing, as if life hadn't tipped on its side. As Henry returns to his food, I dig my nails into the wood, waiting.

"Kids, you're free to go," my mom says in a calm voice as she rises to put her bowl in the sink.

I stand so quickly my chair tumbles backward and crashes to the floor. "What about that email?" I point an accusing finger at Sadie. "What about what she did?"

My three younger brothers stand and scurry into the living room, probably to wreak havoc in the room my mom just cleaned. I'm glad they're gone, so they don't see Sadie and me fighting.

"I'd like to stay," Xander says, a smirk lurking in his expression.

Dad ignores him and turns to Sadie. "Sadie, I don't know what you were thinking," he says. "I think you should apologize."

"I'm sorry, Bree," Sadie says. When she looks at me, her face is downcast, her shoulders slumped in a perfect picture of misery, but it's not enough.

"Why did you send it?" I demand.

"Now, Bree–" Dad begins, but Sadie stops him with a raised hand.

"It's all right, Dad." Sadie averts her eyes and talks to the floor. "Bree has a right to be mad. It's just that you've been waiting around for your professor like you've waited around for Teddy. It hurts to watch." Her voice trembles. "I just wanted to fix it."

My anger thaws at the sincerity in her voice, and I'm angry at myself for not holding strong. Instead, my eyes well up, and I rub at them to stop a teardrop before it falls down my cheek.

Sadie has always been a lighthearted prankster and a fierce friend. I always regretted not listening to her advice.

Through the years, I've been grateful for her guidance when I went to my first dance, dated my first boyfriend, and picked out outfits for the first day of school, especially the stranger ensembles suited for junior high mismatch days. On mismatch day, I had refused to endure such blatant discomfort when my sister presented shorts to wear over my jeans, but when I went to school, all the popular girls wore exactly what Sadie prescribed. The first time Teddy took off to hang out with his friends rather than call me, she told me to hang out at some other boy's house and tell him about it afterward.

This last year, Sadie's smile became fringed with ice when she saw Teddy, though Teddy does his best to charm her. He charms everyone else without effort.

Was Sadie right about Teddy, too? Was she right to email the professor?

"I'm glad you two have worked things out," Dad says with a smile too broad for my current level of forgiveness.

Xander leans forward, as if to remind us of his presence. "If you end up going to your special school, Bree, you'll want to look into the dress code. And you'll need new pants. Everyone over there dresses formally. Jeans are an obvious sign you're American." Xander visited England for a few months after he graduated from high school, and he's overly proud of the fact.

I can't tell if he's teasing me, but I take note.

Mom returns to her chair and steeples her fingers beneath her chin, her elbows on the table. She has thick, dark hair and a firm mouth. You don't raise six adopted children without being severe, and I admire her for it, so long as she isn't being severe with me. "Bryanna, how come you never told us you wanted to meet Bryan?

We could have set something up."

Child services thought I was three years old when Professor Reeve found me, so my birthday became the day he found me, minus three years.

My mom gets upset whenever my siblings bring up meeting their birth parents.

*I weathered all those sleepless nights. I nursed you when you were sick. I kissed your tiny feet. You're mine before you're anyone else's,* my mom always says. My older brother's girlfriend didn't appreciate this language. She thinks my mom is overly shackled to her kids.

The professor has no biological relation to me, but he's the only connection I have to any other life. I'm sure she sees this, too, which is why I never asked to meet him.

She stares at me with an expectant eyebrow raised. I still haven't answered her.

I fish for the right words. "I just wanted to know if he..." My voice trails off as a hole opens inside me, and even as I take a deep breath, the hole doesn't fill.

"If he cares," Mom finishes. She nods as if she expects this. My cheeks burn as she meets my gaze. "He does care."

I leave my desire to learn more about the day he found me unspoken as Mom and Dad stand, and Mom squeezes my shoulders before leaving the kitchen.

Sadie waits until they're both gone, with Xander following them out. "Bree?"

I look up, uncertain whether I should continue ignoring her or not.

"I truly am sorry," she says.

I nod, though I wish I could take the email back and pretend none of this happened. Little do I know, solemn dinner conversations are inescapable for one such as me because one week later, Sadie returns home for one last visit before her semester picks up again. My mom sits beside my dad at the head of the table and dismisses my brothers with a wave of her hand. As I stand to go, she clears her throat. "Bryanna, Sadie, can you both stay a minute? Dad and I need to talk to you."

Sadie casts me a questioning glance, but I shrug, just as confused as she is.

Mom turns to Dad, and there's something off in her voice, the kind of off rail that sends trains careening over precipices when they've lost hold of the world. "John?"

Dad strokes his chin with one thick hand. "After Sadie sent your email, I received a call from Bryan Reeve's boss. She was interested in you, Bryanna. Excited, I'd say. She didn't know the professor rescued another kid, so I guess that means there's somebody else with a similar story."

Professor Reeve found another kid? I lean forward, the edge of the table biting into my ribs, ready for more. If I had names, I'd stalk Facebook and Instagram pictures all the way back to the embarrassing albums they posted in junior high, though they likely call it something else in England. I'd know everything about them. "Really?"

"Yes, but she didn't give me details, in case that's confidential. But I guess the school is opening a program for students with disabilities and other learning difficulties." Dad winces as he finishes, as if realizing he said too much.

The heat of humiliation chars my excitement. I don't require special treatment. "ADHD isn't a learning disability."

Mom's frown deepens. "Just listen," she says.

Dad continues. "Bryan's assistant mentioned she could get you into the program if you want to go, bad grades or not, and you'd get to meet the professor. You'll spend a year in the country you're from, and you'd be in a situation to kick your grades up, so you can go to college."

I don't know where to look. They think I need special treatment, and I've never heard of anyone getting sent to boarding school. That's something they do in old classic books, not in real life.

How does a single drafted email come to this?

Even Sadie stares at Dad with wide eyes, as if she didn't quite expect her joke to go this far. She glances at me with an open-mouthed expression.

But I still have a choice, don't I? They aren't forcing me to go. I simply have to say no.

"What do you think, Bryanna?" Dad asks. He reclines in his chair, his ankles crossed above his muddied boots. "Your mother and I already talked, and we've agreed this could be good for you."

My mom grimaces. "Hardly. Your dad had to do some convincing, but I think he's right."

"If the school doesn't see effort on your part," Dad continues, "they'll send you home, so it'll be up to you to make this work."

I study the wood patterns on the table. I have always wanted to go to England; I've always wanted to meet the professor; I've always wished I could study as hard as everyone else and get the same grades. But I can't leave my home, Sadie, my family, my job, or Teddy. And boarding a plane to another country has a lot of unknowns. I've never flown in a plane alone. My chest tightens.

"I don't want to go."

Sadie's face relaxes while my stomach churns.

"But maybe," I add. I'm not sure I want that door to close. Not completely. "I'll…I'll think about it."

# CHAPTER THREE

THE OPEN DECISION of potentially going to England paired with Teddy's non-response haunts me as I take my math test at school the next day. It takes all my energy to focus on the questions.

Some of my favorite stories originate in England. Every few months, I reread *Jane Eyre* through the night, but it doesn't fill the need to go to England myself. With six adopted children and a struggling lumber business, my family never spends money on travel, but I still dream of escaping the twenty-first century, returning to the olden days to sail giant ships to places where stories happen.

Thinking of England is much more interesting than math problems.

After what feels like several hours, I hand my test to Mrs. Allred, and she holds up a hand while she scans my answers from behind purple winged glasses, her hair pulled into a tight bun. I divert my eyes to the organized bookshelves and black chalkboard behind her desk as she writes a score in red ink and circles it. She writes the score down for her own records and hands me the paper back, but I don't look at the red.

"Thank you," I murmur.

As my teacher's eyes slide away, I toss my test into the trash.

"Bryanna?"

I cringe at Mrs. Allred's exasperated tone as I turn and meet her eyes, wishing I could walk out the door into an empty hallway where no one will bother me.

The eyes of the other students rise to survey the situation. Many desks are empty as most of the students have finished and gone, but heat still creeps up my neck.

I pretend not to notice the attention Mrs. Allred has drawn to me. "Yes?"

Mrs. Allred's gaze slides to my fingers where I fiddle with the chain of my tree pendant necklace. I force myself to stop.

She beckons and turns on a fan, so the room is filled with a subtle whirring noise, likely to cover whatever she has to say. My feet are stiff as I force them to move toward her, and she raises an eyebrow.

"Bryanna," she begins in a low voice so no one else hears, "if you don't try a little harder, you'll be nothing more than average." She taps her paper where she wrote a "D." "This is an average grade. Is that what you aspire to be?"

This sounds an awful lot like my conversation with my parents at the dinner table, and it makes me fidget.

At least it's not a failing grade, like my last test. If she expects nothing, she won't be disappointed. So what if she thinks I'm capable of more?

Mrs. Allred waits for my answer, but when none comes, she sighs. "All I'm asking for is a little effort. It won't hurt you to try. You've only got two years to impress colleges. Or maybe you don't care to go to college?"

I don't, but she doesn't need to know that. I wouldn't fare any better at college than I would here, and it might be too late for me to impress anyone, anyway. "Yes, of course."

"That's good to hear. I expect to see that reflected on your test scores from now on."

I nod and turn my back on her. She doesn't dismiss me, but she doesn't call me back either as I walk out the door. Hurrying down the hall, I find my locker and twist the dial. My fingers remember the code before my brain does. The mechanism clicks, and as it swings open, my books tumble out onto the floor.

The hairs on my neck rise.

Every time I sense someone watching me, apprehension knocks against my ribs. I flip around, and a girl across the hall turns her face away. To her right, a few feet back, a boy does the same. I ignore them and face my locker, but I don't know how falling books merit such lengthy, solemn stares.

As I swing the metal door shut, Abbey, one of my friends who shares this hour of my schedule, stands behind it. I jump, laughing as my heartbeat settles. "Were you trying to scare me? Cause you succeeded."

She grins, but her smile looks forced, like she's dreading Spanish even more than I am. "Absolutely, I was. Are you ready?"

"Let's go."

My phone buzzes, and I glance down at a message from Teddy.

Sorry, just saw your message. I've been busy with home-work, but maybe next time. Tell Sadie I said "hi."

My pleasure sinks at the distant tone of his message, but at least he responded.

I tuck my phone into my pocket and sling my backpack over my shoulder.

Abbey follows at my side. "Who's that?" she asks.

"Teddy."

She purses her lips and nods.

More stares stalk our progress down a boring hallway decorated with nothing but gray walls and cement floors. I used to think people didn't know who I was. Perhaps I imagined it.

"I've caught three people staring. Are they looking at you, Abbey?" I ask. "Did something happen you haven't told me?" I jostle her shoulder, but she doesn't laugh. She's usually more chipper.

"I don't think they're staring," she says, a little too quickly.

I look sidelong at her, and she avoids my eyes. There's no reason for her to act so guilty, at least not that I can think of, but I rack my brain for what I'm missing.

As we round the corner for Spanish class, Abbey abruptly stops and thrusts out an arm, so I'm forced to stop, too. I follow her gaze, and the top of my boyfriend's messy brown hair sways over everyone else. I smile at Teddy, especially at how tall he is. He used to be shorter than the other kids in our classes, but he shot up his freshman year.

A thin girl with bluish-black hair stands at his side, a few inches away, but close enough to touch him. My heart skips a beat as I see them standing together. The happiness I felt at seeing him dissipates.

My feet slow.

I'm not sure why. They aren't holding hands. They aren't even looking at each other, but I can't shake the feeling that something's wrong. Maybe it's the soft expression on Teddy's face that he used to reserve for me. Maybe it's the quiet way she's smiling, or maybe it's simply because Teddy hasn't texted me in days, and I feel like I'm about to see the reason.

I shove Abbey behind a set of lockers as Teddy scans the hallway. I don't want him to know I'm watching.

Abbey's eyes are wide. "I think we should skip Spanish today," she says in a panicked voice. She looks from one side of the hall to the other.

I ignore her, though her panic sets me on edge.

Teddy leans toward the girl and whispers in her ear. She smiles shyly, her mouth moves, and she steps away to disappear into a classroom.

He didn't kiss her, but his expression says he wants to.

Acid burns my tongue.

"Bryanna..." Abbey's hand touches my shoulder, but my anger flares as I shove her off.

She knew Teddy before me, so I'm certain she only cares to protect him. I thought I had better friends than this, and I hope she sees her betrayal written in red on my face. "Just stay away from me."

"I didn't know how to tell you," she says.

I ignore her and step out from behind the lockers, straightening my shoulders, so I'm standing tall. I need to make him feel as small as I do, make him regret ever treating me this way. We've known each other for years. I helped him through his parents' divorce. I made him cookies when he called me, crying. I went to every single one of his boring basketball games. But I just stand there in the middle of the polished hallway, my tongue embarrassingly limp and pathetic.

Teddy turns and pauses as he sees me. His face pales, and the soft expression dries up to one of panic. "Bryanna, what're you doing here?"

Judging by his expression, he forgot my class schedule. My Spanish class is only a few doors down the hall.

His eyes flick between Abbey's and mine and doesn't wait for an answer. "I was just walking a friend to class, that's all. Lynn and I are not together yet."

The "yet" says it all.

He opens his mouth and closes it. "Honestly, I was going to tell you, but I knew you'd take it hard."

*You were going to break up with me?* The question resounds in my head, but my lips don't move. There are a thousand creative insults I could use, but none are vulgar enough.

This is why he ditched me.

Teddy shifts from one foot to the other. "We're waiting until I had the chance to…" His face contorts, as if he can't think of what else to say. "You're just so nice, and you don't have a lot of friends, and things between us have gone cold. Do you know what I mean? I'm sure you've felt it, but you've been clinging to us and our relationship. I couldn't do it to you. I care about you. I just care about Lynn a little more. Can we be friends?" He holds out a hand.

I'm too nice to deserve common courtesy? A simple text would have been better than this.

I stare at his open palm, his long fingers. I used to hold those hands between classes. They were my rock, my pride. They made existence in high school bearable.

Does he really think we can be friends after this? I meet his gaze one last time, and the answer stares back in his eyes, blue as forget-me-nots.

And I walk away.

⬦

I sit by myself at lunch the next day. Two tables down, Lynn sits by Teddy. As he wraps an arm around her waist and pulls her against him, my insides clench. They look good together. Easy. As if they've dated for years.

Eyes settle on my back, and their gazes beat against my skin, squeezing my heart. If I stay here any longer, I'll suffocate. I can't eat my lunch at this table every day like I used to. I sat in this exact spot, day after day last year, and it's only the beginning of the new school year. Teddy knows my habits. He has to know I see him, has to know his actions hurt me.

Teddy isn't mine anymore, nor is he the person I thought I knew. I can't avoid him, but I can leave him behind. Far behind. An ocean behind.

I stand and leave my lunch untouched, hurrying out the door onto the grassy hillside. As I stop to breathe, my chest rises and falls like I ran a marathon. The air sticks in my chest, dry and hollow, as if I not only lost that marathon but tripped over the finish line.

People stop to stare, and I turn my face away. I run down to the parking lot, jump in my car, and speed home. As the street signs pass, my face burns with hurt and humiliation. I roll the windows down and let the hurt consume me as the wind whips my face. When I pull into my driveway, I fight to pull myself together.

I have to look sensible when Mom sees me, but that doesn't stop me from rushing into the kitchen.

Mom chops chicken at the counter and doesn't look up. Her hands are a cyclone of knives, though she doesn't move with the aggression that courses through me.

"I want to go," I say in a rush as I stop in the doorway. My hands clutch the frame so hard my fingers hurt. I'm breathless from running. I think I'm sweating, too. I'm hot everywhere.

She glances up, and her eyebrows rise. "What?"

"I want to go to England, to that school."

"The boarding school?" Her brows almost disappear into her long bangs.

"Yes, I want to meet the professor. I'll get good grades, and I'll put in my best effort. When would I leave?"

Mom offers a hesitant smile. "You do seem eager. Why the change of mind?"

"I thought about it, and I really want to go."

Mom purses her lips. "You'll do your very best?"

"Promise." I'll promise anything at this point. I never want to set foot in my high school again. I'd rather set it on fire.

"Let me talk to Dad." She gives me a long look and sighs. "I don't like you leaving, but it could be good for you. Dad and I will arrange it. Bryan's boss thinks this is the perfect program to help you turn around your grades for college."

I never told Mom I have no intention of going to college, but now isn't the time. Only the tiniest bit of guilt at letting her hope plagues me. I swallow the guilt and nod quickly.

"I can pay for the flight," I say.

Finances are tight for my parents, and it's not like I do anything else with the pennies I make. I never had a boyfriend who bothered to call, so I rarely bought so much as a movie ticket.

I almost forgot about my job at the flower shop—the job that helped me build my savings. They won't be happy when I put in my two weeks' notice, and they have to find someone else to take the night shifts. But it's either that or watch Teddy kiss Lynn every day for the rest of the year.

Mom bites her lip and fiddles with the strap of her apron. "Are you sure?"

"Yes."

She nods and brushes her bangs out of her eyes, while the creases around her mouth deepen, making her look older than her fifty years. "Start thinking of what you need to pack, but don't pack yet. We'll need to find out if Bryan's assistant can make the transfer. I'm sure their year has started."

This requires me to leave my family behind, but I can write and talk to them.

There's no way to make getting to know new people in a strange place easier. I'll have to deal with it.

Walking into my room, I scan the closet for anything I should bring. There are old CDs with dance tutorials hidden in a box, but I gave up on learning to dance in the privacy of my room ages ago, and I don't own a CD player anymore. It's 2016, and no one uses CDs, but I can't convince myself to get rid of them. I never told anyone I wanted to learn, not even Sadie.

I stuff a duffel with pictures of Sadie and leave the ones of Teddy. I should tear them up or toss them out, but I'm not ready for that yet. I grab a few t-shirts and sweatpants. I don't need much, I just need to get out of here.

The door creaks open, and Sadie leans against the wall beneath my bookshelf. Her eyes are watery, but she doesn't avoid my gaze like Abbey did. Her bleached hair frames her face in a fashion pony, without its usual flounce. "You leaving home wasn't my intention."

Seeing her eyes water makes mine water, too. "Mom told you?"

She nods. "What happened?"

"Teddy and I are done. I saw him with another girl, and he said I'm too nice to break up with." I walk to her and give her a hug. "I can't go back there." She has to understand. My high school is sheer misery.

"I'm sorry, Bree." She holds me tight.

I bury my face in her shoulder and try not to break in half. I'm a mess, but I can't pull myself together, even as I rub moisture from my eyes.

"You never liked Teddy as much as you think," Sadie says. "You'll get over him. Or you could transfer to a different school here. I'm sorry, I know this has been hard for you. I know you were with him for a long time, but he was the worst to you. I'm glad things between you two are over. I just wish you weren't fleeing the country because of him. You do know that leaving isn't going to fix anything, right?"

"I know." I don't want to fix it. I don't want to deal with it, or him, at all.

Maybe I'm overreacting, but I can't imagine anything worse than another afternoon in the cafeteria across from Teddy and Lynn, except a foxtrot to the jail cell that was junior high. Flying to a foreign country is a lesser evil.

Sadie pushes back and meets my eyes, her hands on my shoulders. "Mom and Dad think this will be really good for you. It would be selfish of me to dissuade you if they're right, so I won't try. But I'm sorry if I had a hand in making you leave. In fact, I'm more than sorry. I'm pretty pissed at myself, to tell you the truth."

I give her the best smile I can muster, though it hurts my cheeks. "Write to me."

Her eyes shine. "Every day."

# CHAPTER FOUR

Two weeks later, I'm at the airport. Finding the correct terminal frightens me, but transferring at JFK terrifies me even more. As I arrive at Heathrow Airport, I understand how terminals work and follow the neon signs, pretending to know where I'm going. The pretending gives me the courage to smile at people as I pass glass windows and fancy stores I'll never afford. The polished floors gleam, reflecting the lights above.

I take the train with a sign that mentions Burnley School and sit on faded seats. Holding one of my suitcases on my lap, I raise and lower my heels in anticipation.

Hours later, the train stops, and a bottle rolls across the floor, clinking against the far wall. A middle-aged woman stares at me across the aisle. Our eyes meet, and a chill chases away my exhilaration. Everyone else is quiet, staring at the ground, but when a horn blares, everyone stands up together. The doors squeal open, and I file out after the crowd onto the train platform.

A bitter wind whips through my thin jacket, and I pull it tighter around me. In the distance, a spire pierces the clouds that hide a timid sky. I pull my suitcases after me, toward the spire and the little town surrounding it.

I've left my mountains behind for flat grass and the occasional rolling hill. Every plant is fresh and green, but it's unfamiliar, and I'm hesitant to accept it. Especially the wetness that hangs in the air and clings to my clothes. Dewy droplets seep into my fabric shoes. It's a different kind of cold to the dry freeze in Colorado.

I walk faster, ready to examine every medieval structure and every curve in the sidewalk. I want to breathe it all in and make it familiar.

The spire of the school grows as I near, revealing a network of stone buildings at its base. A wide river cuts around the perimeter where moss-colored water ripples from the occasional raindrop, but the flow stays as stagnant as a modern moat. Trees dangle lush leaves. Bridges cast long reflections. Not a single boat drifts through the water.

Unease slithers down my back as a man in a hoodie strides toward me, hands shoved in his pockets, shoulders hunched. He's tall and strongly built, with copper waves that stick out of his hoodie, but the hood shields his features from view.

Normally, I wouldn't notice him. I rarely notice anything beyond my nose, but my nerves are tense, and he's big enough to drag me away without effort.

I shouldn't have left the main road. No one would look for me if something happened.

Why does he feel the need to cover his face?

*You're being paranoid. Everyone wears hoodies.*

I force myself to relax my shoulders.

He makes no effort to give me wide berth, so I train my eyes forward and watch him in my peripheral vision.

The man looks up and gives me a reassuring smile that assuages every concern.

He's young, my age or a year older, and his eyes twinkle, as if they hide a secret joke. That twinkle is so familiar, as if I've seen it on television or in an article. I haven't met him in person, that's not possible, but perhaps he resembles an actor. I can imagine myself ogling someone like him.

The edge of a rock catches my foot, and I trip. My carry-on

suitcase tumbles and splits open, so the contents spill to the ground. Books and notepads soak up water in the grass. I have a knack for falling at the worst possible times.

The boy crouches at my side and rights the suitcase. Without asking, he gathers my scattered belongings while I pick myself up and brush grass off my clothes. My cheeks burn as he examines a pair of books before he tucks them inside and zips up the suitcase. "Your Austen collection is ruined," he says in a thick British accent. "It's a shame."

Swoon!

If Sadie was here, she'd laugh at me for going from utter terror of this guy to drooling over him in 3.2 seconds. If he means to kidnap me, I'd voluntarily follow him into his trap now, especially with the accent. I could listen to that accent all day. "You've read them?" I accept the handle of my luggage as he hands it to me.

"Yeah, they're really good. Light but clever."

"Oh, wow." I didn't expect that answer as I've never met a man who reads Austen. Fumbling for better words, I say, "I feel the same." I want to say more, but the sting of Teddy's rejection catches my voice. I'm sure all he sees is a lost American with an unmanageable suitcase. "Thanks so much for your help."

His eyes glint with gold flecks swimming in the hazel. "You're welcome. I'm Hadrian, by the way." He holds out his hand.

As I shake his hand, electricity shoots through me. It's more of a painless, tingling jolt, but I stifle a gasp as I say my name, "Bryanna DeLacey."

Hadrian's brows pinch. "Can I walk you to wherever you're going?"

"I'm not going far." My voice is still strained. Maybe I picked up some static electricity from the grass or even from the station. I want to ask him if he felt it, too, but I don't want to be creepy.

Hadrian reaches for the bigger suitcase. "May I?"

A gorgeous boy with a sexy accent wants to escort me and help me with my luggage? Yes, please.

I step back as he takes the handle of my suitcase and mute my mother's warning voice about strangers. I'd never admit it to my mom, but I'd follow this guy anywhere.

We continue down the sidewalk side by side, and the suitcase wheels drown our footsteps. It's much easier to drag one suitcase, rather than two. "Thanks for your help," I say to fill the silence. "I appreciate it."

Hadrian nods. "Where're you from?"

It's funny to think I'm the one with the accent. The idea fills me with a touch of unease. I don't like standing out. "Colorado. Was it the accent?"

"Yes, sorry." He points to my dress pants. "You're dressed up for travel."

I look down at myself and then at him. He's wearing jeans. My brother told me no one wears jeans in England, which is why I wore slacks.

My cheeks heat. Why do I ever listen to anyone? "My brother played a joke on me. He said everyone dresses formally here and jeans would shout 'American!'."

Hadrian grins but doesn't laugh. "I think I'd like your brother." The suitcase rumbles behind him. "Is Colorado closer to California or New York?"

"Definitely closer to California."

"I'd love to go to California. I bet it's warm where you're from."

I never would have thought anyone in a place like England would consider my home interesting. I indulge in a brief fantasy about taking him to school, so everyone sees me at his side. But as soon as this occurs to me, I banish the thought. First, that would be weird. Second, I'm not going back to that school. "Definitely not warm."

Furrows crease his brow. "How far is Colorado from California then?"

"Fourteen hours, maybe?"

His eyes widen. "Not close at all, then."

I studied English maps and train schedules before coming, and everything did seem a lot closer here. England is small compared to America. "It's a long car ride, for sure." I've made the drive a few times before. Once, I got sick from eating too much licorice and threw up in the back of the car. I haven't eaten licorice since.

A trace of cigarette smoke wafts from groups of people chatting by the roadside. In the distance, a gate towers with spikes of weather-stained stone. The details sharpen as we approach, revealing a shield that marks the entrance with griffins, a gold clock, and some old text that must be Latin.

*Cavete virtutem eorum qui nunquam moriuntur.*

Hadrian glances sideways at me. "I imagine Burnley is quite different from schools in the states." He points down at his clothes. "One benefit to Burnley over other schools here in England is that we aren't required to wear a uniform, unless you're in Reeve's honorary program. Our school is more relaxed than others."

It never occurred to me that schools in England would mandate uniforms. It sounds horrible, so I'm glad to hear this school doesn't require that level of subjugation. "There are different houses here, right?" I'm not sure how they group girls and boys in their dormitories. "Which are you in?"

"St. James."

Disappointment stings, and I struggle to keep my displeasure out of my voice. "I'm in Sharona." It might mean I'll never get to see him, but I don't know that yet. I like this gorgeous boy who reads Austen and helps me with my suitcases.

We pass a kid in a hat and jacket, reading a book beneath a tree, then more clusters of people. The numbers increase as we reach the gate, which opens into a courtyard with a statue at the center. Stone structures loom, including a chapel with carvings that web across a series of tall steeples like immortal old men with straight backs.

Someone bumps into my arm, and I stumble sideways into Hadrian. He steadies me with one hand as two more people shove around me. I lead him out of the crowd to a patch of grass, so I can fish for my map of the school.

Hadrian eyes the rumpled page as I tug it out and smooth it. "Do you need the administration desk?" He points to a set of tall, carved doors with fading paint. "It's just inside Wilbur Hall, through those doors right there. Will you be okay from here?"

"Yeah, sure, of course."

"I have to work, but I'm sure we'll see each other again. It was very nice to meet you, Bryanna."

Not just "nice" but "very nice." That has to be a good sign.

"Nice to meet you, too," I say.

"Welcome to Burnley." He gives me a charming smile and a slight wave before he leaves for the gate. The crowd of people part, then engulf him so only the top of his head surfaces.

With Hadrian gone, the ancient spires on the buildings paired with swarms of unfamiliar faces make me squirm. Everything towers, casting me into shadow.

I shake the feeling and follow a path of wet footprints inside Wilbur Hall. As I take off my sweater, droplets spatter onto the marble floor, and I can almost see Hadrian's face mirrored on the shining surface; light freckles and loose, wavy curls. When I close my eyes and open them again, the face is gone.

With so much to distract me, I can forget Teddy. The realization strikes hard, and I have hope for the first time.

I cross a room filled with rows of tables. Behind the tables, stained wood covers the walls, and portraits of scholars in matching white wigs, like old women with perms, hang between glass sconces.

At the far end is an open door with a gold plaque above it, "Administration."

Two middle-aged women stand behind a desk. One smiles as I approach and drums her fingers on the tabletop.

I try my best not to sound nervous, especially in my ugly dress pants. "My name's Bryanna DeLacey, the new transfer student from America. Am I in the right place?"

The woman's eyes light up. "You are indeed. We've been waiting for you."

I hand her my papers, and she gives me a brass key and a class schedule. "It's just down that hall and up the stairs." She points. "You're in Birdie's Court."

I hesitate before I go. "Is Chelsea here?" I ask. "I'd love to meet her." I should thank her for getting me in, but I also want to ask if Bryan Reeve is around as well. I bite my tongue before vocalizing the last bit. If he wants to meet me, he'll come.

The attendant's professional smile widens. "She's not, but she's excited to tell Professor Reeve you're here. He gave her seats to fill for our special education program, and she wanted it to be a surprise."

I'm shocked Chelsea wriggled me in without Reeve knowing, but I hope he's happy when he finds out. What if he's not? The question fills me with dread. Chelsea doesn't know Reeve hasn't spoken to me once since he shipped me off. She couldn't know if he had a reason for it. What if he doesn't want to meet me?

What if I made a huge mistake?

My stomach churns, and my previous excitement wavers as I follow the attendant's directions through a library, passing a few more administration offices, and then up a set of stairs with polished wood banisters to the third floor of Birdie's Court.

At the door numbered sixty-two, I pause. A tingle of anticipation runs up my arm as I reach for the smooth, brass doorknob with intricate designs. Despite my concerns, I feel more alive than ever.

The thick wood creaks and swings inward.

This is my new room.

A swell of voices from a river below penetrates the window, and a musky smell envelops me. I peer in at a small, cozy room with a writing desk and a springy mattress wedged into a corner. The sight of the bed reminds me I haven't slept in almost twenty-four hours. Dozing upright on the plane doesn't count.

My eyelids droop like a shelf piled high with heavy books. I drop my suitcase and lie down.

*Tap, tap.*

I bolt upright and fight a wave of irritation. All I want is sleep, though I know it's still midday.

I stand, rub fatigue from my eyes, and pull open the door to confront a curvy girl with long lashes, wiry chocolate hair, and rosy cheeks pockmarked with acne. "Are you Bryanna?" She sounds American. I'm happy to have a small slice of home to make me feel less out of place.

"I am."

The girl extends her hand with a bright smile. "I'm Noelle. I heard another American was coming. I'm the only one, besides you." She glances over my shoulder at the barren room and crumpled bed behind me. "Did you just get here?"

"I did."

"Well then, I guess I'm your first friend at Burnley." Noelle steps around me into the room, plops onto my bed, and bounces a few times. The decaying wood frame groans. "This is nice. Mine's stiff as a board. I have my own room, too. It's great cause not all the rooms are single."

I sit on the edge of my desk chair as Noelle gives me a soft smile. She probably wants me to say something, though I'm too shocked to think, nor am I in the mood to be social.

"Thanks for coming." I try to relax and look like a normal, friendly person.

"I hope we can be friends." Her smile is as airy as it is sweet, and I'm awed at her statement, at how simple she makes something so difficult sound. I would never walk into someone's room and sit with so much comfort. I envy the ease with which she does it. "Do you have your class list yet?" she asks.

"They gave me an itinerary." I don't know what to do with my hands, so I tuck them beneath my legs. I want to know how long she's been here, if she has fun, if the classes keep her up all night studying, if there's hope I can succeed within these old walls.

She cocks her head. "What classes do you have?"

I know I should have looked at the list, but I haven't. A part of me dreads looking, and I don't want to tell Noelle I'm part of a special program. "I heard the school has a botanical garden," I say instead. "I managed a flower shop back home. Do we get to go there often? I love plants."

Her eyes brighten. "You can go anytime. I'll take you. You should totally see it."

She would take me?

"I would love that."

No words could express how much.

"I'll put it in my calendar." Noelle reaches inside her purse and brings out her smartphone. "When would you like to go? I can't go tomorrow night. There's a store opening I have to check out. How about after? Monday at 5:30? You'll be out of class by then, right?"

My smile squishes my cheeks, but I can't help it. "Yeah, sounds good."

"Can I get your number?" She waits with a finger over her screen.

I recite my number and add Noelle's when she finishes. Good thing I got an international phone plan before I left.

"I'll see you in the cafeteria sometime," Noelle says, "or in the library. Don't hesitate to sit by me if you see me around." She stands.

"Of course."

"I'll be looking for you."

I shut the door after Noelle leaves and do a little fist pump. I've already made a friend. Perhaps this change is not only good, but necessary. I'll make new friends and leave the memory of Teddy in the dirt for the worms. I belong here. I fit in better than I did at home.

The only thing for me now, besides doing well in my classes, is to meet the professor. Though I know Noelle isn't the professor, meeting her gives me hope that my first meeting with him will go well, too. After all, everything has gone better than I dared to imagine.

Perhaps Reeve will go so far as to answer my questions about my birth parents, which makes me wonder if my birth parents are people notable enough to warrant hiding who they are. Would they be ashamed of me for getting into Burnley Boarding School with a special needs scholarship?

The idea of meeting them and explaining the special needs program makes me cringe, so I push the thought away.

# CHAPTER FIVE

Only moments later, another knock shakes the room, and my limp limbs tense again. The knock isn't soft like Noelle's, but so hard and urgent it rattles my insides.

I wish I had a peephole as I shoot to my feet and swing open the door. A man faces me, his face pale. Fiery anger ignites his eyes while blood drains from his lips, his hands balled into fists. "What are you doing here?"

My stomach drops to the bottom of my chest cavity, where I wish I could curl up and hide.

"What do you mean?" Though he seems to think he knows me, I don't know him, and I certainly don't know why he's here looking at me as if I did something wrong. He looks too old to be here anyway, at least college age. "I think you're at the wrong door."

A drip of perspiration slides down his face. His anger makes him less handsome. "You must leave this place now."

"I think you have the wrong room." I try to close the door, but the man grips it so tight that my fear ricochets. This man doesn't need a hoodie to terrify me.

"I have the right room," he says through gritted teeth. "You must leave."

His eyes drop to my neck where my fingers twist the chain of my necklace, and his face droops, as if all his anger has ebbed, leaving behind an exhausted shell of a man. I drop the necklace faster than a burning coal. I don't want him to know that I'm nervous.

He releases the door with one hand and massages his forehead. "I sent you to America for a reason. You shouldn't have come."

*Wait...*

"Professor Reeve?" I'm so shocked, I take an involuntary step back. He's far too young to be the man I've heard so much about. The professor would have to be more than twice my age to be old enough to handle my adoption.

"Yes," he says simply, as if his name isn't one I've heard all my life.

Excitement, bewilderment, and pain whirl inside me. I envisioned my first meeting with the professor to include a smile, at least, even if I couldn't picture it. Mom and Dad never showed photos of him, and none exist online, though I searched for years.

I imagined a different man, short with spectacles and a long beard. This man is tall and lean with a crisp, fitted suit. His cleanly shaven cleft chin reveals a square jawline, a straight nose, and proud, twisted lips. Eclipsed by a mass of wavy, black hair, his dark brow arches.

Professors shouldn't be handsome, nor should they be college age.

"Why did you come here?" Professor Reeve demands.

I gesture at our surroundings. "For school. Why else do people come here?"

"There are plenty of schools in America." The anger and frustration return to his face. "Why did you come to this school?"

This is a man who calls to check on me every few years. Even if he didn't want me at Burnley Boarding School, he shouldn't be this angry.

I look down at my feet, afraid he'll see the shame creep into my face. Somehow, I don't suppose blaming everything on Teddy is an answer he'll accept, nor is it an answer I want to give, and the special education program is a secret I'd rather bury. "To see the country I'm from."

"You're serious? This is a vacation for you?" His tone is so condescending that I look up and swallow the flames rearing from my mouth.

At this point, I don't like him enough to admit wanting to get to know him, but I have to come up with a better reason than sightseeing, or he'll never believe me. "I, uh—wanted to meet you."

"Meet me?" he scoffs. "Whatever for?"

I knew he might refuse to answer questions about my origins, but I never thought he would laugh at my desire to meet him face-to-face. I want to shut the door and hide my humiliation behind it, but I don't. I won't give him the pleasure of thinking I care. "Fine then," I say, my face growing hot, "I want to know where I come from. That's all."

Reeve rolls his eyes. "You didn't come from anywhere. If you met your parents, you wouldn't see a single resemblance. Their names wouldn't tell you anything you don't already know." He pauses and takes a deep breath. "No, there's a better way. It's not what you think. Look, I'll refund your tuition money. I'll buy your plane flight home. I have connections at different schools in America. I'll get you into whatever school you want."

"I just got here." My voice climbs in pitch. Everything went so well until now, until this moment I looked forward to most.

"You're in danger here. You need to leave."

I haven't seen or met anything to cause me concern, except the professor himself.

"What do you mean, danger?"

Professor Reeve yanks a phone from his pocket and taps the screen. "There are no flights tonight you'll make in time. I'll buy your ticket for first thing tomorrow morning. Be at the airport at six, and I'll send the confirmation email to your mother."

"I'm not going."

"I can force you to leave."

He's right. My brain scrambles for something to cling to. I could throw a fit and destroy my room, except I couldn't force myself to ruin something so beautiful. I could leave a terrible review. Would anyone care?

My brain lights up, and the best response I can come up with rushes out. "Then I'll find a different school in England that'll accept me, and I'll leak to the press that you kicked out one of your special education students before they could even start, for no reason."

His eyes narrow.

I'm not sure my threat holds weight, especially here in England, but I let the threat sit between us, watching his face for any hint that it affected him.

He keeps his expression neutral.

"Al—" he coughs, "Bryanna." His voice deepens. "I need you to trust me."

I haven't done a lot in my life to be proud of. I never played sports, never received any plaques at work. But I'm proud of myself for flying to England on my own, for starting at a new school, knowing no one. I wouldn't have considered doing this a few months ago. Now I'm excited to be here. I'm ready. I'm not going home.

"No."

"What do you mean, 'no?'" His eyebrows rise.

A weight settles on me. My thoughts retreat, and my brain wraps me in a cocoon. Rather than speak my mind, my throat bends to silence, just like it did when I watched Teddy walk his new girlfriend to class.

Maybe I shouldn't have come.

Teddy said I'm too nice to break up with, but I don't want to be nice. Not right now.

"Why should I trust you? I don't know you. You've never bothered to speak to me." The harsh words spill from my tongue.

"I did," he shoots back. "I kept contact through your mother and planned to visit when you were older, even looked at positions at Colorado Universities, but enough of this. What can I do to convince you to leave? Money for college? For your family?"

I wedge my metaphorical heels hard into the dirt. I'm angry, I'm tired, but worse, I'm disappointed. It's a disappointment that bleeds through me and makes me wilt, like a cut flower. "You can tell me where I came from and why you want me to leave."

A muscle in his jaw twitches. "I can't do that—"

"Then there's nothing else you can do."

He cocks an eyebrow. "If you won't talk to me, I'll call your mother."

He has nerve, but I'm upset enough to challenge him. "Call her then."

The professor lifts his chin and stalks down the hall. But dread buries itself in my gut.

I close the door and lie in bed again as despair replaces the excitement from earlier. I didn't want the professor to see how he affected me, so I only showed him anger. I pretended to be certain of my decision, but he planted weeds of doubt.

What was I thinking? So, Teddy takes off with someone else, and I decide to flee the country and hope the professor who never bothered to talk to me will be excited to see me? It's laughable.

I don't know what the professor was referring to when he said I was in danger, but I've certainly made a fool of myself. Perhaps I'm in danger of flunking out of a British school, too, and there's no returning from the double shame.

But if I left, it would give the professor what he wants.

I wish I had Sadie with me. There's a seven-hour time difference between Colorado and London, which means it's morning there. But I need Sadie's advice, or at least her voice, to calm me down.

I snatch up my phone, and the metal edge digs into my ear as it rings.

"Bryanna? I'm skipping class right now to talk to you." Sadie's hushed voice is as good as a balm. "Is everything okay? You've only been gone a couple of days. How was your flight?"

I hold back a wave of tears, but the dam I built is in danger of splintering.

"I'm fine," I lie. "But," my voice hitches, "I need to come home."

"Bryanna." This time, Sadie's voice is stern. "You spent thousands of dollars to get out there. You can't turn around and come home. Give it a couple weeks, at least. I doubt you have the money for the flight, and you know Mom and Dad can't afford it."

"You don't understand. I met the professor, and he doesn't want me here. He came to my apartment and told me to go home the moment I arrived."

Static cackles through the other end as Sadie sits in silence. She must think it's bad, too.

"That doesn't make any sense," she says at last.

"I know." The corners of my eyes burn. "I shouldn't have come out here. He doesn't want to get to know me."

"You have no reason to stay, then?"

Hadrian and Noelle come to mind, but I'm not sure they're enough, though I don't like the idea of returning to the school I shared with Teddy, either.

Sadie takes my silence for a response. "You need to push through this, Bree. It doesn't matter what your professor thinks. He'll love you if he gives you a chance. Don't make a rash decision to leave. Give it a few weeks."

She's right. I'll find opposition wherever I go. I simply traded Teddy for Reeve.

"Thanks, Sadie. I miss you."

"I miss you, too."

I end the call and sprawl on my bed.

Though tired before, I can't close my eyes. My conversation with Reeve replays in my head, louder each time. He doesn't want me here. He doesn't want me.

What if he comes back and tries to kick me out again?

A squeak from floorboards out in the hall sends a wave of panic through me, and I sit up so fast my head spins. No knock comes, and I rub my aching eyes. I can't stay awake all night like this. My phone taunts me from the desk beside my bed. I could call Noelle, the girl who visited earlier, but that's embarrassing. I'd rather die in a hole.

I close my eyes and stare at the back of my eyelids until I'm standing alone in a room of stone. A noose dangles from the ceiling above my head. Smoke stings my nostrils, but when my eyes fly open, the burning smell evaporates. I breathe loud and hard, as if I've just run the mountain trails behind my home in Colorado with a bear behind me. Except I'm in England, thousands of miles away.

No, I don't want to die in a hole.

I dial Noelle's number, and my finger hovers over the green phone icon.

*Just do it.*

She acted so friendly. Surely, she wouldn't mind, but my chest compresses, and I can barely breathe.

I push the green button, and the phone rings.

A sleepy voice answers. The airy lilt Noelle tries so hard to maintain…gone. "Hello?"

I almost hang up, but I steady my hand. Sadie says I overthink these conversations, and Noelle herself made it sound so simple.

"Hey, Noelle, this is Bryanna." My voice quivers at too high a frequency. "We met a few hours ago. Would you mind staying with me tonight?" I swallow. "I'd love some girl time, and I could use the company."

Noelle doesn't speak for a long moment. Does she think me childish? I wouldn't blame her. "I'll bring some blankets," she says. "Be over in a few."

Relief fills me to the brim, and I've never been so grateful to have a friend. "Thank you so much. You're the best." I hang up. Whatever Noelle thinks, she's coming, so I won't have to brave the night alone, especially if Reeve returns.

No way will he intimidate me with another student at my side.

# CHAPTER SIX

I LET NOELLE into my room and shut the door behind her, wishing I had chocolate bars to make tonight feel more like a party and less like Noelle babysitting.

She dumps her blankets in a pile on the side of my bed and kneels to arrange them, her long, dark hair creating a sheet over the side of her face, so I can't read her expression to know how she feels about staying with me tonight, rather than sleeping in her own bed.

Sleeping on the floor isn't anyone's idea of fun, but I'm glad she doesn't say so.

"Thanks again for coming," I say, standing beside my bed, rather than sitting on it.

She looks up and flashes a charitable smile. "I'm sure you're not the first to get homesick on your first night here."

"Did you?"

"No." She turns back to arranging her blankets and pats the layers before laying down.

I've missed my family since I said goodbye in the airport, from the moment I turned the corner. It's sad that Noelle doesn't have that relationship with her own family.

Noelle mentioned she's from Florida, but never said why she came here.

"I never asked, but what brought you to Burnley?" I finally allow myself to sit down. Picking up a tassel on my floral-patterned bedspread, I twist it around my finger.

"I didn't want to go to the same private school my brother goes to," she says as she buries her head in her pillow. "And I watched this show where a girl goes to a boarding school in England, or at least I think it was England, and meets hot vampire boys. So, I asked my parents, and they said 'yes.'"

"Have you met vampire boys, then?"

She meets my gaze and laughs. "No, but I keep an eye out."

I try to imagine Hadrian with fangs, but it doesn't suit him. He's too warm and red-haired for Dracula. As I pretend to check for vampires under my bed, Noelle laughs again, this time with her head thrown back.

"You joke," she says, "but when the day comes that I finally meet my vampire boy, he'll fall so madly in love, he'll want me around for eternity. And when he bites me and gives me that porcelain skin, I'll have all the other vampire boys chasing after me, and I'll be a heartbreaker. That's the dream."

"That's quite the dream," I say. It would be nice to be the heartbreaker, rather than having my heart broken. I like the idea of reversing that role. "Breaking hearts and taking names. I broke up with my boyfriend right before coming out here." I cringe as I say it. Though I did break up with him, it doesn't feel that way. It feels like he broke up with me long before, even if I didn't know it. "It's a big part of the reason I came."

"I've never had a serious boyfriend. I'm too picky, but I asked a guy out here a few months ago."

"You asked him out? I'm impressed. I'd never do that."

"Why not?"

I'm surprised by her question. Isn't it obvious? Maybe not to her. "Because that takes courage. And confidence. I'd worry I'd get turned down, and then I'd be embarrassed."

She hesitates. "I've been turned down…" Then she shrugs. "Their loss, not mine."

Her response reminds me that not everyone is as awkward as I am. Looking down at my finger, the threads of my bedspread are unraveling around my skin. I drop the tassel and tie a knot where the threads have come loose.

"That's brave of you." I fish for something else to talk about. "So, you don't like your brother much?"

"I like him fine." She looks away as she says it.

"My siblings drive me nuts sometimes, too," I say to comfort her in case it's a sensitive topic. I could tell Noelle what happened with Sadie, but that's a long story, so I tell her about the dress pants instead. "My brother told me that English people only wear dress clothes, no jeans. So, I didn't pack anything normal." I gesture to my pants. "I've got about five pairs of these in different colors, but that's all."

She doesn't laugh like I expect her to. "They have cheap stores here you can buy clothes at. We can go to Primark. They'll have jeans. I haven't shopped there myself, but I've heard about it."

I'm grateful she didn't laugh, and I salivate at the idea of experiencing the city I've heard so much about, the very streets where Professor Reeve found me. "We can grab food, too. I'm sure the food here is amazing."

"Don't get your hopes up. Unless you like Thai or Indian food, it's mediocre." She shrugs. "It makes me miss the fancy restaurants my parents used to take me to. We went out all the time."

That can't be right. England is fantastic in every way.

Scrambling to correct her statement, I say, "What about the bread, cheese, and chocolate? I've heard the yogurt is good, too." I strain to remember everything my brother raved about. Every time someone talks about England, I hang on to every word.

"They're fine. But my parents imported better stuff at home."

"Oh."

My siblings and I ate squished peanut butter sandwiches my

mother hauled around all day. Feeding so many kids amounted to expensive bills if we ate out every time we left the house. I have six siblings, which amounts to a conversation topic all on its own.

"That sounds incredible," I say.

"They considered making connections very important. We knew a lot of big names."

Hearing Noelle's tales of her upbringing doesn't make me feel bad about my own, but I'm surprised she feels the need to elaborate.

"I'm not so big a name, but I hope it's worth you coming here tonight."

Her smile lights up the brown of her eyes. "Of course, it is. I got to know you so much better. But you never told me, what fictional species is your dream boyfriend?"

I picture Hadrian. A human? But that's not what she's looking for. "A leprechaun. Because they're short, chubby, and green."

Noelle laughs again, tears springing to her eyes.

"He can point me to the gold at the end of the rainbow," I continue, fighting a laugh of my own, "and I'd convince him to let me skip the rainbow part. Just send the money. Post marked to my address, please."

"Gold digger," Noelle says between laughs.

"I can live with that." I chuckle into my hand. "I'm joking, of course. I'd feel too bad to do that, even with a leprechaun."

Noelle snorts. "Don't. They wouldn't feel bad for us."

The bitter note in her voice chips at my smile. I let it falter.

"Did anything happen with the boy you asked out?"

"He's from a family my parents would be excited about. And he's one of the good ones, you know? I don't have the best dating history, and this guy seemed a decent choice."

I can't tell if she didn't like him or doesn't want to admit to liking him. Either way, it's not my place to pry, though she didn't exactly answer my question.

Letting the conversation fall to a comfortable silence, I lay back on the bed. Noelle shifts under her blankets, rolls to her side, and then returns to her back, staring up at the ceiling.

"What happened to your boyfriend?" she asks.

I flinch. "Mine?"

Though I understand her curiosity, talking about Teddy still hurts.

"Your ex, yes. Unless you'd rather not discuss it."

"We dated a long time," I begin, and falter, but as I start again, my voice gains strength. "But in the last year or so, he stopped calling me. And then weeks would pass where I wouldn't see him. I'd text him to plan dates, and he wouldn't respond. He avoided me in the hallways, but never broke up with me. I figured he'd come to eventually tell me what was bothering him. I was naïve to think it had nothing to do with me and something to do with things going on at home. The truth was, he just didn't care about me anymore."

Letting the story out to a complete stranger recalls the full weight of the last month, but I'm stronger with distance. It's a burden I can shoulder without stumbling.

Noelle nods. "It's hard because you'd think when they got to know you, they'd like you more, not less. Because you're more human to them. You love the people you're familiar with and comfortable around. But it doesn't work that way because new things become old. And to him, you're an old thing."

I'm speechless. She said she hasn't dated much, but this boxes up Teddy in reinforced, steel packaging.

"Have you had that happen?" I ask.

"I've had everything happen." She sighs. "But yes, we move on and get over these things, but I do wish…" She pauses and takes a deep breath. "I know it's terrible, but I hope that one day they regret not liking me. When that day comes, I'll be more than good enough, and it'll be too late."

Noelle's bitterness surprises me because she hasn't been so open with me before, nor would I expect her life, the way she talks about it, to be anything but smooth. However, I can empathize.

Sometimes it's nice to be chosen, rather than left behind. I don't want to be the one who fell short either, but as I wonder if I'll ever be good enough for Teddy, a part of me wonders if I care.

Noelle turns over in bed. "I'm tired," she says. "Let's call it a night."

I fold my arms beneath my neck, staring up at the yellowed paint on the ceiling. "Thanks again, Noelle, for making me feel so welcome here."

"Of course."

I smile at how her pillow muffles her voice.

As I try to get my brain processes to slow, my thoughts move from how glad I am Teddy isn't here to Hadrian's and Reeve's faces.

Hadrian's hauntingly handsome and familiar features.

Reeve's scowling from the darkness.

I fall into a fitful sleep. Though I squeeze my eyes shut, the visions stay, lingering like a burn. My heart picks up every time I hear a noise but slows as the sun creeps into the sky, illuminating the spider webs outside my window.

With the light comes tranquility, though I know it won't last. I'll still have to face Reeve again, but for now, I'll live in the present. I have Noelle with me, and I'm behind a locked door.

My eyes, heavy as a thick blanket, close.

I imagine Hadrian meeting me at lunch and sitting beside me. He tells me we have all the same classes and invites me to sit beside him. He has a hard time listening to our teachers because he's looking at me instead.

"I'm here to leave it all behind," I tell him. I want to become someone new, to not be the person who struggles with her grades, and everything else besides.

He leans toward me, and warmth washes over me as he whispers a secret in my ear.

"Me, too," he says.

*Bang, bang.*

The door shakes with the angry force of someone's fist, and I spring upright.

# CHAPTER SEVEN

"WHAT THE—" The floor groans as Noelle rolls over. "Who is that?"

The sharp thuds come again.

"Don't know."

But I think I do.

Panic creeps in as I stand, straighten my pajamas, and crack the door open. Professor Reeve stands on the threshold with a woman beside him. The woman wears baggy pants with a loose t-shirt, and her hair twisted into a tight bun, her expression both confused and annoyed.

I hang on to Sadie's encouraging words and force my face to stay smooth. "Yes?"

The woman pulls at her shirt. She must have slept in it. "Hello, Bryanna, I'm your superintendent. Professor Reeve said you've been told to leave the school. I must ask that you pack your things and vacate at once."

I take a deep breath to calm my fluttering heart. "On what premise? I've done nothing wrong."

"I asked her to go." Professor Reeve gives me a hard look. "That's reason enough."

The woman's face pinches. "Professor Reeve has asked you to leave, Bryanna." She sounds like she wants to go back to bed. Come to think of it, I do, too.

"I'm not going." I can be stubborn if I want, though I already threatened bad media. There has to be something else I can try, even if it means going to Chelsea Craig, the headmistress, directly. "If you force me from this room, I'll stay with someone else." I open the door a little wider, so Reeve can see into my room where Noelle sits on her blankets with the covers pulled to her chin. "You can't kick me off campus without reason. You're not the headmaster of this school."

This is the sass I wish I'd shown Teddy. This is the me I want to be.

Reeve's eyes narrow as the superintendent glances between us.

"You can go," Reeve says to the superintendent. "I'll speak to Miss DeLacey in private."

Noelle shifts on her blanket pile, and the professor's eyes flick to her. "Who are you?"

"Noelle," she says in a small voice.

"Return to your dorm."

Noelle stands and edges out the door. I can't expect Noelle to stay, not after the professor gave such a direct request. But the bravery I mustered knowing she was behind me deflates as she turns the corner.

I clench my fists at my sides. The professor's determination to make me leave only makes me want to stay more.

"Come with me," Reeve says as soon as she's gone.

So he can dump my body in a dumpster?

"No, thank you."

I've wanted to meet him my whole life. He might as well have slapped me in the face when he told me to leave the moment he saw me, but the hostility he's showing now is next level.

Reeve takes a step closer. Too close. His eyes bore into mine.

I take a step back, but his mouth moves, and my feet freeze in place. Words tickle my ears, but I don't understand what he's saying. All I can see are his eyes, the pupils widening until I'm enveloped in soft darkness. My shoulders relax, then my back and legs.

I blink, and there are walls around me, blurring into people moving on my left and right. A car door slams shut. Buses pass, then hedges, a parking lot, marble floors, a lineup of suitcases, then red seats. My arm lifts a piece of paper, and a woman accepts it.

"Welcome aboard."

The woman wears a neck scarf and smiles broadly. I walk down a hallway, and people pass by. Posters of planes hang on the wall, like I'm inside a jet tunnel. I slow as an attendant stops in front of me. "Excuse me, miss, the plane is about to depart. You need to get on and find your seat."

"Plane?"

I'm so confused. My brain pounds, and the world whirls around me.

"Yes, you need to board your flight."

I inhale, and memories from this morning sharpen. Professor Reeve's livid glare is stamped behind my eyelids. "I'm not supposed to be here." I struggle to piece it together. Professor Reeve came to my room, and now I'm at an airport?

I'm at an airport...

He drugged me, hypnotized me, or manipulated me somehow.

"What did you say?" the attendant asks.

"How did I get here?" I struggle to keep the anger out of my voice, but it boils inside me. He'd be in so much trouble if I reported him.

The attendant cocks her head. "You walked in a few minutes ago. Are you okay, miss?"

He took this too far. Whatever I thought of him before, my childhood idol has fallen hard. At least if I don't like him, it makes it easier to stand up to him.

"Your boyfriend asked me to escort you through security and to your seat."

"Who?"

The attendant gives me a concerned look. "He said he was your boyfriend."

Gross! "Is he still out there?"

"Do you need him?"

"No, I'd just like to know if he's there."

The attendant shrugs. "He said he'd wait until the plane takes off if you need anything. He's just outside of security."

My head hurts, but I push the pain off and lower my voice. "Please, ma'am, help me? I can't board this plane. I just started school here, and he's trying to force me to leave." If the attendant can get me out of the airport without Reeve seeing, he won't know I didn't board the plane. He'll find out eventually, but I can deal with that when the time comes.

The attendant's lips purse. "I suppose I can't force you to board, and we have a few on standby that would love your seat. What would you like me to do?"

"Take me back to the airport, somewhere he can't find me."

Two more attendants enter a side door and collapse strollers. The attendant glances over her shoulder at them. "Let me talk to my coworkers about this. I'll be right back."

I give her my best tight-lipped smile. "Thank you."

She stops her coworkers with a wave of her hand. As she approaches them, the female attendant glances sideways at me while the other purses his lips.

My head pounds, and the tension in my neck moves into my shoulders as neither attendant responds to the first for a long moment. Then one nods, and the other opens her mouth, though I'm too far to hear what she says.

Pointing somewhere to my right, the male attendant motions like he's saying to take me back. Take me back? To Professor Reeve?

The tree pendant on my necklace digs into my skin as I squeeze it.

I want to stay so bad that it hurts. Noelle was so kind and welcoming, Hadrian, too. But the history behind every marble arch fascinates me. This is where I belong. I feel it in my bones, in the weight of my necklace. I have so much to discover, to see. England is my heritage, my story.

Inclining her head, the first attendant turns toward me and

beckons me to follow. "This way. I'll take you past security where he won't see us. Just stay behind me."

I can hardly contain my relief. "Thank you, thank you."

She takes me down the gangway, and we re-enter the main building. Signs speckle the walls as polished floors reflect them. Suitcases roll. Cell phones flash.

The attendant leads me through a side door. "He's over there." She indicates the front of the security line with a nod of her head. "So don't go that way." Pointing overhead, she says, "If you follow those signs, you should be able to find train stations, buses, or whatever else you need."

"Thanks again."

She nods. "Good luck."

I follow the signs but don't breathe easy until I squeeze onto a train.

The doors beep as they close, and I exhale as the train slides from the platform.

Uncertain where to look, I find my seat and divert my gaze to the floor. I certainly don't want anyone to see the anger, confusion, and fear warring on my face.

*Did that really just happen?*

I never expected my absent relationship with Reeve to turn to a battle of wills, with him resorting to insane and creepy extremes to put me on a plane home.

Despite everything, I'm still here.

I wrap my fingers around a set of handles and press my forehead to my arm.

Perhaps if I show I can succeed here, he'll accept my demand to stay. Either way, I'll reconnect with the headmistress and hope she'll side with me over him. She was the one to get me in, after all.

❖

After an exhausting series of trains to arrive finally at Burnley School, I call Noelle. As I wait for her to answer, I drop my suitcase beside my bed and run a finger along the intricate designs of my writing desk, grateful for the opportunity to see it again.

"What happened?" she demands the moment she picks up.

"He tried to force me to leave, but I'm back. I'm not going anywhere."

"So, you're in your room? Stay there. I'm coming over."

I'm glad for her company. The scare from earlier makes my hands jittery, and I can't sit down. Everything feels surreal, like I'm a reflection of myself watching my life unfold. Nothing like this has ever happened.

"Okay," I say.

Within minutes, Noelle walks into my little room without knocking, her expression determined. "You have to tell me everything."

I explain it to her, ending with my train ride back.

She cocks her head, drumming her fingers on my desk. "And you still want to stay? Why?"

"Why does anyone want to stay?"

She gives me a disbelieving look, both eyebrows raised.

"Fine," I say, but I pause, uncertain how to answer, or if I want to answer.

My reasons for staying aren't because of Teddy, not really. It might be because of my heritage, but that's not the whole of it. I suppose it's because I know who I am if I go back. Here, I can change shape, I can create a new persona, I can start over.

But I don't want to tell Noelle that.

"I just really like it here. I fit in."

Noelle nods with a small smile. "You do." She drops herself, once again, onto my bed, as if my admission reestablishes familiarity and opens the path for further questions that only Noelle can get away with. "How do you know Professor Reeve?"

I pace the length of the floor. "He knows my parents." My blood stews too much to explain the entire story.

Noelle's eyes follow the path my feet take. "Really? All the way out in Colorado?"

"Yep."

"Are your parents rich?"

My parents' finances shouldn't matter. Reeve paid for my adoption because my parents couldn't afford it, or at least that's what they told me. "No, why?"

Noelle plays with her sleeve. "Professor Reeve knows everyone worth knowing. He's the jewel professor at one of the top boarding schools in the country, and a renowned lawyer, to boot."

"Then I guess he knows people not worth knowing, too."

She meets my gaze. "Why does he hate you so much?"

Her words make me pause. I don't like to think he hates me.

"He said he means to protect me."

She arches an eyebrow. "From what? Overeager boys?"

He never explained anything beyond the "danger" part.

"Vampiric schoolboys?"

I laugh, and Noelle chuckles with me, until her expression turns thoughtful.

She purses her lips. "I've seen Reeve around school," she says, "but I've never spoken to him face-to-face. He keeps to himself and his honor students. The headmistress lets him do whatever he wants. I never expected to have such an...interesting experience with him."

That makes two of us.

I turn to the window. The river weaves through the grass like a molten snake while giant chestnut trees spread scraggly fingers over the water. Clouds cast long shadows and wring life from lush colors. "I didn't expect to meet him that way, either."

The floor creaks as Noelle stands and bends to pick up her blankets. "I can't believe he bought you a flight home. That's insane." She shakes her head. "I'm heading to bed. My head's pounding. Thanks for my blankets."

"You don't want to stay?" If Professor Reeve returns, I'll be alone.

Noelle shifts her feet. "Not really. I didn't sleep well last night, and I have class tomorrow." Her eyes flick to the scars on my wrist as I bend to help her. I can see the question in her eyes, and I sigh inwardly.

White scars, like veins, spider across my wrist, and I pull my sleeve to hide them. I've had teachers invite my parents to private conferences to express their concerns that I'm hurting myself. However, my parents know I've had the scars since I was found. The marks have faded, and people rarely notice them anymore, but when they do, the conversation is always awkward.

Teddy asked me about them once and never brought them up again.

I give my typical answer to her unasked question. "It's a vein problem." Maybe I'll buy a few rope bracelets to hide them better.

Noelle nods, but her brows remain furrowed.

I help her gather her blankets. "See you at breakfast."

"See you."

Noelle hauls her blankets down the hall while I fight the returning claw of dread.

Professor Reeve thinks I left, meaning he won't come tonight. Will he?

If he does, I won't answer the door, but I can't ignore him forever. There's only one thing to do. Sitting down at my desk, I draft a quick letter to Chelsea, the headmistress.

Hi Chelsea,

This is Bryanna again. I just arrived at school, and Professor Reeve tried to force me to leave...

I backspace every word until the greeting. How do I explain this?

I arrived at school today and have every expectation of loving it here and doing well in my program. My only concern is that Professor Reeve doesn't seem to be excited about my arrival. I hope you know that I intend to be a contribution to the school, and I hope you'll explain this to him as well.

—Bryanna.

I hesitate for only a moment before sending the email. Chelsea's response comes within the hour.

Bryanna, I assure you Professor Reeve is very excited about your arrival and has every hope you'll be an asset to our programme. There's no need to worry.

Chelsea Craig
Headmistress, Administration
Burnley Boarding School, UK

I scan her words again and again. Does this mean she spoke to him? I'm not sure, but at least the headmistress is aware and can intervene. Whether or not she will intervene is a different story.

No incidents occur that night, so when the sun brightens the sky the next morning, I meet Noelle in the great hall for food, ready to walk confidently down the tables where not a single face resembles Professor Reeve. However, what I actually do is creep like a spider down the tables and double-check each face to make sure Reeve isn't among my peers. I may have fooled Reeve into thinking I went home, but the deception won't last.

Noelle spoons food onto her plate as I slither into the chair beside her. "You can stay with me if Professor Reeve is a jerk again."

I snatch a slice of toast, take a few bites, and eye the crowd. "Thanks, I'll let you know."

"I'm sorry you didn't have more time to tour the school before class."

"I'm sorry, too." I drop my toast onto my tray. The time wasted driving to the airport with Reeve and boarding the train back consumed the time I might have spent getting to know the halls and grounds. I hoped to have a day or two of the weekend for that.

"We'll make up for it this week, don't worry."

I force a smile as she digs into a pile of yogurt on her plate.

After swallowing, Noelle gives me an encouraging grin. "I have to go to class, but I'll see you later?"

"Sure, thanks."

Noelle stands to leave, but a boy passes and smacks the back of her head. "Hey, zit face, did you brush your hair this morning? I can't tell." He and his friends laugh, and the group of them leave.

I should have said something, but I sit frozen in horror. Back home, bullying happened, but I never saw it get physical. Especially not boys with girls. Does this happen to her often?

Noelle's eyes are shining, but her cheeks are dry.

I stand. "Noelle, are you okay?"

"I'm fine." She doesn't look at me but hurries off.

My fingers are stiff as I clear my plate. I dump my leftovers in a garbage can and tug a map from my pocket to locate my first class. The excitement I had before is dampened by the scene I witnessed with Noelle. Instead, apprehension slows my feet as I stride out the door and across a courtyard to a dull, red-brick building that stands out like a bruise against the fabulous architecture of Burnley School.

I want to know what class is like, but I'm nervous that the special education program will make me feel special in a way I don't want to be.

Pushing through the glass doors, I scan the halls for Professor Reeve. No one resembles him, and I let out my breath as I press on.

As I stop in front of the classroom door, I peer inside. The room is a wide half circle with rows of chairs and a long, thin desk that mirrors the shape of the room. There's a vacant seat at the far end. I shake out my trembling hands and move toward it. No one gives me a second glance as I sink onto a plastic chair, and I'm grateful for it.

There are quite a few people in the room. Do they struggle with school, too? I scan each of their faces, but their life stories aren't so easy to read in the shapes of their noses or the thickness of their eyebrows.

The teacher enters from a side door. She has dark skin and brown hair with streaks of gray woven into a thick, loose bun. She turns to face us, and her rich, amber eyes warm as she smiles. Her crow's feet deepen, as if she's the kind of person who would bake you cookies and give you hugs for stopping by. "Welcome to your British studies class. Here we learn about the history of our great country." Her gaze finds me, and her eyes gleam.

She turns around and writes on the board. Two dark holes appear in her graying hair, and the curves and craters become the glaring features of Professor Reeve. Round, black pupils constrict, and a voice whispers, *why are you here?*

As I force myself to blink, the vision of Professor Reeve vanishes.

I look around at the other students, but they're focused on the professor as if they didn't notice the strange mirage. Hearing voices isn't normal.

I can't decide if I'm going crazy, or if Reeve is literally haunting me.

The teacher turns to face us. "Does anyone know the answer?" She shakes the stick of chalk in her hand, but I don't remember hearing her ask a question.

I've never hallucinated before. I used to have nightmares about suffocating and fires. In fact, I've been terrified of small rooms and flames my entire life, but I've never seen a dream or nightmare so clearly.

My neck prickles, and a bead of sweat trickles between my shoulder blades.

I shrug my shoulders, as if such feelings are easily pushed aside. Unfortunately, the feeling lingers.

Papers ruffle as the students around me bow to their backpacks to retrieve notepads. They open them and scribble notes, so I do the same, writing as fast as my fingers can keep up. So, if my brain doesn't pick up on the words, at least my notes record everything.

The girl in front of me writes a few lines and draws pictures. I squint to see the details of little flowers growing over stylized block letters. Her fingers nimbly shadow the shapes of fairies leaping from one letter to the next. The fairies have sharp little features with extravagant wings. They remind me of the little fairy figurines we sold at the flower shop for customers with kids or grandkids to put in their gardens.

I wonder about the grandma who bought flowers at the shop before Sadie came. Did her little dancer love her flowers?

The boy on my left coughs into his hand, and I jump at the sound.

I haven't been paying attention. Gripping my pen tighter in my hand, I hurry to scribble the last few words the teacher spoke and hope it all makes sense when I review my notes later.

Forcing my eyes away from the drawings, I bite my tongue to keep myself on task and keep writing.

After class, I walk down the sidewalk to my room and dormitory in Birdie's Court and try to breathe normally. I have thorough notes, so I should be prepared for the next class. And I haven't seen Reeve yet, which may mean I won't today.

*Small blessings.*

My phone flashes with a notification.

**Noelle: Are we still going to the gardens tomorrow?**

Before Professor Reeve ruined every waking moment, I looked forward to going. My chest warms. I almost forgot we'd planned this. I hurry to type out a "**yes,**" but as I look up, the bottom of my stomach plummets.

Professor Reeve stands across the lawn, his eyes narrowed beneath the brim of his hat.

My feet freeze in place, my heart stuck between beats. I hoped to prevent him from seeing me for a few days at least, but since I didn't, I'm glad I planned out what to say. I rehearse the first few lines in my head again. I'll tell him he has no business kidnapping people, and I ought to report him to the authorities. I can do this. I can confront him. I can be mature.

His lips press into a firm line as he shakes his head slowly, his eyes never deviating from my face.

I open my mouth, but my resolve evaporates. Instead, I turn and run.

# CHAPTER EIGHT

I N MY ROOM, I tie a rain jacket over my ugly dress pants as I wait for Noelle to take me to the Botanic Gardens. No knock comes, so I perch on my bed and open *Emma*, the book that fell in the mud when I met Hadrian. I read a whole page, but the words don't stick.

A knock sounds on the door, not loud like Reeve's. I leap to my feet and swing it open. Noelle looks different. Her hair hangs thicker than the day before, longer. The dark color shines as rich as melted chocolate. "Excited?" She beams.

"Did you dye your hair? It looks good."

"No, I went to that new store on Mill Road, Mystic Cosmetics. Their formulas are like magic. It's supposed to improve your hair. I'm not sure how it all works, something to do with collagen." She combs her hair with her fingers, as if she's remembering what the boy said to her in the lunch hall about not brushing her hair. "They're a big brand in the states, started on the East Coast. Or maybe it was France, I dunno. I'd never heard of them before yesterday."

"I haven't either." I close the door behind her.

Mascara is all I ever buy at cosmetics stores. That, and the soap bars with fancy bits of not-soap floating inside.

"A decent hair dye would go a long way with you. I'll take you there," she says.

*My mousy hair color has followed me across the ocean.*

That's what I get for buying cheap drugstore shampoo.

Noelle talks about the different products Mystic Cosmetics sells while we walk out Burnley gate to the closest bus stop. An iconic, double-decker bus rolls to a stop in front of us, and two doors squeal open.

It looks like a regular bus, except with a spiral staircase that leads to a second floor. A few students sit at the far end, their backpacks on their laps.

The bus moves as we sit down, and my heart does a somersault as the driver pulls into traffic on the wrong side of the road. I've been told about the reversal of traffic rules, but that doesn't stop my stress from trying to leap out of my ribcage. Traffic rolls in the direction the bus moves as more students bike alongside us.

"Bryanna, are you listening?"

I jerk at the sound of my name and snap my eyes away from the road to Noelle.

"Did you hear what I said?" Her brow furrows as I scramble for a way to pretend I hadn't accidentally tuned her out. I do this to my siblings all the time, and Sadie hates it more than anyone.

"Sorry, I got distracted," I say and try not to wince.

Noelle sniffs. "There are two parts to the Gardens," she says slowly. "The outdoor gardens and the indoor greenhouse. I thought we could tour both."

"I'd love that."

The bus sways as it stops in front of a massive glass greenhouse—so much glass that it's a wonder the building stands without additional reinforcement. Trees and other foliage press against the reflective walls. We walk inside, and fresh, humid rainforest scents open my lungs. I pinch myself to make sure it's real and am grateful for the bit of pain that says it is.

Noelle drags me toward the first exhibit. "This is *Rotheca myricoides*. It's native to Uganda. The purple leaves are my favorite."

I run a finger along a smooth, plastic sign that illustrates the flower in its natural habitat. "It's beautiful."

"Do you have a favorite flower?" she asks.

"I like roses. I've always liked them."

She glances at me. "Any particular reason?"

I raise my shoulders. "They're pretty and sweet." Yes, they can be dark and creepy, and I love them for that, too. But they're also thoughtfulness in one setting, beauty in another. Appreciation, support, longing.

"If you like thorns."

"What?" I strain to remember what I said.

"Roses. They have thorns." Noelle faces the purple flower again. *Sweet, but not harmless.* "Right. I just like the look of them."

Noelle doesn't seem to notice that I tuned her out again.

She motions me to the next garden, and I follow her to a fresh array of plants and flowers, more tropical than the last.

"That one there's called the titan arum flower." Noelle gestures to a bloom whose tallest petal stands a half foot shorter than me, which means the plant claims a height over five feet tall. It reeks of rotting flesh, and a nasty taste lingers in my mouth.

Noelle chuckles. "It's prettier than it smells." She scans the other greenery. "Want to try the outdoor gardens?"

I nod and walk beside Noelle out the glass doors to grounds filled with neat walkways and overhanging trees with cascading limbs, waterfalls of green.

Noelle leads me down a rock path that parts bushes trimmed into perfect squares and circles, shading flower beds blooming with tiny yellow buds. We spend over an hour investigating the different kinds of plant life.

"Let's find the Scented Garden," Noelle says after sniffing a strange yellow flower with purple veins. "It has a cozy bench in the middle, and I wouldn't mind sitting down for a minute. Sometimes it's nice to relax and breathe it all in. And you can tell me how your first day of class went."

"That sounds great."

We walk deeper into the grounds, following signs that point to the Scented Garden.

Noelle stands straighter as she walks, her eyes gleaming with excitement. "We're getting close. There's a pond back here, I remember."

The path rounds a tree with a massive, knobby trunk, and I slow as the Scented Garden comes into view.

Hadrian, the young man I met when I walked through Burnley's gate for the first time, inhabits the cozy bench Noelle described, a book in his hands.

I falter, stuck in a bittersweet space between joy and terror. I want to see him, but I don't want to stumble on him this way. Will he think I'm stalking him?

Smoothing my hair, I wish I had a mirror. Meanwhile, he continues to read, completely unaware of my discomfort.

His eyes dart across the pages, and his brows knit together, a question squished between them. Loose strands of untidy hair hang over his brow.

He's wearing straight leg pants and a jacket.

In his left hand, he twists something silver on a chain around his neck. The smooth metal reflects the sun in flashes of brilliant light. He looks up, puts the book down, and tucks the pendant of his necklace inside his shirt.

Our eyes meet, and he jumps a little.

Uncertain if there's something more I should be doing, I raise a hand and give a slight wave. His mouth twitches into an uncomfortable smile. Is he unhappy to see me?

"Oh, how embarrassing. I'm going to the bathroom." Noelle's voice comes out of nowhere. "Maybe he'll be gone when I come back."

"I met him the other day. He seems nice."

Noelle purses her lips. "He's nice, that's for sure, but avoid him. I'll be back. Wait for me."

I'm not sure what to think of what Noelle said. She wouldn't say what she said without reason, but I can't ignore him after he made me feel welcome my first day at Burnley. On the other hand, he didn't act excited to see us. Maybe he doesn't want another chat, but I have a secret desire to talk to him again.

My lungs stiffen as the air in the garden settles, and Hadrian pulls out his cell phone. Not a stem moves. Not a blade of grass.

I picture Sadie standing in the corner with an eyebrow raised, furiously gesturing toward him, and I almost laugh aloud.

Hadrian looks up again, and this time, his smile is more genuine. "Aren't you going to say 'hello?'" he calls.

I hesitate for only a moment. There's the chance I might embarrass myself, but I want to get to know him better, and I don't know how many chances I'll get. I eye the book beside him as I cross the space between us. It's a Bible. He shifts his leg, as if to hide it.

"Have you been enjoying yourself?" he asks in a light voice.

"They haven't made me stand on a stool with a sign yet." I chuckle, but his brow scrunches. "Like Lowood, Jane Eyre's boarding school." Clearly not my best joke. "Sorry, it's not funny if you don't get the reference."

Recognition lights his eyes. "Is that what you were expecting?"

"No, not really." I scan the plants for Noelle, but she hasn't returned yet. I need a reset button.

"Do you want to sit down?" He gestures to the bench. "There's room."

"Thanks." I sit so slowly my knees creak, and I cross my hands on my lap. I want to say something clever, but I'm not off to a good start. "It's not so bad here," I say at last. "Except the creeper who snuck up on me my first day."

Hadrian's eyebrows shoot up on his forehead. "It was the hoodie, wasn't it?"

"Possibly."

He laughs. "I'll never creep again." His hand moves to the edge of the Bible at his side, though his eyes stay on me.

"What are you reading?" I ask. My parents are Christian, and I follow their faith, but I've never encountered a high schooler reading the Bible unless it's for a religious class.

His smile stills. "Nothing exceptional." The awkwardness between us snaps back like a rubber band. "What brought you to the gardens?"

"Noelle wanted to show me the plants." Again, I scan for Noelle. He leans back on the bench too stiffly, with his chin raised and his mouth slightly pursed, as if I've made him uncomfortable somehow.

His shoulders relax, and he drags his fingers across the book cover. Then he picks the Bible up and flips it over. "I'm reading about Solomon. The Bible is full of questionable stories, like here I read that King Solomon had his brother killed for asking to marry his father's nursemaid."

He watches my face as I try to keep my expression as neutral as possible. When I sat beside him, I never anticipated discussing such a topic, though I talked to my dad about this exact scene a long time ago. It didn't make sense to me, either.

I remember the night well. My dad sat on his recliner by the TV, and my mom scolded him for the mud on his shoes. I asked my dad why Solomon would do such a thing, but I haven't spoken about a religious topic like this one with anyone else.

"I suppose you have to understand the culture at the time," I say. "Taking the old king's concubine was like declaring your right to the throne. Solomon was protecting his right from his older brother. That doesn't necessarily make it right, but it does make more sense."

The furrowed brows return, and I can see Hadrian's thoughts circling. I've never made spirituality the center of my life, but I get the feeling that religion is important to Hadrian. "Am I the only one who thinks about these things?" he asks.

"No." I try not to laugh.

Creases appear between his eyes. "I'm sorry I brought it up, but I'm glad you're familiar with the topic. I didn't expect you to be. I don't usually…" His eyes dart to the far end of the garden where Noelle walks down the path toward us, back from the bathroom. She's so quiet, I'm not sure how he noticed her.

As she nears, she glances between us and stops a few feet away. "I'm glad you two are such good friends," she says in a tone I can't quite interpret.

My face warms.

Hadrian scrunches his nose. "I creep on her from time to time."

Noelle hugs her purse to her side, her lips pursed. "Well, let's go, Bryanna. I'm ready. Nice to see you, Hadrian."

She wants to leave so quickly?

Hadrian inclines his head.

As Noelle clutches my arm, I allow her to drag me down the walk, but I glance over my shoulder for one last glimpse of Hadrian. He's still sitting on the bench with a quiet smirk. He winks, and my cheeks warm.

Noelle rolls her eyes. "If you want to avoid Professor Reeve, you'll want to avoid Hadrian, too. Besides, there are lots of hotties here at Burnley. You don't have to sell yourself short."

Reeve and Hadrian are two completely different people. "How're they connected?"

Noelle pushes her way out the glass doors. "They all know each other. I heard Reeve made a special request to get Hadrian in."

It bothers me more than I'd care to admit that Reeve made a special request for Hadrian when he wanted to kick me out.

We walk to the bus station, where Noelle pulls at her hair and stares at the schedule. "Fifteen minutes till the next one." She turns to me. "We don't have time tonight, but do you still want to go to Mystic Cosmetics sometime? I'll introduce you to Jane and Ellen."

"Sure. Remind me who Jane and Ellen are?" I want to see the store that Noelle talked about on the bus, if only to understand why her eyes light up every time she mentions it. I mean, it's a cosmetics store. How great can it be?

Noelle stands with her back against the bus sign. "The owners. There's a tonic for weight loss I'd like to try, but it's expensive. And I heard they have stuff for acne, too."

"My sister, Sadie, had issues with acne," I say. "It took some time for hers to clear up, but it did, and the treatment was affordable. I can call and ask her about it if you'd like?"

"No, thanks. I think I'll try the tonic. Everything at the cosmetics store works. And not only does it work, it works right away. What are your plans for next week? We'll plan a day to go. This Saturday I have a group project I can't miss, and I'm meeting a friend for lunch."

"Next week? Let's see. I think I'll go to class, eat some food, sleep a little, and do some extra important walking around my bedroom."

Noelle's eyes crinkle. "Think you can squeeze me in next Saturday?"

Smiling, I give her a teasing sigh. "I guess so."

Of course, I can squeeze her in. I'll clear my schedule for anyone who'll keep me company in the middle of the night when I'm scared. Besides, it's not like I have anyone else to make plans with.

She laughs. "Good. Let's go to Mystic Cosmetics and watch a movie afterward. Make a night out of it."

The bus stops, and we climb aboard. As we sit in our seats, Noelle asks, "Do you really like that guy Hadrian?"

I don't like being observed. "What?"

"You're thinking about him, aren't you?"

My cheeks and ears burn. "No," but I say it too quickly.

"He's a bit weird, but if you like weird, I can set something up. I know a close friend of his."

Why would she set me up with him if she doesn't like him?

"I thought you weren't a fan of Hadrian."

She stares at her fingers, twisting and untwisting them. "Remember when I told you I asked a guy out? Well, that was Hadrian. He turned me down, but I've thought about it, and just because things didn't work between us, doesn't mean they can't or shouldn't work out for you. I can get over the awkwardness of it."

I'm glad she told me, but now I feel odd about liking him. Is it weird to date a guy your friend asked out first? I guess it doesn't matter if Hadrian doesn't like me, either. "That's nice of you. But are you sure?"

"I'm sure. So, you want me to set it up?"

I do want her to set something up if she's willing. "Yes," I say. "Thank you."

She half-smiles.

We return to Birdie's Court, and I climb the stairs to my room, waving goodbye to Noelle. I open my computer to check my email for any messages from home before going to bed, and the notification for a new message flashes on my screen. Clicking on it, a white page greets me with a single sentence from Professor Reeve.

You should have gone home.

# CHAPTER NINE

"**B**RYANNA? I got a voice message from Professor Reeve about you coming home. What happened? Please call me when you get this. We're worried."

Clicking stop, I cut off my mom's voice. I don't have it in me to tell her the professor wants nothing to do with me. When I talked to Sadie last night, I avoided the topic with her as well.

I drop my phone, let it bounce on my bedsheets, and I pack my backpack. Hurrying to my morning class in one of the newer buildings, I go through the glass doors and up the stairs, though I stop at the hallway intersection to peer around the corner. There, I scout for the dark hair and crisp suit of the professor.

Gleaming floors reflect student artwork on the walls, but no Reeve.

"I admire amateur artwork, too, but usually from a less irregular angle."

My chest jolts as I spin around.

Hadrian offers a playful grin. "You see it much better when you stand directly in front of it."

My insides squirm. "I'll be sure to remember that." I suppose it's me doing the creeping this time, though I hope he doesn't ask why I'm peeking around corners. While I can explain my relationship with Professor Reeve, I'd rather not. Honestly, I don't want to talk about Reeve at all.

He gives me an odd look. "Where are you headed?"

The tension in my shoulders eases. He asked an easy question. "Biology."

His face brightens. "That's where I'm going. Join me?"

I nod, and he turns for me to walk beside him. I match his pace, and we sit together at the back of the classroom. Hadrian sits upright in his chair and presses the tips of his fingers together. His eyes dart around the room, from one door to the other, and then down the lines of students.

It's my turn to ask him questions. "What are you doing?" I ask.

He looks at me, his eyebrows raised. "I'm not certain what you mean."

"You look like you expect a bomb to go off. Should I be concerned?" I like to think I'm funny sometimes.

He relaxes into his chair, as if to show me I'm wrong, and gives me an easy smile. "If I thought a bomb would be going off, I'd not sit and wait for it to happen. Would you?"

"No," I say.

The overhead lights dim as the professor strides forward. "Quiet please."

Hadrian repositions himself and rests his chin on his fist. I catch myself studying his profile and make myself look away before he sees. I take notes with stiff fingers, though heat bridges the gap between us.

He twirls a pen in his fingers and doesn't write a word, though his eyes sweep the room.

"Were you listening?" I ask as the professor finishes his slideshow and turns the lights back on.

I would forget in a minute.

Hadrian stands and stretches. "I was."

"Aren't you worried you'll forget what he said? We have a test on this."

"I'll remember." He stifles a yawn with his hand and turns to me. "Thanks for the pleasure of your company. Perhaps I can convince you to join me again." He flashes a smile that doesn't meet his eyes as he shuffles into a side aisle, joins a throng of students, and disappears.

Was it something I said?

I tuck my notebook into my backpack and follow. I make it down the hallway and halfway down the stairs before a hand grips my shoulder and pressure builds in my blood.

"I need to speak with you," says a familiar, agitated voice.

I whirl to face Professor Reeve, and a whirlwind of fear and anger whips through me. "How dare you talk to me after what you did? I should report you." I want to smack him and run from him, but I'm too scared and angry to do either.

Annoyance ignites his eyes and then vanishes as if he jerked a shade over his emotions. "For what?"

"For harassment, kidnapping me. Take your pick." I stoke my anger to keep the fear at bay.

The professor straightens a black fedora over his hair. "I made a mistake. I'm sorry, I shouldn't have forced you, and I'll not do it again. I realized what I did wasn't the best approach, so I decided to give you space and think long and hard about how best to explain. Now that I've come to a resolution, I have something important to show you. Please, come with me."

"I'm not going anywhere with you."

He steps toward me. "Please."

"No."

Despite my determination, my feet move without my permission and won't stop. I can't scream either, no matter how hard I try. I've never heard of a drug that controls limbs, and I can't think of how he gave me anything. There's no explanation.

"I need you to understand," he says as we step out on a stone pathway.

But I don't trust him.

He directs me to a rounded, contemporary structure with windows framed in black metal, reflecting the cloudy sky. It's crisp, new, and modern, reminding me of the fancy schools the state built on the other side of town back home. The gleaming dark gray bricks are a stark contrast to the lighter stone buildings that are so old they're worn smooth.

We walk through a set of glass doors to an enormous door made of oak. Inscribed into the gold surface is the name: "Professor Bryan Reeve, BA, BCL, LL.M, DPhil, PhD in History, PhD in Political Science."

Professor Reeve opens it and waits while I fight to control my feet, but my legs continue until Reeve closes the door behind me. He tosses his hat at the coat hanger, shrugs off his suit coat, and hangs it on a rack.

My legs buckle beneath me, and I reach for the wall to catch myself. "What was that?"

"What do you mean?" He folds his hands on his lap.

"I don't want to be here," I say between breaths. "You forced me to come."

"I never touched you. You came of your own volition. And I have video cameras to prove it." He points to two cameras mounted on the wall above our heads. "You should feel safe knowing these are here, too."

Knowing he owns the footage doesn't make me feel safe at all.

I shouldn't be here. "I'll call the police and tell them what you did. You'll lose your job."

He arches an eyebrow. "Will I?

"Yes."

A smile quirks his lips. "Go ahead. You can borrow my mobile to phone the police." He sets his cell phone on the desk. "It's there if you decide to use it."

No one would believe me, and Reeve knows it. I survey the office. There has to be a way out.

Diplomas and awards cover the walls. Pencil holders, a fancy bottle of brandy, and organized compartments of papers line the mahogany surface of his desk. A nameplate announces the professor's identity in gold letters.

He motions to a cushioned chair. "Are you going to sit down? I have no intention of buying you another plane ticket."

I don't want to sit down, but I'd rather bend my knees on my own, so I lower myself into the chair. My right index finger throbs from twisting the pendant on my necklace, but I keep twisting anyway.

The professor has too many awards. The plaques date back to 2008, 2010, and another 2010. One faded diploma says 1980. Perhaps it belongs to his father—another pretentious jerk, no doubt. The man pacing the carpet doesn't look a day over twenty-five. "You should be older."

Professor Reeve's mouth twitches. "How much older?"

"I don't know." Not a man who can fit in with his students. "Why do you want me to leave?"

"I told you—you're in danger."

"From what?"

He shakes his head. "I can't answer that."

I bite back my frustration. "Why bring me to your office, then?"

Professor Reeve sits down, and his eyes bore into mine. "I'd like to try one more time to convince you to go home. Is there nothing you want?"

I clench my hands to keep from screaming. "You can tell me why I'm in danger."

He glares at me in silence. Finally, he exhales. "There are," his face contorts, "persons here who would harm you should certain circumstances come to pass. And these circumstances cannot be prevented at this school without constant diligence on my part, which I haven't the time for."

"That tells me nothing."

He shrugs, and his eyes flit to the silver necklace hanging from my neck. "It's all I can say. I learn from my mistakes."

"Are there people here who don't like Americans?" I can't think of any other reason. I'm a nobody at home, but I'm even less than that here.

"Potentially." His face remains smooth and impassive, despite my increasing agitation.

I don't like his refusal to offer specifics, and it doesn't build my confidence in him. As I struggle to think of another way to force him to talk, my ideas run dry.

Again, his eyes move to my neck, where I've started twisting my pendant again. "Can I see your necklace? I'd like to study it."

"Why?"

A muscle in his cheek twitches. "Please." His tone is condescending, and it makes me more obliged to refuse.

"You've given me no answers, no explanations. And you want me to give you my jewelry?" I've worn this necklace since before I can remember. I'd feel naked without it. If he wants to borrow it, even for a moment, he has to earn my trust.

His mouth curves down as he rubs his chin. "I'd be willing to make a trade." He unlocks a drawer in his desk and pulls out an old piece of parchment.

I crane my neck for a better look. "A trade for what?"

Professor Reeve holds the parchment in his hands with the surface turned so I can't read it. "I've done a fair amount of research on the history of Lancaster, particularly in the fifteen and sixteen hundreds. That's how I discovered you."

I stare at him in shock. I didn't expect any hints about my origins, but I'm a sucker for it.

He holds out his hand, palm up. "Give me the necklace, and I'll explain what the letter is."

I can't let my necklace go for so little, but I study the fine lines in his open palm and hesitate. There's little reason I should keep it, except that I've had it for so long, and it might have meant something to the person who gave it to me. On the other hand, it could give me answers, and I want answers most of all.

"I'll give it back," he says, "and you'll get no further without this trade, I promise you."

Unable to resist, I unclip the necklace, but hold it in my fingertips. "Explain first."

He sighs. "I found you when I was doing a study. I'm renowned for the findings I made in that study—for the Lancashire Witch Trials. You are a descendant of the woman who wrote this letter."

I'm not sure what I expected, but having a lineage that stems from accused witches wasn't it. Both shocked and ravenous, I want to drink the entire story.

Professor Reeve touches the letter where a name has been written in a curling script.

*Alice Grey.*

My arm hairs prickle, but I'm leaning forward, my chair squeaking from the redistribution of weight.

I've heard the name before.

"How do you know we're related?"

Professor Reeve inspects me with furrowed brows. "I took a few blood tests and established it."

My desire to leave Reeve's office evaporates as fast as sweat. "You have DNA from this Alice Grey?" I tried DNA tests before, and they only told me of an Anglo-Saxon ancestry.

"I do."

"But if you know that much, can't you find out who my parents are?"

Professor Reeve grimaces. "Bryanna, if your parents wanted you to know them, they would have left me a name, not to mention they wouldn't have left you wandering the streets. Will you give me the necklace now?"

"Not yet." I shake the necklace, so the pendant dances. "Why were you studying this woman, the woman I'm related to?"

This time, when Reeve speaks, it's slow, as if I'm scraping the words out of him with a scalpel. "The purpose of my study was to determine whether the records of the witch trial are correct. Alice Grey was supposedly released before the trials, though I found accounts that claimed she died in prison. There are no records of her having children before the trials and no records of Alice Grey's life after the trials. You proved some of the records are wrong, and it became my goal to discover what really happened."

He picks up a pen from his pencil holder and bends the plastic with his fingers. "You were left on my doorstep, which is why I sought a home for you. I don't know the reason your family left. I don't know who they are, either."

My energy withers as I set the necklace on his desk by his nameplate. He answered my questions, even if his answers were unsatisfying. "Listen, professor, I don't want to go back home. I swear I'll do everything I can to keep my grades up, so I can stay."

Professor Reeve raises an eyebrow. Silence stretches.

A knock sounds on the door.

"Come in," the professor says without looking up.

A stunning young woman with long red hair steps into the room. Her green eyes have puffy circles, and black mascara streaks run down her cheeks, as if she's been crying, except her eyes are too sinister to be the type to cry.

The professor jerks and clutches his chair. "What could you possibly want from me now, Jane?"

The woman's eyes flick to me, and she stops, though she doesn't bother to hide the mascara smudges on her cheeks.

"Bryanna, it's time to go," the professor says. "Take that with you. Read it and meet me here tomorrow night. Same time."

Jane's eyes narrow. Her gaze snaps to Reeve's face, and her expression transitions from sad to suspicious faster than I can leave the room.

I clutch the letter as the door closes, leaving the necklace behind and hoping I made the right decision to entrust it to him. It's just a necklace, though my intuition says otherwise.

My rapid breathing eases as the distance between me and the glass building grows. Reeve asked to see me again tomorrow but hasn't forced me to go home. Not yet.

And he gave me a piece of my past.

I stride through Birdie's Court and unlock my apartment door. Despite the piles of homework on my desk, I dump my books and papers and shove everything aside. The anticipation builds as I tug the old parchment from my backpack. At the bottom corner is a date.

*—1775—*

*Ink stains. Parchment preserves.*

*Beneath the earth & tombstones at Moorhill Cemetery are mounds of piled bodies. A past incarnation lies among them. I will remember her if no one else will. How could I not, knowing her fate parallels my own? I will relive the horrors of her life in full.*

*In another time, yea, years before this woman was born, a younger woman walked the ancient paths of England. So prominent was her character in our story that my tale ceases in significance.*

*Her name was Alice Grey.*

*Many an eye would follow the belle's footsteps as she crossed the forested expanse of rural Pendle, growing more agreeable with each step and every swish of her skirts.*

*Affluent men courted her as she came of age, despite the disparaging situation from which she emerged. Young or old, married or unmarried, no one escaped her charm. Even the prominent judge, Altham, could not ignore her—he who passed through Pendle on business countless times.*

*Much changed in the years before the witch trials.*

*— Marguerite Dye of Birmingham*

The letter stops with strange suddenness. The scrawled date and name at the bottom contrast the careful writing at the top while the more hurried script in the last paragraph shows a different hand finished the letter.

I've never heard of Marguerite, and she couldn't be my birth mom if the letter was written in 1775. She might be another ancestor, but I'm not sure. While the letter mentions Alice Grey, it doesn't say much about her.

I'll have to research Alice if Reeve thinks she's so important. I wish the letter told me more.

After stewing over each individual word in the letter, I get frustrated at the lack of any information, other than a brief intro of Alice, and tuck the piece of garbage into a drawer in my desk, only to take it back out and smooth it flat. I read it a few more times, until the stars wake, and my eyelids droop, and there's nothing left of my brain to dedicate to the words.

# CHAPTER TEN

As I head to my history class, I'm grateful to be here. I receive no indication that my "special" classes are any different from any other class, even as I return to the brown-haired teacher's room. She stands with a half circle of students in front of her.

"It's time to turn your assignments in. Please, pass them to the students on your right, and I'll collect them on the aisle over here."

Sweat cools my back as she points to the far side of the room, clasps her hands in front of her dress, and smiles.

I search for someone else as confused as I am, but everyone has their papers ready. Pages crinkle as they're passed from one hand to another.

I must have tuned her out when she gave the assignment at the end of the previous class. I want to smack myself. It'll be hard to get the grades I need if I miss the first assignment, though I've been to every class since I arrived. *So much for a special education program.* I hoped they'd give me free passes in these scenarios. Even as I reflect on my expectations, I know they're ridiculous.

If I talk to the teacher after and ask if she can give me an extra day, I have to admit I wasn't listening when she gave the assignment. She wouldn't like that. There's no way to tell someone nicely you weren't listening. Whatever I do, she'll be offended.

The teacher picks up the piles of papers, and my neck gets hotter as she moves further away. It's too late.

I close my eyes and inhale. Even if she's offended, I have to try.

The teacher points a remote at the projector, and I force myself to pay attention, though I can never tell how well I'm listening.

She talks about the Germanic tribes and Anglo-Saxons who settled Britain, how people lived in tribes and kingdoms.

"We'll talk about the important queens and kings, even the mythical ones," my teacher says. "Starting with our famous King Henry the eighth."

She shows us slideshows of artifacts in museums, and we discuss styles during King Henry's reign, and how styles changed through the years. It makes me excited to potentially see the artifacts in person if we visit these museums.

After the lecture, the projector flicks off, and the lights turn on, throwing the room into tungsten yellow.

I stand and hesitate as rows of students file out the door. The teacher waits by the first aisle. Her eyes rove over the students until she finds me. I almost turn away to hide my embarrassment, but her smile grows, and she beckons me. After a moment's hesitation, I push toward her.

As I descend the stairs, she waits, elegant in her fitted dress.

I stop a foot away and try to look confident. "I'm sorry, professor. I didn't do the assignment. I must have missed when you talked about it. Is it possible for me to still do it, even for half credit? Will you tell me what I can do? And what the assignment was about?"

"You may call me Professor Karina." Her smile stays firmly in place.

"Thanks, I will." She seems kind, but I wait for her response before I pass judgment.

She meets my gaze. "Your name is Bryanna DeLacey, right? You're my special education student."

"Yes." Perhaps she didn't hear my questions.

"I have a few students enrolled that I keep track of, and I thought you might come to me with this concern." She hands me a sheet of paper with a brief paragraph detailing the assignment. "This should help."

"Thank you." I'm so relieved, I want to thank her a dozen times, but rather than be annoying, I add it to my bag, so I have it later.

She tucks a stack of papers under her arm as she leaves the classroom, and I make my way to the library to do some research, rewrite my essay, and study some more. It's a longer walk than I'd like, and I spend most of the time looking over my shoulder to see if the people Reeve warned me about are following me. I'm not sure if I should believe his warning. Why would anyone care about harming me?

When I get to the library, I stride down the halls, searching for a room with computers to write my essay on. I find one with a computer table surrounded by bookshelves that stretch to the end of the room, illuminated by fluorescent bulbs. I finish my essay and open my browser. *England adoption records.* The results list the government's website. *For all adoptions outside of England and Wales, call the General Register's office.*

I submitted a request for contact once in an attempt to discover the names of my birth parents, but I wasn't old enough. I'm not eligible now either, but I have another small lead.

*Alice Grey.*

I type the name from the letter Professor Reeve gave me and pages of results pop up. The townsfolk of Pendle accused Alice of witchcraft in the trials. Professor Reeve did mention something along those lines. Some sites claim the judges acquitted her; others argue she died.

I've always wanted to know the identities of my birth parents, and hitting this dead end makes me want to know even more.

I keep digging and find tales of the ruler at the time, King James, who wrote *Daemonologie,* a book that practically stated God would never allow an innocent woman to be accused of witchcraft, which made it easy for people to kill off their enemies without the use of knives or swords.

A young girl with the surname of Device supposedly cast a spell on a peddler named John Law to get pins. She was the granddaughter of an unpopular woman called Demdike who made a living off begging and extortion. Grandma Demdike feuded with another infamous old woman, Chattox, who Demdike claimed stole from her family. The two families dragged each other into the witch trials.

One of the other accused women outside the Device family, called Widow Nutter, owned a tempting parcel of land.

Essentially, the witch trials were a convenient way for the local magistrate and lawyer to take the land they wanted and rid themselves of the local pests.

It seems Alice was a girl caught in the crossfire. She was accused of witchcraft, but was related to neither Chattox nor Demdike, owned nothing, and had little to do with any of the feuds.

This all happened in the 1600s. How does Reeve have Alice's DNA?

I'll have to ask him. I'm supposed to meet with him tonight.

I open Ancestry.com, a site I've used many times in the past, but I'm not sure which family branch to follow before Alice Grey. After Alice, the line ends. The DNA sample I took a long time ago connects nowhere and says I have Anglo-Saxon ancestry, which only tells me what I already know.

A video call alert pops up on my phone's screen, and Sadie's photo appears in the corner. I jab "end." I'll have to call her later. I need to study before I get distracted again.

Pulling out my notes from class, I review everything I learned and quiz myself on dates, until my brain leaks information it can no longer retain. Then it makes no difference if I stay five hours or one.

I leave the library and pass through Birdie's Court to the great hall. Carved arches fan like spider webs, and the scent of roasted chicken saturates the air. A vacant table beckons amid the lineup of tables with students eating their lunches.

"Bryanna!" Noelle waves while her other hand balances a tray piled with leafy greens. Behind her stretches the lunch buffet. She makes a beeline toward me, and her hair shimmers with each movement; longer, thicker, and darker than the previous day. I need to ask her for some tips.

"You weren't in your room earlier," Noelle says. "I tried to find you. You could answer your phone, you know. I ran out of shampoo. Want to come with me to Mystic Cosmetics? I told you I'd bring you Saturday, but do you want to go this afternoon instead? Like right after lunch?"

"Sure." I attempt to imagine my hair as a silky chestnut brown, but the image falls flat.

"Ellen makes the best shampoo. Get your food and meet me at the table." Noelle points three tables away. "I'll be over there." She hurries off.

I load my food and sink into the seat Noelle saved. Going somewhere with a friend, even a makeup store, would be a good respite from thinking about Reeve. I still have a few hours before my appointment with him.

Noelle returns and tucks a hair behind her ear as she sits. "Are you okay?"

I wear my feelings like an emo t-shirt. "I'm supposed to meet with Professor Reeve tonight."

"Oh." Noelle tugs a brown curl. "Why?"

"He says he has something to show me."

"And you're going?"

I raise my shoulders. I don't want to explain my adoption as it'll only incite more questions. "I am, but can you make sure I make it home afterward? If I don't, look for my body somewhere by the law building." I give a hollow chuckle, though I know Reeve would never actually hurt me.

Noelle grimaces. "That's not funny, Bryanna. Let's get going, so you're back in time."

I stand with my tray. Seeing the cosmetics store might not be as fun as the Botanic Gardens, but it's better than the inside of my textbooks.

◇—◇—◇

I ride with Noelle on the bus to Mill Road. When it stops, we step off onto a narrow street with Victorian brick houses, the occasional awning, terraces, brightly lit signs, and chained bikes outside shop doors. Several stores open their windows to admit the fresh evening air. Most of the streets I've seen in Burnley are varying shades of modest brown, but Mill Road employs splashes of color, like the owners wanted to mimic the inside of a travel book.

Noelle pauses on the sidewalk. "Coming?"

"Yes." I hurry after her.

A bright purple awning bears the words, "Mystic Cosmetics," in black, spiky letters with a large, gnarled vine growing around it with sections that twist and reach into the upper stories. Huddled about the window, a group of young men press their faces to a wide crack in the glass where fumes escape to swirl into the sky. Not a single guy steps into the store. Instead, they linger around the threshold.

The number of boys far outranks the number of girls.

"Isn't this a cosmetics store for women?" I ask.

"It's for both," Noelle says. "But you're right, it's usually women you see shopping here."

We circumnavigate the group and make for the door. A spoon sways from a knocker with strange symbols inscribed into the convex side. Dried parsnip hangs from the handle.

Inside, dozens of fruity scents churn in the air. Bars of soap organized by color decorate rows of wooden tables. Bundles of lavender, basil, dill, and chamomile dangle from the ceiling, some fresh and others dry. A circular counter stands in the middle, covered with old-fashioned pots and silver spoons. A clock with an oval face chimes with two large hands, painted with fancy eyes. Perched on top, a raven cocks its head. Three tiny black eyes fixate on me, and a shudder runs through me.

Is it a mutant raven? A fake, robotic one? I'm not sure, but its beady eyes look too real for comfort.

About a dozen women crowd in the far corner behind a sign that says, "Demo today only. Make your own soap. Sign up for lessons now." A young woman leans over and sniffs a platter of soap bars with dried herbs drizzled over the top. All the women in the store are beautiful with long, thick hair and perfect skin.

I've never felt the shame of my freckles and boring hair color more than I do now. My hand goes to my necklace, but it's missing from my neck.

Noelle tugs on my arm and wheels me to face a young blonde woman behind the counter. The woman has glossy hair, ivory skin, and ice-blue eyes. In one hand, she stirs a concoction over an electric stove. If she didn't run a cosmetics store, I would have guessed she was my age.

Something squishy strikes my foot.

*Scrieeee!*

A rat darts out the open door as I stumble sideways.

Noelle steadies me with a smile. "Don't mind that. It happens."

I don't trust myself to speak. The little hairs on my skin refuse to flatten, and I can't stop eyeing the crow while it watches me. I take a few steadying breaths. I'm overthinking this. The store owners must have added the crow to set a mystical mood. It's in the store's name, after all. So perfectly normal.

*It's not like I'm afraid of rats.* I try to laugh at myself, but it's not funny.

Noelle steps toward the blonde woman. "Hey, Ellen, I came to get more of your hair product."

"I'm making it now," Ellen says in a tone that would make anyone hide under a rock.

"No hurry, I can wait."

"Excuse me." A man wedges around me and rubs his fingers on the counter. His eyes track Ellen as she crosses the room for more plants. The men outside the door continue to watch, barring the exit.

Ellen turns to him. "Are you here to buy?"

"No." The man tugs on the neckline of his shirt. "I'm here to—"

"Tell me your name." Ellen waits with a slanted brow.

His expression brightens. "Tom—"

"Get out." Ellen returns to her pot of bubbling product as the man shuffles his feet.

His face falls as he sticks his hands into his pockets and looks around. He leaves, and the door slams shut. The young men around the window step back, crane their necks, and regroup.

Ellen holds her chin high. "Just blonde hair to them," she mutters.

"Who're you looking for?" I ask.

Noelle shakes her head as if to silence me, but it's too late.

Ellen looks up, and her eyes narrow. "What do you mean?"

"You asked for his name," I say. "Are you expecting someone?" Clearly not a Tom.

Ellen sniffs, but her haughty expression relaxes as she returns to stirring. "Hadrian Bristol, or at least that's what I hear he calls himself. Seems every man comes to see the Bierley sisters, except the one I care about. I don't suppose you know him?"

My gut twists at the thought of Hadrian standing outside, gawking at Ellen like an idiot. Or looking at any of the women here, for that matter.

"No," I say.

Ellen's upper lip curls back as she leaves her pot. She thrusts aside a set of curtains behind the counter and vanishes.

Noelle stares at the shifting drapes until Ellen returns with a bundle of supplies under one arm.

"I'd also like to get cover-up for sensitive, light skin and try it on my friend here."

I don't remember discussing this. "That's nice of you, Noelle, but I don't have the money for—"

"I'll buy." Noelle winks.

Ellen points to the far wall, and Noelle follows her silent direction to study the different hues of foundation. I suppose if Noelle wants to buy the cover-up herself, it's her prerogative, but I'm mortified she thinks I need it.

I wander the perimeter of the store. Near the door, a collection of photos features glaring women with bruises for eyes. It's high fashion.

A low, circular table displays stacks of soaps. I pick up a bar and turn it over.

*Bloodroot, mandrake, lavender, wormwood, fingernail...*

Sweat tickles my skin as it drips. It's a joke, of course. I shouldn't worry. I set the soap down, and a spider crawls from a crack in the pile and almost brushes my hand. A squeal tears from my lips as a sharp elbow shoves me aside.

Ellen sweeps the spider into her hands and dumps the black, sprawling ball of legs into her pot. She stirs with her spoon, and a loving smile caresses her face.

My stomach roils. I must be hallucinating, and I pinch myself to make it stop.

Ellen drops her spoon, her eyes on me. "Would you like to learn how to make those soaps? We're selling lessons."

Noelle claps her hands, and a wide grin splits her face. "Will you teach your secret recipes?"

"Yes." Ellen waves a hand over her pot, and the scent of lilac fills the room. "But only to a select few. If you bring the man called Hadrian Bristol, I'll give you 50 percent off."

The spider's gone, so there's no more need for pinching. I let the smarting skin loose. "But why Hadrian?"

I regret speaking as Ellen stops stirring. Her eyes focus on me, and I feel like someone dumped a bucket of ice on my head.

"We saw him earlier this week at the Botanic Gardens," Noelle says.

My blood runs a few degrees colder at the thought of being the one to bring Hadrian here.

Ellen's red lips spread thin over white teeth. "He used to be quite the gentleman."

"Used to be?" I have every reason to believe Hadrian still merits the word, archaic or not.

Ellen ignores my question. "Tell you what, bring him today, and I'll give you 70 percent off."

"Today?" Noelle's brows pinch together. "I don't have his number."

Ellen shrugs.

Noelle can't be serious. Hadrian would have no reason to come here. I give Noelle a pointed look, but she ignores me. He's too kind to dupe into coming to a cosmetics store to satisfy Noelle's vanity and pocketbook.

"I'll try to find him." Noelle pauses. "Would I get a discount on the products, too?"

I grab Noelle by the hand, the same way she grabbed mine at the Botanic Gardens, and tow her outside before Ellen replies.

"Certainly," Ellen calls as the door chimes shut.

We leave the purple awning and the door with the dried herbs behind until the fuss of the store admirers blends into the general noise of the street. We stride toward the bus stop. My cheeks are on fire. Even if we wanted Hadrian to come, he wouldn't agree to it, would he?

Noelle stops beneath the bus sign. "I don't know why you were so anxious to leave. You acted like you'd seen the devil."

I flinch away from Noelle, stung by her words.

"Look," Noelle says, "we'll go back and get some stuff for your hair. You could use the color boost, and we'll have a discount." She pulls her phone out of her purse as compact cars rumble by. Beside me, a pole supports a plastic case with missing person pamphlets. Someone pasted a photo of a smiling kid on the front.

I don't need fixing, and I don't like Noelle analyzing me like I'm an art project she wants to paint over for a better grade.

"I'm not going back there," I say, struggling to stay calm.

Noelle purses her lips and jabs at her phone's screen.

I wait for her to finish before I ask the question that nags me. "Are you friends with Ellen?"

"She's nice."

I bite my lip at the blatant falsehood.

Noelle drops her phone into her purse and sighs. "I don't know where Hadrian lives. How could I have known to bring him? And how am I going to convince him to come? Maybe you can talk him into it?"

Ellen, in all her blonde beauty, would wait in the doorway for Hadrian to arrive. Her long curls would spill over her shoulders, and her lips would expose straight, pearly teeth. Those chilling eyes would glitter as they devoured him with a glance. I may never admit it aloud, but I don't want that.

"I thought you didn't like Hadrian," I say.

"I told you I'd get over that. I decided to forgive him. Anyway, you like him, so I have to like him, too." She pauses, her face screwed up with desperate deliberations. "I know someone who knows him. She'll know where he lives."

"It doesn't matter," I say. "I can't go back. I have to meet with the professor."

Noelle chews on her lip. "I forgot about that." She plays with her phone. "We'll bring him back another day. Maybe on a group date. Fifty percent is still a good deal. And any guy will go anywhere for a pretty face."

Why the "pretty face" again?

"I'm not going back. I don't want to take Hadrian to Ellen. Honestly, it's weird that she'd ask."

Furrowing her brows, Noelle says, "I don't think it's weird, but if that's what you want…I still think a group date would be fun. Maybe not a date, but a hangout. I'd like to introduce you to my friend Mika, too."

Noelle's willingness to let go of her discount eases the tension that grips me as the bus appears down the road and draws closer with traffic.

Noelle studies my face. "If we do that, I'll have time to give you a makeover. Then when we go out, everyone will see how pretty you are."

Her stacked comments about my looks fester beneath my skin until Ellen's striking face returns to mind. Everyone in that store looked like they dropped out of a fashion show, with perfect outfits, hair, and teeth. If their products work, I suppose a makeover wouldn't be so bad. Maybe Noelle's trying to help.

"Sure, but no going back to the cosmetics store."

Noelle rolls her eyes, but she promises nothing.

# CHAPTER ELEVEN

THE PROFESSOR STANDS outside the high and mighty oak door of his office with his fedora and suit coat already on as I approach. Perhaps he doesn't intend to stay long. That would be a relief.

I hold out the letter. "This is all you've got? If so, I'd like my necklace back, please."

"No to the necklace." He locks his office door. "And the rest of the journals are at the library."

"The rest?" My curiosity stays me. There's more?

"Yes, like the one I showed you." Professor Reeve strides toward the doors that lead outside and motions for me to follow.

The previous letter gave me no answers, but "the rest" might. Despite my better judgment, I begin to hope, but it's not enough to make me move. Though my brain is often on vacation, I'm dragged back to earth when strange men invite me to go alone with them. I'm not trusting and haven't been, even before Teddy.

"The library isn't far from here, so we can walk together." He glances over his shoulder, an eyebrow raised. "Are you coming?"

My distrust and curiosity war with each other as he waits for a response. The desire for answers is overwhelming. I want to know who I am. I want to know my full story and the people backstage. What is knowing worth?

I take a step, and this time, I command my own feet. If he doesn't intend to force me to come, I'm more willing.

Reeve gives me a dazzling smile, and my irritation stirs. He must know I can't resist, and, Lord above, I wish he wasn't right.

We walk along a path that borders a biking trail and some tall hedges that later become lofty, overhanging trees. A brick tower emerges over the tops of the highest branches. Then the trees part, and a stone pediment crown for a long gray building surfaces, reminding me of colonial buildings on the American East Coast.

"Why do you need my necklace?" I ask.

Reeve casts me a look I can't read and changes the subject. "I found a collection of works made by a man with a guilty conscience—the same man who recorded the history of the witch trials I told you about yesterday. His name was Thomas Potts. He collected journals from the ruined homes of those that died, and I've added a few entries I discovered on my own. When you put them together, you get a clear picture of what happened."

His tale piques my interest, but I'm still bothered by him ignoring me when I asked about my necklace. I don't like it, but I don't expect demanding it back will get me anywhere. Not with Reeve. I'll have to think of another way to reclaim it that won't get me expelled.

The professor walks beside me through a door into the lobby and beneath a cream-colored, arched ceiling. Fine lines intersect on golden stars while antique cherry bookshelves whisper of dusty volumes.

Reeve continues up two flights of stairs to a locked door in a remote corner of the third floor. He unlocks it and ushers me into a room with rectangular panes of glass that frame the distant grounds. Against the wall stands a printer and scanner. Two large leather books rest on a circular table. One has a black cover inscribed with a tree surrounded by runes. The other is a simple brown.

Professor Reeve picks up the black book and motions to the other. "I put this in here for you. It can't be taken out—it's too valuable— but you can come here anytime you like. You won't be able to read it in one sitting." He lifts the brown book, tears out a page at the end, and stuffs the torn page into his coat pocket.

I follow his movements with my eyes. I would never tear the pages of any of my books, even the ones worth the cost of my lunch. It makes my insides writhe.

"If it's so valuable, why tear it?" I ask.

"It's very valuable. You are correct. Here's the key to access the room." He offers a small brass key on the palm of his hand.

Sidestepping my questions only makes me want to hound him with more. I swallow more inquiries as I accept the key and grip it in my fist. If I pester him, he'd only evade me again. "Can I copy them?"

"Yes, it won't hurt the book. You can take the copies home, too."

An even more important question hovers on my tongue, and I can't hold this one back. "Will it tell me who my birth parents are?"

The professor's eyes bore into mine. "It'll tell you who you are. And when you make the connection, hopefully, you'll leave."

Knowing who I am has everything to do with the identities of my biological parents, though. "But—"

"When you're ready to leave, come to me. I'll get you wherever you want to go, the moment you want to go. This is all I can do, short of strapping you to the seat of a plane and calling all the powers of hell to hold you there." His mouth jerks into a rare, almost pained smile. "Believe it or not, I care about you, Bryanna. I'd like to keep you alive."

Icy shivers scuttle from my dry throat. Life or death again, and I still don't know if I should believe him.

Professor Reeve tucks the black book beneath his arm and turns to go, but I call after him. "What about that one—the one you're holding? Don't I need it, too?"

Professor Reeve pauses in the doorway. "The book on the table is sufficient."

The black book looks far more interesting, with intricate carvings and signs inscribed into the jacket.

"What are those characters on the cover?" I ask.

"A language few know."

He must enjoy being cryptic. I'll have him know I've smacked my brothers for less. "And you know it?"

A smirk steals over his lips. "I do." He closes the door behind him.

I have homework to do, and I can't be late on another assignment, or Professor Karina won't give me another chance. Professor Reeve told me to scan each page, so I can take the scans home. Yet an insatiable hunger for knowledge gnaws at me as I trail a finger over the book's soft leather cover, stained with age. I open it to reveal a description written in fancy calligraphy.

*The compiled works of Thomas Potts.*

*A collection of true accounts in an attempt to right a terrible wrong.*

*All works have been honestly claimed from the homes of victims or given by the families of those accused.*

*Other accounts have been provided by the son of Magistrate Nowell, in his later years of service.*

*Though I know none will believe this account, I feel I have done all I can to atone for mine part in this heinous transgression.*

*The Pendle Witch Trials and curse of the Mekori.*

A note at the bottom says, *The Pendle Witch Trials and curse of the Mekori.* I grab the letter from Marguerite Dye out of my backpack where I'd tucked it when the professor refused to take it back. The signature matches the more recent handwritten note, which means the same person who signed Marguerite's name also wrote the subtitle for the journal.

I put the letter down.

No one knows my origins better than the professor. Somewhere in this book, the professor has something for me to understand.

I check the clock on my phone. I have time to read a few pages before the library closes, and I'll make copies before I go.

Above the first letter, a preface written by Thomas Potts spans the page in a curling script.

*I did not believe in witchcraft until the trials here in Lancaster. Read and be warned lest you be accused of witchcraft or fall and become one of the devil's followers yourself.*

His words sound consistent with the beliefs in witchcraft during that era. I continue to a journal entry further down the page.

*—June of 1603—*

*I crested a hill that overlooked Trawden Forest. Blue haze drifted over the tree line, a crowd of dancing ghosts. The road descended into the trees and disappeared, though my map indicated the road should lead to Cox Colne, the local alehouse.*

*I glanced behind me. No one had followed, but dread breathed in my breast.*

*My horse, Dantes, pawed the soft dirt and let out a low whinny as I promised him we wouldn't stay long.*

*I brought out the cross from where it hung around my neck. The smooth metal usually gave me a sense of bearing.*

The cross reminds me of the one Hadrian wore, so I pause at the mention of it. A sense of meaning grips me. But lots of people wear crosses, especially when this letter was written. It means nothing. Dismissing the thought, I dive back into the letters.

*Dantes pranced back and forth. I dismounted, leaned against him, clasped my hands, and prayed with an earnestness I have never before known. I prayed for the Catholics. I prayed for the Protestants. I prayed for the king, though, in my heart, I have not forgiven him. Most of all, I prayed my name might remain in God's keeping.*

When I remounted Dantes, I spurred the horse
to trot into a landscape of boughs and muttering
breezes. Branches creaked and skeletal leaves
fluttered to rest in a grave of deteriorating mold.
Creatures slithered through needles as a crow
sprang from the canopies and squawked.

I leaned forward to hasten Dantes, but a soft mew
made me pause. A black cat slunk through the dead
foliage, its tiny legs keeping pace with the horse.

I laughed at my uneasiness, but my mirth rang
hollow through the forest, and I let the sound die.

A woman's voice came from behind, asking me to
pardon her intrusion. I turned and before me stood
the most beautiful woman I ever beheld, carrying
a broom, which was strange, for she had nothing
to sweep but dead needles. She wanted to know if I
was from Colne.

I fumbled with the brim of my hat as I said I was
foreign.

Her long locks flowed like a golden waterfall down
her back, and she had a smile as pale as the glit-
tering moon over the Basque Coast. Fine jewels
and ruffles adorned her neck.

*After I dismounted Dantes, I stooped to kiss her thin fingers, but my lips met stone, and I pulled quickly away.*

*As if to explain the strange texture of her hand, she told me a lady's hands are always cold.*

*Eager to accept her explanation, I swallowed a lump of fear and communicated my desire to travel to Cox Colne Alehouse for the night and that, on the morrow, I shall continue to Liverpool.*

*She asked if I needed directions, but I had a map and knew the way.*

*Out of politeness, I asked her name. She answered with Ellen Bierley. An angel dressed in folds of satin and lace.*

*When she asked for my name, I gave her "Guido," and she wanted to know where I hailed from, if not here.*

*I come from many places, I told her, nonetheless, I considered Flanders and Spain home for many years. I didn't want to say too much of myself in case anyone came to this village asking questions.*

She observed my face closely as we spoke, and I grew uncomfortable with the number of questions she asked, though she said she does not often find gentlemen in her path, especially not in Samlesbury where she comes from. She wished I would stay longer, though she asked if I had seen a child with yellow eyes.

When I said no, Ellen smiled, but she had no warmth to melt the ice blue of her eyes. I will quote her next words exactly because they chilled me to my core. "I could not leave Master Guy Fawkes alone on the road," she said, "looking so handsome in his hat."

She knew my true name without me speaking it aloud.

A bird somewhere overhead chirped a warning crescendo. "Guido," I corrected her.

She said she knows who I am, and I should not be disturbed by it, that she will keep my secrets. Yet she repeated my worries in the exact phrases I thought them.

All warmth drained from me, down to the sodden earth. She knew too much without me saying a word. Then she extended her hand and asked to see my map.

I reached into my saddlebags, but instead of a map, I found parchment folded into the crude shape of a cat. I crushed the little feline in my fist as she asked in a smug voice if I lost it.

I could barely speak. Such ill luck couldn't belong to me.

She begged me to trust her, but I clutched the crucifix beneath my coat and told her I must go.

Her face hardened as I urged Dantes on. She demanded I stay, and I thanked the Lord I had checked and rechecked the map throughout my journey. The roads endured in memory while Ellen's eyes bored into my back.

I did not expect to find a living soul until Marsden, the nearest village. However, several miles down the road, an old woman stirred at the foot of a wizened tree and begged me for coin, her crumpled legs surrounded by empty or broken *bottles. Wrinkled fingers clawed the air while a milky white film covered the old woman's eyes.*

*She said her daughter is lame. Indeed, her daughter sat beside her, meeting my gaze with unbalanced eyes. One looked up while the other bounced without direction.*

*I drew several small coins from my pocket, but the elder woman seized my coat and beseeched me for milk, though I promised I had none.*

*A figure emerged from the trees with ebony hair, calling the woman by "Demdike."*

*I ripped my coat from Demdike's grasp, remounted my horse, and the two of us fled, eager now for the shores of Liverpool. We didn't slow until the dim silhouette of the alehouse appeared across the road.*

*— Guido*

I touch the name, *Ellen*. The woman in the cosmetics store shares the same name. "Guy Fawkes" sounds familiar, too. Surely, the reason Reeve wants me to read these will become clearer as I read further.

"Excuse me, the library is closed," says a snappy voice from the doorway.

I twist in my chair to face a woman with blue curls and round glasses. She must be the librarian. "Sorry, I'll get going." I reach for the book and stop. Reeve said I couldn't take it home. He suggested I make copies, but I haven't given myself enough time.

*Crap.*

I'll have to come back to finish. I scoop up my backpack and shut off the light. "Sorry, again."

The librarian only nods.

When I close the door, it seems I leave a part of myself behind.

# CHAPTER TWELVE

HE NEXT MORNING, I go to class and walk in moments before it starts. Professor Karina watches me sit down and glances at me several times during the lecture. She must plan to talk to me after, and she does.

As soon as she dismisses everyone, she meets my gaze and holds up a hand. I press my back into the seat and try to get comfortable. I'm not sure what she's going to talk to me about. Was my essay bad?

She sits slowly at my side, wearing another dress more tight-fitting than the previous one. She hands me my essay, and there's a green "C" on it. Disappointed expectations carve a hole in my stomach. It's not a terrible grade, but it's not good either. I suppose it's what I expected.

"What did you learn about King Henry VIII when you wrote this essay?" she asks.

I should be able to remember what I searched. "He married a lot of women he didn't like and never had a son." That should sum it up.

"What were you trying to convey about King Henry when you wrote about him?" She peers at me with an intensity that makes me feel like I missed something.

"Well, he married Catherine of Aragon." I pause, trying to remember them in order, and am surprised to find all the names within my grasp. My voice grows stronger. "Anne Boleyn, Jane Seymour, Anne of Cleves, Catherine Howard, and Katherine Parr." English people back then all had the same names.

Professor Karina's voice is overly kind in her response. "But why does that matter?"

"Because…He was a jerk?"

The professor's raised brow says she fishes for a deeper conclusion.

"Because nothing he had was ever enough," I say.

"Exactly." Professor Karina smiles. "Let me tell you a secret. Start with that statement, end with that statement, and organize your thoughts between. Your essay jumps around a lot. Be sure to make your points flow and transition coherently. You have a lot of interesting facts, but I know you have something to say about them. Don't be afraid to say it."

That makes sense, and it gives me hope that it's something I can fix.

"I'll redo it," I say. "I can do better, if you'll let me."

"Good." She seems to like my response. "I don't want you to get discouraged. People like you are often the most creative, hard-working students." She gives me an encouraging smile, and it makes me feel better.

It's nice to think she sees potential in me.

"Is that why you chose to teach here?" I wince at my hidden question. Did she want to be a special needs teacher?

Her smile widens. "Part of it, yes. I joined Burnley at the start of this year, so I haven't been here long." She pats my hand. "Good luck on your essay. I know you won't let me down."

When she leaves, her faith in me settles, thick and heavy. What if I don't live up to her expectations?

I push the thoughts back as I walk out the classroom door.

"Bryanna? What class did you just come from?"

I jump as Noelle's familiar voice comes from down the hall and force a welcoming smile. Professor Karina doesn't seem to teach just special needs kids, so I think it's safe to tell Noelle the truth.

"Professor Karina's history class."

"Oh, I love her. She's so nice."

If Noelle is familiar with Professor Karina, I'm curious whether Noelle knows about my program. "She teaches the special education class, right? Have you heard of that?"

Noelle nods. "Oh, that's a joke. A journalist wrote an article on Professor Reeve's honorary student club, and the school got trashed on a few blogs and newspapers. The headmistress was furious, I heard. The special education program was introduced as a way to deflect attention and save face, in my opinion. I don't think it's real."

My neck heats. Professor Karina didn't act like the program was a joke. Honestly, I don't want it to be. I search for a way to change the subject. "Have you talked to your friend, Mika?"

Noelle glances down the hall and shakes her head. "Yes, but I have to run. I'll talk to you about that later. See you!" She hurries off. Since I don't want to talk about the special education program anymore, this solves my problem.

I don't have another class for a while, so I head straight to the library. I find the private room Reeve showed me. The journal waits on the table. I make the copies, tuck them into my backpack, and leave the ancient book behind. After going to a room with computers, I start by chugging a cup of coffee and then work on my homework. Within a half hour, the caffeine coursing through me makes me feel alive and focused, like nothing else does.

I reach for my backpack to start reading the journals, but the slap of a volume hitting the floor makes me turn. A book lies on the ground by the bookshelves. No one picks it up. Silence grins, and my skin tingles.

Forcing an exhale, I let my shoulders drop and grab my backpack. I'll read the letters at home.

As I head for the bus stop, I glance over my shoulder, and Reeve's warning about nefarious persons intending to harm me scratches at my thoughts. The faces of the people that stroll down the sidewalk behind me vary. No nefarious stalkers follow.

I'm being paranoid again, so I let out a flat chuckle that doesn't make the eerie feeling go away. The impression clings to me as I take the bus to Birdie's Court.

I glance over my shoulder again as I enter my dormitory and close the door behind me. The hair on my neck refuses to stop prickling. Sitting at my desk, I bring out the copied journal entries but set them aside. I study for several hours before I allow myself to soothe the itch that has plagued me since last night.

When I finally stuff my homework in my backpack, it's a relief to have my studying done. The letters are my reward.

The next letter in the pile, written in June of year 1603, bears the signature, *James Altham.*

## —*1603*—

*Townsfolk gestured to my carriage through the window while the gentle, steady clop of the horses' hooves brought me closer. Trees. Peasants. Lacey collars here and there beneath plain faces.*

*Then the whistle of a flute and the smashing of mugs on wooden tables penetrated the walls of the carriage. We reached Cox Colne at last. The carriage doors opened, and my driver stepped aside.*

*The alehouse entry stood open, devoid of flouncy dresses. No heads peered over the windowsill to* see what manner of man arrived. Inside, nothing changed. Grubby mugs littered the floors with a group of wooden tables thrown together. The magistrate's son lounged in the corner alone with greasy strings of hair slapped across his face.

Behind the boy, a maiden danced between tables. She made her way to me as the sun's dim rays streamed from the window. Dust stirred like glitter. She twirled and slammed against my chest while her breath rose, hot and stale. I pulled her in for a kiss and requested a drink as she left with money clenched in her hand.

Behind the dancer sat a woman with unreal red hair and a low neckline. Her eyes brightened as I sat at her side, close enough to smell her perfume, a splash of nutmeg. She had to be at least twenty years my junior.

She introduced herself as Jane Southworth. I have heard of her on my travels to Samlesbury, for she is the wife of John Southworth.

Her unparalleled beauty would cause any man to risk disownment. John's family—all devout Catholics—contested his marriage to a Protestant.

This was the gossip only six years previous. Could their marriage have been so long ago? Jane looked young. And what is she doing in Colne?

Curiously, she asked if I had seen a young boy with yellow eyes. She seemed to seek someone specific, and I could not help her.

After apologizing for not being useful, I told her I had heard much of her loveliness, and she answered that she knew of me as well and felt I could be very useful indeed, for she could be the wife of James Altham, Serjeant-at-law if I wished it. She said, "Only heaven attempts to record the countless marriages that have been consummated over the ages. We both know that neither of us will end our lives in heaven, seeing as thou hast three wives thus far."

Her response made a bead of sweat trickle down my nose.

No one knew this, not even my wives. I traveled so far, so often; I doubted any of them would ever discover me.

She might have slapped me, for I felt the sting of her insinuation, and the horror that anyone else might have suspected me.

When I demanded to know where she heard this blasphemy, she claimed that she discovered all she could upon my arrival.

"I know much of thee, Altham," she said. "I would not mind becoming the fourth wife, so long as all thine fortunes are imparted to me upon thy death."

The server brought my ale, and I guzzled the drink. I could have used a few more drinks, too.

She smiled as she told me that man's life is fleeting, and that I should die like all the rest. Her own husband does not have long to live, and he is younger than me.

When I stood, my gut tumbled from my breeches, and I let it.

I demanded to know if she intended to threaten me, her superior before God and our king, but she did not seem disturbed by this. Instead, she asked if I am afraid of death.

My embarrassment spread, heating my collar to my boots.

Jane trailed a finger down my arm. Her eyes flickered red, and her cheekbones hollowed. All the musculature and skin wasted away until only rows of white teeth grinned.

Laughter broke through the hellish hallucination. Two girls passed outside the window. They walked arm in arm with humble dresses. One had patches on her skirts, but her loveliness surpassed even Jane. I needed to speak to them, to get their attention in any way I could. So, I pushed Jane aside and met them outside the door. They turned when I called.

The several drinks I downed made it difficult to hold my legs steady as I bowed to them and asked to be an escort.

The pretty woman with the patched skirt and dark ringlets curtsied. A silver necklace hung from the girl's neck with a tree pendant—too elegant for her homespun dress. She told me no, but thank you.

I asked for her name, and she said, "Alice Grey."

*Leaning toward her, I whispered the directions to my residence and bade her meet me there tonight. She couldn't possibly deny me with a rank so high above her own, and with her attentions, I would have no need for Jane. So, I turned to the ale-house where Jane waited, paused, and made for my carriage instead. The woman's fiery hair and eyes seared holes in my back as I left her behind.*

*—Sir James Altham*

Alice Grey's relevance must be more than proving errors in history books. Otherwise, Reeve wouldn't give me these accounts. The tree necklace mentioned is curiously similar to mine, which, as much as it frustrates me, Reeve still has. He distracted me before when I asked for it back, but he won't again.

The letters continue with another entry from the same man.

*—1603—*

*My sheets lay smooth and cold. The absence of bare feet do little to warm the thick rugs. The oval mirrors reflect no curves. Stars wink outside the window, mocking me.*

*The girl at the alehouse, Alice Grey, with the dark curls and pale skin, never came. Miserable folk trudge down the street below. She is not among them. Even in Pendle, the women won't have me, only Jane, who desires money.*

*I will not allow this embarrassment to sway me. I am not at the end of my career. Alice will give herself to me, and youth and beauty will be mine. There is a way.*

*—Sir James Altham, Barrowford*

I sit back in my seat, eyes aching from the strain of reading.

Why would Jane need money? She must have been desperate to go after someone as pathetic as James Altham. And something must have happened between Alice and James to set Alice in the witch trials. She clearly survived, otherwise, I wouldn't have been born.

As I reach to turn the page, a knock sounds, and I stand to crack the door open. "Hello?"

Noelle's eyebrows rise. "Aren't you going to let me in?"

My shoulders relax, and I breathe a sigh of relief as I open the door wider. It's not Reeve. "Yes, sorry."

Noelle glances at the papers on the desk. "What's that?"

"Homework," I lie. I bundle the papers and stack them beneath my textbook. I don't really feel like explaining this part of my life to her. "What's up?"

"Is that Professor Karina's assignment? You're in history, right? How did you do on it?"

"I got an A." The lie comes so easily.

"Me, too," she says.

How could she have? I studied far more than she did. I want to be happy for her, so I smile and open my mouth to offer congratulations, but no words come.

Noelle sits on my bed like she did the first day we met. "I tried calling you, but you don't answer your phone anymore. You spend way too much time studying these days. So, when I saw the light on in your room, I figured you were still awake. I have our group hangout all planned. I talked to my friend about it, and we planned for tomorrow night. Does that work with your schedule?"

I look down at the copied pages. I want to read the rest of these, but I also have more homework to get done. I've spent hours on it the last few days to impress Professor Karina.

"Hadrian's coming." Noelle's smile doesn't quite reach her eyes.

I can't say no to that. "I'll make it work."

# CHAPTER THIRTEEN

A BALL OF ANXIOUS ENERGY wreaks havoc in my stomach as I walk down the hall to Noelle's dormitory. The hangout Noelle arranged starts this afternoon. I stand in front of Noelle's door, knock, and smooth my linen shirt until the door opens and waves of sweet perfume roll over me.

As the door swings to reveal Noelle, I do a double take. She wears large, gold earrings and a casual dress, but what throws me off is the reflection of my face in her dilated pupils, like giant black ice ponds spreading cold down to my toes.

I shake the feeling off. Maybe it's the dark. My pupils dilate indoors, too.

Behind Noelle, shoes are arranged in a perfect lineup inside a small closet. Dresses dangle in an ordered rainbow. The bed is made with a quilt tucked at the sides. A heart-shaped frame on the bedside table displays a fluffy puppy.

"This way." Noelle leads me across the hall to a small bathroom where even the makeup is organized into plastic shelving. A flatiron perched on a stool waits beside a box of organized makeup. Noelle gestures to a narrow stool. "Sit down."

I sit. "Thanks for doing this."

"You're welcome." Noelle's voice is light and airy. She reaches for a black pencil and pulls my eyelid down. "You'll look so good when I'm done."

Noelle outlines both eyes, and I dig my fingers into the stool to keep from fidgeting. "Did you get all these products at Mystic?"

I don't like the idea of wearing Mystic products, especially if they're made with spiders. Unless, of course, Ellen meant to scare me, and they're not actually made with insects…they probably aren't. Of course, they aren't. How could they be? The store wouldn't be so popular if spider legs were actually in their soaps.

If Ellen knew how well her scheme worked, she'd laugh at me.

"Not all of them," Noelle answers. "Their products are expensive, and I've spent too much on them already." Noelle pauses. "See how pretty you look?"

Dark eyeliner borders my gray-blue eyes. Noelle adds a creamy powder to my face and blush to my cheeks. "I can't believe you don't wear mascara. I never leave my room without it. What do you think?"

"Um…" I look good enough to go to a cocktail party. A smile steals over the reflection of my face in the mirror. I can't wait to see Hadrian.

Noelle's phone buzzes. "Oh, look! Mika texted me!" Her mouth splits into a grin. She mutters incoherent words as she types her answer, and then looks up. "I want you to know I'm okay with you dating Hadrian. It's a bit awkward between Hadrian and me still, but I've moved on to his friend, Eser." Noelle pulls on her fingers, her smile fading. "Anyway, let's get going. Mika's waiting. She's the only one who can drive unsupervised."

Despite Noelle's graciousness, her comment makes me uncomfortable, and I'm not sure if I should feel bad for caring about Hadrian. But if she's okay with it, I can be, too, right?

Doubt squirms in my stomach.

"You should try the other products at the cosmetics store," Noelle says as we descend the stairs.

"I just might. Thanks again for the help."

We cross the courtyard and start down the road where the tallest tower of the library emerges over the trees as the road turns. A girl on the front steps rises to her toes, waves, and rushes toward us.

I fidget as the usual dread of meeting someone new creeps in.

"Noelle!" The girl hugs Noelle and embraces me as well. A strong, vanilla perfume clings to her long, black hair. She wears jeans and a plaid coat, and I can picture her walking down Oxford Street with an expensive bag on her arm.

"Hey, Mika." Noelle grins. "I've missed your beautiful face. And your clothes, actually."

"Thanks, Noelle." Mika's dark, almond eyes wrinkle at the sides. Her voice is sweet with a noticeable accent. She faces me. "I don't think we've met."

"I'm Bryanna." I'm not sure if they shake hands in England, so I offer.

She smiles and takes my outstretched fingers. "Mika."

Noelle checks her phone. "Mika's making us snacks to take with us, and we'll have lots of time to talk at the boys' dormitory. We need to get going."

Motioning for us to follow, Mika glances over her shoulder at Noelle. "You bought the tickets?"

"I did. And made a dinner reservation at a restaurant." Noelle squeezes my arm as we walk.

Excitement and apprehension war for space in my head. I hope we're doing something active that doesn't require me to stumble through conversation.

"Where are we going?"

We round a curve in the sidewalk, where rows of cars fill parking spaces. Mika rummages for keys in her pocket. "We're going fishing. I thought the boys would like the idea. And I clearly forgot the water part when I put these shoes on this morning." She points her toes to show her leather heels. "I'll have to make do. Anyway, I'll mostly be watching."

Mika nods to a Peugeot. "That's me. I hope you don't mind if it's a little messy—"

A whistle comes from behind, cutting Mika off. "Hey, girls. And Noelle, I've missed our conversations."

We all turn as a group of students snicker behind their hands. The boy at the front looks me up and down and winks. "You look fit, my sweet."

I turn away in disgust.

Their raucous laughter fades as Noelle drops into the passenger seat and slams the door shut. I melt into the back, where the scent of new leather clings to the seats. Mika starts the car, which is so clean, I couldn't find a crumb if I wanted to. So much for being messy.

Noelle's lips are pale, and she bounces one of her legs on the seat. "Are you okay?" I ask.

She brushes her hair over one shoulder but doesn't smile. "I'm fine."

Mika's brows draw together. "Are you su—"

"Yes," Noelle snaps, and Mika pinches her lips shut.

I can understand if she doesn't want to talk about it, so I change the subject. "How do you know Noelle and Hadrian, Mika?"

Mika straightens in her seat. "Hadrian and I have known each other for a long time. I never had brothers, so he, Eser, and even Robbie are as close as I'll ever get. Noelle and I have classes together."

"Bryanna and I saw Hadrian at the greenhouse," Noelle says in a flat tone.

Mika turns the wheel and backs out of her parking stall. "He goes there sometimes." There's something off in her voice. She maneuvers the car out onto the road, makes a few turns between streets, and pulls into another parking lot where she lets the engine die. "Cliviger Fishponds is one of my favorite places. I'm excited for you to see it, Bryanna."

"Me, too," I say.

I know so little about England, and the more I discover, the more excited I become, though it separates me a little more from home.

Mika parks in front of a building that resembles a skewed gray block with black squares for windows. I squeeze between the door and the neighboring car to get out. With the heels of Mika's shoes clanking, we ascend a worn marble staircase.

Given the upscale details of the building, I expect to hear classical piano wafting through the floors, but instead, it sounds like an action flick on the other side. "Get out of there. It's going to blow," comes one voice, then a series of muffled gunshots. "Where's the bomb?" someone else asks. "Other side. Go, go, go!"

Mika scrunches up her face at Noelle and me while she knocks. "They're at it again. I'll never understand the gaming appeal."

The action scene on the other side of the door quiets.

Noelle taps her toes on the floor.

"Eser, go get the door," a muffled voice says.

Another boy's voice comes loud and clear, just on the other side of the thin wood. "Why is it always me? You're closer. Or why not Hadrian?"

The floor creaks, and the door squeals open.

I pull at my shirt to smooth the wrinkles.

A young man with a hooked nose, wearing a fitted sweater, looks down at me. Beneath his feet, shag carpet stretches wall-to-wall. Behind him, velvet brown couches and a wood coffee table with water rings sit haphazardly against the backdrop of oak bookshelves lined with Lego spaceships. Few things scream "decorated by boys" quite so well.

A guy with mussed, sandy hair reclines on a La-Z-Boy on the far side of the room with a controller in his hands.

The sweater guy at the door eyes Noelle and me with a disapproving scowl. "Hiya, Mika. I see you've brought friends." His dark hair swoops into a stiff peak, and his black, pointed shoes gleam.

I wave. "Nice to meet you. I'm Bryanna."

"Eser," sweater guy says with a flinty smile.

*Way to make us feel welcome.*

Hadrian appears in a doorway on the other side of the room, and suddenly, I don't care who else is here. Flutters multiply inside me. "I've got it ready for you, love," he says to Mika. He sweeps a hand behind him. "The kitchen is yours to command."

I know it's an expression I should get used to, but my stomach pitches when Hadrian calls Mika "love." I force myself to smile.

Mika claps and squeezes past Eser, her heels sinking into the shag carpet. When she reaches Hadrian, he steps aside and follows her into what, I assume, is the kitchen.

This leaves me with Noelle and two guys I don't know, which wouldn't be half bad if Noelle wasn't gazing at Eser like he's the eighth wonder of the world.

I follow Mika with slow footsteps until I'm in no-man's-land, close to the kitchen, but still in the main room, uncommitted to either space.

My whole body twitches as I wait to be invited with Hadrian. Meanwhile, Noelle starts a conversation with Eser, the sweater guy. The open doorway casts me into shadow as Mika and Hadrian chat in front of the oven, but they don't turn to see me standing there like a misplaced statue. As the minutes lengthen, I decide I've stood at the edge of the kitchen too long. If they notice me, they'll feel bad, and I'll feel worse.

Swaying in my shoes, I oscillate between the more confident me, who should walk into the kitchen like I own the place, and the more realistic me, who gives up and clings to the only person I know, Noelle. It takes half a moment before the natural me wins.

I take a step toward Noelle as she tucks a strand of hair behind her ear, batting her long lashes. "How's the season going, Eser? Have you had any wins?" She uses a lower voice than I'm used to hearing, and it sounds so false and uncomfortable that I cringe inside.

Eser's lips quirk. "A few."

"What teams?" She leans toward him, as if to close the gap between their bodies, but the tension in Eser's face and shoulders reveals an emotional chasm the size of the Great Barrier Reef. I examine the polish of his shoes and the careful style of his hair. Maybe Noelle doesn't know any gay guys. That would explain why she doesn't seem to notice.

"A few," Eser repeats, his eyes focused on the TV instead of Noelle.

Noelle laughs and slaps Eser's arm. "You said that before."

Eser flinches and steps back as he smooths his sweater.

"I love football," Noelle adds. "And I'd love to be invited to one of your games."

I feel like I should warn Noelle, but I'm not sure how, nor am I certain Eser is gay, since I don't know him personally. Rather than watch this awful exchange unfold, I opt for a cozy spot on the couch near the guy in the recliner that I haven't been introduced to.

Gripping his remote, the boy in the recliner faces an enormous screen with roaming zombies and rags that whip in an eerie, virtual wind. He's too invested in his game to spare me a word, and I'm grateful for it.

Watching him play recalls the nostalgia of sitting behind my brothers as they played growing up, and I'm almost comforted, until gamer boy takes his socks off, and the whole room fills with the smell of sweaty feet. I do my best not to wrinkle my nose in front of him, but I can't stay. Instead, I flee the room to the kitchen, whether Hadrian and Mika want me there or not.

The kitchen greets me with the much cleaner scent of flour and butter, and I take a deep breath to expunge my lungs of the feet smell.

The quaint room has dark cabinets with tiny carved details near the handles, black composite countertops, and a fridge half the width of one from the states, but just as tall. Piled in the kitchen sink, a mountain of dishes threatens a landslide.

"I didn't ruin the dumplings, did I?" Hadrian asks Mika, his back to me.

"No, no, they're just as I left them, thank you." Mika must have heard my overly loud feet because she looks over her shoulder. "There you are. Hadrian, have you met Bryanna?"

He turns and meets my gaze. As he grins, butterflies erupt. "I have," he says and nods toward me. "Lovely to see you again."

I give Hadrian what I hope isn't a shy smile.

He steps closer and lowers his voice so only I can hear. "You look beautiful, even in makeup."

Before I can stop myself, I touch my skin where blush colors my cheeks. I hope he doesn't guess that I dressed up for him.

Hadrian fiddles with the slender chain of his necklace, probably the crucifix, like he did at the Botanic Gardens, and returns to Mika's side. "How may I help?" he asks.

"Sorry, but you're complete rubbish in the kitchen." She casts him a sly glance. "Please, just enjoy yourself."

Hadrian does a little bow and smiles at me again.

"What're you making?" I ask, leaning forward to see better.

Mika kneads a chunk of dough into a log. "Steamed dumplings."

I inhale the steam, savoring the fantastic scent of fresh dough.

"They look so good," I say.

Hadrian watches me the way he studies a room, like he's trying to memorize my face and expose every hidden corner. It makes me feel like I should say something more than fluffy compliments. "I'd love to make them at home," I say, "if you'll give me the recipe. I'll need all your tips, so I don't mess them up."

"Just buy pre-made dumplings and save yourself the trouble," a voice interjects.

I turn as the gamer guy sidles in through the kitchen door, Eser and Noelle close behind, their eyes scanning the kitchen.

"Pre-made? Pre-made?!" Mika wrinkles her nose. "That's twice the cost with half the flavor."

"But it makes twice as much with half the conversation," gamer guy says. "I'll never understand why you put so much effort into making your food pretty. It tastes the same either way." He grabs milk out of the fridge and pours himself a cup, raises it like you would a glass of champagne, and chugs it.

Mika rolls her eyes. "I'd be offended by that, except I know you'd eat cow dung if it meant you never had to get off the couch, Robbie."

The gamer's name is Robbie then. I'll have to remember that. I enjoy their playful bantering, but it makes me sad I didn't have friends like these at home. I never had a meaningful relationship with Abbey, though I do have Sadie.

Mika rolls the dough on a cutting board, cuts the dough up, and loads the balls into a steamer with the care and precision of an artist.

Noelle stands beside Mika and watches her close the lid. "I'm surprised you don't measure the ingredients," she says. "Maybe that's why the dough looks so flat? Did you not use enough yeast?"

Mika's brow wrinkles. "I don't measure because I don't need to. The consistency's fine."

Noelle raises a shoulder. "My parents bought a restaurant back home. They say the best way to make food is to manage someone else who cooks it, and I think I'm doing a good job of that."

Mika doesn't look up as she grabs a basket. "You certainly are."

I'm not sure why Noelle feels the need to tell Mika how to cook, or that her parents bought a restaurant. It feels out of character for her. Surely, she meant no offense.

"My parents bought a boat, too," Noelle adds. "A really nice one."

I don't want Noelle to do or say anything she'll regret, nor do I want Mika to uninvite us the next time, but Noelle seems determined to dig a trench around herself.

Mika looks at me, and I talk to fill the silence, knowing full well that talking isn't my strong suit.

"Speaking of boats," I say. "Will we fish on a punt? I watched people punt in an English movie I watched. It was a romance…but never mind." I blush. Trying not to look at Hadrian, I scramble for something to erase my romance reference, in case Hadrian wonders why I mentioned it. "I'm excited to go. It's been years since my dad took me fishing."

Eser chuckles. "Romance movies, eh? But tonight will hardly be a movie worth watching."

*He's determined to make this hangout unsalvageable.*

Sweat gathers on my forehead, and I take a deep breath, imagining I'm in my comfort zone at home with Sadie beside me. "Only if you're a bore," I say, but as soon as the words leave my mouth, I reel in shock.

*Did I really just say that?*

Eser smiles as Robbie elbows him.

"Think this girl can stick around, eh?" Eser says.

Noelle glances between us. "You're not a bore, Eser," she says in a serious tone. "I don't think you are."

Eser's smile fades.

Mika checks the dumplings in the steamer. "We'd understand if you chose not to come, Eser," she says in a voice full of meaning. "We all know Hadrian and Robbie are not your type, mostly since Robbie is no one's type. Burnley football players are far too fit for the likes of us."

Grateful for Mika's ability to communicate what I couldn't, I nod my appreciation, and Mika winks.

Noelle watches Mika's face, her brows drawn together.

Leaning against the fridge, Hadrian wears a serene smile. "I'm happy to come if you'll have me. I enjoy the company of everyone here, and I like dumplings."

Noelle glances at Hadrian, and I struggle to read her expression, though I wonder at her levels of bitterness. She hasn't said much to Hadrian or looked at him.

A timer rings, and Mika shuts it off. "Well, my lovelies, they're ready, and it looks like Hadrian's the only one who'll get one. Bryanna, too."

Noelle frowns. "What about me?"

"Don't worry," Mika says. "I only tease. Everyone can have one, no matter how clueless they are."

Eser laughs.

Noelle's frown stays as Mika puts the dumplings in a basket and ushers us out of the kitchen and dormitory and into the hall. "I can drive four," she says.

"I've got a car." Robbie shakes his keys at Mika as he pulls a mismatched sock over his toes. "And it's much nicer than your Peugeot."

Mika chuckles. "Your car is much like the boy who drives it, a complete mess. But let's remind you that you're still a baby, and you don't have a driver's license." She shakes her keys back at him. "You've got another full year."

Robbie gives her a dirty look. "You don't have room for all of us in your car, and it's not like we're driving far." He leaves with his car keys in his pocket.

Hadrian and Eser both shrug and follow him, apparently deciding they'd rather drive with an underage driver than get ferried by girls.

I'm just glad I don't have to drive. While I got my license before I left, I can't imagine driving on these backward streets. Even picturing it brings to mind head-on collisions and ambulances.

"Are you wearing those socks by themselves?" Noelle points to Robbie's feet as we descend the stairs. "What about shoes?"

He looks down in mock surprise. "Do you not like them?"

Noelle shakes her head. "Not really."

"But they add a pop of color, don't you think?" He swaggers down the stairs to the parking lot, as if he doesn't hear Noelle's scoff.

Before I can follow, Mika pulls me to the side. "Can I talk to you for a second?"

Noelle looks over her shoulder, and Mika motions her on.

"Meet us by the car," Mika says. "Will you?"

Noelle's mouth pinches, but she shrugs and continues down the stairs, following the boys into the parking lot.

Leaning toward me, Mika speaks in a low voice. "Did something happen with Noelle?"

I haven't known Noelle for that long, but we've talked a lot. However, Mika seems to know something I'm missing. "What do you mean?" I reflect on the last few days, trying to pinpoint something Noelle may have mentioned.

Mika's eyes flick toward Noelle and back to me. "Is something going on with her? She's always been a bit odd with Eser and Hadrian, but tonight has been a whole new level. Did something happen? Was it that boy who teased her?"

We talked to Hadrian in the Botanic Gardens, we went to the cosmetics store, but I can't think of anything else outside of the teasing. Would any of those occurrences cause Noelle to act the way she did tonight? I'm not sure, and I can only raise my shoulders in response.

# CHAPTER FOURTEEN

W E PILE INTO Mika's and Robbie's cars and drive down Burnley Road until we reach a flat-topped ridge with what looks like ripple formations in the rock. Trees throng where a crease forms in the hills. Peeking out from behind fluffy clouds, the sun hovers high in the sky, though it's on its way back down.

I squirm as I leave my seat and shut the car door. Noelle and Mika are already out and waiting. Though I care little about fishing, I'm excited to share this experience with Hadrian.

Noelle checks her phone. "We're right on schedule. After this, we'll go to dinner on Mill Road and take a quick side trip to the cosmetics store on the way. This is all going so well."

Her plans yank me from my happy thoughts.

Cosmetics store? I must not have heard correctly.

"I thought we weren't taking Hadrian to the cosmetics store," I say.

Mika glances over her shoulder at Noelle. "What store?"

Noelle gives me an innocent smile, and her lipstick gleams like polished plastic. "The new one that just opened. There's something I need to pick up if that's all right with you. Would you two come with me? We could go as a group?"

"Whatever you need," Mika says.

"I don't want to go there," I say. I don't want Hadrian to see Ellen and recognize how much I fall short of someone like her.

"Thanks, Mika." Noelle looks straight ahead.

"Why are you ignoring me?" I ask. She hasn't acted normal since we met up with Mika, and it makes me wonder if I did something to upset her.

This time, she looks me full in the face, eyebrows converging. "Can you give me a legitimate reason not to go there?"

She waits, and my tongue knots up. I don't know what to tell her, and I bounce between feeling awkward and embarrassed for having brought it up. My reasons are far from legitimate, but I wish she'd listen to me without making me explain myself. I don't want to go. Isn't that enough?

She turns and walks off. Mika gives me an apologetic shrug but does the same. She probably doesn't understand why either of us care.

I hurry to keep up as we walk across the street toward a wooden fence with wandering sheep behind it. Further down the road, we follow a stone wall to a tiny door made from wood posts where a set of stairs descend to a walking path behind it. As we walk, I'm so angry I can hardly look at Noelle.

The path takes us to the edge of a large pond, bordered by lush, overhanging trees that harbor the musky scent of mud and moss. A platform or dock juts out over the water, and dumped across it, a pile of fishing poles waits. Hadrian crouches beside the poles, attaching bait to the line.

He stands, so sturdy and confident that I can't look away. In my distraction, I trip over a misplaced stone and have to lean on Noelle to steady myself.

Noelle pushes me away. "Pull yourself together," she says.

I stare, dumbfounded, as she walks off.

Mika's right. What happened to the friendly girl who welcomed me to Burnley?

We spread out a blanket on the grass near the shoreline, and I sit down just as Eser steps off the dock into a pile of mud. His shoes make a squelching sound similar to what I envision a bad French kiss sounds like. While everyone else laughs at the horrified expression on Eser's face, I imagine Teddy making that noise with his new girlfriend, and I'm not able to smile with them.

Hadrian hunkers down on the picnic blanket, and Robbie sits beside him, the stripes on one of his socks very much out of place.

"A penny for your thoughts," Hadrian says, with his eyes on me.

My brain is a ship I have to steer from Teddy. Before my thoughts dive involuntarily into bad waters, I have to change course. I have no desire to talk about my ex.

"I didn't mean to put you on the spot. You don't have to say," he says quickly.

"I'm just happy to be here with you—all of you." I mean it, even if that wasn't what I was thinking.

He smiles, and his eyes crinkle. I wish his expression would stay always. "We have Noelle to thank for setting this up."

Noelle nods. She sits across from me, beside Eser.

Eser's polite smile is more pained than friendly. He and Noelle could make a cute couple, except he doesn't look at Noelle at all, and he never will.

I rest a hand against the grass and play with the individual blades, Mika at my side.

The silence on the picnic blanket perches thick and unnavigable. No one moves or seems inclined to break it.

Hadrian reclines against a tree trunk, his head resting against the bark. I wish I could warn him of Noelle's plan to take him to the cosmetics store, but he would probably want to meet Ellen as much as every other boy does. Especially once he sees her.

Noelle shreds a leaf between her fingers.

As falcons flit between branches, the leaves grumble at the disruption. Mink scurry from bush to bush, and Eser points with animation when a deer peers from behind a tree trunk.

Robbie moves to start fishing and accidentally splashes us as he flings his line into the water. As droplets rain onto Hadrian, one falls from Hadrian's hair and slips into his shirt, where the shape of a cross sits against his skin. It's the necklace he wears. He shifts to one side, and his eyes meet mine.

I jolt upright when he notices me staring. "The trees are very pretty," I say, and my cheeks warm. Did he ask me something? I can't remember.

His cheeks stretch with a grin. "Couldn't agree more."

I must have said something stupid, but it's too late for me to fix it. I press my lips together to keep myself from saying anything else.

"Late lunch," Mika says, pulling out the basket of biscuits. "Be sure to save room for dinner."

I start with one and follow it with another as my mouth fills with soft dough spiced with ginger and cilantro. Within minutes, I've devoured my share. "These are the best," I say as I finish the last bite. "Thank you, Mika."

Everyone else nods.

Hadrian takes the last dumpling without apology, and Mika grins, absorbing the praise with relish.

"How do you three know each other?" Hadrian gestures to Mika and me, still holding his dumpling. His eyes linger on Noelle for a half-second longer.

I hope Hadrian doesn't think I obsess over him. "I met Mika through Noelle," I say. "Noelle befriended me on my first day." She's usually a lot more friendly, I want to say, but I don't expect Noelle would appreciate that.

Mika leans back on her hands. "Noelle and I met on one of Professor Reeve's field trips."

Reeve never told me he conducted field trips. He didn't say anything outside of "leave now," really.

Hadrian swallows his food and gives Mika a strange look. "You've been on one of those?"

"Reeve's field trips? Of course. Haven't you?"

Hadrian shakes his head. "He invited me once, but not since. I think our lovely professor may not have the best opinion of me."

I can't imagine anyone disliking Hadrian, not even Reeve, though Noelle seems to dislike him, only because he rejected her.

"Aren't you part of his honors class?" Noelle asks, her tone a bit patronizing. "I doubt Reeve invites people he doesn't like to be part of his club."

A dark cloud passes over Hadrian's features.

"I don't know why he wouldn't invite you," I say to offset Noelle, if only to reclaim his good humor.

He meets my eyes, and an electric current charges through me as warmth floods my cheeks.

I avert my gaze, pretending I haven't been caught staring again. Hadrian notices too much and doesn't let me get away with anything.

How embarrassing.

Robbie hands Eser his fishing pole and offers Hadrian's, but Hadrian shakes his head. Rather than join them, Hadrian folds his arms behind his head, so his cross presses against the fabric of his shirt.

"Is that cross important to you?" I ask. "I noticed you wear it a lot."

Hadrian looks at me with an eyebrow raised, as if trying to decide whether my question needs an answer. I squirm beneath his gaze. Was it a bad question?

"My nanny gave it to me when I was young," he says.

"Your nanny?" I press my mouth shut to contain any further dumb questions. Just because I never had a nanny, doesn't mean other people don't.

"Mum wasn't around much," Hadrian says. "Why do you ask?"

"I was curious."

I'm grateful he's willing to share that part of his life with me, though my hands sweat as I grab handfuls of blanket in my fists. I hope I didn't prod too much into Hadrian's personal business.

Hadrian holds out a hand.

I hesitate, uncertain what he wants me to do. What's he offering? After glancing between his hand and his face, he chuckles and drops a chain on my palm with the heavy weight of a thick metal cross. "Take a look."

The weight surprises me, and I almost drop it. I can't believe Hadrian carries this around his neck all day without falling over. The details are faded, the edges worn smooth, like it belongs in a museum, not around a teenager's neck.

"Cool," is all I manage to say as I return it.

Hadrian slips the chain over his head and stands. "The fish are jumping." With a quick nod, he hurries to the platform where Robbie and Eser fish and grabs his pole. I push myself to my feet, ready to join them. Mika and Noelle follow to the platform, and Mika sits on the side, dangling her feet in the water where no fishing lines can catch her toes. I sit beside her, my arms around my knees, while Noelle borrows Robbie's fishing pole.

Hadrian holds his pole aloft. "Would either of you like to try?"

I eye the pole. While I've fished before, and watched my dad fish many times, I'm not sure how many ways there are to humiliate myself with such an activity, but I'll find a way. I would enjoy it, though, especially the opportunity to stand closer to Hadrian.

Mika shakes her head, and I find myself refusing along with her. "No, thanks," I say.

Hooking another piece of bait, Hadrian tosses the line out, seemingly not bothered by our refusal, though it sticks on my mind because I'm not sure I actually want to refuse. I force myself to focus on the scenery instead.

The water on the lake reflects the green of the trees on either side of the river. The green here is a different green than the darker green of canyon leaves at home. It almost looks unnatural, and I have to remind myself that I'm technically from a desert.

The sun deepens in the sky. Colors creep into the clouds, captured by the water. Here, the world pauses to breathe.

When everyone tires of fishing, we pack up the gear. Robbie offers me his hand as I leap off the platform, taking care to miss the mud. As I land, I grip his fingers, and Robbie steadies my wobble. I open my mouth to thank him, but Hadrian pulls me from the puddle's edge.

Hadrian's eyes meet mine, and he doesn't look away.

Heat sweeps up my arms, and my fingertips tingle beneath the light pressure of his hands, until Robbie pushes between us. "I'm not interrupting a moment, am I?" He grins as he helps Mika, Eser, and Noelle off the dock.

Hadrian's ears don't even redden as he reaches for my hand again. But this time, he turns it palm up where my scars mark my wrist. "What are those?"

I jerk my hand away. "It's a vein problem. I've always had it."

Hadrian cocks an eyebrow.

"I booked Indian food," Noelle says from behind. "There's a place on Mill Road I'd like to try."

I wince. Noelle hasn't given up on Mill Road. The words to warn Hadrian jumble in my mouth, every variation of them insipid.

"I love Indian food," Mika says. "Let's hope the chef is decent."

Hadrian still stares at my wrist, his brows pulled together.

"I'm gonna get going," Eser says in a loud voice. Several steps down the footpath, he straightens his sweater and waves, a guilty grimace on his face. "Thanks for the invite, but I had something come up."

Robbie waves him off. "See ya."

Mika and Hadrian just nod, though there's an unease to their silence that tells me they know the reason Eser wants to leave as well as I do. While I'm sure he came to appease Mika and even our numbers, he's tired of Noelle. It was only supposed to be a group hangout.

Noelle gapes at Eser's back as he strolls down the path to the road. "What?"

He's handsome and a football star. I understand why she likes him, but if he doesn't like her, that's not going to change. "He's probably meeting some people," I say to soften the blow.

Noelle's cheeks color. "Fine, let's go to dinner then. I just need to stop by one store on the way before it closes. Park next to us on the corner where the new cosmetics store is. We can walk to the restaurant from there."

Hadrian follows Robbie up the stone steps to the road with only one glance my way. Trees sway from the gust of a slow, pathetic breeze. I lost my chance to warn him. The boys file into Robbie's car parked along the street, and Robbie starts the engine.

I let Noelle and Mika walk ahead as we cross the street to Mika's car. I might not be able to avoid a visit to Mystic Cosmetics, but I don't have to see Hadrian's face when he sees Ellen. I'll look away. If he likes her more than he should, I'll have to move on or figure out how to afford expensive cosmetics products.

I drop into Mika's car as the engine hums to life. We pull into traffic as fading rays of sunlight blaze through the window. Noelle lowers her visor. Robbie follows in his car, close behind us.

As we drive into town, a familiar purple awning appears around the buildings, and Mika parks. When we get out, the car lights flash once and go out.

The crowd outside the store has dwindled to only a few men conversing at the building's corner. Inside, a young woman waits at a cash register. Dried bundles of sage and lavender hang overhead. They brush against Ellen's hair as she counts bills.

Robbie's voice carries from across the street where the boys climb out of his car. "We'll meet you at the restaurant and save you seats."

My tension lifts. If Hadrian doesn't come, I stressed about nothing.

Noelle's lips purse into a red line. "No, it'll only be a second. Just come with us." She rounds on Mika. "Get them to come."

Mika gives her a black look. "Why? They won't want to."

Of course, they wouldn't. They're boys. Even if Noelle asks, they'll refuse.

"They're going to have to get over themselves," Noelle says as Robbie and Hadrian stride further down the sidewalk.

"Noelle," I say, "this is ridiculous. They don't want to come."

Noelle's eyes narrow. "Why is this such a big deal to you people? It's a cosmetics store. Not a porn shop."

This new, scathing side of Noelle feels like a slap because I've seen a much better side of her. She's part of the reason I stayed in England when Reeve demanded I leave. "We don't want to go in there."

Mika gives Noelle a long look, then sighs and calls out, "Robbie! Hadrian! Will you join us? It'll only take a second. I'd prefer we stay together."

Robbie's mouth turns down. His lips move, and Hadrian gives a single nod as they cross the street. Their eyes rise to the window where Ellen arranges dried flowers on the other side of the glass. I can't prevent him from seeing Ellen's hair as it tumbles over her shoulders. A weight drops in my chest.

Bells chime as Noelle lets herself into the store. They chime again for Mika and me, and then Hadrian and Robbie, too. Hadrian stands at the threshold, glances at me, and steps inside. He'll never look at me again with girls like Ellen to turn to.

I promised myself I wouldn't watch, but it's like turning away from a horrible car accident. I have to witness it.

Robbie stands frozen beside Hadrian, facing the store counter. "What was I thinking not wearing women's makeup all these years? Are you seeing what I'm seeing?"

Hadrian scans the store. "What are you seeing?"

Robbie nods toward Ellen. "The woman behind the counter."

"What of her?"

Robbie gives Hadrian an incredulous look. "I might not be the most appreciative person of perfection, but she's as close as I've seen."

Hadrian's obliviousness means nothing. He'll get charmed soon.

He studies Ellen. "Is that so?"

Ellen glances up from the register. "How may I help you?" Her tone is mild, almost polite.

The curtains ruffle, and a woman with red hair elbows through, a bundle of fresh herbs in her arms. I recognize the small, sharp face and green eyes. The woman came to Professor Reeve's office. "Ellen, are you being nice to our customers?"

"Yes," Ellen snaps.

"I could hear your tone from the back room. Sorry, boys, what do you need?" The woman winks. "Welcome back, Noelle."

"Thanks, Jane." Noelle flashes a smile brighter than any I've seen tonight. "I came for the discount you promised."

"Oh?" Jane drops her herbs into a pile on the counter and sorts them. Fresh lemons permeate the air as she stirs the leaves. Meanwhile, the tension in my neck and shoulders builds.

"I've brought Hadrian—the one you wanted to see."

Hadrian jerks. His wide eyes focus on Jane, then on me. He must think I took some part in this, that I planned this night to drag him to a cosmetics store for a discount. Invisible snakes crush my stomach.

It's one thing to use someone, but it's a shameful thing to do it for a discount.

Robbie slaps Hadrian on the back. "The ladies call for you now, eh?"

Hadrian's attention returns to Ellen, his face unreadable.

"Hadrian." Ellen rolls the name on her tongue. "Hadrian Bristol. I've been looking for you." She pushes Noelle aside, reaches for Hadrian's neck, and tugs out the chain he wears. The crucifix catches on his shirt, then swings free.

I want to snatch it from her hands, but my feet remain glued to the floor.

Ellen watches the crucifix twirl and lets it drop.

"Who are you?" Hadrian asks. While he appears unaffected, a nervous edge catches his voice.

"I'm Ellen." She smiles. "I own this shop with my two sisters."

"Do we know each other?"

"I've wanted to meet you, that's all." Her eyes rove his messy hair. "You look just as I thought you would. It's been too long."

"What has?"

"Since I first heard about you. And I've heard so much about you, Hadrian."

His mouth forms a hard line. "From whom?"

"Professor Reeve. He's known you a long time, hasn't he?"

"He has." Hadrian's eyebrows draw together as Ellen steps back.

"You're welcome to come in anytime you like," Ellen says. "I'll make something special for you, and I'll give you a better discount than Noelle gets on the days I like her most. And we do more than just hair products. I can get you anything you need. Anything at all."

I'm not sure what I expected Ellen to do when we brought Hadrian, but I didn't expect her to act like an ominous schoolgirl with a crush. It makes her seem almost human, like me, but even more socially inept. I should appreciate my levels of awkwardness more. I could be so much worse.

Jane touches Ellen on the shoulder and shakes her head. Ellen bites her lip, hands Hadrian something small, and withdraws. "I'm here. Don't forget me, Hadrian. I haven't forgotten you."

Hadrian opens his hand where a paper folded to resemble a cat rests on his palm.

The paper cat strikes a chord deep inside me. Didn't the journals mention a paper cat? And the second witch in the journals goes by Jane, too, but that's a common enough name.

Hadrian stuffs the paper cat in his pocket and retreats to the door.

"Did you get her number, mate?" Robbie asks as he hurries after Hadrian.

Only Noelle remains to pick out the products she plans to buy with her well-deserved discount. I leave with Mika and Robbie, and the door tinkles to a close.

"What was that?" Mika asks.

Hadrian's face is pale, but everyone looks at me. Noelle is my friend, and they want an explanation.

I heave a deep sigh. "Ellen bribed Noelle with a discount to bring Hadrian here." I can't feign ignorance. "But Noelle promised me she wouldn't do it."

Mika lets out an audible exhale. "Why?"

"I don't know."

"Strange." Mika surveys the store's windows. "Their stuff is great, though. How much is Noelle buying? Enough to make up for all this nonsense, I hope."

"Not a lot, I'm sure," I say. "It costs an arm and a leg."

Robbie leans over Hadrian's shoulder as Hadrian continues to stare at the little paper Ellen gave him. "Is it her number?" Robbie asks again.

"No," Hadrian says in a flat voice.

Robbie's face falls. "What is it then?"

"A cat."

"No, it's not." Robbie snatches at it, but Hadrian pulls it out of his reach.

Hadrian unfolds a little origami cat and holds up the paper. Smooth. Blank. Black.

# CHAPTER FIFTEEN

Hadrian stirs his chicken sauce and stares at his plate. Noelle is as bright as a rearview mirror reflecting the sun into my eyes. She opens the top of her gift bag and shows us wrapped bundles of handmade soaps and shampoos in thin cardboard wrappings and colored bows.

The waitress refills our drinks, but Hadrian's water is still full, so the waitress moves past it to mine.

Robbie finishes the last bite off his plate and eyes Hadrian's chicken. "You plan to finish that?"

Hadrian startles, as if he didn't expect Robbie to address him. "No."

Hadrian's distraction worries me. Whether he's daydreaming, thoroughly spooked, or mad at me, I wish I could change what happened. It's not like him to tune out. That's my job.

I hope he's not mad.

"Thanks!" Robbie pours the contents of Hadrian's dish into his own bowl.

Hadrian's peaked face takes on a green tinge.

"Are you okay?" I ask. It's almost as if he knows that a witch by the name of Ellen gave a similar cat to someone called Guido hundreds of years ago. But, of course, he wouldn't know that, and it's my fault he ended up in the cosmetics store.

"Yes." He speaks too clearly.

"Are you sure?"

He scans the room, and his lips pinch.

I never thought speaking to Ellen would affect him so negatively. A part of me is glad he didn't drool like Robbie did, but my gratitude makes my insides squirm because this is horrible to watch, too. "Look, I'm sorry about the cosmetics store—"

"Not to worry." His smile is strained as he brings out the black origami paper that was once shaped like a cat. "I've seen this cat before." He touches the folded edges. "But never with my eyes open."

I'm not sure what to say. And honestly, I'm not certain I understand. Does he see the cat in nightmares? Tingles run down my arms like cool water. I suppose I can't be the only person who has nightmares.

Hadrian tosses the black paper onto the carpet. "I'd rather forget about it."

I stir my curry. I want to say something to comfort him, but I don't know what. "Siamese cats make excellent ugly house pets, especially the black ones. I'll one up Ellen and get you one of those."

Hadrian's face lightens, and he chuckles. "Please, don't."

"So…you don't like Ellen then? You don't think she's—" I pause. This will make me sound petty, but I plow forward anyway. "Pretty?"

He shrugs. "I've no idea what she looks like under all that makeup. I can't even imagine it."

I lean against my chair and let out a slow breath that I hope he doesn't hear.

Makeup isn't my thing, and I'm glad he doesn't prefer that level of maintenance.

The waiter distributes checks, but Hadrian swipes mine before I can reach for it.

"My treat." He hands the waiter his card.

Relieved he's not mad at me, warmth blooms in my chest. "Thank you."

It's dark outside as we pass old buildings and compact cars parked along the streets. A gentle drizzle coats the car window, and I admire the way the light reflects off the water pooling in the road. I'm warm all over.

If Hadrian paid for my dinner, did he consider tonight a date? Did he want it to be?

I want to ask Mika and Noelle, but Noelle stares out the window with a weird grin, as if dreaming of using her Mystic products, still clutching her bag.

It's still strange to me that the passenger seat is on the wrong side of the car.

Mika glances at Noelle as the buildings turn to grassy fields and stone fences, but she doesn't break the silence, either.

Mika turns right, and the car screeches to a stop. "Can't they let one more car through?" A construction crew sets up cones around a bold "road closed" sign.

Flashing lights burn my eyes as they illuminate our windows. Just beyond the crowd of cars, a group of teenagers slumps on the pavement with their hands behind their backs. Several police officers stand over them.

Noelle sits up straight. "Just take the other road. It's only a few minutes longer. I bet that's a drug bust."

Mika flips the car around and turns left.

As the full moon emerges from the clouds, trees flash by, their lines broken by a bridge with balustrades. Black water glimmers below.

My intestines twist as a sickening smell invades my nostrils, coming from nowhere and yet all around me. I clutch my abdomen. Something rotten lingers on my tongue, like fermented blood.

"I think I'm gonna throw up," I say.

"What?" Noelle turns and surveys me. "Mika, pull over. I think she's serious."

Mika slows, and as soon as the car stops, I push my door open, stumble out, and rush across the road to lean over the bridge's edge. The cool touch of the concrete columns eases my stomach while darkness mixes with the water under me.

"Did you have something off at dinner?" Mika asks at my side.

Noelle joins me on my other side, her hand on my shoulder.

Rough, wet cement digs into my fingertips. "I don't know." I lift my hands, and my fingers quiver. Only minutes ago, I felt so light. Somehow, the happiness dissolved, replaced by an unaccountable sense of dread. "We should go."

Noelle lurches forward and snatches at the empty air as a tiny light drops over the edge and goes out. "My phone!" She leans over, and her hair tumbles around her face. "We have to get it."

I shake my head and step back. "No." The dread claws at me, and my lungs collapse with the weight of it.

"It could be halfway down the river," Mika says. "And it might not even work anymore."

"It's waterproof, and I need it. Besides, we don't know if it fell in the river. It might have landed on the rocks." Noelle strides to the end of the bridge and calls over her shoulder, "Are you coming?"

They don't need me. There's no reason for me to go.

Mika starts ahead, but glances back. "Bryanna?"

My feet have solidified into the pavement. Fire flares from the thick trees. Smoke curls around the bridge and fills my lungs. A knife lies at my feet, its edge dull and bloodied. My face reflects off it, except with hair that is dark, and curly while blood runs from my nose down to my chin.

"Bryanna?"

I jerk. The blood clears, quick as a breath of air, and gone like a gust of wind.

My eyes water, and I clear my throat. I don't want Mika to see how much this bridge upsets me, especially when I don't understand it myself. I've always been a bit jumpy. My brothers make fun of me for it all the time, but I'm not afraid of the dark.

Trying to keep my voice from shaking, I ask, "Can't we come back in the morning?"

"You can stay if you need to," Mika says.

Shame for my cowardice sprouts in my abdomen and flowers into wilted leaves.

I can't allow myself to shut down for no real reason.

Forcing my feet forward, I catch up to Mika and Noelle, so I'm not alone. "I'm coming."

Noelle presses on down the riverbank while Mika and I follow, though my courage frays more with each step. A sigh of arctic wind rattles gnarled branches. Brambles shelter the water's edge. Trees sway, tall specters trooped in a dark netherworld, as the chilly air prickles my skin, damp from the light patter of continuous rain.

After scanning the bushes, I force my feet to keep moving.

*I'm not afraid, and I don't have anything to prove to anyone.*

Lying to myself never works as well as I hope, but is going back to the car really so terrible?

Mika's voice carries as she calls, "Can't you try calling it?"

"Can you? I'd do it myself, but as you see, I don't have a phone," Noelle says in a clipped tone.

Mika doesn't respond but holds her phone as she dials and continues walking through the reeds. "All I see is a load of trees." Mika yanks leaves back, and water shimmers in the moonlight. "I don't think we'll find your mobile, Noelle. Not with so many bushes and only our phones for torches."

Noelle rubs her arms with a pained expression. "I swear I saw it land by some rocks, but you're right. I can come back first thing in the morning."

"We can help you," Mika says.

That's permission enough to leave. I make a beeline for the road.

Mika and Noelle follow close behind. My feet move faster as I will the car closer. I swerve around a willow tree, but the end of a torn trash bag makes me stop. To the right, a limp foot sticks out of the brush. I knew I had cold places inside me, but my insides plummet somewhere so frigid it's unrecognizable.

"What's that you found?" Mika's hesitant voice comes from behind.

I hold out a hand to stop her. My mouth is dry. "You won't want to see it."

My chest hurts as it rises and falls.

"Is it my phone?" Noelle splits the weeds. I'm too far away to stop her.

Her scream splits the air. Mika rushes to Noelle and yanks me after her. I stumble. My legs are numb. My hands are numb.

Noelle stands frozen, gaping downward over the split grass. The moonlight presents a face in the water. Black, curly hair frames dark skin while empty holes glare from gouged out eyes. The girl's exposed throat and upturned hands reveal deep slashes while fresh blood trails from the wounds and darkens the water. I close my eyes to squeeze out the image.

Mika's voice rises. "Oh my gosh, oh my gosh. What happened to her face? You don't think the murderer is still here, do you?"

I force my eyes open again to scan the darkness. Nothing moves but trees and whispering wind. I bend over and touch the dead woman's cheek.

Warm.

Mika coughs and a splash follows. Then she wipes her mouth and straightens on wobbling legs. "We need to call someone," she says in a gravelly voice.

"Let's do that in the car. We have to leave," I say. Urgency grips me, and I repeat the words, "We need to go now."

Noelle stares at the murky water as Mika rubs at her lips. Neither of them heard me, so I take hold of their elbows. They don't resist. We move like zombies. I pull harder to spur us into a run. Noelle and Mika snap into their senses and run faster than I do.

We crest the hill. Inside the car, I lock the doors behind us and rest my forehead in my hands. "Call the police," I say.

Mika fumbles for her phone, dials a number, and presses the device to her cheek. "Hello? Hello? My name's Mika Song. There's a body here. We've found a body on the river. Where? Behind…" Mika stops and looks around. "I'm sorry, we're on a bridge." Her voice quavers. "Wait here? But—yes, I understand." She cups the mouthpiece. "They want us to stay on the line until they arrive."

I shut my eyes.

An eyeless face with a noose around her neck stares back from behind my eyelids.

This can't be happening. It can't be real.

"Sure," Noelle says in a distant voice.

The hum of crickets fills the car. A buzz echoes as Mika puts her phone on speaker.

"Yes, I'm still here," Mika says in a small voice.

Lights flash as cars arrive. Someone raps on the window. Mika rolls it down, and the person on the other side considers me with bloodless lips and empty pits for eyes. What happened to the eyes?

"Bryanna, he's talking to you." Mika stares at me from the driver's seat.

I blink, and the demon face dissolves into a man with a concerned smile, dressed in an officer's uniform.

"They want a statement from each of us," Mika says.

I feel myself nod. "Fine." If I stay sane long enough.

An ambulance, a fire truck, and an SUV park on the bridge. Officers accompany medics while one man pushes a stretcher with a blue bag. Blue and white tape wreathes the bridge. They'll alert the girl's family soon. Someone's daughter will never come home.

"They want us to get out of the vehicle for a moment," Mika says.

The officer watches me open the door. I stand on wobbly legs and press my back to the cool metal of the car. He asks questions. Answers slide out of my mouth and float away. Nothing I say will help them find the person who did this.

Another officer kneels to pass me a card, and I realize I've slumped over, the weight of the night dragging me downward. "This is our department psychiatrist," he says. "Don't be ashamed of seeking any help you might need."

"Do you have flatmates? Anyone you can stay with?" the first officer asks.

Mika's voice reaches from somewhere on my left. "She can stay with me."

I won't be alone.

The officer stands. "Good. You'll want the support tonight."

An officer drives us to Mika's dormitory while another follows in Mika's car. The officer parks, and Mika leads us up the stairs and unlocks her door on the second floor. "My flatmates are out."

We enter a small room with a kitchen and a pristine living room, and I'm grateful that Mika invited me, if only for the company. A large TV screen hangs against the far wall while rows of framed pictures parade the Beatles and Elton John. But when I blink, bloodied eyeballs populate the frames instead.

Mika turns on a movie and lets it play. We spread blankets and pillows on the floor, and then Noelle and Mika disappear into the kitchen.

I need someone to talk to, someone to tell me everything will be all right, so I dial Sadie's number.

"Hello?" comes the sleepy answer. "Bree, it's early here."

"Sadie?" My sister's name comes out as a sob. Tears spill from my eyes, and I blink them back.

"Is everything okay?" The drowsiness in her voice dies.

"I wish you were here."

"What happened?"

An explanation hovers on my tongue, but I reel it in. I can't afford for her to tell our mom, who might get scared into demanding I come home. Reeve would win. I might as well escort myself to the airport, and I don't know yet if I want to leave. I've tried so hard to do well in my classes. "I just miss you so much."

*Tell me I'm supposed to be here. Tell me I did the right thing in coming.*

Sadie's voice sharpens. "What are you not telling me?"

She knows me too well.

I scavenge my brain for an answer. "School is hard, and I'm tired of studying, and the people on the river outside are too loud, and I keep finding spiders on my window, and—"

"Oh, Bree. I want you home, but you can handle a few spiders. What's going on, really? Is that special education program giving you tutors or something to help?"

If I went home, I could give up on trying so hard with my homework. I wouldn't have to spend hours every night writing essays. I'd never see that bridge again, never have to bear the dry stir of wind or see bloodied pits that were once eyes. I could return to work where the most frightening thing I would deal with are thorns on the flowers. Teddy's new relationship doesn't even matter anymore.

Mika's and Noelle's voices carry across the flat. They appear in the doorway, and the worry in their eyes warms my heart.

"I have a teacher who helps a lot," I say into the phone. "I just wanted to hear your voice."

I hear her yawn through the receiver.

"I'm always here for you, Bree, you know that."

"I do."

"You're sure you're okay?"

I pause because I'm not sure at all. "Yes, thanks for listening. Get back to bed."

"I love you a million chocolate strawberries," she says.

"I love you, too. Bye, Sadie." I end the call and stare at the red telephone icon. A part of me wanted to leave when I started the call. The feeling hasn't gone away, but I try to convince myself I belong here.

"We didn't mean to eavesdrop," Mika says.

Noelle bites her lip.

"It's fine." I set the phone down and bundle up with blankets.

Mika and Noelle lie down and drop off to sleep before long. I stare at the figures on the screen. They blend together and blur.

I'm walking along a bridge. Water saturates the ground for miles on either side. The road curves, dusty and full of loose rocks. Trees spring from a swamp with branches that grow shadows as the sun sinks below the horizon.

"Alice," a small voice calls.

The water drains to a boggy marsh. Mists rise and fall like white serpents as a boy emerges. He holds out a rose with bright yellow petals that match his smiling eyes. The boy's smile fades as the flower withers.

"I didn't mean to," he says. Tears spill down his cheeks, and he vanishes, leaving nothing but the outline of the trees in the encroaching twilight.

I wake up, and the TV is off. Noelle's and Mika's forms are a few feet away. I grasp the blanket Mika left for me and roll to my side.

It's just a dream.

# CHAPTER SIXTEEN

"Wake up. Mika's making us breakfast." Noelle's brisk voice pierces my sleepy fog.

Something solid prods my shoulder, and fuzzy cream blurs into textured carpet. I force myself upright and wait for my eyes to focus.

"I've got eggs," Mika calls from the kitchen.

The world teeters as I stand. I clutch the couch and shuffle to a small circular drop leaf table. Mika's kitchen is the same size as the boys' kitchen, but nicer, with white cabinets and clean, speckled countertops. The managers of the dormitory must have known that girls have opinions about their living spaces.

"Thanks." My arm can barely lift the milk jug as I pour myself a glass.

"It's all over the news." Noelle scans the screen of Mika's phone. "Her name was Ava Lange. The detective was right. She'd been dead about fifteen minutes when we found her, with missing eyes and toes. Yuck! They found traces of hallucinogens in her blood, but nothing else. No one knew she was missing. Her friends said she walked home from a party on Mill Road and insisted on being alone."

Mika brings a plate of eggs on a fancy gold-rimmed platter and sets them on the table. "Poor girl."

"We're in here, look," Noelle says. "'Three students found her body at approximately 8:00 p.m. last night and called the police.

Police officers arrived on the scene only minutes afterward as several of the officers wrapped up a drug arrest only a block away. The detectives on the case have yet to say whether these two incidents are related, but they found no traces of the confiscated illegal drugs in Ava's blood or on her body. The hallucinogens above mentioned were not among the drugs confiscated, nor does Ava Lange have any prior history of drug use. Police are now searching the river for the bodies of two more students who have been missing for several weeks in case the disappearances are connected. More information to follow—'"

Noelle looks up. "How soon do you think people will hear about this?"

"I don't know, but I can't believe there've been others," I say. "How have I not heard about this?" I vaguely remember a "missing persons" sign on Mill Road, but no one talked about students vanishing. That should be a major topic for discussion.

Especially if the dead students are missing their eyes and toes. Hallucinogens and slashed wrists; missing persons; cut-off eyes and fingers. I think I'm going to be sick.

Mika raises her shoulders. "I heard about it, but no one suspected they might be dead until now. I think one of the missing students was thought to have run off."

"What do you think the school will do?" Noelle chews on her lip. "This happened on the edge of school grounds. All the students and parents will find out."

I grip my mug so tight my knuckles ache.

Moving to stand by the counter, Mika stirs her coffee and leans against the cabinets. "I think they'll tell us to be careful and not go walking at night alone. The police will handle it. It's not like it happened inside a school building."

Noelle pours a mug of steaming tea as I sip from my cup.

Mika's phone buzzes, and she answers. "Hello, yes, good morning, love." She pauses. "As well as can be expected, I suppose. Bryanna? Right here. I'll put her on." She passes me the phone. "It's Hadrian."

When I take the phone, I'm hesitant to talk. I don't want to revisit that river even in discussion. "Hello?" I say in a small voice.

Hadrian's voice comes through like the distant roll of waves. "Mika told me what happened, and I saw it in the news. Can I do anything for you?"

"I really appreciate it," I say, "but I have to finish some homework. I'd love to hang out with you all soon, though."

"You'll not take a break?" Hadrian sounds surprised.

"No, but thanks again." I hand Mika her phone back.

Mika chats with Hadrian for a minute before hanging up, and then stabs her food with a fork. She keeps her plate by the kitchen sink, as if prepared to abandon it at any moment.

"I think I'm just going to buy myself a new phone," Noelle says.

Mika offers her a half-smile. "Might be a good idea."

I stand, and my plate clinks as I set it in the sink, avoiding Mika's gaze as I pass. "I've got homework to do, so I'll get going. Thanks for letting me stay the night."

Noelle's eyes widen. "It's Saturday."

"I know," I say.

Mika considers me with understanding, as if she sees the dull, detached ache inside me. I can only hope a distraction might rectify it. "We're here if you need us," she says.

"Thank you."

It's difficult to step outside where I'm no longer cocooned in the safety of friends. Dewy droplets seep into my shirt as rain patters over the cobblestones and fans the ground in tiny ripples. Cars drive by and splash water while two students wait by a bench on the side of the road, huddled beneath umbrellas.

Images of the night before crash down on me. Bleeding eye sockets. Dark, swaying trees. Slow-moving water, black as tar. I've never seen a dead body before, let alone one so desecrated.

A walkway leads me through a line of towering trees. The clouds hold their breath. No voices weave through the leaves. No students appear. No backpacks. No shift of air to stir the hair on my neck.

The students likely heard about the girl's death. Had I been alone on Mill Road only an hour earlier, I might be the one floating down the river with no eyes.

My stomach curdles.

I wait at the bus stop and ride to my dormitory and then make my way to my room. At my desk, I sit and write. The sun blares through the window. Students call out to each other below, and I struggle to tune them out. Life goes on with a merriment that doesn't fit with our morbid reality.

I toss aside paper after paper. The waste basket fills with my failed attempts. Daylight wanes, and I turn on the tungsten lights in the room.

I have a few weeks to write this paper, but I know it'll take me several drafts to make it perfect. And I need this paper to be flawless when I'm done. I need it to be full of hope for a better future and not the mark of a bitter end.

# CHAPTER SEVENTEEN

"Are you okay?" students ask.

The news leaks, as well as my association with it, and catches fire across the school. Faculty members study me with concern as I trudge down the halls, and I know what they're thinking.

I have no cuts, no bruises. I'm not the one floating in a river, but I'm not okay. I ignore the questions and head to my dormitory to hole up in my room.

I set aside *Northanger Abbey* and read my favorite Austen novels that I borrowed from the school library, the lighthearted ones that pull me out of any funk. When I had bad days at home, I used books as distractions, but not even Eliza's wit or Darcy's aloofness can bury the girl in the river beneath piles of regency dresses. The pale faces and gouged out eyes burn in on the edges.

I have to try something else, so I pull out the journals Professor Reeve gave me and immerse myself in its impossible puzzle.

*—June of 1603—*

*I tied Dantes outside the alehouse. Dusk crept into the horizon, and cool air brushed my cheeks. I rounded a corner and collided with a pair of skirts.*

Someone gasped.

I stumbled, and my breeches brushed the hem
of a lady's dress. As I righted, I apologized and
helped a laughing lady with fair curls to her feet.
Another woman with darker hair, gentle eyes, and
glowing skin supported her arm. Both had merry
smiles—breaths of fresh air after months of smog.

The dark-haired woman asked if I was lost, but I
was found. That's the problem. I knew not where
to hide.

I told her I was travelling and planned to stay the
night and continue on the morrow.

She promised to pray for my safety on the road.
As she inclined her head, the two ladies stepped
past me.

They did not know me, so they had no reason to
stay, though I would have liked it very much. I
needed company and fresh conversation, specifically from women who did not waylay me in the
forest with cats. The bright rays of the setting sun
settled to dull greys. No lady should be out after
dark, so I called after them to stay.

They turned as I offered to escort them.

The fair-haired woman's smile widened and introduced herself as Katherine, and the other as Alice.

Alice's mouth curved with a shy smile that brightened her eyes.

I told them my name is Guido, and they asked if I have a surname. I lied, of course, and said that I did not.

They both gave me odd looks, and any fool would know they did not believe me.

"We shall call thee Master Guido, then," the girl called Katherine said.

Whatever they called me, it made no difference. There was something behind Alice's expression when she looked at me; a secret room in a chapel; a buried sorrow.

I led the two women to Dantes, and Alice stroked his nose while the horse snuffled and shook his mane. She told me her brother would love my horse, for he has only seen one, that of his father's.

Katherine gave Alice a quick look, and a faint pink seeped into Alice's cheeks. I did not know how to interpret it, so I asked where we should go as I helped the two girls climb onto the saddle.

Directing me to West Close, Katherine said she wanted to introduce me to Chattox, for she thought it might be advantageous for me to hear my fortune. She said this with a laugh and a wink, and I realized she was joking.

I had never heard of Chattox, nor did I care to meet a seer. Nothing but ill lies in my future.

A hesitant smile broke through Alice's subdued expression, but she shook her head and said she would not choose to travel near Chattox for the world. Thus, Katherine decided on Foulridge instead.

I led Dantes as he trotted along the road with two riders on his back. The surrounding trees created a jagged silhouette against the dusk. An owl hooted while the steady clop of Dantes' hooves filled my ears.

*We passed yew trees with knobby trunks wider than I am tall, the bark ancient as the Bible. The wind carried their creaking whispers along the dirt road.*

*Alice looked down at me from the saddle and asked where I will travel on the morrow.*

*I told her Flanders.*

*She asked if Flanders is my home.*

*Flanders is more home to me than any place in the world. I escaped my childhood and religious persecution in Flanders. It allowed me to become someone new.*

*Perhaps I should not have been so forthcoming, but Alice gazed upon me with such interest I could hardly deny her answers. Soldiers follow commands. Few ask what goes on in their minds and hearts.*

*Alice promised that Pendle would astonish me, and that it could use gentlemen such as myself instead of men like the serjeant-at-law.*

*I caught hold of the word "serjeant-at-law." A serjeant here, in Pendle?*

This was God's intended solution laid before me. The very answer to my prayer. I pulled on Dantes' reins and begged her to take me to him.

I forgot about the impropriety of such a request until Katherine complained she must get home. Of course, I should not place them in harm's way, and I apologized for asking so much of them.

Alice studied me with her lips pressed together. When she spoke, she spoke slowly. "If meeting with the serjeant is what you desire," she said, "I shall take thee. I am not concerned with propriety."

While I appreciated her willingness, I asked if she had a relative to go in her place, but she said there was only her brother at home, and she could defend herself against strangers better.

She is fortunate to have family, for I may as well have none.

My news was both urgent and sensitive, so I accepted her offer, though I wished I had a choice.

We left Katherine at her ancestral home. As I mounted Dantes behind Alice, her back tensed against me as I reached for the reins. Her discomfort stretched between us and lasted more than half the ride to Burnley, though she did not watch me in the way of someone afraid for their life. I have seen fear in the eyes of those I have fought. Her fears stem from a different source, from a general nervousness.

The dirt road stretched on, smothered with trees that boast of bark as green as their leaves in the daytime. But at night, they lean into us, dark and foreboding, stealing away the space to breathe.

I promised to take her home as soon as I had spoken with the serjeant and asked if she knew him well. Having some understanding of his character may help me appeal to him, but I sensed she considered him ill-mannered.

She called him an "arrogant man." She said, "He believes he is owed whatever he desires."

He is rich, I am sure. Luxury often makes life more pleasant, but I have never lived with such ease.

Hopefully, he is the type of rich man who will understand my urgency.

From Alice's clouded expression, I gathered something more happened than her words conveyed, so I asked if the serjeant made her an offer. It was not my business to ask, but I wanted to understand her frustration with him.

She told me no.

Relief swept through me, though I cannot understand the source of it. I will be gone soon, and we are but acquaintances.

According to Alice, the serjeant hooks poor wretches with promises of fine dresses and titles, but if she had a wart on her nose, she would have no place in Pendle. The serjeant-at-law would see to that.

I promised the serjeant wouldn't be dissuaded by so trivial a thing, for she would be lovely with a wart.

She turned, gave me a slight smile, and her shoulders relaxed.

Meanwhile, Dantes crossed into an estate where a road led to a mahogany door with a stag's smooth body projecting from the surface. Carved into the wood, a pack of wolves bared their teeth. The pack leader leapt from the door's face, a ring in its mouth, while a thick pewter handle gleamed in the faint moonlight.

I dismounted Dantes and reached for the knocker, but Alice backed away and wanted to leave before the serjeant saw her.

"He cannot know I am here," she said.

I told her to take Dantes, and I would find her.

Alice gave me directions to her cottage, which borders the very forest I promised to never stray into again. She urged me to remember her words. Otherwise, no villager could direct me. Perhaps she lives somewhere remote, for that can be the only explanation for her strange warning. I did not have time to ask further questions.

Chattering crickets swallowed the gentle clop of Dantes' hooves, and Alice disappeared into the darkness.

After rapping a fist against the cool wooden door, it creaked open.

My interaction with the serjeant-at-law felt cold, and my message was not well-received, though I did deliver it. The rest is in God's hands.

—Guido

Likable as Guido is, I doubt Altham cared to speak to him, but I've spent too much time reading. I have to recover my grades.

I want an "A" on this upcoming quiz. So what if I've never had an "A" before? It's not impossible. If everyone else can do it, so can I, if I study enough.

Somehow, it feels like if I succeed with my grades, it'll straighten everything else out. It's something I can control, so I spend all day studying, all night, and all morning the next day. When laughing students in the hallway yank me out of my reverie as they pass, I take a break to clean my room, snack on chocolate, and trim my toenails. Every time I sit down, my leg bounces unbidden, until I finally stand and walk in circles, faster and faster.

*This is getting me nowhere.*

I stop and leave my room, taking the stairs two at a time down to the first floor of Birdie's Court to get a drink from a vending machine. The machines line a wall close to the administration offices, alongside photos of the professors, including Professor Reeve and our headmistress, Chelsea Craig. Fortunately, most of the students will be at lunch, so this hall should remain uncrowded, which means I won't have to see anyone.

And I really don't want to see anyone, not right now. I don't want more questions about dead bodies.

As I scan the options in the vending machines, I look for caffeine. While my parents drink caffeine on the daily, they discourage my siblings and me from drinking it. My mom calls it the "downward slope," but I down caffeine when I desperately need to focus, and now is one of those times.

My expectation deadens as my eyes reach the end of the drinks. There are no caffeinated drinks available. I guess even in the UK, they have concerns for the health of minors. Or, maybe, they don't have them in stock right now. Just my luck.

A pile of trash on the ground behind the vending machine sparks my irritation, so I stoop to pick it up. As I straighten and turn,

Professor Reeve emerges from the administration office, scanning the hallway. He pulls Jane from Mystic Cosmetics behind him.

My astonishment slams hard into me, and I stumble back against the wall, the vending machine between us. What are they doing here?

While Reeve seemed afraid of Jane before when she interrupted us in his office, his face splits into a boyish smile I didn't know he was capable of.

I press against the wall and try not to breathe. I don't want Reeve to know I saw him, and I don't want to give him a reason to corner me again. But I stay because I want to understand the reason for his smile.

"I should thank you," Jane says as the door clicks shut behind her. "I hoped you'd help me, but I didn't expect—"

"Shhh."

I peer out from behind the vending machine to stare as Reeve presses a finger to Jane's lips. Frozen in place, I don't even care that my jaw hangs open.

He takes a flirtatious step closer to Jane and says, "There are ways to show appreciation." His voice is light and teasing as he pushes her against the closed door.

Jane's sincere expression morphs into a smirk. "Is that so? But we're in the middle of your school. One of your students could come around the corner at any moment."

I shrink against the wall again, my lungs squealing for air.

"You're right." Reeve sighs, and the heels of his shoes clatter against the polished floor as he takes a step back.

Chancing another hopeful peek to see if they're leaving, I catch him letting his hand slide down the oak wood door with the "administration" plaque. His smile returns, and he presses his lips to Jane's, holding her fast before breaking away. "But it makes this more interesting, doesn't it?"

Jane pushes Reeve away with a tinkling laugh, her red hair curling around her heart-shaped face. "I've always loved a bad boy, but I only kiss the men I want to play with. Play time ended for us years ago, my sweet." She walks down the hallway without a backward glance, Reeve trailing behind her.

As they disappear around the bend, I flee to Birdie's Court. I don't know what to think of what I saw. I'm confused, and heavy, and I wish my world view could return to what it was. Everything seemed brighter and simpler a few days ago.

If I struggled with studying before, it proves impossible now. My brain bounces between corpses and images of Reeve and Jane kissing. I pace worse than ever and make the trek to the library, hoping I'll focus better. But even in my remote room behind the copy machine, away from the crowds of students by the river, the daylight drains from the sky faster than it would between my fingers.

Tomorrow, I'll track down caffeine, even if I have to walk to London. Until then, I give up.

Allowing my curiosity to dictate my actions, I pull out the next journal, written by Altham.

## —*1603*—

*Late in the night, a knock reverberated through my halls. She came at the last moment.*

*In an earlier rage, I had reduced my extravagant bedchamber to chaos. I scurried about the space to rectify it and stuffed drinks and articles of clothing into every crevice I could find as I imagined the finest woman ever invited to my quarters. I remembered each face intimately, and hers outshone them all.*

However, Alice slunk away, hiding behind a horse as she led it by the reins. In her place stood a tall, broad-shouldered man with long, brownish-red hair, and a pointed beard and mustache. His thick leather boots and gentleman's coat were dirty and travel worn. The feather in his cap wilted and straightened with the pull of the breeze.

Bowing with manners too refined, he introduced himself as Guido of Spain. He apologized for the late hour and asked if he had found the serjeant-at-law, for he had urgent news to discuss.

My age weighed heavier than my thickest, most expensive coat. This man was young and strong, the kind of man Alice would want.

I suggested with a cold cordiality that we should reconvene on the morrow, but he said he would be gone to Lancaster by the time the sun rises. Apparently, God himself willed him to come here tonight.

Guido could not know what God wills and does not will. Perhaps Guido lied and did not intend to leave. Perhaps he expected to steal the women of Pendle from beneath my boots.

He suggested that my lord, the king, is in danger, and that rebels plot to take the king's life within the year.

To his credit, his news had me reeling for several long moments before I could respond.

I did not believe it. Or did I? The king betrayed and persecuted the Papists. I suppose I could expect retaliation. But how did Guido know this information? Why would they plot such a thing?

Guido had an answer for why, at least. He and his friends did not agree with the king's agendas.

When I asked if his friends were Papists, Guido hesitated before answering that they were Catholics.

Guido preferred the kinder name. How interesting.

I asked if he was Catholic himself and, after a moment's hesitation, he confirmed my suspicion.

He was a rebel, no doubt. The king would have his friends' heads, and Guido intended to abandon them, passing their fates to the empty hands of his God.

Too many men left their affairs to nameless deities, but I knew better. I stood behind religion when I saw a benefit. My god is a fiscal one.

The religious group was gathering followers to promote their religious freedoms. They planned to crown the king's daughter in King James' stead to reestablish a Catholic monarchy. The treason!

When I pointed this out, Guido eyed me with a cool expression and said treason was entirely dependent on perspective. He served God, not man. He was as self-righteous as any Papist.

I told him the king was the head of God's church, but he answered the pope was the real head of the true church.

It did not matter if he agreed with me. What mattered was that I used this information well.

I asked why he abandoned his plan. He explained that he wanted war and went to entreat Spain for King Philip's assistance. Yet the King of Spain lost much in the Spanish Armada and could not come to their aid. Now their plot threatened innocents in the House of Lords, some even that were

Catholic sympathizers. He voted for a fair fight with trained soldiers and did not consider this God's way.

Their plan involved rooms rented beneath the House of Lords. They filled these rooms with barrels of gunpowder disguised as food stores, ready to blast.

I knew those rooms. I owned a few myself. The thought of all my stored items being blasted to smithereens made me sweat.

Guido's friends thought him best suited to kill the king because he was once a veteran, a trained assassin, but he refused.

A killer.

Guido told me his friends expected him to attend a meeting at the Duck and Drake on the Strand in May of this year. Soon, they would assign him the task of lighting the gunpowder. If he did this, he, his allies in the House of Lords, and many innocents would die. If he did not go to the Strand, the rebels would seek him out and kill him. And someone else would light the match.

*Guido did not intend to go to the meeting but planned to vacate England. He needed me to alert the king's guard. How kind of him to think of me, that I might take credit for saving the king. Or he meant to trap me. What would he gain from it?*

*I told him the night was late and asked where he planned to go.*

*He said he needed his horse and would walk to find the woman he lent him to.*

*Few knew where Alice lived. Her father kept the cottage's location a secret from everyone, excluding the magistrate and myself. Perhaps Guido did not know that when Alice told him where she lived, she gave him secret information.*

*Alice must have not understood how much I could discover in so short a time, or she would not have scorned me so.*

*Guido was a man with strength and combat experience. Yet I had power and influence. If Alice would not have me, I would ensure she had no one. I planned to exercise my advantages against Guido and prove which skills were deadliest.*

*—Sir James Altham*

I hope I'm not a descendant of Altham, too. That would be awful.

If James Altham killed Guido, did he kill Alice, too? Professor Reeve mentioned he thought she died. What happened to Alice has to be the key to unraveling the mystery of Alice's significance and application to my life.

*—1603—*

*The magistrate arrived with alarming reports. His son disappeared frequently into Trawden Forest. Rumors and complaints stemmed from Demdike and her association with the Bierley sisters in Samlesbury. And more interesting still, the magistrate discovered bodies in the forest with missing eyes, fingernails, and toes. The villagers were frightened. Some called for action, and it was incumbent upon me to separate fact from fabrication. Yes, fact lay in these claims somewhere. With everything that happened with Alice, the world gave me an opportunity, the kind of opportunity where only the ambitious can benefit.*

*—Sir James Altham*

I stop reading. Missing eyes and fingernails…The dead girl in the river had gouged out eyes and cut-off toes. I stand and pace the room, pause before the table, and walk in circles a few more times. Are these journals about witches and not Alice Grey?

Perhaps this is the danger Reeve spoke of, and something happened at Burnley before I came. He should have told me, instead of leading me down a blind ancestry hole.

I open my laptop, connect to the library's Wi-Fi, and search the web for "Mystic Cosmetics." Nothing pulls up. They don't have a website. I don't know their last names, or I'd look those up, too.

The web can't be my resource.

I stack the copied letters and stuff them into my bag. I'll bring the journals home and research everything I can about the cosmetics store. Staying at the library too late would be dangerous. If I don't find what I need to know, I'll pay the cosmetics store a visit and see what I can learn in person.

I leave the library the same way I came and follow a path through the trees toward Sharona dormitory. Mist clings to the bark. The bright hues of the leaves fade to a deep evergreen. Behind me, a branch cracks, and my hands ball into fists as I spin to face my intruder. I won't be the next girl floating in a river.

Professor Reeve stops a few paces away, his fedora askew. Rain droplets roll to the brim and fall to the wet grass. "Sorry, I saw you from my window."

I forgot his office overlooks the footpath. Perspiration drips down the back of my neck as my pulse slows. Does he know I saw him with Jane? Would he care if I did?

"I wanted to ask if you've read any of the journals since I showed them to you?" His right foot taps against the pavement.

He must know, or he wouldn't have tracked me down like this, acting so agitated.

"I have."

His mouth curves upward. "I think it might help for you to experience the place where the witch trials happened. I'm taking a tour group to Lancaster on the second of October. There's limited space, but I could accommodate you if you'd like to come. Would you want to come?"

He either doesn't know, or he's pretending not to, and I don't have a good enough reason to bring it up yet, though I'll find one soon.

"October second?" I ask, "Next week?"

He hasn't given me much notice, but I can't pass up the opportunity, no matter who he kisses in his free time.

"If you'd like to attend, be at the car park outside my building at 6 a.m.," he says. "We'll take the bus." The professor readjusts his computer bag over his shoulder. "Read the journals. The sites won't mean much if you haven't."

"I've read a bunch already."

He nods several times. "Of course you have." He shifts from one foot to the other and grimaces. "You've done well since you started here. I checked in with your old school and saw your report card. I thought you'd struggle here, but you haven't failed, not yet. That's not to say you won't. I still plan to find a way to get you home. Some of my methods may not be pleasant."

I'm not sure if he's threatening or complimenting me.

Professor Reeve inclines his head and turns to leave, but I call after him. "Bryan?"

He stops and turns. I'm not sure if using his first name is too much, but I need him to be honest. "Are the journals about witches? Are they the danger you meant for me to see?"

He purses his lips. "Keep reading."

And he disappears through the trees.

# CHAPTER EIGHTEEN

FTER REEVE extends his invite, I call Noelle to join me for dinner, but she doesn't answer, so I eat alone.

When I return to my room, chocolate wrappers are scattered across my desk. The mess bothers me, but I leave it and lie on the bed. Reeve thinks I've done well, better than expected if not failing is considered "well." I let his words sink in and close my eyes, but the river girl's mutilated face burns through my eyelids.

There's a danger lurking at Burnley School, and I need to uncover it.

It's in the river, in the trees. On Mill Road.

I stare at my ceiling, count the individual cracks, and force my eyes open. Or I try to, but dusk settles over me, and I'm not in my room anymore.

I reach out to the rough texture of stones that forever occupy my nightmares, and my fingers find the shapes of letters. An "H," followed by a "U." A name. Hugh.

The wall dissolves into a deep forest where only a pair of yellow irises look out at me, blink, and vanish, leaving a cold emptiness that thrives between tree trunks.

My eyes fly open. Feeble light shines through my window, and the clock says it's six in the morning.

I'm not sure if it's a dream I should ignore. Whatever it is, these are windows and doors I can shut. I want to know if my suspicions about the cosmetics store are true, and if I can find proof that the owners connect to the journals.

I hurry to an early breakfast, squeeze in some homework so I'm caught up, show up for each class, and take the first bus to Mill Road when class ends. I find a coffee shop across the street from Mystic Cosmetics. The wooden chairs by the window dig into my legs, but I have a clear view of the cosmetics store's purple awning.

I open my history book and rest it on the table. I'll do homework while I wait, though I have no idea what I'm waiting for.

Bikers and cars whiz by. A line stretches out the cosmetics store's doors and down the sidewalk. The line shortens, and the letters in my textbook grow harder to read until one of the coffee shop attendants flips on the light. I buy another drink in case my extended stay becomes too obvious.

Ellen chases a group of men out the door. As the men run, Ellen looks up and down the street with a forlorn expression and goes inside.

Though I doubt she remembers me, I pretend to be busy by scribbling some notes in my notebook.

A waitress wipes the table behind me, and I twist to face her as she finishes. "Excuse me." I point to Mystic Cosmetics. "Have you noticed anything odd about that store over there? Such as anyone leaving with oversized garbage bags?" Body-shaped garbage bags? "Or lights upstairs at night?" Signs of rituals?

The waitress pauses and gives me a look that makes me realize the oddness of my question. Then she shrugs and balls her rag in her fist. "No. They sell quality stuff. Just expensive."

"So I hear."

The waitress nods and wanders to the back room with her spray bottle. When the last customer leaves, I sit alone.

The final rays of daylight disappear behind the buildings' silhouettes before a recognizable figure with long, dark hair rounds the corner and hurries into the cosmetics store.

Noelle.

The lines die down, and Noelle reappears with two bags filled with expensive products only a few minutes later. Unless her parents are paying for the makeup, I'm not sure how she affords it.

Noelle may have been rude the last time we talked, but she's still my friend.

I clean up my stuff, don my backpack, and chase Noelle down the street.

My footfalls resound against the pavement, and she turns with wide eyes. "Bryanna, what're you doing here?"

"I'd ask you the same question." I don't mean to sound rude, but I don't like that she's supporting Mystic Cosmetics. It's a creepy store, doesn't she see that?

Noelle opens her bags and shows the contents. "I bought more hair dye and a few soaps and shampoo. It really works. I told them I'd be a testimonial if they ever needed one. Oh, and I bought lessons."

"Lessons?" Why would she need lessons?

"I bought soap-making lessons. They teach you how to make it yourself. You'd think they'd want to protect their trade secrets, but they're not about that. They're trying to create a community."

"A community for what?" This had to be the rod that reeled in Noelle.

"A community of women and men who've found love for themselves because they've become everything they dream of being." Noelle's eyes shine. "It gives me hope I can get there, and when I do, that I can belong." Noelle doesn't wait for me to respond before she continues. "If I can make the soap myself, I'll save a bunch of money, and I'll have a support group, too."

Was I so terrible a friend that Noelle needed a different group to spend time with? I remember her being the rude one the last time we were together, not the other way around.

"A support group?"

Noelle considers. "It's more like joining a sorority. There are initiation rituals, and then you become part of something with purpose."

My gut fills with acid. "You don't think that's weird?"

Noelle's brows rise, and her expression becomes petulant. "Why would it be?"

"Because their hair is perfect all the time, they sell potions with spiders in them, and they have crows and cats. The name of the store is Mystic Cosmetics."

"And?" Noelle asks in a cool voice.

I try a different angle. "Look, we found a girl with her eyes cut out very close to here. And you're walking around alone at night. Doesn't that bother you?"

"Doesn't seem to bother you."

The stubborn furrow in Noelle's brow tells me I won't convince her tonight.

I exhale. "Can we go home together?"

Noelle's tone toes the line of friendly. "Sure."

We take the bus, and I walk Noelle to her room. As I return to my desk in my room, I slide the letters out of my backpack, and the top page flutters to the floor. It's the first journal given to me by Professor Reeve. I pick it up and scan the contents. The writer mentions danger, and a place called Moorhill Cemetery.

I run a quick search on my laptop, and my browser shows moss-covered gravestones and maps of York. The initial search item displays, "Find a grave." I type, "Marguerite Dye," the author of the letter. No results.

I examine the letter again and try two other names. "Alice Grey," brings no results. Not even "Gray," the Americanized version. Marguerite's hurried signature at the bottom, however, shows, "M. Dye." I search that, and one result remains.

"I don't believe it," I say aloud, though there's no one else in the room to hear. Someone named M. Dye is buried at Moorhill Cemetery.

I write the directions to the graveyard on a scrap of paper and tuck the note into my pocket. I'll go to York and see the truth for myself. I'm not sure what I'll find, if anything, but the strings have to connect somewhere. Maybe there's something inscribed into her gravestone. Who knows? If nothing else, I might find confirmation that someone named Marguerite Dye existed.

⊸◇⬦◇⬦◇⊷

The next morning, I debate how and when I will get to Moorhill Cemetery as I climb the stairs to my classroom. I can go Saturday and take a train. I already looked up the route.

Tripping over the top step, I drop my bag.

"I do that all the time."

As I straighten, Hadrian smiles at me, and my cheeks burn. He's wearing an expensive-looking wool coat that pairs well with his scarf.

I purse my lips and shake my head. "Lies, but thanks all the same."

He waits for me to catch up and walks at my side. "Are you busy Saturday?"

A ball of excitement explodes in my gut. Is he asking me out? I planned for my trip to Moorhill Cemetery Saturday, but… "No, I'm not busy."

"Good. I'm driving to York. Remember when I promised to take you? Do you still want to go?"

A thrill surges through me, and I can hardly keep a grin from crushing my cheeks. "I'd love to." I pause. I'm not sure if what I'm about to ask is appropriate, but if I can make both my Saturday plans work, I'd prefer not to have to take two trips to York. "Can I drop by one spot while we're there? I've been wanting to do some family history work but haven't made it to York yet."

"Where at?"

"It's a graveyard."

Hadrian's brows scrunch with confusion, and I don't blame him.

"For research," I add, by way of explanation.

"If that's what you want," he says.

"I'll make it short, I promise."

"Take as much time as you need. I'll pick you up at six in the morning. We'll have to leave early to make a day out of it."

"I can work with that." I'll down some cold water to wake myself up.

"Good. Let's get to class then."

For the full hour, I sneak glances at Hadrian. Again, he takes no notes and scans the rest of the room more than he looks at the slides. He taps his pencil on the table and twitches at the slightest noise.

He almost seems nervous, except that when the lecture ends, he turns to me with a sparkle in his eye, as if nothing in the world could concern him. "See you Saturday." He dips his chin and leaves with a book tucked under his arm.

I watch him go, looking forward to Saturday with renewed excitement.

# CHAPTER NINETEEN

ON Saturday, I pull my raincoat tight across my chest as the cold seeps through the layers down to my bones. I almost prefer the dry Colorado snow to the bitter rain that bounces up my jeans. A black compact car slides to a stop on the side of the road, and the back window rolls down.

"I've got the heat on." Hadrian sits in the back seat of the car. His jacket and blue jeans carry no signs of water.

In the front seat, a man I don't know sits in the driver's seat wearing a suit.

He has his own driver? Then again, Noelle did say he has money, or at least his parents do.

My laugh is a nervous chuckle as I climb into the back passenger side, toss my useless turned-out umbrella onto the floor, and inspect the car. The discolored tan ceiling has holes in places, and the steering wheel bears shabby streaks. He has a personal driver and a dumpy car? "I thought—"

"You thought my car would be nicer?"

"Kind of."

The driver pulls into traffic.

"Sorry to disappoint," Hadrian says. "But I like to use my own."

He thinks I care about fancy cars.

"No, no disappointment. I'm glad, actually. I don't have to worry about ruining it."

Amusement flickers in his smile. "What would you ruin?"

"You never know. I could use some hot cocoa right now, and if we got some, I might accidentally spill it all over your seats."

"We need to get hot cocoa then." He puts his hands on the driver's seat. "Silas, can we make a quick stop at a coffee shop?"

The driver turns off the road, parks, and Hadrian gets out to disappear into a corner coffee shop. I stare out the window while I wait. Fifteen minutes later, he returns with two drinks and water streaming down his jacket. "Spill as much as you like," he says as he hands one to me. Rain drips from his hair onto the seat cushions.

"I will." I take a sip.

There are creases in his cheeks from smiling. His cheerfulness warms me as hot cocoa slides down my throat.

The driver starts the car again as Hadrian slides on sunglasses. His curly hair tumbles around them. "While you're at that graveyard, I'll run a few errands. My dad wants me to pick up stuff and smile at a few people. Just call me as soon as you're done, and I'll come right back."

That would entail a lot of driving. "I hope it's not too much of an inconvenience."

"Not at all." His smile is reassuring. "My dad will thank you."

My dad rarely asked me to run errands for his business, but he had my mom's help. "What does your dad do?"

"Parliament."

He says it as if it's a job title all on its own and needs no other explanation. Noelle called him a rich snob, but I've never met anyone less snobby.

I take another sip of hot cocoa. "And your mom?"

"Mum's a lawyer."

High society people. Would he disapprove of my parents' failing business?

"My parents co-own a lumber business." It's a subject not worth delving into. "So how long have you known Mika, Robbie, and Eser?"

Loose hairs brush the ceiling above Hadrian's head. His car is almost too small for him. "My whole life. They're the closest I have to siblings."

"I have too many siblings."

He glances sidelong at me. "How many?"

"Five."

His brows go up over the brim of his glasses. "Five?"

"Yep." Most people respond that way when I tell them.

Our driver merges onto the highway, and several cars pass. I want to tell Hadrian about my garden at home, my dance tapes I had in my closet, my sister, Sadie, and how glad I am to never think about Teddy. In fact, I could see Teddy and his new girlfriend right now and not be bothered.

I want Hadrian to get to know me, and I want to know him better, too. On the other hand, I don't want to vomit all the details of my life in his car on our first outing together because what if the connection is only on my side?

What if I'm not as stylish as Mika, as friendly as Noelle, as funny as Robbie, or as athletic and chic as Eser?

What if I'm just me?

"What're you thinking about?" Hadrian asks.

I blink. "What do you mean?"

"You're somewhere else."

I can't help but grin. "I was thinking you have such different experiences than me, and I'm glad to be here sharing them with you."

"I'm glad, too." He reaches for my hand and squeezes it.

I grow roots, my breath trapped between wanting to escape the anxiety that comes with opening up to someone new, and the feeble hope that he wants me here beside him as much as I want to stay.

I wish I could forget about Moorhill Cemetery and spend the rest of the day at his side, but I can't dismiss the nagging impression that I need to go.

"Do you..." Hadrian hesitates. "Do you ever think about different perspectives and experiences? Like what life would have been like to grow up and live here in England?"

I used to contemplate how my life would have been if Reeve adopted me. "All the time," I say.

"Have you heard of the Gunpowder Plot?"

"I haven't." It's usually me who dives out of the clouds to say something random. I wonder what brought this subject to his thoughts.

Hadrian's shoulders curve inward, and his face falls, as if he just remembered that while I speak English, with an accent, our cultures and histories are different, and he's disappointed. "It's a historical English event, but never mind."

I don't want the disappointment to linger, so I touch his arm. "I'm happy to listen." Even if I didn't grow up here, I can still learn the history.

His eyes glaze as he looks out the window, and I'm not sure if he's considering my words or thinking of something else. Then his eyes snap to the road signs. "This exit, Silas."

Silas swerves, and a car honks. I clutch the sides of my seat.

"I'm so sorry," Hadrian says as our driver continues driving without a change in his expression. "I wasn't paying attention."

Laughter erupts from somewhere deep inside. "You spaced out for a second. I've never seen you do that."

Only once have I seen him absentminded, after Ellen gave him the origami cat, but I'd rather not bring that up.

Hadrian's face goes red. "It might not be appropriate to blame a passenger, but it's entirely your fault."

"My fault?"

"You are a lovely distraction, Bryanna."

Happy goosebumps make me squirm, but in a good way. "Thank you."

After driving over two hours and chatting about everything from Mexican food to the books we love to read, Hadrian tells the driver to park close to a pub in York. In the distance, a monstrous building with columns and domes stands tall over the city, with stripes of metal and wood used as lifting equipment for construction workers.

A line of cumulus clouds drifts across the sky, casting the imposing building into brighter, dreamier light. Fresh air expands in my lungs from recent rain.

"Welcome to York." Hadrian steps out, opens my door, and extends a hand. "Walk with me?" His stance is relaxed.

I clasp his hand in mine, a thrill of excitement running through me at this simple sign of affection. "I'd love to."

We walk through the cathedral, and my brain reels with stone pillars, paintings, and gorgeous staircases. As we leave, a crowd forms around someone famous selling artwork. Hadrian leads me away, though I have an irresistible urge to hound everyone around me for signatures in case they're someone important, too.

We find a tiny street called Shambles, full of preserved, timber-framed buildings that look like something out of a fairytale. When Hadrian takes my picture, I dwarf the doors and windows behind me.

As we walk the length of the city, we follow the line of city walls, still intact from Roman times. I'm amazed at how much history is here, and so well preserved, opening my imagination to processions of soldiers holding banners aloft, escorting kings and queens wearing dresses heavier than my backpack.

I catch Hadrian watching me, but when I catch his eye, he looks away with a satisfied smile.

Crowds of locals play soccer and sit on benches by the lake, making me feel like part of a community.

When we get to the road, double-decker buses squeal past pedestrians. I take cheesy pictures, and Hadrian humors me, giving me a goofy grin from behind a telephone booth.

Later in the day, we linger on the grass overlooking Clifford's Tower, like a squat chess piece perched on a hill. Rain drizzles as the sun sinks below the buildings and their rooftops. Hadrian matches my stride as we rejoin the crowds on the sidewalk and pass tourists taking in the scenery from behind lenses. Locals observe it with their eyes, and I try to soak it in as they do, truly part of it.

When we stop beneath a tree, I press close to his warmth as wind whips hair around my face, rain thick in the air.

Clouds dot the sky, rimmed with gray, as dwindling rays of sunlight fall on the water. I inhale and hold the air in to make the moment last.

Hadrian buries his chin in my hair. "I thought you might like this place. There are twenty acres of gardens here and a shop where you can buy rare plants to take home."

"Will you take me?"

"Don't you have to go soon? It's getting dark."

I press closer and sigh.

He laughs, squeezing me tight. I feel like I'm in a convertible with the top down, passing through a new world with my hair blowing wild. It's cold outside, but I'm warm in his arms. I nuzzle my nose into his neck and rest my cheek against his collarbone. I fit there, as cozy as my hand around my hot cocoa.

"I hope you've found York to your liking." His breath caresses my skin.

"I have." I should say more, but I'm enjoying his attention too much to interrupt.

Hadrian looks out at the water. "If you don't mind me asking, what made you decide to come to England?"

I'm not sure how much to tell him.

"To escape," I say. "I had a boyfriend at home that I needed to get away from."

His arms tighten around me, but I haven't told him the full truth, though I'm not fully positive I know it myself. Teddy isn't the only reason I'm here, even if he was at first.

"My parents wanted me to get a better education. I wasn't doing well in my classes at home, and they were worried about me. Professor Reeve got me into," I clear my throat, "well, he got me in. Or the headmistress got me in, or something like that."

I check his face for his reaction, but his features are smooth. I'm not sure if it's his close proximity, or how well he listens and absorbs, but I ramble on. "And I guess I wanted to come for myself, too. I felt like a piece of me is here."

"Let's make a trade," he says, his voice slow and teasing, without the condescension I feared. "You join the honors program in my place, and I'll join the rest of the students. Just prepare to be ignored. It's quite nice, since the kids in the program are a bit..." He trails off with a grimace.

I told him I didn't do well in my classes at home, and he didn't fixate on it, but moved on.

He doesn't care or doesn't seem to.

Beyond this observation, I've lost track of our conversation, and I scramble to remember the last thing he said.

*The kids in his program are...* "What?"

"Strange," he finishes. "Though I don't enjoy saying that about people. They're nice."

Nice? "Are they though?"

He laughs. "No. Are you ready?"

My lips chill at the suggestion. "No."

What else could I tell him that he would take in stride? I want to find out.

His chest shakes as he chuckles. "I thought you wanted to go to your graveyard."

I did, but I don't want this to end.

He squeezes my shoulders. "Thanks for coming with me, but I don't want you at a graveyard alone after dark. Which graveyard was it you wanted to visit?"

"Moorhill Cemetery. Do you know where that is?"

"I do."

It sucks to separate, but I have a lifetime of curiosity tied up in the graveyard, and I know as well as anyone that being there after dark isn't safe. After what happened on Mill Road, I don't want to push my luck, but I also don't want Hadrian following me through graveyards for hunches I can't explain.

Hadrian's driver takes us to the cemetery and drops me off on the side of the road. I wave goodbye as they drive away before turning to face an entrance flanked by two grim columns and a rally of spindly trees.

Discomfort sloshes in my empty spaces, but I attribute it to the images of dark rivers and empty eye sockets that return to haunt me at every reminder of death. I may be at a graveyard, but I'm likely safer here than at Burnley School, close to Mill Road, where the disappearances happen.

Inside the gates of the graveyard, elaborate crypts with stone guardians protect the graves of notable authors and poets. M. Dye's tombstone wouldn't be with the poets, so I pass them by. Groves of trees surround gravestones with black weather stains and faded carvings. Crisp leaves huddle in corners and crevices.

Across the grounds, the gravestones shrink and grow less distinct, like soldiers in broken formation, tilted from the shifted soil, with layers of rotted foliage at their feet. Over the curved tops lies a tombstone so small it could be a rock.

I leave the crypts and stroll toward the smallest stone, to where trees cast long shadows on the grass.

Beside it, a woman stands alone with a hat that shades her eyes. After standing behind her for several long, uncomfortable minutes, I step around her and hope I don't disturb her mourning as I crouch beside the smallest gravestone. Someone inscribed a list of names into the face, faint and hardly legible.

M. DYE & A. BURBIDGE

On a larger stone beside the first, a faint inscription glimmers. SOME STORIES DON'T END.

Beneath that inscription, in tiny letters I almost don't spot, it says, YOU'RE BEING WATCHED.

I turn around and check behind me, but there's no one there. It's probably a joke, but what a creepy thing to inscribe into a gravestone!

I take out the old letter I brought from Professor Reeve and confirm the name matches. Marguerite Dye was a real person, and, somehow, I found Marguerite among thousands of crypts and gravestones without direction. A glacial finger touches my heart, but I brush off the feeling. It can't mean anything.

Suppressing the urge to wrap my arms around myself, I turn, but a loud thump makes me pause.

What was that?

I turn back.

Resting on the stumpy blades of grass, a purple leather book waits, as if someone dropped it from the trees. Except there's no one in the branches above me. I'm hesitant to pick up a random book by a gravestone that wasn't there two seconds ago, but my curiosity wins, and I reach for it.

The book has a tree inscribed into the front, like the one on my necklace, and a complex lock shelters its contents. A note tucked into the pages says, "Protect yourself and the people you care about."

The leather cover warms beneath my fingertips as if an energy emanates from the book, or an awareness, I'm not sure.

Holding the book beneath my arm, I turn around, half expecting the owner of the book to be standing behind me, but there's no one. Even the woman in mourning has left.

I should put it back, but my fingers wrap around it. Someone left it for me, maybe the mysterious woman. Maybe not. It has the symbol from my necklace on the cover, so, obviously, I have to keep it.

Right?

Hadrian's black car slows against the sidewalk. The door opens, and I grab the handle and step inside. I shove the book I found into my bag and drop it on the floor.

"What's that?" Hadrian asks. His gaze lands on the backpack.

I shrug as I buckle my seatbelt. "A book I want to read. I found it."

"Where?"

"On the ground."

Out the window, the trees in the graveyard sway, and a few leaves flutter to rest in the grass.

"Are you all right?"

I'm not sure how to explain the weird feeling I got when I held the book. I just want to sit and think, but I can't not make conversation.

"Yes." I force myself to turn toward him. "How was work?"

"I shook a few hands and organized some events and speeches. It's Reeve's favorite way to make me useful."

I force my voice to fluctuate how it normally would when I'm fully attentive. "That sounds great."

"It's not." Hadrian eyes me. "But there are perks. Someone invited me to a party next week. It's a Halloween dance of sorts. Would you be interested in coming?"

My focus sharpens on his face as I realize what he's asking.

*He wants to take me out on a date?*

I study the gold flecks in his eyes, the sincere turn of his full lips. How he relaxes against the leather seat, as if he asks girls out all the time. As if dances are a regular thing for him to attend.

An image of twirling across the dance floor with Hadrian sticks in my head like the highlight of a movie. It begs me jump into the screen. "As long as you don't mind bringing someone with zero rhythm, I'd love to go."

Hadrian's driver turns up a street and accelerates.

"Not to worry. My dad's not much of a dancer, either," Hadrian says, his arm on the window ledge.

My breath flees at the thought of an introduction to someone so important in Hadrian's life. "Your dad will be there?"

"He mentioned he might pop by. Is that a problem?"

I search Hadrian's face for his thoughts. "Do you want me to go?"

"If you're comfortable doing so."

My grin is so broad, it aches. "Let's do it." I can avoid dancing, and it's not like we're an item. We just had our first date. His dad might not speak to me at all.

"There won't be anyone you know, but there'll be food and wine. And dancing if you're into that."

"I can sway from side to side."

He chuckles, reaching across the center seat, and winding his fingers through mine.

I lean against his shoulder, and his lips brush the top of my hair, though the idea of the driver watching makes me feel odd.

We hold hands on the return drive to Burnley, and stars glitter out the window. I step out of Hadrian's car in front of my dormitory and reach for my backpack. The old leather book tumbles out. Hadrian's gaze fixes on the tree inscribed into the cover as I stuff the book back into my bag.

"That's an interesting cover."

"It is, isn't it?" I consider telling him about my suspicions with the cosmetics store for the briefest of seconds but dismiss the idea. He'd think I'm crazy. And, honestly, talking about it will bring up what happened on Mill Road, and I'm not ready for that.

He cocks his head. "Have a lovely evening. Thank you for making my monthly trip to York loads more enjoyable."

I wave and shut the door. The gravel crunches as they drive off, and two red lights disappear in the night.

I heft my bag and hurry to my room, close and lock the door, and slide the book I found out of my bag. The tree has an eye at the bottom. Branches intertwine and a star crowns the top. It's too witchy and creepy for a normal book you'd find at a bookstore, but the lock has the shape of my necklace, too, and I can't help but think my necklace might be the key.

If I want to open it, I suppose that dreaded conversation with Professor Reeve has to happen.

# CHAPTER TWENTY

I LURCH OUT OF BED in the morning and rub my eyes. The professor scheduled the buses to leave at six o'clock in the morning, and my clock shows twenty minutes till. I throw on clothes, wash my face, and brush my teeth in record time. Then I rush out the door and cross the grounds to where two buses wait in the parking lot by Professor Reeve's office.

As I board the first bus, I scan the rows of seats for a familiar face. Disappointment washes through me when no recognizable faces smile back, not even Mika. I hoped Mika would come.

I sit in the back and rest my head against the seat.

The bus door opens, and a group of people enter. In front strides Professor Reeve. He searches the seats until his eyes fix on me. He inclines his head, but his expression burns cold. When he sits in the front row, Hadrian steps out from behind him and flashes a wide smile.

My stomach erupts in flutters as he walks to the back of the bus, sits beside me, and stuffs his backpack under the seat.

I didn't expect to see him, but I'm glad he came.

He messaged me after our date, but I've been busy. I have so much homework, and I've rewritten my essay a dozen times. I've explained this all to him, and he's been patient.

"I thought Reeve didn't like you?" I say. "You said he never invites you."

"Mika talks so highly of these field trips, I decided to give it a go. My parents called, and he actually told them 'no' at first, but my dad can be quite persuasive when he wants to be. Seems like you were invited."

"I was, yes, but I'm not sure why he would invite me and not you, unless he feels obligated."

He chuckles. "Why would he feel obligated? I'm not sure Professor Reeve has ever felt obligated, not in his life."

If I've told him about my struggles with school, I suppose talking about my adoption shouldn't bother me. After all, it's a large part of my life, and not something I'm ashamed of.

"He found me as a kid and adopted me out. Maybe he feels responsible for me."

Hadrian stares, eyes wider than his eyes have room to be.

"What?" I demand.

"He found you?" His stunned expression makes me shift on my chair, impatient for an explanation.

"Yes, I'm adopted."

He puts his elbows on his knees and leans forward. "So was I."

Now it's my turn to gape, and the shock lingers longer than his. I don't know what to say, except that I never expected this, not ever.

*What does it mean?*

Professor Reeve doesn't strike me as the type of do-gooder who searches streets for abandoned children. Surely, he doesn't adopt out kids in his free time.

Hadrian winds his fingers together. "I was abandoned, and Professor Reeve discovered me. My father is a friend of his. My parents couldn't have kids, and they were looking to adopt."

"When?" I ask.

He scrunches his face. "What do you mean?"

"When did this happen? When were you adopted? And where?"

His face clears, and his mouth turns up at the corner. "August twentieth. Old Street."

My blood crystalizes. August twentieth is my birthday, or the birthday my parents assigned me, though they only ever said Reeve found me in London.

If Professor Reeve found two discarded babies and not one, Hadrian might be my brother. I study his face. He has green eyes, not gray. My mousy hair doesn't have an ounce of his copper red. I'm small and scrawny, while Hadrian stands tall and broad shouldered. Nothing suggests any relation except the date Reeve found us.

Hadrian chuckles. "Looks like you're as surprised as I am."

Hadrian claims Professor Reeve likes me better, but it was me that Reeve sent to strangers across the ocean, not Hadrian.

"I'm sure you've wondered who your real parents are," Hadrian says, his voice hesitant.

"All too often." The mystery of my parentage has always felt like a scale, oscillating between fairytale and tragedy. "Do you know who yours are?"

"No." Hadrian watches me pensively, like he wants to say more.

The bus lurches, and Hadrian's eyes flick to the front of the bus where Professor Reeve sits, and then back to me. I wonder what Hadrian's thinking.

I tuck my bag under my seat. "Professor Reeve says I have family from Lancaster," I say. If Alice Grey is family. "That's more likely why the professor invited me."

"Then it'll mean more to you than to me."

So, he doesn't have family there. Good.

Reeve's deep voice resonates over the commotion of students. "I think that's everyone, then. Feel free to go when you're ready."

The engine starts, and the bus lurches.

When it rounds a sharp corner, Hadrian slides into me. "Very sorry," he says.

I blush as he rights himself. His jacket brushes my fingertips and brings back the fresh scent of the breeze at the fishing pond and the kiss of the wind on my cheeks.

He's all ease and warmth, but I'm stiff as an arrow stuck in the snow. We held hands only days ago, but I can't imagine reaching out and touching him again, though a drop of my hot cocoa from our date still stains my ramshackle purse.

"I'm glad you're here, Bryanna," he says.

He doesn't put his arm around me, but his smile is a warmth that blows aside the dust of past relationships. It's nice to be the one he messages, rather than the one he ignores.

I scoot closer.

Outside the windows, stacked stones make fences to contain wandering sheep. The sheep wander the hills in groups, like fuzzy balls on a grass blanket. The road curves toward a green-and-purple plateau, crowned with a gathering of clouds.

Twenty minutes later, the bus halts at the top of a hill. Professor Reeve stands and points to a white dome in the distance. "Attention students, what you see there is Gallows Hill. I've done a lot of excavation in this area, especially regarding the famous Pendle Witch Trials in 1612. I was the first to find the possible remains of Malkin Tower using old land ownership documents. That's what this tour concerns.

"In 1612, Pendle was a remote and humble area full of uneducated people. Some were Catholic, others were of the more popular Protestant faith. Unfortunately, faith, among other things, caused schisms to grow between friends and families. Disputes with politics, land, money, and inheritance widened the cracks. Then an unfortunate girl walked down a lonely road as an elderly man had a stroke. The poor wench didn't know what to do to help him and was later blamed for having maliciously triggered the stroke by magic.

"There was an uproar in the town, and the magistrate at the time, Roger Nowell Senior, took advantage of the unrest. Here, on that hill, the town brought the innocents in a cart to be hung, drawn, and quartered for their crimes, which means they were hung until they were barely alive, dragged through the dirt at the end of a cart, and then cut to pieces. Alive till the end."

I shiver at the imagery, but in the back of my head, a little voice whispers.

*But Alice Grey survived.*

"Malkin Tower," Professor Reeve continues, "was where the witch meetings allegedly took place. It was said the witches met and plotted against the more righteous villagers to capture their wealth and kill them off. After the hanging, Malkin Tower was burned. I studied land ownership records and have reason to believe that before the tower was burned, it was located at Black Moss Reservoir, which is where we're headed."

The bus shudders as it rolls over bumps in the road.

Small villages lie nestled against the landscape. If Alice Grey lived in the valley beneath the plateau, her descendants could still be there. I may have aunts, uncles, and cousins minutes away.

The bus drives down a road that winds between old Victorian homes, with flower boxes in the windows. We even pass a sign with a witch riding her broomstick, hanging over an inn. After parking by a picnic area, Professor Reeve beckons as he passes the bus driver and descends the stairs. "Come along." He waits for us to disembark, but as soon as my shoes touch the wild earth, he's off, leading everyone past a café, across grass, and then a bridge, before turning down Barley Lane.

It's a short walk from there to the reservoir, which reflects Pendle Hill in lovely green and blue hues.

"This way." Professor Reeve gestures to the woods. "It's a bit off the beaten path."

He leads us into the trees, which start out sparse, with the occasional tree carved into an elaborate sculpture, cylinders stacked on top of each other, trees creating metal and wood arches, and people with blank eyes.

We pass them all by as the trees grow more numerous.

No paths or signs mark the direction between knotted trunks coated in moss. Enormous roots peppered with mushrooms tangle the earthy floor until the trees become so dense, they squeeze out the light. Gulping down my fear, I glance over my shoulder at Hadrian. With him close, I'm less worried.

I search for signs of Professor Reeve. Surely, he won't take us any farther? He must be ahead because the other students plod along, as if they know where to go.

I squish between two trunks and stumble into a clearing filled with broken brambles, dead grass, and a row of crumbling stones. The wind dies, and a stale stench settles. Crows caw in the distance. A twig snaps.

"This is the spot." Professor Reeve's discordant voice echoes. "See the rocks here?" Black scorches streak the stones. "Now, what do you think? Do you believe in witches?"

Hadrian casts Professor Reeve a funny look. "It's a bunch of rocks."

Someone might've made a campfire—that would explain the black scorch marks. Yet the stones look familiar, like I've seen them on a camping trip in Colorado. They also feel wrong. Displaced or marred.

"True, but it's the only remaining evidence of where Malkin Tower once stood." The professor meets my gaze. His voice sounds light and carefree, but his eyes remain somber.

Raw, fresh marks cover the crumbling rocks while no growth replaces the circle of dead grass. I can attribute it to rambunctious teenagers or a recent forest fire, except the other trees should have burned, too. Perhaps the earth hasn't forgotten what transpired, has seared the event into its corporal memory. A scar.

Frigid gusts of air encircle me. I lift my arm and turn my wrist up. The scars on my skin glare back. The stones seem to morph into brick walls. They block out the sun. Fiery tongues of flame reach up the bricks. Heat licks my skin, and wood crackles beneath my heels. Then a door slams shut, and the clearing returns, the rocks motionless as before. I stagger and catch myself before I fall.

Reeve's face comes into focus as he lifts his chin. "It's what happens to people who get tangled up with witches, Bryanna. There are no shortcuts in this life. And no second chances."

I scan the students in the clearing, but no one else seems to have heard what Reeve said. If they did, they don't react to it. Though he clearly has something he wants me to see, I can't tell if he's referring to Alice, the cosmetics store, or something else entirely.

Professor Reeve's brows gather, and he faces the group. "Let's eat lunch by the bus, everyone, and we'll head to our next destination. Stay with me, please. I don't want you to get lost."

"Are you feeling well?" Hadrian asks again. He waits with one hand outstretched.

I nod a few too many times and wobble past him, but he stops me with a touch.

"Allow me to help," he says, wiggling his fingers. "There're roots everywhere, and you look like you're going to be sick."

He stays close until the trees thin, and the bus appears between leaves. Bagged food bursts from a plastic bin on the ground. I snatch a lunch and eat it on a rock.

Perhaps Reeve's warning involves my parents, and the aftermath of the trials Alice was caught up in. My parents might have died in a fire when I was a baby. That would explain my nightmares.

Hadrian sits beside me and nibbles on a sandwich. "Why're you so quiet?"

I shrug. A dark cloud seems to have settled over me, and I'm not in the mood to wade out of it, or to explain myself. I'd rather sit alone with my thoughts.

He leans back on his hands, either unaware of my silent plea for solitude, or unwilling to leave me. "You know, Reeve received so much notoriety from his research here. I thought there would be more than a bunch of burnt stones. I hope the next stop's better."

"This stop is creepy." Too busy staring off into space to pay attention to what I'm eating, I bite into my orange and cough as I spit out the bitter peel.

Hadrian stifles a laugh. "Sorry, I've never seen someone try to eat an orange like an apple."

I'd hoped he didn't notice, but of course, he did.

I strip the rest of the peel and eat the orange slices the way a normal person does.

Professor Reeve's voice rises over the group. "Let's go. We don't have a lot of time."

I board behind another student, and we drive another hour until the spiked tips of a medieval fortress surface over the treetops.

The bus stops across the road from a row of old buildings and apartments with white lattice windows and bricks the same uniform color as the castle walls. Grass, trees, and cobblestones weave to the fortress, where columns welcome us like smiling teeth on rotten gums. A weathervane and flag flap in the wind.

The shadows cast by the walls cool my skin.

Reeve ushers us beneath the arched entrance. "This is another favorite spot of mine. I can tell you many stories about this place. You've heard of the Pendle witches, but have you heard of the Samlesbury witches? Both groups of witches were tried here in the Lancaster Assizes.

"The Samlesbury witches were three of many witches tried here. The magistrate released them after they convinced the jury they'd been the target of a Catholic plot. A clever bunch. The other women accused did not prove so lucky. The jury moved the condemned witches from here to the gallows on the moors above the town, where they were hanged for all to see.

"We'll tour the jails, so you can see for yourselves just how dismal they are. This was where they held the witches before trial. One accused witch you never hear about was Alice Grey. It's generally said she was acquitted, but I have reason to believe she was imprisoned here for seven years."

I don't have to look at him to know he's speaking to me, and I know I should be excited to see where Alice stayed, but I'm not.

There seems to be an invisible wall my body doesn't want to cross, because my legs stiffen as we approach.

He continues. "After seeing her jail cell, you might comprehend, just a little, how terrible such a sentence must have been. Nowadays, Lancaster Castle is still used as a prison and courtroom, but also for much lighter affairs. There's a museum, and a lovely café, and sometimes they hold music festivals, marathons, and Christmas fairs."

Christmas wreaths and prisons.

I turn to Hadrian. "Is this place more to your taste?"

The corners of Hadrian's mouth tick up. "I see places like this all the time, but I'm glad you're enjoying it."

Despite the uniformed castle courtyard and paid actors gallivanting in knights' uniforms, a sinister impression slithers beneath the green grass and spectators in raincoats. Maybe it's the threatening rain clouds, or the shapes of the stones. Or the knowledge that Reeve planned this whole thing for me, for a reason.

I push off the feeling because it ruins a trip I'm determined to enjoy.

Hadrian walks close beside me as we cross the courtyard and enter the castle through a dim corridor with short ceilings and dark halls.

The professor pauses outside a door and slides a key into the lock. He turns it with an audible click. Hinges groan, and the wood swings inward, revealing a puff of musty air that makes me quiver. The stones have rough edges and decaying hollows.

"These are prison cells," Reeve says. "See the marks carved into the walls?"

Scratches mar the surfaces. I step inside and run a finger over the coarse corners. The prisoners tallied their anguish and unfounded hopes into days. Some marks cut deeper than others to create grooves time cannot erase.

I turn my hand, so the thin, white lines show etched in my skin. "Next room."

I jump at the sound of Professor Reeve's voice as he directs the other students to another cell down the hall. "Not many are permitted in these rooms, so do not touch anything, please. I don't want my privileges revoked."

Forcing myself to follow, I stop in the doorway.

A rock drops to the bottom of my abdomen.

Someone gouged the name, "Hugh," into the wall.

The hauntingly familiar name steals my breath.

*Hugh.*

The walls of the prison press in from all sides. I reach forward and touch each of those carved letters. Icy chills ravage my body, and pain lances through my right forearm, though my lips are locked so no sound escapes. I'm drowning in a pool of skeletal dreams.

"Bryanna?" Hadrian's urgent voice is faint. "We're not supposed to touch…"

This is the same room, the same low ceiling, the same smooth stones. The complete absence of light and windows. Unlike my dreams, there are no scorch marks. Just carvings. Someone wrote a scriptural reference by Hugh's name. "VENGEANCE IS MINE. I WILL REPAY, SAITH THE LORD." Scrapes, like trenches made by nails, deepen the words into the rock.

Putting one hand against the wall, I try to steady myself, but my fingers leave streaks of red.

I stare at my wrist in horror as fresh blood drips to the ground.

Black shining shoes tap the floor. I look up into Professor Reeve's full black eyes. Heat flashes through me, wild and hot. I want to seize his neck and wring the life from it. Watch the skin gray and the eyes pop from their sockets. I choke on the emotion, and the heat redirects to my cheeks.

Faces all around. Hot tears make them blurry.

Hadrian stands beside me with an expression full of concern. He thinks I'm crazy, and he might be right.

I turn and flee down the hallway, out the open doors, across the courtyard, and into the closest bathroom. I crouch in the corner with the stall door closed. My teeth chatter, and cold sweat drips down my neck. I clench my hands to keep from shaking, my arm bleeds from scratches made with my nails.

"Bryanna?" Hadrian's voice carries from outside the bathroom. "Are you all right?"

I take a shaky breath. "I'm just sick."

"Shall I fetch a doctor?"

A doctor is the last thing I need. I rub at the tears and push myself up. My knees wobble as I open the stall door. "No, I'm coming." I keep my head down as I leave the bathroom.

"You look pale. What've you done to your arm?"

I shove past him. "I feel awful."

"Let me help. Stay here." He disappears into the bathroom and reappears with a wad of toilet paper. He presses it to my bleeding skin and wraps an arm around me.

"Thanks," I say.

More staring as we pass crowded tables in the courtyard and board the bus. I curl up on my seat cushion.

"Do you feel well enough to keep going?" Hadrian hovers over me. I haven't left him any room. "There might be another stop planned."

"I don't know."

If he stops talking, I can close my eyes and forget all of this.

"I'll tell the professor. Maybe he can send one of the buses back early. It's worth asking."

I rest my forehead against the cool metal panels as Hadrian sits across the aisle. In any other circumstance, I would want him to sit beside me. Now, I want to be alone even more than before because I don't want him to see me this way.

Hadrian's voice rises over my tremors. "I get it, you know. You don't need to be ashamed. To me, they're stones and old buildings. But some places have weird effects on us. I've always loved cathedrals. Time slows. I like the quiet. But when I was a kid, my parents took me to Westminster Abbey, and I couldn't stand being there. Don't know what it is about that place, but…"

The other students' feet clomp against the floor as they board.

I shut my eyes, and the hollowed eye sockets wait on the backside of my eyelids, with fire and scorched stones behind them. All of it building up to consume me.

"I went into the women's toilet to get paper for you," Hadrian says. "I hope you remember that. I wouldn't do that for anyone else."

My sickness recedes, and I almost smile.

Professor Reeve's voice rises over the chatter. "Students, we'll cut this tour short. We're returning to campus." His feet move down the aisle until he stands over me. "I'm sorry," he says in a low voice, "but I wanted you to see it, to remember. If you've read the journals, you know this place. It's real. It's not just a story. You need to go home, Bryanna." He glares at Hadrian before he turns and leaves.

Another threat, warning, demand, whatever he wants to call it, but a name from a nightmare won't make me leave any more than a dead body can.

The buzz of chatting students grows louder as more students board.

"What's that about?" Hadrian asks.

I sit up and rub my forehead. I wish I could explain. I wish I could state the reason Professor Reeve works so hard to scare me away. "I don't know."

The rest of the drive passes in a blur, with me spending most of the time with my face pressed to the metal siding on the wall where hundreds of greasy fingers likely left germs. When the bus rocks to a stop in the parking lot, I wait until all the students have left before I stand to follow them out.

Hadrian walks me to my room, his concerned eyes tracking me as I open the door. "Call if you need someone to talk to."

His words touch an ache from Sadie's absence that I didn't know I had. "I will."

Velvet strands of hair hang in his face as his eyes lock onto mine, curiosity smoldering behind them. Silence crowds my ears.

I reach for him and press a hand against his jacket.

Hadrian grasps my hand with both of his, and the muscles in his forearm flex. His lips purse, and he brushes my chin with his fingers. "I hope you feel you can talk to me," he says, dropping his hands. "And I hope you feel better soon."

"Thank you."

He's hesitant to leave, but I need solitude.

"I'll text you," I say.

He backs out of the room, and I listen as his shoes thud down the hallway, and the scent of him fades. I ease the door shut and drag myself to bed.

The sheets look comforting, like a hug. Instead of falling into it, I lift the mattress to expose the purple book beneath. The eye on the cover stares. I don't know why I thought of it, but I bring it out. In order to open it, the book requires the key.

I need to research Alice Grey, the cosmetics store, and now Hugh. Hugh is important. The feeling resounds in my bones, I don't know why.

Slipping the book beneath the mattress again, I can almost feel the intensity of the eye through the sheets. Perhaps the tome references Hugh.

I need my necklace.

# CHAPTER TWENTY-ONE

THE LETTERS on the pages run together into one muddy pool. I squeeze my eyes shut and open them again. Hugh's name must exist somewhere, and I hope to find him in the journals. Otherwise, I don't know where else to look.

I read from where I left off, beginning with Guido as he departs from the judge's house to meet Alice.

—*1603*—

*I followed Alice's directions and arrived at daybreak the next morning. Though I planned to leave as soon as I arrived, Alice showed me that Dantes gained a slight limp from our travels. I cannot risk further hurt to his leg, so I agreed to stay a few weeks longer to allow Dantes time to heal.*

*Ellen's meddlesome smile plagued my dreams, but I assured myself it was not her who caused my horse injury. This happened naturally often enough.*

Alice claimed I looked worn as well. She was correct, I was exhausted. In fact, I may have been delirious.

Lady Ellen had been following me. She was keen to have me visit her, but I refused many times. In addition to her, I met Alice's younger brother, Hugh. Alice doted on him as if he were her son. However, there was something wrong with the boy.

If I believed in magic and superstition, I would have said Hugh was not human. The resemblances between sister and brother were difficult to see. His eyes were an unnatural, livid yellow, the color I suspected Ellen was searching for when we met in the woods. When he looked at me, his gaze bore through me.

Strange things happened when he was around. He ran faster than I deemed possible. Once, he ran into a tree and leapt away unharmed. He picked a flower for his sister and wept as it withered in his hands. Alice would not allow Hugh to step outside the cottage without his boots for fear he should kill the grass.

*Animals of prey flocked to him. A wolf appeared in the trees with a rabbit in his mouth. Hugh accepted the gift and sent the beast away. Dantes refused to go near Hugh and neighed when the boy came too close.*

*At first, I was wary of Hugh, but after weeks of staying in the village nearby, we became familiar. I realized he needed me, though I have never been needed before. While he was loved tenderly by his sister, the boy lived without a father. I understood that emptiness.*

*My visits to Alice's cottage increased to daily trips, especially since Dantes stayed there.*

*Alice did not allow Hugh to leave the meadow surrounding the cottage, nor did he have acquaintances, save for a young girl I saw sneak into the garden to play—though I never spoke of her to Alice.*

*As Dantes' health improved, I took him on gentle walks every evening before the sun went down. One night I glanced back at the cottage as a hooded visitor slunk to the doorstep. The door opened to admit the stranger, only to shut quickly behind him.*

*Alice did not mention a stranger coming, and while Alice's affairs are her own, I felt odd about it. While I have never been a jealous man, I believe I have gained this fault.*

*I waited for the stranger to leave. He did not stay long. When the door opened again, the hooded figure stooped over Hugh's bent head, and then hurried toward town.*

*When I asked Alice about him the next day, she seemed both surprised and upset that I saw the stranger but readily identified him as her father.*

*What kind of father visited his children in the night?*

*—Guido*

I clutch the paper in my hands. Hugh isn't a fabrication of my mind. Not only does Guido mention him, but he describes him as someone extraordinary and important to Alice.

My chair squeaks in my eager rush to pick up the next letter.

*—1603—*

*A wild man with rags for clothes and wicked eyes watched the house from the trees. I warned Alice, but she assured me all was well.*

*She gripped the fine silver branches of a tree pendant she wore around her neck and said, "This necklace is protection. Iduna gave it to me."*

*I did not know who Iduna was, but Alice checked her neck often, perhaps to reassure herself the necklace was still there.*

*Today I spotted another stranger in the woods around the cottage, a woman I glimpsed at the alehouse. She had long, fiery red hair and bright eyes that glimmered in the twilight. The sight of her turned my blood cold. I ran to the trees to speak to her, but she disappeared. While saplings and giant oaks fortified the cottage on all sides, we were exposed.*

*Alice tried to hide her anxiety from me, but I saw that she lived in constant dread of a threat she would not reveal. Hugh played in happy ignorance, hunted rabbits for fun, wrestled with*

*wolves, and, occasionally, ran into the woods
with a little girl who came to find him.*

*Dantes' leg improved, and he was ready for travel,
but I delayed my journey to the continent until I
knew that Alice and Hugh were safe. I could not
leave Alice there alone. Though Alice commanded
me to go before dark each day, I returned at dawn.*

*—Guido*

Guido mentions a too familiar necklace, and the journals note the names of the women in the cosmetics store. They're common names though, so does that mean anything? Guido talks about a woman with red hair in the trees, which sounds an awful lot like the Jane I know, but that's not likely.

Most important of all, it mentions that Alice's necklace was protection. If her necklace and my necklace are the same, this might be why the necklace is so important. Is this why Reeve wants it? If he's worried about my welfare, why doesn't he want me to keep it?

Two sharp knocks make me jump, and I set the journals aside, rising to answer it.

Reeve stands in the doorway and rakes his fingers through his slick hair so many times it stands on end. His eyes have a wild look as he twists the fastenings on his coat. Around his neck, the branches on my necklace glimmer, making my blood warm. Does he mean to torment me?

I reach out a hand to snatch it from his neck, but he sidesteps out of my reach. "Give me my necklace back."

"Have you read the journals?" he returns in a grating voice.

He eludes my demands so easily, it frustrates me all the more.

"Yes, I read that the necklace is protection. So why don't you give it back to me? And what're you doing here, anyway?" I need to invest in a peephole.

Reeve's eyes flick down the hallway.

If he came to make sure I'm all right after my dramatic reaction to Lancaster Castle, I haven't been kind to him, though I'm not sure I want to be. I just wish he would explain himself. He might have a reason for clinging to the necklace, but why does he not say?

"I'm fine, really," I say. "You didn't need to check up—"

"That's not why I came."

My tone cools. "Then why did you come?" He can't harp on the same demands and expect me to succumb to them. If he were less rude, I'd be more likely to listen.

"I saw who you were with yesterday. Has anything happened between you and Hadrian?"

"What're you talking about?"

Being told to leave the moment I arrived was crazy enough, but to have a professor demand to know about my dating life is ludicrous.

"Answer the question." His frightening tone makes my treacherous limbs tremble. No professor should be allowed to ask these personal questions, not even one who claims to be connected with me.

I glare at him. I don't know what he'll do if I don't answer his question, but I don't care either.

"If you know what's good for you, you'll stay away from Hadrian," he says.

"Unlike you, he's been nothing but kind to me."

Reeve's eyes almost burn holes through me. "Of course, he has."

"And what about Jane from Mystic Cosmetics? You think she's good for you? You were terrified of her when she came to see you."

"What do you mean?" His eyes are wary.

"I saw you two together."

The confusion on his face morphs into a death stare that could sharpen a knife. "It's how I keep tabs on them, and it's none of your business."

"Exactly." I shut the door in his face and lock it.

It feels so good.

⬦—⬦

I heft my backpack after a long afternoon of classes. All morning, I search "Hugh Grey" online and find nothing while Professor Reeve's words and the characters in the journals clash for space in my brain.

I hurry down the hall for my next class, students parting around me.

"Did you hear about that girl that disappeared on Mill Road? They found her in a river."

"That's why you don't go out walking at night alone. She was asking for something like that to happen," another student says.

I've heard the whispers for weeks now, but this one in particular bothers me. No one deserves what happened to the girl we found in the river.

Too angry to look at their faces, I shove past them.

My phone buzzes in my pocket. No one calls, except my mom and Sadie, and I don't have time for a long chat right now. I reach for the device and check the tiny screen on the front as Hadrian's name flashes on a neon background. Nervous anticipation makes me fumble as I flip the phone open. "Hello?"

"Bryanna, it's Hadrian."

I struggle to control the frustration from the conversation I overheard, and the nervous excitement filling my voice. "Hey, Hadrian."

"Remember that Halloween dance I mentioned to you?"

"Yeah?" I assumed he forgot.

"It's tonight. Do you still want to go?"

The phone bites into my hand as I squeeze it. I'm a mess of anger, chronic uneasiness, crazy excitement jumbled with nerves, and a dash of disbelief that he still wants to go with me after witnessing my breakdown on Reeve's excursion. "I would love to."

I need this.

"Good. Do you have something you'd like to wear?"

I envision my closet of awful dress pants and swallow hard. "I'm sure I can find something." My uncertainty leaks into my voice, despite my best effort to sound lighthearted.

"Anything you have should be fine."

My lip twinges as I chew on it. How humiliating is dress pants at a party? I guess I have no other choice.

"That sounds like fun." I turn away from passing students. "What time?"

"When's the earliest you can get away? It's in York, so it'll be a drive."

"After my last class should be fine. Around four? Will Mika and Robbie be there?" I ask, hopeful to see familiar faces. Mostly, I want Mika around in case I'm forced to make conversation with anyone outside of Hadrian.

"No. This is—" he hesitates, "an even more elite crowd. But it should still be entertaining if you like cocktails and dancing."

Elite? My phone slips in my sweaty hand. "I do." I love dancing more than I admit, though I wish this dance included the friends I love and am familiar with.

"Also—" Hadrian pauses again. "My dad invited us and really wants us to come. He reminded me several times."

"Us?" I perk up at the thought of his dad requesting me. It makes me feel welcome, and my stress cloud thins.

"Well, he wants me, specifically, to make an appearance. But I'd like for you to join me. It would make going more bearable, and my dad wants to meet you."

"Why?"

What do I mean to Hadrian's dad? Or to Hadrian himself?

"I suppose he fancies meeting the one person who can tolerate me for longer than an hour."

I laugh, though I wonder if there's more he's not saying. I squirm at the thought of Hadrian caring for me enough that his dad notices. "Pick me up at four," I say. "Right after class."

"I'll see you then."

I snap my phone shut, walk through the door to class, and let the warmth sink in. I'll see Hadrian's infectious smile in only a couple hours, and there's nothing Reeve can do to prevent it.

# CHAPTER TWENTY-TWO

HADRIAN AND HIS DRIVER pick me up at the street corner right on time. He leans across the car to open my door, and I toss my pack into the back and climb in.

"You're not wearing a costume?" I ask.

He raises both brows. "Neither are you."

Shrugging, I gesture to my pants. "I dressed up as a businessperson. There you go."

Hadrian laughs. "Well played. My dad is bringing my suit." He draws a simple, thin white mask out of a shopping bag that would only cover his eyes. "This is all I need. If the mask were a bit bigger, I'd draw a mustache. With a bit on the chin, too."

I nudge him in the ribs. "How about not? Where is this party?"

His smile turns roguish. "It's not at Burnley Boarding School, if that's what you're asking. You can't run off to do homework tonight. You're stuck with me." He checks his watch. "The party starts now, and we have a two-hour drive, so we've got to hurry."

"That doesn't answer my question," I say.

His response is simple. "You'll see."

We drive and talk as the countryside turns to buildings and then to tall, narrow apartments. Hadrian's driver parks on the side of the road before a squat, turquoise store, and Hadrian helps me out of the car. Cold, wet wind tears through my sweatshirt, and I pull it tighter.

The store has big, glass windows with mannequins draped in ball gowns. A few Halloween dresses have bats, stars, monsters, and jewels sewn in, and interspersed between them, glitter more extravagant dresses with silk, gold, and sequins.

I need one of those, rather than these ugly dress pants, but I keep my mouth shut as Hadrian leads me past the store windows further down the road, pressing a hand against the small of my back. A slow burn travels up my spine. "Shall we?"

Hadrian slows before a tower of glass windows, with lights shining bright as beacons. He takes my hand. "You can change inside."

My hands shake as sliding doors sweep open to admit us, along with a wave of heat that melts the outside frigidity.

Hadrian kisses my fingers. "Don't be nervous."

"I'll try."

We step into an elevator that carries us up several flights and keeps going.

"It's just a small party," Hadrian says as the elevator dings. "Bigger parties are usually at someone's country manor, like Blenheim."

"What's Blenheim?"

Hadrian smiles, as if my question is funny. "Can you wait here for me?" He leaves for the bathroom and reemerges wearing black. His suit compliments his broad shoulders and trim form.

"You look handsome," I say. My dress pants and sweater look like an oversized circus tent next to his.

"You're absolutely stunning," he says, as if it's a line he isn't expected to say.

"Thank you. How did you change so fast?"

"Lots of practice." He offers a hand. "My dad's waiting."

The time has come, and the insecurities I pushed to the back of my mind rise.

*Will Hadrian's dad like me?*

My stomach rolls. "Give me a minute." I pull away, ready to run back down the stairs, but Hadrian winds a hand around my waist.

His lips press against my forehead and traces of pine needles fill my lungs.

I can't resist him, but my anxiety isn't so easily dispelled. My heart still thuds.

A door down the hall swings wide. "Hadrian, there you are. I see you've brought her!" A man in his early sixties strides toward us, also in a black suit and white collar. He stands so straight, his back must be made of oak.

"Father," Hadrian says.

Hadrian's dad clasps my fingers. "Bryanna," he says with a small, formal bow. "I'm delighted to meet you."

I hope he doesn't notice I'm wearing boots, not fancy heels. "Nice to meet you, too."

"You're from America?"

"Colorado."

His forehead creases. "How lovely. And you're at Burnley School. Are you an honor student as well?"

I open my mouth, but the lies scramble and lodge in my throat.

Hadrian fills the silence. "She's very bright. She astounded me with an exemplary essay just last week."

My cheeks flush.

Lord Bristol gives me a satisfied head bob. "Come join the party. Everyone is eager to meet you."

Everyone?

I search Hadrian's face for an explanation, but he doesn't look at me.

Lord Bristol ushers us through the doors into a glass sports bar with black leather seating. Suits and a plethora of colored dresses whirl around the polished floor, with fairy wings and goddess circlets. Champagne glasses clink. A piano composition of the Phantom's "Masquerade" drifts from hidden speakers, and York's city lights wink through wall-sized windows. A balcony overlooks a river, and several couples lounge outside.

Eyes turn. Mouths stop moving.

Lord Bristol makes his way toward the bar and returns with two sodas and lime. He offers one to me. Hadrian accepts his and eyes the crowd over the top of his glass. As Lord Bristol pulls me into a circle of people, he introduces me to an older woman wearing a bracelet with more diamonds than I've seen in my life.

"Miss Downey, this is Hadrian's new friend, Bryanna."

"Nice to meet you."

He introduces me to several more circles of people, and I smile until my cheeks hurt. Lord Bristol seems to know everyone, and their eyes survey me with a little too much interest.

After several more introductions, Hadrian stops his dad with a hand on his shoulder. "Please, give us a minute," he says. "We'd like time to ourselves."

Lord Bristol inclines his head and steps aside. "Be sure to introduce your lovely guest to your mother. She's on the balcony." He raises his cocktail. "It's been a pleasure."

I nod as Lord Bristol moves on to a group of partygoers by the door.

"Why did he want me to come when he doesn't know me?" I ask Hadrian.

Rather than answer my question, Hadrian presses my knuckles to his lips. "You promised me a dance."

Hadrian leads me to the floor, where many dancers wear fake eyelashes, have high cheekbones, and move with dainty feet, as if they all made trips to Mystic Cosmetics to gain fairy godmothers.

Hadrian takes my hand and sways at my side with short, slow movements. "I love the gray in your eyes. They're like starlight."

My heart skips, and I can't resist a grin.

The song changes to a low base with piano. I study his feet for a pattern, but stumble over his toes.

Hadrian steadies me with a chuckle. "Do you know any dances?"

"No."

If only he knew about the collection of dance videos I hid in my closet at home, left to rot.

He spins me to face him again, grasps my left hand, and holds it up. Sweeping me into fluid steps, he presses his hand against my palm and moves me with him.

It's not so bad. I stumble a time or two but manage to keep up with him.

When the song fades, his smile is bright as he releases me.

On the next song, he adds a bend. I fall into his movements, sliding as he slides, twisting, twirling, touching only to pull away and draw close again. As we pass other dancers, it's almost easy to ignore their eyes on me.

The melody ends, and another begins as Hadrian sweeps me into another twirl.

When the song stops, a small crowd of people gather around the floor.

Hadrian runs a hand through his hair and messes up the curling copper. "This is far better than homework, is it not?" He winks. "I'll get us some drinks. Wait for me." He disappears into a rainbow of dresses.

I find a chair on the side of the dance floor to sit and breathe.

"Excuse me?" a high voice asks. "Are you Hadrian's girlfriend?"

I twist to look at the speaker, a girl with a mask covered in pearls, wearing pink lipstick. She has full hair and cheeks, a heart-shaped face, and wide, hazel eyes. She's the type of star who can stand beside Ellen and not dim.

"I'm Bryanna," I say, but I don't offer to shake her hand.

The girl's lip hitches upward. "How much do you know about Hadrian?" she asks.

"Enough, why?"

"Curious, is all. Nice trousers." She gives me a smirk and dissolves into the crowd amid a flurry of skirts, closing behind her like curtains.

Hadrian returns with more soda, his smile bright and unassuming.

"Who is that?" I point to the girl with the pink lipstick.

He follows the direction of my gaze and winces. "An old girlfriend. Why?"

I take my soda and sip it, trying to hide how much his casual use of the word "girlfriend" bothers me. Everyone has a dating history, but I wish his didn't include girls like that one. "She came to say hi."

"That's nice of her." Hadrian sits beside me, leans back in his chair, and closes his eyes. "This is fun, isn't it? I'm not sure I've properly enjoyed one of these before. I should have found you years ago."

I elbow him. "So why didn't you? Colorado isn't far."

His eyes open, and he turns his gaze to the balcony and the partygoers outside. "Would you like to meet my mum? I know she wants to see you."

I can't refuse him. "I'd love to."

He takes my hand and pulls me toward the doors and out onto the balcony, which overlooks the dark, rippling water of a river. A light, tinkling song plays as couples chat at rounded tables. Two women laugh beside a pillar, close to the glass railing. One is tall with dark skin and gorgeous chestnut hair. The other is shorter, with graying curls.

Hadrian stops beside the taller woman and squeezes my arm. "Mum, this is Bryanna, the girl I told you about."

Hadrian's mom turns and looks down at me, the laughter fading from her eyes. "Bryanna, it's a pleasure. I'm Raven." She holds out a hand, palm down, and I'm not sure what to do with it, so I squeeze her fingers and give them a little shake.

"It's nice to meet you, too," I say.

"And you two met at Burnley? In the honor program, of course." Her lips spread outward without a curve, as if her smile is on a platter, waiting until a box is checked before she'll confirm delivery.

I open my mouth and do something funky with my lips. I'm not sure what my face looks like, but I'm glad there's no mirror.

"No, mum. She's not in Reeve's honor program," Hadrian says, sounding agitated. He pulls me toward him. "But she's plenty smart. She'd have to be, to get in at all, especially as an American."

His mom's face clears, and a smile dawns.

I don't correct Hadrian because I don't have the heart to do it. Not to mention, I'd be humiliated to tell his mother the truth and see her face darken again.

My heart has become a pancake, flattened at the bottom of my chest. Not only am I not in the honorary program, I'm in the special program—the program the school opened to avoid bad press. If Hadrian's mother knew, she'd escort me out the door. Maybe I should escort myself and save her the trouble.

I press my lips shut.

Hadrian leads me through the doors again, to the dance floor, and turns to me. "Will you give me the pleasure of one more dance?"

I take his hand, but Hadrian's assumptions haunt me. Would he still have feelings for me if he knew the truth? I sway at his side, but the magic is gone, and I can't recall it.

Hadrian searches my face. "Are you all right?"

I nod, but I don't meet his eyes.

"The honor program isn't a big deal, especially to me," he says.

I nod again.

He touches my chin, and this time I'm forced to meet his gaze.

"I'm fine." I attempt to put on happiness the way I put on my clothes, simply taking off the negativity and shrugging on a smile. Easy.

Except it isn't.

"Do you want to leave?" he asks. "We can get gelato."

"Please."

While I love gelato, I really just want to go anywhere that isn't here.

We walk together to the elevator. The door closes behind us, and my stomach jostles as the elevator drops. I look for patterns in the wallpaper opposite me as the elevator lands, rather than look at Hadrian. I'm ashamed, and I don't want him to see it.

As soon as the elevator door slides open, we walk together out the front door. Hadrian's driver starts the car as we approach, and I clamber inside. Hadrian's looking at me, his eyes steady, but I don't meet his gaze.

The air thins. I take a deep breath.

I'm fine, really. I don't need the approval of random people at a ball. It's okay that I'm not an honor student, that I'm just average. Hadrian likes me the way I am, and together we're blue skies and funny conversations.

Hadrian's driver takes us along winding roads, deeper into town, where the roads twist and apartments tower, squished together like passengers on an uncomfortable train.

A slow, drifting melody fills the car as the driver turns music on.

"I'm sorry. I'm not very talkative right now," I say.

Hadrian gives me a small, forgiving smile. "I figured you're tired."

The driver slows in front of a cute gelato shop, with a pink sign and heaping mounds of ice cream behind the glass windows. We park along the road, and cars fly by as we close the car doors and walk toward the shop's entrance.

I open the shop's door, and Hadrian follows me inside. The moment we stop in front of the ice cream display, an associate asks me a question with so thick an accent I can only stare back.

"Which flavor?" Hadrian prods.

"Oh." I point and blush as the associate scoops it up, and Hadrian pays.

It's been a weird day, and I don't care to add the humiliation of my finances to it.

"I can cover this one," I say, but Hadrian raises a hand to stop me. Shaking my head, I murmur, "Thank you."

"You're very welcome."

We sit down at a round table, and I stab my ice cream with the tiny spoon. As it melts, I stir the barely frozen cream at the bottom and create a lumpy mess.

Hadrian watches, his head tilted. "You like gelato, right?"

"I love gelato," I say, letting my voice fluctuate to a high, contented pitch. After such a wonderful night, I don't want to soil it with a terrible mood I can't climb out of.

"That's good, because I was beginning to think you didn't." He leans against his plastic chair. "You're a lovely dancer, did you know that?"

I resist a smile, and the pressure of the night recedes. "Liar."

"You are."

"Thanks," I say.

He says what I want to hear, but I'm grateful all the same.

"Did you notice my dad's friend wore a pig head to the dance? My dad teases him for being pig-headed, and he wanted to poke fun at him."

"I didn't notice, no," I say. My smile comes easier now, and I'm happy being at Hadrian's side.

Though Hadrian's dad seems too serious a man to joke, I'm sorry not to have noticed the pig head.

"I know my mum's a bit intimidating, but she has a soft side, too. She's a lovely person." Hadrian takes our bowls and tosses them. "Let's go. I think we danced the muscles off our feet. I'm sure you're feeling it."

After we leave the gelato shop, we drive to my dormitory, and Hadrian walks me to the door.

I pause before taking my keys out, and he waits with a small smile.

"I had fun tonight," he says.

I picture the doormat scenes and jiggling keys of romantic comedies, and my legs stiffen. Is this the moment when people who aren't formally dating kiss for the first time? I dated Teddy for so long, I don't remember what happens next.

"I had fun, too." I pause as my brain short circuits, thinking of something to say. "Thanks for taking me. Bye." I close the door behind me.

*I blew it.* If I lingered a moment longer, something might have happened. I picture Sadie rolling her eyes behind me.

I definitely screwed that up.

Dragging my feet, I sit on the bed in my room, my shoulders heavy as I stare out the window. The river slithers, too dark to see, and the stars in the sky flicker with little bravado. I imagined this dance being so much more victorious and magical, but I only think of Hadrian and his parents' reaction when they hear I'm not in the honorary program, but the special education program.

I can't fix this, but I can write the best essay for my upcoming assignment that I'm capable of.

Opening my computer to a blank document, I write. Then rewrite it and write it again. Still, I'm not happy. I delete all five pages and let the frustrating black line of my cursor flash on the white screen.

It taunts me as it flashes.

And flashes.

And flashes.

# CHAPTER TWENTY-THREE

Two days later, my phone pings, but I ignore it. I'm still not done with my paper. The sun rose hours ago and set again, and I have class tomorrow. I have to get this done.

I rub my forehead, massage my temples, and close my eyes.

I read article after article on King Arthur. I've read *Idylls of the King*. I've read the *Arthurian Legends*. I've written my thesis and am writing circles around it, but I know deep down that Professor Karina won't accept what I have.

I need to change the way my brain is wired and make it function on a one-way track.

*Was King Arthur's attempts to create a perfect kingdom a failure? Why or why not?*

He failed because he didn't create the perfect kingdom. His round table buckled under the Holy Grail, and he lost everything. So why do I feel like this simple answer isn't sufficient? Like Professor Karina hopes for more?

I scratch my eyelids and run a finger over the dry pages. The words in my open book blur. I'm so tired, but I have to finish. I can't turn in another subpar essay.

Alternatively, I can clean my room, run to the store, and buy potted plants—I haven't cared for plants in so long. I can call Sadie and complain, but she'll have more questions than I want to answer.

Other than Sadie, I don't have any friends outside of my old friend group, including Abbey, but they were Teddy's friends more than mine. The next option involves buying ice cream and moping at another grade that will inevitably slip through my fingers, but that's another expense that won't help anything.

As I stand to empty my trash, a light knock sounds on my door.

It's probably Noelle coming to check on me because that's the kind of person Noelle is, despite her recent behavior. Right now, I really don't want to talk to anyone. I'd rather hole up alone in my room, but if I become too much of a hermit, Noelle will know something's wrong. Best to pretend my essay is going well.

I'm careful as I pry the door open, after all my mishaps with Reeve. But it's not Noelle or Reeve.

"Noelle told me you'd be here." Hadrian tucks his hands into his pocket. "I wanted to make sure you're okay. You haven't responded to anyone the last couple days. Can I come in?"

I glance down at myself. I'm wearing sweatpants, and I haven't brushed my hair in two days. I run my hand through my hair and try to comb it out, but it's tangled around the nape of my neck.

I check my room over my shoulder and am disappointed that no magical mice have cleared away the papers that litter the floor. A plate with a slice of bread sits on my desk. A devoured box of donuts is on my bed. "Come in." The invitation is rough coming out of my mouth.

Hadrian steps around the junk and sits in my desk chair. There are no flowers to cover my mess.

"What're you working on?" he asks.

"My history essay."

He peers at the books on my bed. "Is it going well?"

I sigh aloud. "Not really. I'm the worst at writing essays. I'm sure you could sit and write one in an hour, no problem, and it would put mine to shame."

Hadrian offers a smile that's close to a grimace. "Do you really think that?"

He hardly tries, and he's in Reeve's honors program. Yes, I think that.

He shakes his head at my silence. "Our own faults are always the most visible. Since I'm obviously an expert essayist, though you haven't read a single essay I've written, may I offer to help?"

I sit on the bed across from him and bury my face in my hands. "I'm supposed to write about King Arthur and whether he ultimately failed in creating Utopia."

"What have you written?"

"A bunch of facts. And then a yes." It sounds dumb saying it aloud.

"Is this the *Arthurian Legends*?" He pulls a book toward him. "Oh, *Idylls of the King*." He flips through a few pages, runs a finger down the paragraphs, and points to one. "This is a favorite of mine."

*To me He is all fault who hath no fault at all:*
*For who loves me must have a touch of earth;*
*The low sun makes the colour...*

It sounds fancy. "Why is it your favorite?"

His smile is small but patient. "Think about it."

I read the paragraph again, as well as the paragraphs before and after. It's what Guinevere says about King Arthur to explain why she doesn't love him. She says he's so perfect, he's boring.

If perfection is the goal, and it's the path to perfection where we live, perhaps King Arthur didn't fail. Not entirely, because reaching perfection wasn't the point. Each stride along the path is a success. Every failure is an opportunity to learn. Life is a collection of experiences.

Guinevere says there's color in imperfection. It gives character. It provides something to look forward to and something more to look back on.

The journey is the low sun that creates color.

I grab a notebook and scribble some notes. My hand twinges as words spew onto the page. I struggle to keep up with the thoughts that tumble out of my head.

"I see you're onto something. I'll leave you alone." Hadrian stands, and I don't stop him, though I want him to stay. I don't expect him to sit and watch me, and I can't have distractions.

"Thank you," I say.

He stands in the doorway. "Let me know if you need anything."

I look up and catch the concern in his expression before he wipes it away.

"I'm fine," I tell him. Or I will be soon.

After writing all night, I pass my paper to Professor Karina the next morning in class. I don't hear from her for several days until she pulls me into her office.

"Please, take a seat," she says.

I sit down and cross and uncross my legs, unable to tell if she's happy or angry. Was my paper terrible? Or perhaps she thinks I plagiarized it.

Professor Karina picks up my paper. "If I apply this to myself," she reads aloud, "it means I should allow myself to learn at my pace. There is no bar to measure myself against, no expectation. Life is a continual path of progression." Her lips split into a smile, and her eyes shine. "Bryanna, this essay is leagues better, and I can tell you're passionate about your thesis. I'm impressed. You've really outdone yourself, and I want you to keep up the good work."

There's sunshine in my heart. I wish she would repeat those words a few more times, so I can bask in the light and grow petals. I'm warm all over.

"Thank you," I say.

After everything that's happened since coming to Burnley, I need this win.

Professor Karina hands me the paper as if it were a trophy or a graduation certificate, and I hug it to my chest. It's as good as a trophy to me.

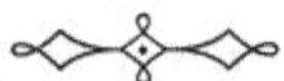

I need to celebrate, so I take a bus to the grocery store and load up on European chocolate. After bringing the stash to the library, I steal away to the room Professor Reeve lent me and munch at the table, trying not to think about how I must have looked when Hadrian came to see me the other day.

Still, I want to take this moment and treasure it.

I set my bag down. The true treat will be finishing these journals. Here, I can read undisturbed by anyone, including Noelle, and ensure my mind doesn't drift.

Bringing out the copies I made, I find the next letter in the series and set it on the table.

The next journal beckons, written by Sir James Altham.

*—1604—*

*I posted watchers at the Duck and Drake but heard nothing until the twentieth of May when the man I pursued, a Catholic sympathizer called John Wright, was spotted.*

*When I arrived at the inn where my contacts claimed John would be, I found a circle of men in hats and wired collars. They gathered at a low table by a flickering fire, sheltered beneath an iron hood. The wood walls and benches in the room provided an agreeable warmth that should never lend to clever plots and murder.*

I sat in a crowded corner nearby and listened while a man spoke, the sides of his mustache quivering. He said they must act immediately, because the longer they waited, the less likely they would succeed.

The man who called himself John Wright argued that they must build an alliance, because wars are fought with armies, not five men with a vendetta. There are other Catholic countries who can help us place the young princess on the throne. England spurned Catholicism everywhere, and he thought it foolish to act too soon. They should go to King Philip, for he is their greatest sympathizer.

Another man thought King Philip would not assist them, not after the Armada. If he cannot, who else will? No other accessible Catholic power in Europe can stand against England.

A thick silence settled as the men looked at each other, each wearing a hat over dark hair, coats with varying levels of holes and patches, and boots with brass buckles. They were not the type of men I should have wanted to be, but their conversation was exactly what I came to hear.

When none could think of anything more to say, John asked where Guido was. He was supposed to be there. John wondered if anyone had seen him, but the others said they didn't expect Guido to come.

A man called Robert spoke to Guido in Brussels and again in York of an alternative plan, but Guido stubbornly opposed it. In York, he left in a temper, and no one heard from him in Flanders, either. Robert believed Guido forsook them.

The group became very grave upon hearing this news, especially as the alternative Robert spoke of was discussed, which involved loads of gunpowder stored beneath the House of Lords until the proper time. They wondered how they could assemble so great a quantity of gunpowder without scrutiny and without Guido.

Robert had the answer to that. He rented a storage space beneath the House of Lords and employed a servant to ferry barrels of gunpowder to the storage room. His progress thus far went unhindered.

*John asked if Guido did not light the match, who would?*

*A disturbed silence condensed around the men. This was it, the moment I came for. The time I would interject my own thoughts and make them their ideas.*

*I stood and announced my ability to solve that problem for them. The men leapt to their feet. After promising I intended no harm, they agreed to listen to my version of the plan, which involved using Guido, whether he wanted to be used or not.*

*—Sir James Altham*

Altham's scheming makes me fidget in my chair, but I want to know more about Guido and why he's so important to this group, so I turn the page to where Guido's signature curls.

*—1604—*

*I taught Hugh to hunt rabbits and gave him my knife with the serpent hilt, the weapon I carried throughout my conflicts and wanderings.*

> *When I commanded him to throw the knife at an old oak, his aim landed the knife hilt-first in the dirt. I instructed him, and he improved quickly.*
>
> *I could be a father to him. I should be happy to buy Alice a piano and play for her, to watch her dance every night after supper.*
>
> *When her father comes, I shall wait for him on the doorstep.*
>
> *—Guido*

Guido wants to join Alice's family, and Hugh continues to live an innocent, happy life, but something bad happened to Alice. I feel it.

> *—1604—*
>
> *I wrote a fine letter to warn Lord Monteagle, with a date and location that fast approaches. I signed Guido's correct name at the bottom corner with my left hand. No conspirator would be so imprudent as to admit to a scheme with his signature. Yet there are many fools in Parliament willing to believe. I need only one to credit me.*
>
> *—Sir James Altham*

*—1604—*

*Alice is gone. I know not what has become of her.*

*Last night, dusk settled early over the valley.
I knew Alice would have me depart soon, but I
spotted the wild man in the woods again and did
not want to leave her unprotected.*

*We sat together by the fire, and I told Alice and
Hugh stories of my time in Spain. Alice forgot to
dismiss me as she usually did. A whistling breeze
fluttered the resin-soaked linens in the windows as
I finished another story, and the fire blew out.*

*Alice shook herself and glanced outside. "You must
go," she said.*

*I took my time. Alice's father had not come for
weeks, and I needed to meet him, to inform him of
my intentions, and to request his blessing.*

*The door opened, and a young man with fine
clothes and a messy shock of brown hair pushed his
way past me. He barked at Hugh to leave, and the
boy slipped out the window.*

*It all happened so fast. I didn't understand well enough to know how to respond.*

*The door swung inward again, and two men strode into the room. One man I recognized as Sir James Altham. The other I learned was the magistrate.*

*Did James come because of the information I gave him?*

*As I surveyed James' expression, I wondered if I made a mistake in approaching him, but when Alice paled, I knew something was very wrong. I demanded an explanation, but no one spared me a glance, even as several more men filed into the room carrying weapons.*

*Despite my years of warfare, I was outnumbered, and my powerlessness frightened me.*

*—Guido*

Guido wrote another journal.

*—November of 1605—*

*I awoke to the echo of footsteps, a sound I had not heard in some time. A tender bruise throbbed behind my right temple as I gazed up at the stone-walled ceilings of the vault around me. I was surrounded by barrels, firewood, and coals, in a spacious room that absorbed mildew and rejected heat.*

*As I dragged myself to my feet, a multitude of men swarmed the room. One jabbed my leg with his gun. "Who art thou?"*

*"John Johnson," I lied to him. "A servant to Thomas Percy."*

*I wish I let them shoot me instead.*

*—Guido*

It wasn't enough to accuse Guido in a letter. Altham let him be found on site as well, but I want to know what happened to Guido after those men found him. I reach for the next journal, but my phone buzzes. The screen lights up with a message from Hadrian.

Stay put and check the news. They found another body.

Praying it's no one I know, I lunge for my laptop, and my blood pounds in my ears as I search the web for the local news. I click on an article with an image of paramedics pushing a blurred body on a stretcher. Body found near Rowley Lake. Investigators connect finding to a recent murder at Burnley Boarding School. Police discovered a boy with missing hands and a slashed throat. The photo at the bottom displays two mismatched socks sticking out of a body bag, and then another picture displays a smiling boy in an old photo.

My mouth dries.

It's Hadrian's friend, Robbie.

I call Hadrian, and he doesn't answer.

As I stare at my computer screen, a dawning horror spreads to every inch of my soul. A few days ago, I obsessed over attaining a model grade. I didn't expect to look into the vacant eyes of someone I know. Shame and fear fill me in turns. No matter how awful I feel, Hadrian must feel worse.

I text him again.

I'm here for you if you need me.

# CHAPTER TWENTY-FOUR

Y BARE FEET sink into damp moss. Gnarled trees grow in all directions. Shadows form empty shapes, but none shelter the bright eyes I search for. My heart thumps as I stumble into a meadow that should flourish with life and color but holds only the scent of death.

My legs give out. I fall to my knees and jerk awake.

*Not again.*

Rubbing my eyes, I dismiss the sense of loss that clings like residue. My eyes itch, and sores on my lips crack when I move my mouth.

I stand and check my reflection in the cabinet mirror. A scaly, red-skinned, pimpled face stares back, my wrist swollen from the additional scratches I gave myself during the night. It's from the stress that follows me like a shadow. I can't go to class like this, but I can't not go either.

I wash my face, but the scaly skin peels. If only I had the cosmetics store products that helped Noelle, but I'd rather figure this out on my own.

I yank a hoodie over my t-shirt, throw on the dress pants I haven't replaced, and wrap my wrist.

The halls are clear of students as I duck into class and sit in the back corner with my hood tugged around my face. Hadrian's broad-shouldered figure walks through the doorway. A new grimness pulls his mouth into a neutral frown, and his eyes don't sparkle like they usually do.

I should talk to him, comfort him somehow, but I angle my face away.

He sits by another young woman two rows in front with big eyes and bigger hair.

Hadrian opens his backpack and glances over his shoulder. Every molecule in my veins freeze, and I pull my hoodie down closer to my nose.

The professor passes the tests down the lines of students, and I hunch over mine. I forgot we had a test today, but I've studied for weeks. I'm more than prepared.

Hadrian hasn't called me back. He sent a short text. **Thanks. You're a good friend.**

I don't like that he called me a friend. Though we haven't kissed, I hope he thinks of me as more.

Worse, I don't know what to say to him about what happened to Robbie. It's not my fault, but my insides knot up when I think of it, as if a part of me wonders if it might be.

Hadrian scribbles on a paper and doesn't look up. He stands, walks his paper to the professor at the front, and leaves, and my chance to be the friend he needs is gone.

More students follow him out the door, until only empty chairs yawn, and my test waits with empty lines.

I fill out the page, turn it in, and hurry to trudge across frost-stiffened grass. My breath trails in the air as I walk down Birdie's Court where posters cover the walls.

MISSING SINCE SATURDAY. HAS ANYONE SEEN ME?

Robbie, with his mess of sandy hair, smiles from the photos.

The flyers hang with the edges curling into themselves, old and faded. I shudder at the continual reminders I can't avoid.

Why hasn't anyone taken them down?

I can't be the one to do it. I don't want to do it.

Everything around me is spiraling out of control, and there's nothing to do but sit outside the merry-go-round and watch it spin off its rail. Because how does someone as small as I am reach out to stop it?

I hurry down the halls of Birdie's Court to my room and shiver as I shut the door. Sitting at my desk, I move the journal pages I already read aside. My phone dances across the table, and the tiny screen lights up. I flip it open, and a new message from Noelle flashes.

I have exciting news about our favorite store. I need to tell you!

Probably about Mystic Cosmetic's newest shampoo. Doesn't she feel like a jerk being excited about anything after what happened to Robbie? Not this new Noelle, I guess.

I'll answer her later and finish the journals instead. I need to learn everything I can…and distract myself from everything else.

I turn to the entry from James Altham.

*—1606—*

*When I approached Alice last, I gave her an ultimatum. She blinked in the faint candlelight with dilated pupils, knotted hair, and skin slathered in dirt.*

*She knew why she was there but would not accept my proposal. Until she does, she shall remain imprisoned. Perhaps she enjoyed the stale air, stone walls, and restricted light. Could I be so grotesque an alternative?*

*If she refuses to comply, she is condemned, and her little brother may as well be dead.*

*—Sir James Altham*

Perhaps Alice evaded the witch trials while in prison. Altham's curling script continues in another letter.

*—1606, Westminster Palace Yard—*

*No one knew what handsome, eloquent Guido lost on the guillotine, save I alone. I stood in Palace Yard at Westminster Hall as they carried the sentence out. Dense clouds and upraised arms cast shadows on the scaffold. When they forced him to sign his name, he couldn't hold the pen. They dragged him forward, emaciated and broken, and I looked down on him at the end.*

*Behold, the first honest man ever to enter Parliament. And what has his honesty done for him?*

*—Sir James Altham*

Altham's account continues, as if Guido is a pawn to push aside.

*—1612—*

*Alice scratched at herself for months and cut gashes in her arms and legs. I thought she would have given in, yet she made no gesture of acquiescence, not even after seven years.*

*Her skin cracked and bled, and her hair was wild and untamed when I went to see her. She mumbled to herself and flinched at the slightest sound, but I cannot forget her. Her refusal has plagued every waking moment.*

*Perhaps she would love me if I were as handsome as her Guido. Perhaps if I release her, just long enough to taste freedom, she would see me in a new light. Otherwise, I shall dispose of her, so I might never look on her face again.*

*Freeing myself of Alice would be simple, especially as the word "witch" blazes across Pendle to explain every unfortunate event. When I imprisoned Alice Grey on the pretense of witchcraft, many questioned me. Years later, rumours spread of a witch who howled and scratched at the demons in her skin. They called her "Mouldskin."*

*The magistrate, and grandfather of Alice, did not wish her illegitimate connection to him known, so he does not defend her.*

*Claims arose against a simpleton called Miss Preston, whose lover died rather suddenly and suspiciously at a wedding.*

*Witch.*

*A local peddler collapsed in Colne, accompanied by the granddaughter of the infamous healer, Demdike.*

*Witch.*

*Townsfolk have died of strange diseases while village healers boasted of magical powers. More villagers have disappeared by the week and are never found again.*

*More witches.*

*Magistrate Nowell sees the proposed witch trial as a wonderful opportunity. Condemning them shall improve our standing in the sight of not only Lancaster, but the king as well.*

*I needed to rid myself of her. I needed to let her go.*

*—Sir James Altham*

I suck in a sharp breath. Alice went crazy in prison, and James Altham was creepy as crap. Weird things happen around town, and James, of course, took advantage of it, but the prison part can't be coincidence. Reeve mentioned Alice Grey was imprisoned for seven years. I had a breakdown at the Lancaster prison, and my worst nightmares feature prison cells.

My nightmares can mean anything. The magistrate, the witches, and Altham lived long ago. I never knew them and have never seen that prison cell before.

It's not real.

A sharp pain lances through my arm. I glance down as red flourishes from fresh scratches over my scars. Nail biting is preferable to this strange new habit. I clench my fists to stop myself from doing it again and take a deep, shaky breath.

*I'm not crazy.*

I can almost picture Sadie looking at me from across the table with one eyebrow raised.

"I'm not," I say aloud.

I jump at the sound of my voice and scan my room, but I'm not in the library, of course, and no one heard me talk to myself. I exhale and continue with a letter by Altham, dated the same year.

—*1612*—

*We met with accusations of witchcraft as far as Liverpool from some of the most powerful men in the country. These same nobility accepted our proposed witch trial with applause.*

*However, when we received word of a planned village gathering, Magistrate Nowell and I met to discuss it. Friends and families of those accused hope to facilitate the release of the witches imprisoned. The time has come to discharge Alice Grey "Mouldskin." I will ensure her presence at the meeting. No one questions Alice is a witch. No one fits the role better.*

*This is her final chance to change her mind. If the temporary release does not work, then I must be willing to let her die with the rest.*

*—Sir James Altham*

Accusing people of witchcraft must be the prime way to get rid of pests. I can't think of anyone more deserving of being cast into a witch trial than Altham.

Widow Nutter writes the next letter.

*—10<sup>th</sup> of April, 1612, Good Friday—*

*I found a child in the woods, wandering alone, calling out a boy's name in mad desperation.*

*I remember her from before when she was young and sought after. I'm afraid Alice Grey's fair features have turned ragged, though she is no more a witch than I am.*

*She needs help.*

*I brought her to a gathering of townsfolk and introduced her to a group of wide eyes and open mouths. Mildew clung to the walls, and chairs scrapped against the uneven floorboards as I told them of her plight. Wary faces regarded me and then her.*

*My good neighbor, Isabel, spoke first and rebuked me for bringing her, especially with the reputation she carried.*

*I told her we must disprove the rumors. Witch-craft existed only in imaginative minds, but Isabel shook her head. She wanted to appeal to the magistrate. If there were enough of us to protest, we could make a difference there. Isabel thought I should send the girl back to where she came from.*

*"I shall not stay another minute while this witch, this Mouldskin, remains," she said.*

*The candlelight flickered, and many eyes rested on Alice. They took in her rags that clung to her form; the dirt and autumn leaves stuck to the fabric. Her hands trembled, and her lips pressed shut, as if opening her mouth would cause the earth to shatter.*

Another person at the table spoke and claimed the magistrate would not listen but would hang us by association. Nor would he allow our loved ones to be freed.

The youngest of the Device children rose to her feet beside her frail mother. Her eyes lingered on Alice as she suggested we use gunpowder to blow up the jail. The magistrate believed in magic but did not fear it. Once they knew what we were capable of, they would not dare harm or mock us. We could use Alice to frighten them.

Alice's face paled even more, and I reached out to squeeze her hand.

She jumped, looked at me, and relaxed, but only a little.

I told the little girl to worry not, for her family has not yet been sentenced to the gallows, though they currently sit in jail with the rest of our loved ones.

If they feared magic, I told her, they would burn more of us. We must disprove the witch fallacies. We must show them there is no reason for fear. I pointed to Alice. Alice Grey is as innocent as the rest of us.

At the word, "innocent," Alice twitched and took one step toward the door.

The young Device girl folded her thin arms.

I tried appealing to them again. Alice's brother disappeared into the forest seven years ago, and she did not know where he went. I asked of them to listen for news of him.

Isabel asked who Alice's brother was.

Hugh Grey.

Tears streamed down Alice's cheeks at the answer.

Isabel promised to watch for him, her expression sincere.

I thanked them and escorted Alice out.

We would meet in one week's time. Something must be done.

—Widow Nutter

Alice searched for her missing brother while Widow Nutter hoped to protect her by disproving the witchcraft rumors. Instead, they would be hurt by association, as James Altham planned.

Only a few entries remain for Alice to find Hugh, and I'm afraid to keep going, in case I discover nothing. I couldn't bear the disappointment.

Still, I try another.

*—1612—*

*We recaptured Alice Grey, but her answer would not waver. At every turn, I thought I succeeded, only to find my cleverness inadequate. What must I become to influence even the lowest of women?*

*I needed one more chance, so I tracked down the source of reports made about potions and spells and discovered Jane Southworth, the woman from Samlesbury who accosted me at the alehouse, at the center of it. I believe she and her sisters, Ellen and Jennet, sold potions and wares through a network of village healers, including our local Demdike and Chattox. Some wares provided ene-mies with afflictions; others enhanced beauty. I must know how they work, and if they work.*

*I planned to travel to Samlesbury to approach the witches and discover their secrets, but the magistrate exposed my plans and confronted me. He sent word to the king for another witch trial, but he did not receive my plans of a trial well. I suppose he worried that he killed too many of his own subjects.*

*Instead, the king turned a wrathful eye toward the magistrate and myself and revoked his support for trials across the nation, despite his recent publication and its contradictory message.*

*The king stripped me of my title and money, and every single one of my wives wavered in their devotion. My desire for a greater source of power and influence became a requirement. I could not live without what I lost, and I could not impress Alice as a lesser man than I was before.*

*If magic is possible, I will be the first to know it.*

*—James Altham*

I knock several books to the floor on accident, and the crash jars me. The sisters, Jane and Ellen, sold wares to the villagers just as the Jane and Ellen I know sell cosmetics to students. This is too much of a coincidence. What is Professor Reeve trying to tell me?

While the journals mention another sister called, "Jennet," I haven't heard her name among my peers. The entry also talks about recruiting more followers, and how Altham wants to become one himself.

Witches returned to the modern world. Is it too far-fetched?

If this is what Reeve wanted me to realize, why hasn't he called the police? The sisters at the cosmetics store must be the danger he warned me of, causing students to disappear. They're the thread weaving through everything.

Immortality isn't possible. No one lives forever, not even me. Especially not me.

Maybe they're descendants, too?

I lift the mattress and pick up the book with the fancy tree, running a thumb over the cover. The journals said my necklace is protection. I need it back, and not just to open the purple book, but to protect myself from the dangers Reeve warned me of.

Do I really believe this? I think I do, but I need to test this ludicrous theory. I have to know if my suspicion holds weight, and the only way to do this is to investigate the characters involved.

Or ask Reeve.

Shoving the book beneath the mattress, I snatch my purse and hurry out the door. I run across the grounds, down sidewalks, to the oak entrance with the gold plaque, and raise a fist to pound on the door.

My chest rises and falls as I struggle to pull in air.

The wood creaks open, and Professor Reeve stands in the opening with his fedora hat. Waves of sleek hair curl over his ears, and his eyes widen. "Bryanna?"

"I finished the journals," I say.

He arches a dark eyebrow. "All of them?"

"Yes, and I know what you were trying to warn me of. Please professor, we need to call the police. We need to give them a reason to investigate."

His eyes flash. "What are you talking about?"

Maybe I'm way off-base, but it's too late to turn back now, so I keep going. "The women at Mystic Cosmetics," I say. "The witches in the journals."

Reeve knits his brow. "Enough of this, Bryanna. Go home. It's not safe for you here."

"It's as safe for me as anyone else. People are dying. Those students can't know what kind of cult they're joining." If he doesn't care about the safety of his students, I misjudged him.

"They know," Professor Reeve says in a flat tone. "Go home and reread the journals. You've clearly missed something."

"You can't let this happen at your school."

"I can."

I'm stunned into silence. All I can do is gape. "Haven't you seen the flyers?"

"People disappear all the time."

If he won't talk about the witches, perhaps I can ask him about someone else important. "What happened to Hugh then?"

Reeve's brows pull together, and his black eyes darken. "Who's Hugh?"

"He's in those journals."

His eyes are empty, his expression confused, as if I made up the name. If he's teasing, it's not funny.

"Alice's little brother," I add.

Professor Reeve's expression clears. "I've no idea what happened to Alice's brother, and that's the truth. You're wasting my time asking these questions."

"But you do know she had a brother?"

"She did, yes." Reeve leans against the doorway, as if nothing I say will move him. "But that's all I can tell you about him."

If he won't offer answers, he might as well slam the door in my face.

"Fine." I storm down the hall as several passersby cast odd glances. Ignoring them, I bring out my phone and dial the police. I don't need Professor Reeve's help. If I see one more poster on the wall with a missing face, it's my fault.

This is how I help Hadrian.

"Lancashire Police," comes a no-nonsense voice on the other line. "What's your address?"

"No need for an address. I'm calling to report nefarious activities at the new cosmetics store on Mill Road—"

"Mystic Cosmetics?"

They must have them on their radar. "Yes, I believe the owners are behind the recent disappearances and murders."

"What gives you reason to suspect this?"

I cup my hand over the phone so other students don't hear. "I think they're a…a coven of witches."

The officer's voice turns crisp. "I know it's Halloween, but this is not a number for jests, miss."

"It's no jest." How do I explain this? "I think they're the reason behind the kids disappearing at Burnley Boarding School. I have these journals—" Would my journals be proof of anything? Probably not. "They attract people to their store and charge kids astronomical sums for cosmetics."

"That doesn't prove they're behind the disappearances. Do you have a specific reason to suspect them? Have you seen something?" Despite the officer's questions, her disinterested tone suggests I'm losing her.

"No, I just know it's them. Their store is close to where the first girl disappeared."

"Lots of shops are close to Mill Road."

"That's true." I try to think of something tangible I can give them, but nothing comes to mind. "Will you at least take note of this call?"

"It's protocol."

"Oh, right." My arm droops as I clutch the phone. "Well, thanks anyway."

"Goodbye, miss. Thanks for calling."

The line goes dead, and I rub my face with frustration.

With her long, black hair swaying, Mika walks down the hall, stops, squints, and claps her hands. "Bryanna, love."

I struggle to arrange my face, so my emotions won't burst through. "Mika, what're you doing here?"

"I'm glad I caught you." Her eyes shine with an excitement I wish I could feel myself. "Noelle's been trying to get hold of you. Remember that cosmetics store Noelle loved so much?"

Ice crystallizes every vein in my body until I'm stiff with horror. "Yeah?"

"They offered her a job. She's ecstatic. I can't tell you how many times she listed off all their products. I know them so well, I feel like I could be a sales rep myself. Maybe I should be." Mika's expression turns thoughtful. "Don't give me that look, Bryanna. I have no real intention of applying." Mika flashes a smile. "If Hadrian caught me working there, he'd never forgive me. Anyway, call and congratulate her. She's been applying for months."

Noelle got a job. Not just any job, but a job at the store I hope to shut down.

"When did she start?" I ask.

"She started today. It was all rather quick. Are you okay, Bryanna? You're acting a bit peculiar."

"Fine."

Without proof, no one will listen, not the professor, and not the police. Noelle can't be the next victim.

"I have to go," I say.

Mika looks taken aback. "Where?"

To the only place I can find proof that Ellen and Jane contributed to these murders. "To Mystic Cosmetics."

# CHAPTER TWENTY-FIVE

Without wasting a moment, I go straight to the source of my concerns. The bus halts, and I step out onto a street blanketed in midnight. Darkness empties the doors and consumes the roads. Streetlight glints off metal verandas, windows, and white paneling like skeletons dug up by the moon.

The bright purple of the Mystic Cosmetics awning shines among muted greens and browns while a dense, knotted vine clings to the side of the building and snakes to the windows.

I creep toward the front door, shut with a "closed" sign. Lights brighten the windows in a narrow upper level where a cracked opening lets smoke and whiffs of fresh lavender escape to spiral into the starry sky. Murky shapes move behind the glass. I open my phone, press the record button, and stuff it in my pocket.

The rough texture of the vine shifts beneath my fingers as I pull. I jam my foot into the thickest branch and tug again until my chin rises above the door, level with the second-story window.

A circle of silhouettes surrounds a mixture of blankets and trinkets, chanting in some peculiar language. The air throbs with a vocal beat that's both frightening and enticing.

The hair on the back of my neck tingles, and deep inside, warning bells ring.

I shift my feet to get out of the notch in the vine, but waver as the scene through the window changes. A slumped figure is dragged into the room, and every muscle in my body crystalizes.

They drop the figure on the ground, bundle the person's feet, and tie them to a stair post. The people who held the prisoner form a circle as others join from the stairway. The unconscious person disappears behind black cloaks.

Shapes draw closer to the window.

I drop lower. A shock of frantic energy pumps to my fingertips as I slide down the vine, so fast my phone slips out and clangs against the store's metal awning. My body jerks at the noise.

The chanting ceases. I stiffen. My heart roars in my ears.

Every passing moment is a needle on my skin, a hold on my breath.

Nothing.

The chanting resumes, and some of the tension in my shoulders fades. I scurry down the rest of the vine. My legs tremble as I leap to the pavement, and my knees buckle under my weight. My phone is a tiny light behind the store's sign above my head. I can't reach it, but if I abandon it, my whole trip is for nothing. I need the incriminating footage.

Wavering, every molecule in me screams to run.

I still have time.

The store's front door chimes as someone opens it, and a dry voice speaks, "Excellent."

My breath flees my lungs as I turn to Jane standing on the doorstep, watching me. Her blood-colored lips part over her teeth. "I've seen you before."

And I've seen more than enough of her.

Ellen follows with a black cat balanced on her arm. She pats the feline's head. "Welcome, child. I wondered if anyone would try to climb that vine."

The cat hisses.

I have so many threats to make, but I don't remember them, so I turn to run, but two sets of nails grab me from behind and dig into my shoulder.

"You're not going anywhere," Jane snarls into my ear.

As Jane and Ellen tow me into the store, a table covered in soaps tumbles. They shove me to the back of the room where black curtains close and floorboards creak while they lug me up the stairs. Burnt bark and incense grip my lungs. Wood scrapes against my shins.

We crest the top stair, and the two women hold fast to my arms. The room is bare, except for a circle of black-robed figures. They surround frayed blankets spread over the floor, with strange items assembled in a star-shaped sequence. Around the pattern, someone drew a second circle with chalk.

Tied to the post is a boy with dark hair and a black t-shirt. His sliced wrist is smeared with blood.

The world blurs as a scream rips from me. Fingers claw at my thrashing arms, struggling to hold me in place.

"Close the window, or people will hear!" someone shouts.

"The walls and windows are charmed. No one will hear anything."

A set of hands let go. Ellen stoops in front of me, and her eyes flash as she jabs me hard in the throat. Pain slices through me. My knees and elbows hit the ground as I claw at my neck, my lungs crying for air.

Someone's hand touches my shoulder, and I turn and bite until I taste blood. A shriek pierces me, and a slap sends me sprawling. My cheek stings. My throat is on fire. Everything goes fuzzy around the edges.

"Enough!" Jane thrusts me into the other staircase post.

Only a few feet away, the tied-up boy doesn't flinch, doesn't even move. The horror of it expands inside me, until it's all I can do to stay in one piece.

"Don't hurt her!" Hurried footsteps bring the new voice closer, until Noelle's pale face is inches away. A black hood conceals her dark-chocolate hair, and hope springs up inside me as recognition clicks into place.

*Noelle is here.*

Jane glares. "Get back in the circle, unless you want to join her."

Noelle flinches and casts me one last, shameful glance, as she melts into the crowd.

I stare after her, and my hope bows to disappointment.

If Noelle won't save me, no one will.

The chanting swells as the gathering sits in unison, at least fifteen people together, their legs crossed. Sauntering into the circle, a black-robed figure casts shadows over everyone.

The figure kneels on tattered mauve blankets covered in star constellations and stretches sharp fingernails over a set of teeth, knuckle-bones, an enormous crystal, and a pile of feathers. Beside the figure, a wood stump supports a single pewter goblet.

The figure chants in a clear feminine voice, her obsidian hair tinged with purple at the ends. When she finishes, she raises her eyes until they focus on me. The purple in them gleams, though the rest of her face lingers in the shade of her hood.

"Thank you, my children." She hoists the pewter goblet from the stand and raises it above her head. "This is our largest group by far. I am pleased, as is our master. Welcome to beauty and acceptance." Her eyes rove down the group. "To vengeance. To money." Turning to the far end of the circle, she spreads her arms. "To immortality, to excellence. All the worldly things heaven has denied you. We will teach you our ways, which go far beyond simple hair care recipes and fragrant soaps, I promise you. No one will laugh or belittle you or dare steal from you again. The only repayment is a tribute to the master and your sworn dedication to him. Together, the scorned, the ugly, and the forgotten will come to instant perfection and rule God's world."

The chant picks up again, and the chorus of voices arouses dust and smoky fumes. The words accelerate, my heartbeat with them, until every rib throbs.

The woman holds a goblet in one hand and a blade with the other. Her thick eyebrows curve over eyes outlined with heavy, black wings. Dusky lipstick accentuates full, exultant lips while pale skin stretches over high cheekbones.

She approaches, and her robes trail behind her, brushing the backs of other figures who turn their faces away. Strange words seem to bloom from the floor as her heels clack against the floorboards, her cloak swallowing the light. She swoops over the boy, dagger raised high, and clutches his good wrist. He barely jerks as she slices downward, and blood oozes into her goblet. A soft moan escapes his lips, though his eyes remain shut.

Whoever he is, I can't do anything for him, and I can't do anything for myself either. While I can see him well enough, I don't recognize him. I'm glad I don't, and my gratitude horrifies me because whoever he is, someone loves him.

The witches won't let me go after I witness this. My parents will hear from the authorities that they found my dead body in the river with my eyes cut out. I'll never have the chance to tell Sadie goodbye.

The woman with the purple eyes strides away and slices her own palm. She adds a few drops to the goblet and passes the cup to the first person in line, who presses the cup to their lips and hands it off. Each figure in the circle takes a drink. Some shudder, others keep still.

The woman lights candles around the room and motions to Jane, who inclines her head, hurries down the stairs, and returns with a hot iron. The purple-eyed woman touches the tip, and a cruel smile distorts her black lips.

Each person in line extends their arm, and the woman brands them with a curious symbol. They thrash as the iron presses against their skin, but none scream. As the last person is branded, the purple-eyed woman twists her wrist, and her sleeve falls back to reveal several blackened symbols and dozens of rings that adorn her fingers. "Welcome, brothers and sisters," she said. "You have been given the power. Now it is left to you to acquire the knowledge, which we, the Mekori, are here to share."

An evil presence stirs the air, and its energy sweeps through the room. The candles dim, and a strange sensation crawls beneath my skin.

The boy twitches and goes still again.

Her eyes landing on me, the purple-haired woman's upper lip pulls back with an expression that spells death.

A smile splits the woman's lips as she approaches, holding the knife aloft. "I'm sorry, sweetie, but you weren't invited to this party. I suppose if we run out of blood, you can be our spare."

"Jennet, stop," says a deep voice.

*Jennet.*

The third name. The third sister from the letters.

Jennet looks up, and her upper lip curls again, distorting her beautiful face. She glares past me. "What are you doing here?"

Two firm hands unbind mine and encircle me, almost protectively. "I'm taking the girl. You have no right to kill her."

My head lolls against a flat chest, and the rigid jawline of Professor Reeve dominates my vision. His arm slides beneath my knees and lifts me from the ground.

He found me.

He's taking me away.

I'm not going to die, not tonight.

Jennet's eyes glitter. "Is this her then? How interesting." She draws herself upright and wipes her bloodied blade on her robe. "Take your offering, Reeve," she says with a sneer, "but I will slaughter you in an instant if you cross me again. Whether she dies today or tomorrow doesn't matter to me."

He shifts my weight in his arms and touches his neck where my tree pendant hangs on a silver chain. "You can't kill me."

Jennet's eyes narrow. "Where did you find that?" She spits on the floor. "You lying thief, how long have you had it?"

"I didn't steal it from you."

"It's mine. I don't care where you got it. You told me it was lost. How dare you lie to me! That necklace was mine from the beginning."

"How can it be yours? You can't even touch it."

Jennet shows her teeth. "The moment that pendant comes off, I will slit your throat."

He turns his back on her and keeps his eyes trained forward as he carries me down the stairs, his mouth a hard line. The silver tree hangs from his neck, and I have half a mind to snatch it for myself, but I can't now that he's rescued me.

The professor sets me down, and, as we descend the stairs together, I glance back to the silent form on the floor. I stop. The boy they took won't last much longer without medical attention, and he doesn't deserve to float the river either. "We can't leave him."

"The kid? He's already dead." Reeve's voice is a hiss. He drags me forward.

The bell on the door chimes, and frigid air chills my skin as we leave the cosmetics store. A shrieking laugh follows from the open window. "Watch her, Reeve. Watch her closely."

The professor scowls as he yanks open the door of his compact car. My legs are weak, but I lower myself into the passenger side without hesitation. Getting in after me, he fumbles to fasten his seatbelt before starting the car. He backs out, his hands trembling on the steering wheel. We turn off Mill Road, and Professor Reeve flips on jazz music.

I examine my own unsteady fingers and count each breath. Despite the mellow saxophone, every muscle in my body clenches. I can't pass off what happened at the store as a weird cult. They killed a boy right in front of me, and the ceremony with his blood was unnatural and hungry. Worse, it was real.

Snow sprinkles the roads outside, but the raw images of the night bleed afresh, staining everything red.

"I told you to go home," the professor says.

I was wrong to dismiss him. "I know."

"I'm doing my best to protect you," he continues. "But I can't do this again. You have to leave. Surely after this, you wouldn't be so stubborn as to ignore me a third time."

I avert my eyes. Residual fear fills my hollow spaces, inflating until it's all I feel. "I promise I'll go."

Relief smooths the lines in Professor Reeve's face.

I take a deep breath. I can't fall apart with Reeve in the car. "Can you tell me one thing?"

He glances at me and looks away. "I can try."

"Why haven't you gone to the police?"

A bitter laugh bursts from Reeve's lips, and my chest constricts. "The police can't protect you from the Mekori."

"Who are the Mekori?"

If I'm going to leave, I should at least understand why.

Professor Reeve shakes his head. "Bryanna, I'm willing to do anything I can to protect you, short of something stupid. I know you don't know me very well, but I care. Please go home. I haven't maintained many contacts through the years. Though you may view me differently, you're the closest thing I have to family. You're all I have. And now that you've grown up, I plan to keep in contact."

I turn my face away.

What he said is sweet, but family calls occasionally. He never did, and it's a little too late, but that's not important now.

"Robbie died the same way that boy did, didn't he?" I ask. My voice breaks as I say it.

I'm glad Hadrian never witnessed the witch ceremony.

"Maybe." Professor Reeve pulls over at a McDonalds. "Let's get you something to eat." He doesn't ask what I want but orders a quarter pounder with orange juice at the drive-through window and passes it over.

I take a hesitant bite and set the hamburger down.

Reeve watches me with intense eyes, his fingers on the necklace as if he takes solace in the feel of hard metal.

"I need that back." I point to the chain. "I can't leave England without it."

He gives me an odd look. "I'll ship it to you."

I don't believe him.

"No, I told you I'd go, and I plan to. But I'm not leaving without it."

His eyes flash. "You heard Jennet. Who knows which students she controls. The minute she hears from her following that I've taken this off, she'll come looking for me."

Do I trust Reeve? He saved me, after all. Still, I shake my head. He should have no reason to hang on to my family heirloom. If it truly offers protection, I could use that, too. "I'm sorry, but I need it back."

His mouth presses into a flat line, but he unclasps the necklace from around his neck and hesitates.

I hold out my hand, palm up. "I'm not going anywhere without it."

He scowls as he hands it to me.

My fingers wrap around it, and instantly, I feel safer. "Why can't Jennet touch it?"

His eyes linger on my fist. "It was hers once. That's all I know," he says.

"And how did you know to find me?"

"I keep a close watch on you, as well as Jane. If I didn't, you'd be in a dumpster with your throat slashed, not sitting next to me drinking orange juice."

I suppose I should be grateful.

I close my eyes to shut out the image. "Just take me home."

The professor takes the empty orange juice cup and wrappers from my lap, stuffs them into a bag, and stows it on the floor of the back seat. "I'll drive you to your dormitory. You'll be safe inside the gate. I'll make sure of it. But my protection will only last a day. I'd buy a plane ticket tonight if I were you. Those witches have been hiding in plain sight for thousands of years. They know how to keep secrets, and you're a loose end."

*Witches.*

He said it aloud, as though there's no doubt what they are.

He reaches over, touches my cut wrist, and draws away. "I'll come visit you in Colorado, if you'd like. We can talk about your ancestry as much as you want."

I can't think about my ancestry right now, or my grades, any of it.

As soon as he drops me off, I flee to my room and lock the door behind me. An eerie silence squeezes the walls from all sides. Covering my face with my hands, I slide to the floor. Hot tears trickle down my cheeks. Behind my eyelids, cloaked ghosts surround me. They extend their hands to the sky. Gray stone walls grow from the ground, marked with scorches, and, above my head, hangs a single noose.

# CHAPTER TWENTY-SIX

LIGHT CREEPS INTO THE SKY as I stumble into the bathroom. My head aches, and my eyes stare back with bruised circles. I didn't sleep at all because every time I closed my eyes, the nightmares returned. Every noise shook my bones—rattling pipes through the walls, a squeak outside the door.

Who was the boy that died? When will I see his face in the news?

I shuffle into the bedroom, pop Ibuprofen into my mouth, and dig into my savings for the first return flight home. Class doesn't matter anymore now that I'm leaving. I'll have to find a new job in Colorado. If the flower shop doesn't rehire me, maybe my dad's lumber business will have an opening.

I don't want to hear about the boy's death or his grieving family. I'd rather pretend it never happened.

My hands shake as I empty the room of my stuff and toss clothes into a suitcase. Tears sink into my mattress as I lift it to reveal the book from the graveyard. The eye below the tree stares back, and a shudder sweeps through me. Whatever I'm supposed to learn doesn't matter now that I'm leaving the danger behind, but I stuff the journal into my backpack, anyway. I didn't demand my necklace back from Reeve for no reason.

The absence of a phone feels odd, like being stuck outside the flower shop without keys, or checking out customers with no way to speak. I'm not keen about going to the cosmetics store to get my phone back, though.

Without a phone, I can't call my mom, so I send her and Sadie a brief email with my departure and arrival information. It's better this way, I tell myself.

I should send Hadrian an email, too, or go see him in person. But I'm too much of a coward to explain the reason why I'm leaving and seeing him would make the decision harder.

Reeve can figure out any arrangements that need to happen after I leave.

I try not to think about what might happen to Noelle while I ride the bus and then a train to Heathrow Airport, but during the wait at the terminal for my flight, her betrayal punches me.

How could she abandon me to the Mekori, knowing full well what they would do?

I board the plane and doze the entire way to JFK airport and on to Colorado, arriving in metaphorical mental pieces.

As I wait for my mom at the Denver airport, I watch waves of people disappear down the walkway toward the parking lot, or moving to the baggage pickup, until the steady stream thins, and the hall empties to lifeless carpet. Vacant, except for the future that awaits, which is bad grades, teachers who don't believe in me, nights alone in the flower shop, and a hole that Hadrian once filled.

All I want is to close my eyes, open them again, and see Hadrian standing on the empty carpet, waiting for me. But he's not here, and the overwhelming likelihood that I'll never see him again makes me want to cry.

Maybe someday I'll find someone as smart and understanding as Hadrian. And Hadrian will move on.

Except I don't want him to. I want him trapped forever in thoughts of me.

I wipe my face on my sleeve, so my mom doesn't see my misery. If I told her my suspicions about the witches on Mill Road, she'd send me to a psychiatrist in addition to a special needs school.

I made the right decision coming home. The witches will hunt me if I go back, with glaring purple eyes, and daggers raised high. As for Noelle, I never want to see her false face again.

My mom pulls up in the passenger pickup lane a few feet away and helps me load my bags into the back of our old Ford. "You okay?" she asks as she ducks into the front seat. "Why'd you come back?"

"Just ready to be home."

Mom wraps an arm around me and gives me a quick squeeze, making me want to cry again. I contain the despair, barely, as she starts the car, and we leave the airport behind.

Mom tells me about Sadie's latest boyfriend, and her new bathroom cabinets. The jagged mountains grow, and the familiar river rock and logged walls of my home appear around the bend. The air smells of pine needles, like Hadrian, so I roll up my window.

Mom pulls into the driveway.

I drag my suitcases across the pavement, down the stairs, wave at my little brothers, and lock myself in my room in the basement. My old duvet is spread across the bed, embroidered with sunflowers, just as I requested on my eighth birthday. I've loved it for years, even though sunflowers are more weed than flower.

The sunflowers belong here more than I do.

I fish for copies of Austen novels and stop. Austen will take me to England. I'll have to find a new favorite author.

The doorknob jiggles, and my dad's voice filters through. "Bryanna?"

I wipe my nose, open the door, and give him a quick hug, but it doesn't make me feel any lighter.

As I pull away, his eyes shine with concern.

"You hated it, then?" he asks.

"No. Sorry, Dad, but I need a little space. Can we talk later?"

He nods, and I shut the door before he can ask more questions. He'll worry, but everything will go back to how it used to be.

Grabbing a book about high society in New York, I sprawl on my bed. I always meant to read it, so I open it to the first page, but let it fall on my chest.

I close my eyes, and when I open them again, it's dark.

Lurching to my feet, I run upstairs to the kitchen where the first rays of dawn peek through the window and highlight the grass and pine trees outside. My breathing slows a little.

There are no witches here.

I sit at the table and stuff my mouth with toast, dig up a bag of chocolate chips, and munch on the two together. I should look for jobs today, but I think I'll stay sitting in this chair for the rest of my life.

The sun shines in my eyes through the kitchen blinds, and I shift to the left, just as my dad strolls out of his bedroom, circles the counter, and pours a bowl of cereal. "You're up early. Excited to go back to your old school?"

I pop another chocolate chip into my mouth. "Not really."

He shakes his head. "I called yesterday, and they said you could go sit in on your old classes until your paperwork goes through."

"Thanks," I say without looking at him. "I'll go now, then."

Rather than continue this difficult conversation, I grab my car keys and head out the door. Returning to school is inevitable, so I drive my old baby back to the school parking lot and head to my first class. By the time I've left for my second class, I've forgotten everything the teacher said, almost as if the last few months passed in a dream, and I returned to the same seat I zombied through life in months ago.

Avoiding everyone in the hallways, I make it through my first few days without incident, until Friday, the morning of my fourth day back.

I'm sitting at the breakfast table when there's a knock at the door. My dad stands to get it, and the door swings open to Teddy standing on the other side.

Teddy smiles the same smile that used to make my heart race. It's the smile that had me waiting by my phone countless nights. It's the smile I hoped I'd never see again. "Hey," he says.

I drop my fork and nearly spit out the eggs I stuffed into my mouth seconds ago. I've been at school for days, and he could have talked to me there, so why did he come to my house?

My dad looks between us, his brows pulled together in a silent storm above his eyes.

"I'm sorry, Mr. DeLacey," Teddy says, "but can I talk to Bree really fast?"

I tense at his use of my nickname. Teddy never called me that, only my family does.

My dad glares at him.

Teddy looks past my dad, straight at me. "I tried texting you, but you never answered, and you've been avoiding me in the hallways. Can I drive you to school?"

"No," I say.

He grimaces. "Look, I'm sorry about the way things ended, but Lynn and I broke up, and I heard you're back." He glances between my dad and me, as if wishing my dad couldn't listen to his every word. "Anyway, I thought we could go out sometime. Or just hang out, or whatever. How long will you be here? I wanted to catch you before you're gone again."

I guess I should be happy he still thinks of me, but he's likely looking for a one-night hook-up with no obligation. A few months ago, I had a better opinion of Teddy, but now I see through him... to Hadrian.

"Pass," I say in a sad, breezy voice, "but thanks for dropping by." I suck chocolate off the tips of my fingers as my dad shuts the door on Teddy's mortified face.

Teddy and Hadrian don't compare. How could I have ever liked Teddy?

My little brother, Henry, pushes his way through the door from the basement and stands at my side, clinging to my waist. "I'm glad you're back," he says. "Even if you're not happy about it."

I chuckle at his honesty as I squeeze him tight. "I missed you every second." It's not quite a lie.

Dad turns to face me and folds his brawny arms over his chest. "Bree, why did you come back?"

I sigh. "I wasn't doing as well as I hoped." It's the best I can come up with.

The frown lines around his mouth deepen. "That's all?"

"It is."

Wrinkles form on his forehead, but he goes back to eating his cereal. "Sadie's excited to see you. She's coming to dinner tonight."

"I'm excited to see her, too." She's one big reason to stay.

I stand, give my dad a hug, and walk around him to the door. After driving to school, I sit through class. The lecture drags on, until the lesson abruptly ends. The teacher must have assigned homework, but I can't remember. I rack my brain for any recollection of anything she talked about for the last hour, but there's a gaping pit in my memory.

I should ask, but the teacher won't understand, not like Professor Karina did.

Now that I'm back to failing grades, I'll have to beg for my former job back, except I can't imagine myself staying in this little town I grew up in. It's a story I finished, a book I closed, and I don't like the story enough to revisit it.

Can I go to high school and work somewhere else in Colorado? Can I be done already?

My shoulders weigh a thousand pounds as I pick up my backpack. I strain to raise it off the floor but can't.

The classroom spins, and I clutch my desk to stay upright.

My vision blackens.

"In case you weren't paying attention," a familiar voice says at the edge of my consciousness, "the essay is on King Arthur. Did he fail in his goal to create the perfect kingdom?"

Twisting around, I come face-to-face with a smiling Professor Karina, hugging a stack of books.

She drops the books she's carrying, and they collapse into one purple book with a tree. The symbol of my necklace hovers over the lock until it flashes. The pages open, and the book grows, overtaking my vision. It's all I can see, yawning purple and black, until my vision shudders, and the image fades into a room filled with people watching with curious expressions.

I'm going crazy.

Shaking my head, I hurry out the door. Professor Karina won't be in the hallway just like she wasn't in the classroom. She's not in Colorado at all, and if I want to see her again, I have to go back.

I drive home after school, and the TV flashes in the living room as I push open the front door. Striding past the family room, I hurry down the stairs to my room in the basement, where I pull the purple book from my backpack.

Unlocking the latch with my necklace, I let it fall open to reveal sketches of the moon. A paragraph is written in archaic calligraphy, but it's a language I don't recognize. The black-and-white pictures by the text are as fuzzy and indistinct as the stars.

Strange words shift and move across the page as indistinguishable illustrations creep from the corners and curve into paragraphs. Then the words sharpen, and I know the patterns. I know the letters.

The pages flip beneath my fingertips.

The book is full of spells and astrology. It tells of using symbolism from plants, animals, humans, and metals with the power of the planets to create metaphysical power.

It's fascinating, but I don't understand how the materials are supposed to protect me.

I read until my eyes burn, then pace the room.

There's something I'm missing.

A bang interrupts my lonely musing, and my brother, Henry, plows through the bedroom door. "Bree, come upstairs. You've got to see this." He's holding a stitch in his side.

I follow him upstairs to where my brothers watch the news on a bunch of plump bean bags, a shared bag of Cheetos between them.

I'm hovering at the perimeter of the room when the image of Burnley Boarding School takes over the screen. "What's this?" I ask.

"It's that place you went to school," Henry says. "Mom liked to follow the news to check up on you." He points to the headline. "Look."

Another Student Missing!

I scan the description. Is it the same boy I watched die? Or someone new?

*The police have yet to find a body.*

My first impulse is to shrink down the stairs and hide in my room again, but the thought that it might be someone new makes me run for my backpack and return, yanking my computer from an inner pocket onto my lap. I search the web for news articles, anything I can find to give me more details and to tell me it's not a name I recognize.

Parents of students at the nearby boarding school are calling their children home. Headmistress Chelsea Craig, who was just last year accused of dividing students into honorary classes based on favoritism rather than merit, and ignoring students with disabilities entirely, has been summoned to questioning...

Until the culprit has been caught, students should not be out after dark, and everyone should walk in pairs, never alone.

No names.

I close my browser window and shut my laptop.

Even if Hadrian, Noelle, Mika, and Eser are all fine, they're still there in the midst of it.

I never called Hadrian to ask how he handled the news, though he went out of his way to do that for me when they found the first body. The day he needs me, I run away. How can I face him now?

I can't go back, can't afford it even if I wanted to.

When Sadie comes for dinner, I sit at her side.

"Did you have fun in England?" she asks with a little hesitation in her voice.

"Yes."

"But you decided to finish the year here?"

"Yes."

It's all true, I think. I stir my bowl of spaghetti, and the red pasta creates satisfying swirls. I need something to do with my feet.

"Bryanna?"

I jerk and meet Sadie's gaze.

"I said I pooped in someone's mailbox, and it didn't get your attention. You didn't even ask how I managed it. What's wrong?" Her brow furrows.

"Did you really?" I ask.

She waves a hand. "That's beside the point. Why did you come home?"

"Because Reeve told me to," I say.

It's not because he didn't like me, didn't want to get to know me, or because my grades weren't good enough. It's because he worried about me, just like I worry about my friends.

Sadie leans against her chair and nods. "Okay. That's it? You're not going to tell me?"

I shrug and let my silence answer.

Turning on the TV later that night, I focus on the noise, but see Mika floating in the river instead. Noelle. Hadrian.

I pitch forward in my chair, tempted to pull out every strand of my hair, one by one, but it wouldn't be enough if Mika or Hadrian died. I should at least call and warn them, but I don't know if they'll believe me. If something happens and I'm not there to prevent it, I'll never forgive myself.

I may not have joined the witches, but is fleeing from them any better? Here in Colorado, I can't help, can't even try.

Footsteps creak across the floorboards, and my mom's gentle fingers scoop the remote from the couch. "It's almost five," my mom says. "Did you sleep at all last night?"

I didn't realize so much time passed.

Looking away so my mom doesn't see my face, I answer, "Yes."

My mom raises an eyebrow, and I know she doesn't believe me. As she heads to bed, a chasm opens in her absence.

Light enters the room without brightening it. The scent of cooking bacon wafts into the living room, but I'm not hungry. The black TV screen stares back at me, and even though it's off, I can still see the footage of Burnley Boarding School.

However nasty things become in England, the witches know who I am. They'll come after me the moment I return, just as Professor Reeve warned. And what can I do for anyone? Honestly.

Someone coughs from the doorway. Sadie surveys me, a strand of platinum hair tucked behind one ear. She wears overalls, a fad I tried once, until a boy at school told me I looked like an Oompa Loompa. I took the feedback a bit too hard.

She drops an envelope on the side table.

"What is it?" I ask.

"A plane ticket."

I shove the envelope across the table. "I'm not going back."

Sadie heaves a deep sigh. "I didn't pay for it. Dad did. You're not happy here."

Warm tears slide down my cheeks. My chest shakes, but the envelope remains unmoved at the edge of the table, still sealed.

I never fully unpacked my bags, except to stuff jeans in them instead of dress pants. Mom can drive me to the airport, and I can be back in no time at all.

Except I can't go back. I've stayed in Colorado for over a week.

Hadrian doesn't know why I left, because I fled in such terror and humiliation. With my phone gone, I don't have his number any-more, nor does he have any way of contacting me. I can only imagine the pain he feels hearing of his friend's death, and then finding me gone only a few days later.

And then Noelle. Noelle was my first friend at Burnley, and she left me for dead. How do I trust anyone?

An intangible pressure pushes from all directions. It rumbles in my head.

Going back to England is too dangerous. Jane, Ellen, and Jennet might have a ceremony prepared just for me, and I'd walk right into it. Why go back?

Because I'm the only one who knows who those three are, and who will also do something about them.

The whine of my brother's voice echoes from the family room as I yank open the door and rush to where my mom teaches simple addition and subtraction with plastic teddy bears.

"Can you drive me to the airport?" I ask, out of breath.

My mom musses my brother's hair, sets the tiny teddy bears on the coffee table, and smiles. "Let's go."

⬦

My mom parks in the drop-off zone at the airport and touches me lightly on the shoulder. "Before you go, I want to ask you a favor."

My hand hovers over the door handle. "Yeah?"

She takes a deep breath. "I know you see me as Mom first. I know Sadie is way more fun to talk to—"

"I call you all the time."

She holds up a finger. "You called a handful of times. Look, all I want to say is, I want to be a friend to you as well as your mom, and I want to be part of your life wherever you go. I want to hear about the things you care about, even if it's another mother. I want to know if you're struggling, and if you're not."

I never meant for her to think I went to England to find someone else to call "mother." I wanted to escape Teddy. Yes, I hoped to search for my biological family, but mostly to learn who I am, and perhaps prove to myself I'm capable of more. Life moved too fast before, but England showed me I can move with it.

"You're a better mom than I could have asked for." I give her a one-armed hug.

She holds me tight. "Call more, promise?"

"I will."

I pull away, reach for the door, and pause. "There's someone I want you to meet—if I get back, and he'll still talk to me, that is. Will you come visit?"

Mom smiles, and her eyes light up. "I will."

# CHAPTER TWENTY-SEVEN

FTER I LAND in Heathrow, I file past the plane attendants out on the boarding bridge, push my way down the hallway, past security, and grab my bags before heading out the airport doors. Fresh English air fills my lungs, radiant with roses, lush grass, a trace of cigarettes, and thick humidity.

A weight lifts from me.

The train to Burnley comes and departs on schedule. When it delivers me to the school grounds, I drag my suitcase down the hall to my room at the end, just as I did on my first day.

When I left a week prior, I never informed the administration office of my departure, but the door to my room hangs wide open, though I closed it before leaving.

I freeze.

Someone either ransacked my room, or they're here, waiting for me.

I breathe in and out to steady myself.

I made the decision to return, so I'll stick to it.

Fighting a rising panic, I edge to the doorway and peer inside.

Noelle, with her long, thick hair, sits on the mattress and turns her puffy eyes and makeup stained cheeks toward the open door. "Bryanna? You're still here." She leaps to her feet and throws her arms around my neck. "Please," she sobs, "please forgive me. I didn't know. I promise I didn't. I thought you'd gone back, and it was my fault."

Her voice wobbles as she pulls away. "I've been checking this room every day since that night. I didn't know what to do when it happened, I swear, and I didn't drink from that cup."

This girl pretended to be my friend. Noelle looked me in the eye that night before she melted into a crowd of murderous hoods. I'll never forget the gut-wrenching realization that my first friend here, the very person I put myself in danger for, was no friend at all. "They tried to kill me, Noelle, and you stood across the room and watched."

"I know."

"I needed you."

Noelle's eyes shine with tears. "I know, Bryanna. And I'm sorry. I didn't realize what I got myself into. The moment I did, I did the only thing I could think of." She reaches into her purse, draws out two phones, and offers them to me.

"Thanks." I take my phone and test its weight in my fingers, but Noelle still holds out the other phone for me to take. "What for?" I ask.

Noelle unlocks the screen and plays a video, which shows a circle of figures in black. A woman raises a knife and slashes the wrist of a boy lying on the floor. Beside him, I press against the stair post, my eyes wild with horror.

I don't want to relive that night.

When I look up, Noelle lifts her arm to reveal the angry welt from Jennet's hot iron. An elemental star marks her burned and blackened wrist, a sign so hauntingly familiar, it makes me shudder.

"I have proof," she says.

A knock echoes from the door, and Noelle makes no move to get it.

"Are you expecting someone?" she asks, her voice half-choked.

"No."

The knock sounds again, louder this time. My palms sweat as I crack the door open, revealing Professor Reeve on the other side, his black eyes narrowed to slits.

I should have expected this, but dread drops into place, like a spider dropping from the ceiling.

He's sure quick to know when I'm back.

"What are you doing here?" he demands. Spit flies from his lips. "I thought you boarded a plane home. Do I need to buy you another flight?"

"How did you find me?" I demand.

Does he watch my room?

"You didn't answer my question."

"Professor Reeve, I'm grateful to you for saving me from that cosmetics store, but let me make my own decisions, even if you think they're bound to be mistakes. I understand the danger you warned me of, but I have a plan to do something about it."

"Do you really?" His face contorts. "How do you know what you understand and what you don't?"

I can't confront him and remain civil, so I start to close the door.

He grabs my arm. "What do you think you're doing?"

I jerk my arm out of his grasp. "I belong here, Reeve, and I came to defend my friends. You warned me of witches. I'm doing what you should have done. I'm going to get rid of them."

"Look, come to my office. We can talk about this." His mouth pinches, his anger barely suppressed.

"I'm not going to your office, and I'm not running away. Have a good day, professor."

This time, when I shut the door, it closes with a click, and I rest my forehead against it.

Noelle shifts, calling my attention to her as she casts me a furtive look.

"What?" I ask.

"Why does he stalk you the way he does? It's almost…"

"Creepy?" I stuff my wallet in one boot and my phone in the other.

"I wouldn't mind him stalking me." Still pale, Noelle raises her hands to form a picture frame. "But you're right, he's more attractive when he's not yelling."

I shake my head, a laugh pulling at my lips. "I'm glad you can still find humor at a time like this. Let's get going. We've got to pin down Hadrian."

Opening the door again, I check to make sure Reeve isn't still there, and breathe a sigh of relief when I find him gone. Noelle follows me into the hall.

❖

I knock on Hadrian's dormitory door and wait, though no sound comes from inside. Certainly, none of the racket I heard last time I came.

"Is he home?" Noelle asks.

"I don't know."

He never responded to my texts, which I deserve.

I sink to the doorstep, and Noelle slumps beside me, her fists tucked in her armpits. "What now?"

I exhale, and my breath swirls in the dark, foggy air. "We wait, I guess."

"For how long? It's freezing."

Noelle makes a good point, though I don't want to say so. We can't stay here all night, and I have no idea how dangerous riding the bus is, or being here, out in the open. "Let's text Mika then."

"I left my phone at home. I don't want to see how many times the women at the cosmetics store call. I jump every time my phone lights up." Noelle shudders. "Bryanna, I'm scared."

Noelle betrayed me, and might have let me die that night, but she's risking herself now by giving me that footage. I don't want to forgive her, but I can't help but feel sorry for her.

I squeeze her arm because there's nothing else to do. "It'll be okay." Rather than see Noelle's fear swimming in her eyes, I avert my gaze. She has as much reason to be afraid as I do. "I'll call Mika."

I call but only get a voicemail, so I shoot a text off and wait for an answering ping.

"It's not going to be okay," Noelle says in a soft voice. "They'll kill me the moment they find me."

The police may not believe us, and if I go to Professor Reeve, his idea of fixing things is to tell me to run, but Hadrian will help. He'll try, at least, and he has always been a good, nonjudgmental listener. "We'll figure this out, I promise."

Noelle buries her face in her knees. "How?"

"Hadrian knows people, and Mika will get back to us soon."

More than anything, Hadrian will listen.

I should say something to make her feel better, but instead I say, "Let's make this right."

We have to try.

Noelle wipes a tear from her cheek.

The night dissolves when the headlights of a black car illuminate the parking lot. My legs wobble. I'd recognize the gleam of the black paint and the shape of those windows anywhere.

Noelle grips the railing. "Is that his car?"

"I think so."

Hadrian gets out, and his driver takes off. As he nears, his hair shines copper beneath the sidewalk lights. He reaches in his pocket and pauses as he looks up. "You're back," he says.

I stand, sick with the apprehension of knowing I can't mess this up. "Hadrian, I need your help."

"What do you mean?" His voice is guarded.

"Can we go inside?"

He frowns but leads us into his dormitory.

Noelle rubs her arms. While the shag carpet and bookshelves haven't changed, at least the flat has heat, though gusts of cold follow us inside.

Hadrian nods toward the couch. "Please."

I lower myself into the sofa's ancient cushions and tuck my hands under my legs. Noelle sprawls at my side. Hadrian takes off his jacket, sets his backpack down, and still standing, studies us with a crease in his brow.

I take a deep breath. "I'm sorry about Robbie."

His face remains placid. "Thank you."

"I'm sorry I didn't call. I should have checked up on you."

He blinks, but his lips don't move.

I have to get it out.

"I…" I lick my lips, and the words I planned to say spiral into oblivion. "I know you're wondering why we're here so late. I wanted to tell you…" I take a deep breath. My words need to escape the dark room of that terrible night and tumble out in the open where they can drink up the sun. "Robbie…"

Hadrian's face blackens. "Died about the time you left."

His tone implies that he hasn't forgotten how I abandoned him at a time of need. The guilt cuts deep.

"Yes, that," I say. "He was killed by witches. By the women at the cosmetics store on Mill Road. I saw something similar happen."

He stares past me, and I can't tell if he heard, or if he doesn't believe me.

"I went to their store and stumbled on a witch ceremony. They sacrificed a boy to initiate their newest followers, and I'm certain they did the same to Robbie. I know it sounds crazy, but they worship the devil in the most literal way possible, and they're killing people."

His eyes focus on me. "You were there?"

"Yes, but I got away. It's why I left. I was afraid they'd come after me."

Deep furrows cut into his brow, and I search for a hint of his thoughts without success.

Noelle folds her arms. "It's true. They hook you with promises, offer to teach you how to make their products, and force you to do what they say. Then they do a sacrifice and brand you all to join their club." Noelle shows Hadrian the burn on her wrist. "I backed out when they tried to kill Bryanna."

Hadrian studies the burn. "You shouldn't be here. You were right to go back to America. I think it might be best if both of you go."

Does this mean he believes us? Or he doesn't want us around? When I rehearsed this moment, I imagined his response a hundred different ways, but I didn't think he'd do what Professor Reeve did and tell me to go home. Hadrian needs to understand why I came back.

"I'm not leaving again."

He opens his mouth, but I shake my head.

"No, it's not an argument." I tug the journals out of my backpack and pass them to him. "Professor Reeve gave me these when I first arrived. He told me I was in danger, and I should read these to discover why. He also told me to stay away from you, though he refused to give a reason." I hope Reeve wasn't right to tell me to stay away from Hadrian, but I trust Hadrian. I feel in my gut that he cares. "You're welcome to read them," I continue. "I highlighted the important parts, so you don't have to read them all. Maybe you'll see something I don't. They're littered with references to women with the same names as the women at Mystic Cosmetics." I spent the last several hours going through them, so I could point out which parts Hadrian should read, mostly the ones that mention the Mekori.

Noelle cranes her neck as Hadrian grabs the printed pages. He lays them on his lap and leafs through them, his eyes widening at times. After about an hour of skimming through them, he gravitates toward the ones signed by Guido. Soon, that's all he's reading, but that's not what I wanted him to focus on.

I'm about to point out my highlighted sections again when he hunches over the words. "Guy Fawkes?" he asks.

It sounds familiar.

Peering over his shoulder, I ask, "Where?"

He points. "Right here. The man on the horse, going down the hill. It says his name is Guy Fawkes, but he goes by 'Guido.' The Guy Fawkes you always hear about went by 'Guido,' too. It's the Spanish version of his name."

I remember Guido, but I must have overlooked his other name.

Noelle glances between us. "What about him?"

To be honest, I have the same question.

Hadrian's face flushes. "I've been researching him for months, at the Botanic Gardens even. I've felt a connection to him for a long time, ever since I first heard his story as a child. I always loved cathedrals, but a few months ago, I visited Westminster for my dad and walking through Old Palace Yard made me sick. I feel the stories about him are incomplete, and Old Palace Yard is part of it. I have to read these. They could explain so much."

"But what does that have to do with the cosmetics store?"

Hadrian's face falls, and a touch of guilt stabs deep.

"Probably nothing." He continues to read, this time focusing more on my highlighted sections, and doesn't glance up. Noelle coughs, and he jumps, his hands clutching the pages. He scans the room, inhales, and returns to his reading without so much as a grimace. At last, he straightens the stack and hands them to me. Though he doesn't smile like he used to, his forehead smooths. "This version feels right."

I slide the journals into my backpack and zip it up, but as I sit upright, the spark fades from his features.

"You think the women at the cosmetics store are the same women?" he asks.

"I know they are."

"If all this happened at the Lancaster Witch Trials, they somehow escaped. This lawyer, Judge Altham, must have had a lot to do with that. But why do they need more followers? What's the point?"

I hadn't thought of that, but maybe I should have. "I don't know."

He rubs his temple. "All this time I've watched people burn bonfires…Why did Professor Reeve give you these? He could have told you to avoid the witches and might have turned them in himself. He never gave me these journals, never even mentioned them. There's something missing here, and it'll bother me until I figure it out."

I wish I had the answers. "It bothers me, too."

"I've given you my thoughts," he says, "but what do you need from me?"

Before I came, I pieced together the beginnings of a plan, just the framework, and hoped Hadrian could fill the gaps. "I thought with your knowledge of the school and staff, and with your dad's connections, you might advise us on what we should do."

He rests his chin on his palm and stares at the papers. "I need to consider this. Come back in the morning and let's talk. I'll sit on it till then."

"Thanks for believing us."

He gives me a slight smile. "You're about as crazy as I am, which is nothing to brag about." He hesitates, and all traces of happiness fall from his face. "Will you be safe?"

"I'll try to be." I pick up my bag. "We're as safe in our dormitory as anywhere else." The witches won't dare come after me where so many people live, and Professor Reeve will protect me. He seems to know where I go before I arrive.

Hadrian arches an eyebrow. "You're sure?"

"Yes." I'm not ready to go yet. "I'm sorry I wasn't here for you, Hadrian. I truly am. Next time, I promise I'll be wherever you need me."

He takes my hand and squeezes it. "I know."

I stand, and Hadrian walks Noelle and me to the door. He stands aside as we pass him by, and I hope his smile is real. I hope it's a new beginning, an open notebook.

Noelle is at my side as we leave Hadrian's dormitory and enter Birdie's Court. She glances over her shoulder as she climbs the stairs to our rooms, one hand on the banister. "He cares about you."

My heart skips a beat, and I hope she's right.

We separate in the hallway, and I let myself into my room. Heading for my suitcase, I dump my stuff at the foot of my bed, and the purple book tumbles across the floor.

Each page holds the archaic language, formatted like recipes, as if it's a cookbook listing foods I've made so many times. The ingredients are muscle memory. Except I don't remember making them.

I memorize every page, pound it into memory, though the outlines are already there. All I have to do is put the recipes back, like sliding books into empty shelves. Dusting the edges. Organizing them by color.

The book said I need to protect myself and the people I care about. Reeve warned me of danger so often, I couldn't forget if I tried.

I close the book but pause on the first page. Scrawled in the middle is one word.

*Remember.*

# CHAPTER TWENTY-EIGHT

MORNING ARRIVES bleak and cold, the greeting of November. I recognize the nip in the air, the promise of snow. It signals a change in season.

I wrap a scarf around my neck and meet Noelle at the bus stop. We ride to Hadrian's dormitory, and Noelle stands at the front of the bus, her hand gripping a pole so tight, her knuckles are white. Shadows circle her eyes and cut gaunt wrinkles in her cheeks. She aged ten years in a single night.

I touch her shoulder, but she shrinks away.

The tree pendant of my necklace is cold as I twist the chain tight against my neck, let it loose, and pick it up again.

Sadie would say something courageous and spunky to beef Noelle's spirits, but I'm not Sadie, and I don't feel courageous.

The bus stops, and the doors creak open. I follow Noelle off, and we walk to Hadrian's dormitory, just as we did the night before. I knock, and my knuckles are still touching the smooth wood when Hadrian lets us in.

Dropping my backpack, I sink into his threadbare sofa.

Hadrian eyes Noelle. "Neither of you looks like you slept."

Noelle nods and grabs a notebook from her purse. "The ride was fine. Let's just get this over with. We discussed some ideas on the way here."

Hadrian spreads a bunch of heavily marked papers on the floor. "I have some ideas, too, but you first."

Noelle runs a hand through her hair as she stares at Hadrian's writings. "You can read those scribbles?" She wrinkles her nose. "Sorry, I guess that's trivial right now."

At least she recognizes her criticisms.

Hadrian studies his own writing and twists the papers sideways. "At the proper angle, yes. But I must admit, your writing is much finer."

Before Noelle takes us too far in the wrong direction, I say, "We can warn the dean of the college in an anonymous letter. Or submit an unsigned article to the school newspaper."

"Those are good ideas." Hadrian picks up a note. "But would you rather something more direct?" His expression gives nothing away.

"Such as?" I ask.

He shakes the note in his hand. "There's an event going on this week. Burnley School is inviting all local businesses to come on site to post jobs, pitch careers, or educate students on their potential futures." Hadrian points to a catalog of names on the floor. "I called this morning, and the events director gave me this list of attendees. Mystic Cosmetics is on here. They're looking for part-time associates, and at least one owner plans to attend the event."

"Of course you know the director—" Noelle stops herself, and I smile as she gives me an apologetic look.

Hadrian continues as if he didn't hear. "I asked if we could highlight my dad at the event for his work with the town council. Some of it directly relates to local businesses. I told the director that having an important person there would boost attendance, and I'd be more than happy to invite my dad myself. My dad never says 'no' to being openly recognized. Plus, students can ask him questions. He'll be a prestigious career advisor and might even bring internship opportunities to the table. The director loved the idea."

Noelle's brow pinches, as if Hadrian's in a high-speed car that left us both behind since I'm as confused as she is.

"Yeah, so?" Noelle asks.

I'm not sure how Hadrian's dad makes a difference, either.

"So, we can show our dirt on the cosmetics store owners at the event, and a member of Parliament will be there to witness it. If we have strong enough evidence publicly exposed, the cosmetics store will have to be investigated."

The dangerous part comes when the evidence has our names attached.

Cold, clammy hands squeeze my waist. "We have proof."

The Mekori will know exactly who filmed it.

Noelle's face takes on a green tinge, but she nods. "We do." She hands Hadrian her phone with the video of the witch rite.

He takes the little device in his hand. "What is it?"

Noelle's lips turn white.

My stomach coils in a dozen knots. "It's a video," I say, "but it won't be pleasant to watch."

✧⟡✧

I apply mascara and slip my dress pants on, though I actually have the option for jeans. For the first time since coming to England, my dress pants suit the occasion. If anyone wears dress pants here, it'll be for a career event. Right?

Maybe not.

The door opens, and Noelle's eyes glitter as she walks into the bathroom, her organized room like a magazine photo behind her. She fiddles with the threads of the knit sweater she's wearing with jeans and platform boots. "I bought this when I got here," she says in an offhand way, as if her sweater isn't really what she's thinking about. "It doesn't get this cold where I'm from, not very often."

I shrug on a black coat. "Are you ready?" I ask.

Noelle leans against the wall and looks away. "I'm worried," she says.

"Me, too."

Ushering her into the hall, we descend the stairs, hurry through the building, and exit to the street outside. A bus squeals to a stop within minutes of our arrival, and Noelle boards behind me.

We sit across from each other as Noelle laces her fingers over her lap.

I give her what I hope is an encouraging smile.

All we have to do is show up, provide testimony to the video… and survive.

We ride to the career fair building, a blocky, gray brick cube that has so much cement, I wonder how they keep it heated. Riding the elevator, we step off into a modern room with wood floors, more cement, and lots of glass. Framed photos of influential philosophers hang on a white wall, their faces overlaid with color. Tables speckle the floor with medium-blue tablecloths alongside signs that trumpet company logos. Students rove down tables, backpacks on shoulders, and cell phones in hand. A note captioned, "SPECIAL GUEST," hangs from tape on a door.

"What now?" Noelle asks at my side.

I suck in air that reeks of paper and bleach. "We find Hadrian."

Dragging Noelle after me, I press through the crowd. A sign above a booth sways over the others, with lists of various careers for students to consider. Global engineering, project services, manufacturing, electronics.

"Do you see him?" Noelle asks.

"Not yet."

A crowd forms around a bend of tables. Rather than typical signs and advertisements, this table has cauldrons with steaming concoctions, glass beakers, and scales. Ellen stands over them, her blonde curls spilling down her shoulders. Red tinting her pale cheeks, sweat shimmers on her brow. Bubbles issue from the top of a cauldron and float to rest on the tablecloth.

She keeps herself busy and ignores the crowd, but as I approach, she looks up and scans the room.

Intermixed with the students, but rising above them, stands Hadrian. He has one hand in the pocket of his leather jacket, but his broad shoulders face the pretty blonde. In his other hand, he holds pamphlets from the cosmetics store.

Join our support group…

As soon as I see him, I glance at Ellen, whose eyes lock on him as well.

I grab his arm but force my grip to slacken. Ellen isn't a stick to measure myself against.

He starts, but as he turns to face me, he smiles so wide, it travels to his eyes. "I'm ready," he says.

"Then let's go."

Ellen doesn't know why we're here. How could she?

I avoid Ellen's gaze as Hadrian motions for Noelle and me to follow him and leads us away from the crowd to the side of the hall. Near the door with the sign, he turns to Noelle. "We're going to do the video in this room. Can you watch for my dad at the lift? Someone will need to bring him back. Tell him he'll get his award, and students will ask questions at the end."

Noelle nods and makes for the doors.

As soon as she's gone, Hadrian ushers me into a small auditorium. The door shuts, and the noise outside muffles.

We're alone, save for a projector, empty rows of chairs, a podium, and a laptop.

"Can I talk to you?" he asks.

I study the soft lines of his mouth, the brightness of his eyes. We have a plan, so what's there to talk about?

Hadrian takes a step back. He looks hesitant now, as if my silence sucked his confidence. "We have a few minutes."

Perhaps he wants to bring up the night of the dance. Or when I abandoned him and left for Colorado without a word. Or he's concerned our plan won't work or has lost faith in my claims.

I'm not sure which.

"What do you mean?" I ask, dropping my purse on a seat by the door.

"There in the room, you grabbed my arm, and I thought, for a second, that you looked upset."

The walls of the room heighten, leaning over me with leering faces. He wants the truth. "I fought Noelle on bringing you to the cosmetics store, not because I thought Ellen would disturb you, but because…"

He's watching me closely, only a breath away, his curls hanging in his face.

"I thought you'd prefer her over me." I take a deep breath. "I suppose I like you a little."

Hadrian's face splits into a wide grin, and he steps closer, cradling my chin with one hand.

My heart flutters.

"You suppose?" he asks.

"Yes." I'm not sure what to do with my hands, so I stuff them in my pockets. "Hadrian, I'm in a special education program. I didn't tell you because I was embarrassed. I was failing my classes at home, and Professor Reeve opened up this new program, and my parents hoped it would save my grades. It's why I came here in the first place. I'm far from being in Reeve's honorary program."

"And you want to tell me this now?"

I meet his eyes. "Kind of."

"Thank you," he says.

It's as simple as the period at the end of my statement, as if the words, once lodged like rocks in my throat, were smooth stones the whole time, the ones that sink to form the base of the river, rather than block it.

His hands wrap around my waist. I'm smiling when he kisses me, because I'm enough. Because we can be like the vines that spring from the ground, growing together. Always changing, a better person with each new thought. A lifetime of learning.

Or many lifetimes.

New memories shove into my brain.

Running through the graveyard, running through the woods, running across bridges.

Running.

They're not my memories, and I try to breathe normally to force my heart to be still. I've waited a long time for this moment, and I want to cherish it, rather than let the fears pollute it that have plagued me since I found that body near Mill Road.

His lips part my mouth, and my hands tremble as I cling to him.

He's so solid, so safe.

Everything will be fine.

His hand presses against the small of my back. "Don't leave me again, Bryanna." He kisses me lightly on the nose.

The door creaks open, and Hadrian and I spring apart. A man steps into the room, ushering behind him a second man in a stiff, black suit with sharp cheekbones, gray hair, and a long nose. "Here's where you'll be speaking, Lord Bristol. I really can't thank you enough for coming," the first man says as the door closed behind them.

Lord Bristol's eyes fix on my hands, intertwined in Hadrian's. His face remains smooth, unperturbed as any true politician. "Nice to see you again, Bryanna."

I squeeze Hadrian's hand tighter. "Lord Bristol."

"Dad, we have you reserved in this room and scheduled to speak in an hour. We recorded a video to introduce all the startup companies, and we'll begin in twenty minutes. But where's the woman I sent to get you? The video I want to show is on her phone."

Lord Bristol's brows pinch. "I looked for her, but she wasn't there."

"What do you mean, she wasn't there? I told her to wait for you by the lift."

"I didn't see her. Perhaps she went to the toilet?"

The man who brought Lord Bristol gives Hadrian a solemn look. "I found Lord Bristol by the elevator alone. I didn't see anyone else."

If Noelle didn't go to the bathroom, where did she go?

Hadrian shakes his head. "Thank you, director. We'll take it from here." As the director leaves, Hadrian turns to his dad. "I'm going to look for her. Can you wait here for a few minutes with Bryanna? And Bryanna, can you get everything ready?" He points to the stool. "I'll be back before we start."

I've seen too many bad endings not to recognize another one, but I force myself to stand straight.

We're doing what needs to be done.

Hadrian will find Noelle, and everything will be fine, but what if…

I can't let myself go down that dark tunnel.

I set up chairs and start the laptop and projector. As the start time nears, students wander into the room to find seats. Lord Bristol sits at the front of the room and taps his foot on the ground. The room fills, but Hadrian doesn't reappear.

I tell myself there are any number of reasons. Noelle might be anxious and unable to leave the bathroom. Maybe she's sick.

Lord Bristol checks his watch, and I pretend not to notice. I straighten a few more chairs and align the next row. We need to start soon. Someone has to lead the presentation.

Lord Bristol beckons. "Is it time?" he asks as I near.

"As soon as Hadrian gets back."

His brow creases. "I don't think he's coming."

"I'll look for him." I don't wait for his answer, but hurry to the door to peer out. A handful of students linger at the tables outside, though none resemble Hadrian or Noelle, not even a little. Meanwhile, the force of a hundred eyes burrow into my backside.

Applause rings, and I spin around as Lord Bristol rises to the podium and pushes his plaque aside. "Welcome! And happy Guy Fawkes Day, by the way!"

"Remember, remember the fifth of November. Gunpowder, treason, and plot. Those are the famous lines. If you remember the history around the Gunpowder Plot, Guy Fawkes was stopped by members of Parliament and our own police force beneath the House of Lords. Today, I'm here to speak to you about—"

My toes go cold.

Remember, remember.

*Remember.*

My head aches, and I press my palms against my ears.

Remember. Remember. Remember. Remember.

Fire crawls up stone walls. A noose. Words engraved into the rock. Yellow eyes. A judge standing outside the door. "Bryanna," he jeers. Except that's not my name.

A rift deepens inside me.

Remembering hurts.

My feet move, faster. I shove open the door and stumble into the conference hall. The booth with the Mystic Cosmetics sign sits unoccupied. Cauldrons and chemistry tools no longer cover the tabletop.

I run past it, my feet a steady thrum in my ears.

I shove people aside.

Mouths move, heads turn. I find the bathroom, kick in every stall. I shout Noelle's name.

Sprinting to the elevator, I stop cold at the closed door, pivot, and take the stairs.

My heart is pounding feet.

*Faster.*

I skip several steps, and my insides lurch as I round the last corner. At the bottom, a body lies crumpled and broken, a leg twisted backward, the neck bent, familiar brown eyes popping. A scream shreds me, and Noelle's name reverberates up and down the stairs.

Her eyes are open and staring. She's dead.

I stumble down the rest of the steps, dropping to my knees and reaching for Noelle's soft hair. Blood clings to my fingertips, a vivid red. The metallic scent is a familiar reality, as is the faint and fading heat of Noelle's skin. My fingers burn as I hold her.

The world blurs.

*She was my friend.*

Searching Noelle for her phone, I find only empty pockets. They knew.

I never should have brought Noelle or allowed Hadrian to send her away. If I could go back, I'd tell Hadrian to wait at the elevator instead.

*Hadrian.*

Panic clenches me with sharp talons, so fierce I nearly double over. I don't have time to be angry or wonder what I could have done. They might have Hadrian, and they'll kill him as cruelly as they killed Noelle.

I run up the stairs to the room with the projector, and a stunned hush greets me. The seat beside Lord Bristol is vacant. Hadrian hasn't returned.

Without a word of explanation, I snatch my purse from the chair where I left it and flee. Down the stairs, over Noelle's too still body, out the door, and into the frosty night air where my tears crystalize on my eyelashes.

A figure parts from the shadows, and blonde hair hangs in sheets. Ellen smiles, red lipstick dividing over white teeth. A hint of lilac clings to her dusky pink dress with draping sleeves. She extends her hand and opens it to reveal a black origami cat perched on her palm. "For you."

# CHAPTER TWENTY-NINE

LLEN'S RED SMILE THINS.

I snatch the paper and crush it in my fist. "I know what you did."

"I killed Noelle." Ellen's calm voice strikes hard.

Her admission makes it all so real. I'll never speak to Noelle again, never knock on her door for help, never see Noelle waiting at the dining hall, but Ellen doesn't care.

"Why?"

Ellen cocks her head. "I would think it obvious. You, however, I need not kill. You'll meet your end soon enough." She gestures to my hand, which still holds the origami cat. "I gave you a pointer, for Hadrian's sake."

The muscles in my neck seize as blood rushes to my head. "Where is he? What have you done with him?"

Ellen's eyes glisten. "You're quick to point fingers, aren't you? Don't you remember what happened?" Her voice lowers to a purr. "You do remember, don't you? James Altham came, and you were weak. You had all the power you needed, and you failed. Even Jennet didn't think you'd be so easy to overcome."

I keep my face neutral, but her words cut deep, because as she speaks them, I remember who I am.

Frost lingers on Ellen's face as she clucks her tongue. "You must hurry if you want to save him. I'd go myself, but my sisters are watching, and my duty is to them first." All traces of a smirk disappear. "He could have been happy with me, child. He'd be alive. Don't be so foolish as to think everyone is as heartless as you imagine. I care about some things. I care about Hadrian, even if I don't care about you." Her dress flutters as she strides into the dwindling light.

I open my fist and unfold the origami cat. Two words glow in white, cursive letters.

*Moorhill Cemetery.*

Each word carries dread. Of all places to go, a graveyard in the middle of the night? I can't turn away, whether or not I fail. She may be leading me into a trap, but I have no other leads.

I board the first bus heading for the train station, get off, wait for the train, and board again. As the train departs, buildings and trees fly past, dark contours against the stars. The doors open at each stop, and my chest caves a little more.

At eleven years old, my parents reshaped my world and the image I held of myself when they told me my biological mother gave me up for adoption, that the mother I knew didn't hold me the day of my birth. I felt like I'd lost myself and everything I knew about the world. Now I'm a child again, sitting alone on the battered seat, surrounded by unknown faces.

Once again, I don't know who I am.

My identity has been many things: orphan, misfit, awkward, quiet, a girl capable only of dropping out.

I've been Bree. I've been Bryanna. I've been Marguerite.

My fingers shake on my lap, so I bring out the purple book with the eerie eye beneath a tree, still in my purse from when I showed Hadrian. Iduna promised it would help. I need that help now, so I flip it open.

My wrist itches, but I resist the temptation to scratch it.

The feeble outline of an elemental star shines from behind my scars, the same sign the Mekori witches burned into Noelle's wrist. I move my wrist away from the book, and the mark fades.

More memories flood through me.

I'm sitting on the stones of a prison cell as I try to scratch the mark off, gouging through layers of skin with my fingernails. The pain, the responsibility, the realization of who I am won't go away, no matter how hard I scratch.

Alice Grey was a witch with the power to protect and defend. Her sole responsibility was to protect her younger brother, Hugh, but she failed, and Hugh was lost.

I am Alice Grey.

The name slides into place, heavy and whole. It weighs on my shoulders, but it's also freeing.

Images of Hadrian as Guido pummel me.

Guido wears a suit and dances before dozens of strangers. Then he dances with me, just the two of us, in a cottage in the woods as one important child watches with yellow eyes.

A wilted rose in Hugh's hands; happiness in his eyes as he disappears into the trees alongside Hadrian, a gun slung over Hadrian's shoulder, his knee-high boots almost covered by the length of grass.

Hadrian's hands in my dark curls while a crackling fire warms my skin and brightens the flecks in his eyes. A smile touching his lips, honey and lavender on his breath, fresh as the woods outside.

Hadrian, my Guido.

When Alice's father—my father—brought me to the cottage and gave me Hugh to take care of, Iduna, the white witch, came and offered the tree necklace as protection. She stood before me, dressed in purple, with branches weaving through her hair, the scent of lavender wafting from my garden outside.

I was alone in my little cottage in the woods, my father gone, my grandfather unwilling to acknowledge me, and my half brother napping in the other room, unaware of the constant danger he lived in.

My responsibility crushed me every night as I looked out the window and watched the swaying trees for signs of trouble.

The white witch put a hot iron in the fire and took my hand, turning it palm up. She ran a finger over my smooth wrist, but her gentleness only stoked the fear that crackled within me.

"One of my seers foretold that thy brother, Hugh, has the power to defeat the original witch, the head of the Mekori," the white witch said. "If the Mekori discover your brother here, they shall do everything within their power to end him. You must be ready. You must master thine own brand of witchcraft to rise against them, for surely, they will come."

She asked for a teen with little experience of the world to rise against the most powerful witches of all time. Naïve as I was, I understood my burden. The strain moistened my back, my forehead, my hands.

But I had no other choice.

"The Mekori ask for sacrifices of blood and bone," the white witch said, releasing her hold on my hand. "I ask for sacrifices of a different nature. I want your freedom. From this day forward, you belong to me. You will defend your brother with your life and your soul."

Retrieving the hot iron from the fire, it blazed a fiery red. I whimpered but allowed her to lower it to my wrist, biting back a scream when the pain buckled my knees.

I loved my brother. Whatever protecting him required, I would do.

As the wound healed, my days filled with learning spells, nurturing my garden, and discovering how I can use plants to defend myself and my home.

But when Guido came, so did the Mekori.

After meeting with Judge Altham in the alehouse, Jane went to Jennet and told her of my association with him, fearing I would ruin the Mekori's plans to take Altham's money. They investigated me and found Hugh at my secret cottage.

On his daily rounds surveying the woods, Guido noticed Jane flitting through the trees, watching us. When Altham brought his vengeance to our doorstep, the Mekori realized an opportunity to use his jealousy for their own ends.

During my seven years in prison, Altham visited every year.

*Knock, knock, knock.*

The door squealed, swinging on heavy hinges.

Altham filed in alongside the Mekori. The witches with red hair, blonde, and black, black being the queen of them all.

Jennet stepped forward while the rest waited in the lantern light, which cast yellow crescent moons on each of their faces. After years of living in this squalor, I didn't smell the must that grew in the cracks anymore, but I could see it in Altham's scrunched nose.

Jennet gripped my hair in her fist as I tried to shrink away. Years of torture taught me to fear those purple eyes. "Where is he?" Jennet demanded for the sixth time since I came to Lancaster Jail.

"I don't know."

I didn't know anything, except that I failed. While my brother disappeared, it didn't mean he was safe.

She shook me before slamming me into the wall. My head spun, but this move paled to her other forms of torture. In the years before, they dunked me, cut out my moles, flayed me, and let me go, only to recapture me as a reminder of what it is to live.

A year later, they came to release me, but rather than let me go, they brought me to the home of a family who died in the witch trials, since my cottage had already burned down. The tower was circular and tall as the trees, with rafters still intact. They strung ropes from those rafters, looped them over my head, and hung me there, my feet dangling.

Altham made his sacrifices while I clung to life above him.

They set the house on fire, starting with the table beneath me. Flames licked my feet, pain lancing up my legs, until I ran out of breath.

As Judge Altham became a necromancer, the Mekori placed a curse that would bar me from seeing my brother again. This curse has followed us throughout time.

James Altham lost his money, position, and reputation, the basis of his self-image, and sought the power that came with the ability to command the devil and raise the dead. The Mekori required him to sacrifice an innocent to become a necromancer and demanded he continue that sacrifice eternally. I was a target for the Mekori and an obvious choice of sacrifice for Altham.

The moment Guido and I found each other again and rekindled our past with a kiss, Altham began to age. In order to stop the aging process, Altham would be forced to sacrifice us, rather than risk a step closer to death.

So, I am reborn, forced to remember my oaths just as Altham kills me.

Over and over and over.

I never search for Hugh, because I don't remember him until it's too late.

I never live a full life.

One lifetime ago, James Altham, tired of a vendetta long fulfilled, offered the best compromise he could. When I could offer no information on my brother, the Mekori lost interest and ceased their involvement in Altham's sacrifices, which allowed Altham to keep our agreement a secret. The agreement prevented me from meeting Guido, negated the kiss, and postponed my death as long as possible. It should have worked, but England called to me.

I broke my end of the deal.

An image of the white witch, Iduna, in a white cloak, stark against her skin, springs to the forefront of my thoughts. Her soft, purple eyes survey me as she hands me a necklace with a tree pendant.

*Protect him, Alice. You have everything you need.*

The grimoire glows in my hands. New images appear with illustrations I've never seen. Words morph into fresh letters, and a shock of excitement surges through me.

## To Bless a Sick Child with Health.

Instructions follow the label. Every word sticks to my brain, as if I'm breathing it in. The symbolic relationships between objects, liquids, and celestial spheres are there already, waiting for me to reach out.

I haven't held this book in ages, but it knew me when I visited my grave. It knew to return.

I flip to the last page where a sentence is underlined in red.

## When You Fully Understand the Laws, You Can Command Them.

A chill spreads to my fingertips.

There's more here than I've ever known, even during my years in that cottage in the woods, but I don't have time to ingest it all. I only have a train ride to prepare.

I've failed so many times, but I have to try, because true failure is not trying at all.

The train slows to a stop, and I shoot to my feet. The doors open, and I sprint to a street smothered in snow. Frost bites my toes, and each breath comes in a ragged burst.

I don't slow until night unfolds its wings, and I reach a pillared entrance with skeletal white stones. Spindly branches rise to the sky where the moon glows red. Its crescent shape, color, and position are all wrong for the spells I'd hoped to use.

I'm not sure which way to go.

Ellen gave no clues after Moorhill Cemetery, and there are many places my assailants could hide. I scour the tombstones down to my own tiny stone at the end of the lonely row, but there are no recent footprints, nor anyone else around. I pass several famous crypts and search for any structure large enough to hide someone. This life can't end this way. I can't spend hours searching for nothing, and never find him.

My only solace is that while the Mekori would end Hadrian in an instant, Altham wouldn't allow it without my death as well. We have to be killed together to continue Altham's long life. Otherwise, Altham will die a final death.

Closing my eyes, I picture the first letter Reeve gave me when I came to Burnley Boarding School.

*Beneath the earth and tombstones at Moorhill Cemetery are mounds of piled bodies. A past incarnation lies among them. I will remember her, if no one else will.*

I remember being Marguerite, speaking to Altham about our agreement.

I remember where I died, by a stone archway reserved especially for me. This is where they'll wait for me. I know it in my bones. They'll want to remind me of my insignificance, of how it will end as it always does. They want to squash my hope.

I run toward the tombs, then behind them, where the path is forgotten, and the stars sit in hushed silence. Their positions are unfavorable, but I'm glad they're there, watching.

Rows of tombstones stand erect, pale as bones. The path stretches on, past trees and graves, until York's buildings and traffic lights vanish in a dark hush surrounding an empty meadow with a stone arch. Stairs climb up the side and branches weave like spiderwebs over emaciated stones, dusted with snow.

A pressure more frigid than my fingers squeezes my lungs. It's just as I remember it, burning beneath the stones, while a cloaked figure drinks my blood, my Guido, dead on the ground.

The circle has closed.

A hooded person stands beneath the arch and raises their arms over a fire, chanting with old, rhythmic words. Wind sends spirals of smoke into the sky.

I step forward. A branch cracks beneath my foot as I leave blackened prints in the snow. The chant quiets as the hooded person stills. It raises its head to reveal the cleft chin, square jawline, and black, wavy hair of Professor Reeve. Except his eyes are dark circles, and his skin stretches against the gaunt, haunted lines of his skull.

Seeing his face brings clarity. It's just as it was before, except the witches haven't bothered to join us. It's been centuries since they came to witness my death. The students the witches sacrificed to expand their following. Tonight's sacrifice is to continue the cycle.

"Hello, Altham," I say.

# CHAPTER THIRTY

"ALICE." The wrinkles around his mouth deepen. "You remember now. Good. Then you must remember the promise you made."

I promised if he sent me away, I wouldn't come back. Guido and I would never meet, and he wouldn't have to kill us. "I remember."

James Altham circles his fire, footsteps fast and erratic. "You ignored everything I said. What else could I have done short of killing you the moment you arrived?"

"You could have let me be."

"Look at my face. I'm dying as we speak." He claws at his bony cheeks. "What will happen to me when I die and only the devil is there to receive me? I belong to him now, whatever I do, and I'm tired of chasing you, Alice. I don't want to kill you. I truly don't."

He tried to send me home, away from Hadrian and the Mekori.

"I postponed this as long as possible," he continues, stooping to take off his socks and shoes. He shows me purple-veined feet with all the toes missing.

Swallowing the urge to throw up, I turn my face away.

"I sacrifice your flesh as well as my own, and I'm out of toes. It'll be my fingers next, and when I run out, it's over for me. I hoped to get you to remember before it was too late. Every time I delayed this day, I hoped it meant I could kill you one less time. Every time I saved you, I hoped you would see my devotion and return it. You thought I saved you from the streets. I was family already, and so close to having everything I wanted."

No matter how hard he tries, I'll never love him, and I'll never respect him. "You should have told me about the curse."

Shadows cradle his cheekbones as he glares across the flames. "I did once, and you turned on me; ran to your lover instead and tried to kill me. I couldn't let that happen again."

"It doesn't have to be this way. Let Hadrian go."

"Yes, it does." He drops a bone into the fire where it cracks and spits embers. "I gave you your chance, Alice. This time should have been different. You were supposed to live your life and listen to me. You can't blame me for how things turned out."

A soft moan issues from overhead and sends sparks through me. *Hadrian is alive.*

"Go, run to him," Altham sneers. "At this point, it changes nothing."

I race up the stone stairs to the top of the arch where Hadrian lies on his side, his arms shackled behind him, his hair matted with blood. His eyes open as I fall to my knees. Magical chains spring from the stone and arc toward my wrists as I tug on Hadrian's cuffs. I dodge the chains, but one catches my wrist and jerks me backward, dragging me against him.

If it ends here, I hope the grimoire will give me another chance.

Below, Altham extends the pile of wood beneath us and raises his hands. The fire flares, and the heat of it burns the hairs on my legs. His pale lips crack as he looks up and smiles.

The temperature drops even further, until my nose and ears freeze. The air turns dank, and dark shapes swirl overhead. Voices whisper, and leering faces grin and then vanish as vile spirits swoop and careen away. They're meant to watch and hold Hadrian and me in place.

A cold, hard resolve replaces my fear. It builds a glacier around my heart, around the last vestige of my sympathy for him. He made a deal with the devil long ago, and it's time he faces it.

Forcing my eyes down, I reach for Venus and the moon, innocence and childishness, brightness to defy the dark, and allow it to fill me. There's nothing physical to connect the planets to, no plants to draw from, so I harness the energy and let it pass through my core. It's not as strong as I would like, but the spirits withdraw, though I can feel their wrath just out of reach.

As long as they can't see Hadrian and me, and can't get to Altham, they can't alert him. I keep the energy as a barrier between us to blind them and keep them at bay. The effort sucks my strength, but I don't release the spell.

Below us, Altham pulls out a knife and slices his own finger down to the first knuckle. Collapsing into a ball, he screams and writhes.

The next step is the hanging, but that's not what I should be thinking of.

His pain is a distraction, and it won't last.

I focus my power on the manacles that secure my wrists, looking for a symbolic weakness to bend what is strong. When I lived in the cottage in the woods, I used the soft malleable stocks of plants for this, but there's only melting snow on the lifeless stones of the arch. Taking the black piece of paper from Ellen from my pocket, I throw it on the ground.

"Paper soft, Mars is strong, loose my chains, play along," I chant.

Paper is soft, malleable. It should work.

The manacles don't change shape.

*I'll make the metal brittle then.*

"Neptune, furthest from the sun, icy cold would help a ton." I direct the cold into my manacles, but the ice burns my wrists, and I cry out from the pain.

On the grass below, Altham pushes himself to his knees, clutching his hand with the missing finger, and groaning.

Hadrian stirs, his jacket gathering water. Sweat beads down his forehead, but he smiles, as if he knows my poem is garbage and would never be accepted in any English class.

I can do better.

I squeeze my eyes shut and fix my attention on the lock instead of the entire manacle and freeze the mechanisms inside. When the pain doesn't come, I smash the metal against the stone, and the manacles tumble from my wrist.

I gasp in air but push the triumph back. We're a long way from escaping.

Altham staggers to his feet, still in too much pain to focus on anything outside himself. He trusts his spirits and my inability to defend myself.

Hadrian's eyes widen, but I hold a finger to my lips as I break his manacles as well. The effort almost buckles my knees, but he steadies me. I manage to stay upright.

We creep down the steps and crouch behind the stones at the bottom. Altham whispers to his fire, his bloodied hand held against his chest, his eyes popping. The flames burn brighter, growing bigger, though the light turns to smoke and shadow. He's building a cursed fire to sacrifice us.

Hadrian motions to the trees. *Come with me*, he mouths.

I shake my head. I won't run anymore or allow the fear of failure to sway me. Hadrian has to survive. Whether I live or die, the cycle ends here.

I draw energy from the deadened grass beneath my feet. There's not a lot there, but it's enough. The grass dies as I transfer its energy, and I wince at the waste, though the energy expands, giving me strength.

The spirits hound the barrier I maintain, but my magic holds. They can't touch me.

Hadrian ducks behind a stone column as Altham looks up and pauses. He cranes his head, listening as if he hears the cries of his spirits. Reaching into the fire, he grabs a ball of flames and ascends the stairs; the fire floating above his palm. His hood falls back to reveal gray strands in his black hair. Over ten feet above the ground, he crouches so his fingers brush the stones.

"Where are you?" he growls.

A chilly breeze ruffles the fur on my coat as I stand upright and walk into position behind him.

"I'm here," I say.

Altham jerks and swivels to face me, his back hunched, his muscles tense. "And Guido?" The fireball in his hand flickers. "No matter. I suppose I can start with you, so long as you're dead within minutes of each other." He flings the fire.

I wobble on a loose stone and sidestep another fireball as it blasts toward me, singeing my hair as it goes. Several hit my leg at once, and the pain scorches down to my ankles.

Altham steps closer, another flame in his hands. "I'm a lot more powerful than anyone gives me credit for. Even more powerful than most witches, though my sacrifice was greater for it."

"I hope it was worth it."

Altham grimaces. The fire in his hand shrinks as truth burns in his eyes. I was locked in a prison for seven years, but we have both been locked into this curse for many lifetimes. The hopelessness has eaten at him for decades and worn him away from the inside.

"You know it wasn't," he says.

A hand touches Altham's shoulder. Altham turns, and Hadrian meets him with a punch to the face. Snatching a knife from Altham's belt, Hadrian stabs Altham in the side.

Altham's back arches. He coughs, and blood spews from his lips. When he smiles, he leers with red teeth. "I'm immortal, fool." He pushes Hadrian off the arch, and I'm too far to grab him before he falls.

With a grunt, Hadrian hits the ground.

Altham stretches out his arms, his fingers bent toward the earth. The ground creaks. Cracks snake through the dirt, and skeletal hands burst through. Worms hang from loose threads of hair and clothes crumbled to dust as full skeletons emerge.

Skeletons climbing from the graves grasp Hadrian by the arms.

Snow falls from barren skulls as outstretched fingers drag Hadrian into the dirt.

Altham raises a fist. "Goodbye again, Mr. Fawkes."

My terror echoes as I scream.

Legions of empty eyes turn. Pressure builds, and tremors seize my knees as skeletons stalk toward me. One emerges at the front with gray curls clinging to the skull. It's the remains of one of my past lives, clawing, scraping, moving closer.

Bones grate, wind howls.

Evil faces, devoid of life, stare up at me as if they expect me to join them. As if I already have.

I close my eyes and plant my feet. Rather than zombies, I picture water flowing through the dirt, across the bones. Wind. Plant roots and worms. The setting sun. The molecules that create water, that power the substance. The pull of the moon.

Cool, bony hands clutch at my wrists. Daggers rake my skin, and teeth bite into my shoulders. Blood runs in warm rivulets down my forearms.

Hadrian shrieks somewhere beneath the pile of undead. His face replaces the images of water, but I squeeze my eyes tighter. Moon, worms, water, sun. Altogether, a perfect cycle. A seamless process. Professor Karina understood me better than most because she understands how my brain works. I tune things out without meaning to. I struggle to focus, but when I do focus, I focus for hours. When I want to be, I'm tenacious.

My brain locks into place.

*Moon, worms, water, sun.*

It's nature.

Power pulses in my blood, down to my fingernails.

"Bones, they groan, Worms, they eat, Water feeds, and Light is heat. Wear away, groan no more, Burrow deeper than before," I chant.

My voice is strange, but the language that tumbles from my lips is stranger.

Silence presses as the earth, wind, and snow obey. Water trickles from the ground and creates pools at the skeletons' feet. Worms crawl, mold blossoms, and boney pores widen to tunnels for wind to whistle through. Something slimy wriggles against my leg, but I force myself to stand still.

Images swirl in my head, beginning with James Altham before he was handsome.

When he strung me up, barely alive, from the top of a tower, the three Mekori witches stood around him. One carried a bottle of ashes—the remains of Guy Fawkes. Another held a pewter chalice and dagger. Altham drank my blood, and Ellen used an iron to sear the mark of a necromancer, a black skull, on his wrist.

The teeth and jaws that bite my shoulder slacken. Dirt blasts my cheeks, and a piercing scream forces my eyes open.

Altham's clothes and cape remained intact, but his skin peels from his limbs. His face twists with shock and pain. His body fights to reform while magic disintegrates him. Lurching sideways, he takes a gasping breath. "What is this? You're no witch."

"But I am." I touch the tree pendant that hangs from the chain around my neck. "You used this necklace as a talisman the first time you burned me alive, but do you know what it really is?" I hold it up.

His face pales.

"Let me show you."

The tree is more than a necklace and more than just protection.

When the door of my cottage opened, and my father entered with Altham, Hugh escaped. Guido fought with his fists. I rushed for the package of seeds I kept near me at all times and tossed them on the ground beneath the moon. I begged the sky for help, but while the sky twinkled with stars, the moon's light shone cold on my skin, buried in gloom.

I didn't plan for nights with a dark moon.

So, when the guards tackled me to the ground, I had no way to drive them off. James tied me up and led me to the tower, where he stole my necklace and set me aflame. Even Jennet, the head of the Mekori, didn't know he had my necklace, not even when he bound our lives to it with her curse. She didn't know until she saw me wearing it.

The necklace once belonged to Jennet, but she was banished from it. She can't touch it or harm it, which is why the necklace protects the wearer. Iduna, the white witch, took it from her and gave it to me.

James' immortality thrums against my fingertips, like a heartbeat, as I clutch the pendant. The energy of the curse lives at the center. It's Hadrian's misery, Altham's everlasting servitude to the Mekori, and my eternal bondage. I focus on the necklace's chain, which Altham used to symbolize the connection between him and me. As I break the metal links, the magic unravels.

James Altham lets out an anguished scream as his body dissolves into the snow, leaving only a pile of clothes behind. A vacant meadow gapes with a set of yellow lights in the trees that blinks and goes out.

Hadrian lies on the ground, Altham's dagger in his hand, his eyes wild. With the skeletons gone, his fists close on empty air. As I descend the stairs of the decrepit arch, the ragged remains of my dress pants flap around my legs. A soft gust stirs Hadrian's hair and jacket as I kneel beside him.

He turns his head but looks past me.

The cauldron still smokes, but no one stirs it. The danger is a black spot in the snow, a memory, a scar, just like the tower where I died. A glacier in my chest shatters to a thousand tiny shards and wedges in my heart.

"He's gone," I whisper.

After so many lifetimes of being hunted, I'm free. Or, at least, as free as I can be in this life.

I offer Hadrian my hand, and he pulls himself upright and dusts off his pants. His face is pale, and his eyes are still wide. Blood covers his arms and legs from fresh bite marks. He's seen many wars, but none waged by the undead.

Altham's black cloak lies on the sodden ground, perhaps with its own counter-aging spell. I pick it up, and one pocket puckers. Reaching inside, I draw out a page that matches the style of the other journal entries Altham gave me.

*—1604—*

*There has been much talk of the Samlesbury Witches in Pendle, at times referred to as the Mekori. I observed them for some time before I approached.*

*My career teetered on the edge of a pen after my disagreement with the king. Everything I held dear was gone. My money was gone. My wives declared we never married. My reputation became the rags barmaids used to clean floors. And worst of all, Alice still refused me. There was nothing left but to find a way to get it back and end my suffering.*

*I researched the witches and found evidence of authentic witchcraft. They had already been accused of sorcery by Jane's father-in-law, the Jesuit Priest. Demdike, the village hag, was willing to testify for partnering with them to* peddle potions, though I know there is no drop of witchcraft in Demdike's blood. I could present this information to the king and reverse what I lost, but I found a grander prospect.

I have real witches between my fingertips, not just pretend ones.

I arrived at Jane's home with the threat of a solid conviction. Jennet answered the door, and she led me down the hallway, past Jane's children as they pressed their backs to the wall, and into a larger room.

I always thought Jane was the lead of the Mekori, but I was wrong.

In the privacy of the room, Jennet turned to face me. "Thou art meddling in powers far exceeding thine own," she said. "All magyk is derived from me. No mortal can kill me. No fire. No hangman's noose. Nothing you threaten holds sway." Ball, Jennet's black-feathered raven, soared through an open window and landed on her shoulder. "But you may pay for your conversion."

"Conversion?" She spoke as though I wanted to be baptized. "Does the devil do baptisms?" I asked.

"Do not toy with me." Jennet's purple eyes flashed. "I know why thou didst come. Dost thou know the price?"

To her, my intentions were obvious. "Price?"

"I require payment in coin and blood."

A few gold pieces and a slit of the palm—only to be expected. "Of course. And as a necromancer, I shall have command of the devil and his spirits? I shall control the dead, as the stories say? And I shall be handsome and immortal as well?"

"Thou shalt have all the power thou desireth after the initiation is complete, after thou hast drunk the blood of an innocent, burned it alive, and eaten the ashes."

"Drunk the blood?" More than a simple cut. I hadn't expected this but saw no other way. "I will do it."

"There is more. One innocent is not enough. Thou shalt do this continually, for every lifetime. Thine innocent shall be returned to thee every time her life ends, and the sacrifice must be made again."

No single person would be too great a sacrifice, and a lifetime is a long interval. I could make this work. "That does not deter me."

Jennet tilted her head, and the crow on her neck mirrored her. "This innocent must never know love. Alice must never know the joy thou hast stolen from her, or thou shalt die in her stead. Thou hast broken the love she shared once already. Thou must break it again."

"Alice?"

She spoke Alice's name as if she suspected my obsession, but how could she?

Jennet circled me, her pace slow and deliberate. "Alice is the obvious choice."

I need this knowledge, the ability to read what others think. To know if they think ill of me, so I can punish them for it. To be rich again, but stronger. Impenetrable and undeniable.

*A smile twisted Jennet's face. "Thou shalt be all thou desireth. Thou shalt find women even more handsome than Alice, and they shall fall at thine feet."*

*I could picture it. "Is it worth the sacrifice?"*

*Jennet halted, and the raven cawed as she angled her face away. "I shall meet thee at Malkin Tower with the innocent. Do not disappoint me."*

*She escorted me from the room, and I set out to do what must be done. I have become who I am meant to be. My regrets with Alice will ebb, I am certain, and others will take her place. She and Guido are dead, and I am alive for eternity.*

*—James Altham*

Reading his words sickens me, but James Altham will never bother me again. I'll go on living the life I should have had from the start.

Hadrian glances at the letter over my shoulder, his expression knowing.

I give him an inquiring look, and he shrugs. "I always suspected my connection to Guy Fawkes but didn't realize my full history until he called you 'Alice.'"

He does know, but what does he make of it? I fold the page up and slide it into my pocket.

"You're a witch, then?" Hadrian asks.

We've never remembered long enough to have this conversation.

I search his expression for disgust and fear, but only relief shows. "I am."

"I wish you had told me. I'm not sure what it would've changed, but you could have mentioned it."

"I'm sorry."

I never meant to hurt him, but nothing about me was socially acceptable at the time, especially that.

Firecrackers disrupt the black sky in the distance, and Hadrian stares upward. "Remember, remember the fifth of November; fire, witchcraft, and zombies."

I laugh until two firm hands grip my shoulders and cut the laugh short. Hadrian cups my chin and presses his mouth to mine. I relax into him and deepen the kiss.

# CHAPTER THIRTY-ONE

THE WHITE-TIPPED CANDLES, ancient altar, and priest aren't enough. Nor the cathedral full of students who never knew Noelle. Noelle's entire family attended the funeral at a church near Burnley Boarding School, except for a little sister who was too sick to come. After the service, her family plans to send her body to Florida for its final burial in the family cemetery.

Noelle deserves to be alive, not contained in a wooden box. Even with flags, the hearse looks small against the ageless buildings and acres of muddy, half-dead grass. The hearse shrinks as it moves down the endless road out the gate.

Attendants carry bouquets out the church doors, no less lovely than the ones I arranged at the flower store in Colorado. When they pass on either side, gray skies dull the colors. They'll wilt by morning.

Warm fingers intertwine in mine, and the vacuum inside me diminishes.

"I'm sorry, Alice."

The taste of salt lingers on my lips.

"Can I take you home?" Hadrian asks. "Or somewhere to get your mind off this?"

I exhale slowly. "No. I want to remember." I want to remember everything. To cling to the moments that will pass and fade from memory before I can reclaim them.

Hadrian gives me a long look, his brows drawn together. "Are you going to stay, then?"

"Just for a few minutes."

"That's not what I meant. Are you going to stay at Burnley after your mum comes?"

Iduna's face materializes in my head, with lavender eyes and branches in her hair. She probably thinks I'm dead, but if she finds out I'm not, she'll expect me to find her. I lift my arm and study my wrist, where the scars cover my witch tattoo. The grimoire brought the mark back momentarily, but it faded again. I'll have to renew it, as well as my vows.

"I'm not sure," I say.

I could stay while I search for Iduna. The witches on Mill Road haven't vacated. They're still there, luring students into their store. Whatever happens, I have a duty to Burnley Boarding School, so long as the Mekori are nearby.

Though I checked my phone for the recording I took, someone deleted it, so our convicting evidence is gone.

The Mekori have no reason to leave, so why would they? I have to give them a reason, but I can't do that without regaining the full power I once had.

"I need to find someone," I say.

"Who?"

"Someone I knew a long time ago."

"Where are they?"

"I don't know."

Hadrian raises an eyebrow.

Even when we lived in the cottage and Iduna came to visit, I didn't know where she came from. "I'll figure it out. I promise I'll tell you everything I know."

I wish I could bring Noelle back, but I can't. I can, however, look for Hugh. I have to discover what happened to him. With his affinity for immortality, he may still be alive, though I squash the hope before it sprouts leaves too green. Iduna might know more.

"Will Iduna help with the murder investigation?" Hadrian asks.

"I doubt it."

A student discovered Noelle's body at the bottom of the staircase. The police locked down the building, interviewed students, and posted security guards on every corner of campus. However, the police are no closer to solving the missing persons case, though the case gained more attention when a highly esteemed professor, Professor Reeve, disappeared, too.

Many students have been called home by their parents. My parents haven't called, but they don't live here and might not have seen the news yet about Reeve, though I'm sure they will soon.

Hadrian tugs me toward Mika and Eser, standing beside the church doors, waiting for us. Mika waves, and Eser turns, his sweater fitted and unwrinkled, as usual.

Mika nods.

"Can we go and take a moment to be happy?" Hadrian asks. He gestures to Mika and Eser. "Can we live the lives we lost?"

I study Hadrian, the gold flecks in his hazel eyes, his shoulder-length, copper hair, the sturdiness of his footsteps. The kindness of his smile. The strength of all the years we've endured together.

He's my *Aster* flower, my undying love, my unassailable attraction. With or without a curse, I'll chase him through lifetimes. I'm happy so long as I'm with him, but I'll never be content until I've redeemed myself.

I can't lie to him, so I say nothing.

Putting on a smile, I allow a soft chuckle, but my lips rehearse the vow I made all those years ago, tweaked to the version I'll speak when I find the white witch, Iduna.

As we walk down the aisle of the school's church to the courtyard on the other side, a reverent hush settles over us. Filled with carved wood and stained-glass windows as old as my story, the nave showers the room with rainbows.

*The low sun makes the colour…*

I want a normal life, too, but I also want my brother back. And I'm all he has.

"I, Alice Grey," I say under my breath, "accept the blood of the witch tree, the source of all magic. I am the protector of my brother, and I will not fail again."

# LET'S BE FRIENDS

If you enjoyed this book, please leave a review on Amazon and on Goodreads so other readers can find it! One line is plenty!

**Follow me on**

@brookeclonts

@brookeclonts

Novels & Nooks Channel

brookeclonts.com

For early access to deals and announcements, subscribe to my mailing list.

# ACKNOWLEDGMENTS

THANK YOU to Tami Mandarino, Chase Davies, Emily Coleman, Karlie Dalton, Jenny Flake Rabe, and all the writers in the Bountiful Writing Group and WereX/Scott Forman Writing Group for beta reading my book through its many revisions. This book has been through so many writers, it's embarrassing. Thanks so much to Rachel Lopiccolo and Eran Pickering for helping me keep the content true to the history and area (if you haven't checked out Rachel's books on the witch trials, look her up!). And thank you to Kelley Riegert, Fiona McLaren, and Kim Autrey, my editors, for polishing it! Thanks to Ben Dougal for creating this incredible cover that I've hung on to for over seven years! And Seth Weinheimer for convincing me not to throw this book away after revising it for the tenth time. Where would I be without you all?

# ABOUT THE AUTHOR

Brooke Clonts was born in Salt Lake City, Utah. Her passion for writing started as a kid when she spent most of her time hiding in her bedroom with a book. Her cousin recommended she try writing, and it became her obsession. She has a degree in exercise science she's never used, is a self-taught software engineer, left her job as a software engineering manager for Adobe to start her own businesses, and is a wife and mom to the most beautiful boys in the world. She often writes late at night after her sons go to bed. But her stories follow her all day long.

Brooke uses her writing to empower young girls to see their worth, whether it's in showing girls how they can support each other, or by giving them characters who discover how they're smart and able to overcome obstacles.

Brooke firmly believes that everyone is smart in their own way. They just have to figure out what that way is.